Mad shouts...Screams of pain...

Conscious only of the others running in different directions, Casey blinked awake. He hopped up, cocooned in his sleeping bag, then pitched forward on his face. Despairing howls and wild activity surrounded him.

A snarl ripped the night.

He grabbed the flashlight, switched it on, swung it wildly about the clearing.

The throb of the crickets. Everywhere. The throb of blood rushing in his ears. Deafening. The mistiness was not his vision—thin fog curled through the clearing. He realized someone had been shrieking the same thing over and over, but he couldn't make out the words. There was movement. "Jenny, where are you?" Swinging the tiny arc of light, he stumbled bleeding into the pines, and they closed around him. Crickets rose to a dense pitch. He could hear running. Cries came from all around him. But, near fainting with shock and pain, he could see no one, the flashlight providing only fleeting, distorted glimpses.

Now he heard something else, a growling, a thrashing. The child's white face, blank with fear, flashed at him, then vanished, lost in the blackness.

"Amelia!" Sickened with dread, he held the flashlight out in front of him. The beam thrust forward, the shaft of light striking...

...a visage out of a nightmare.

THE PINES

ROBERT DUNBAR

LEISURE BOOKS NEW YORK CITY

A LEISURE BOOK®

November 2008

Published by

Dorchester Publishing Co., Inc.
200 Madison Avenue
New York, NY 10016

ISBN 10: 0-8439-6165-1
ISBN 13: 978-0-8439-6165-2

The name "Leisure Books" and the stylized "L" with design are trademarks of Dorchester Publishing Co., Inc.

Printed in the United States of America.

10 9 8 7 6 5 4 3 2 1

Visit us on the web at www.dorchesterpub.com.

DEDICATION

This book is dedicated to the ogre who lived in my bedroom closet. It's for the wormy things that crawled the floor around my bed at night.

This book is dedicated to Lizzie Borden and the Headless Horseman of Sleepy Hollow. It's for Crypt of Horror *comics and for the summer wind in the linden trees out front, for "The Damned Thing." It's for evenings when the doorbell rang, and there was no one there.*

I wrote this book for hitchhikers who vanish, leaving only their jackets behind, and for dead linemen who prowl the turnpikes. It's for The House of the Seven Gables. *It's for "The Black Cat" and "The Dunwich Horror" and for all those forbidden, sleepless, childhood nights I spent reading* Something Wicked This Way Comes *beneath the sheets by flashlight.*

And, especially...I wrote this book because of mist-shrouded nights on Owl Creek Bridge, nights when you meet the weeping little boy who tells you he's lost...and slowly you realize he died long ago.

ACKNOWLEDGMENTS

The author wishes to express gratitude to Madge Spreng, captain of the Lindenwold Ambulance Corps, for her moral support and detailed advice. Heartfelt thanks also go to the historians and folklorists who have explored the Pine Barrens in their work, particularly for the invaluable information found in Henry Charlton Beck's "Forgotten Towns of Southern New Jersey" series, in John McPhee's *The Pine Barrens*, and in *The Jersey Devil*, by John McCloy and Ray Miller, Jr.

This is entirely a work of fiction, although based in part on the authentic folklore of southern New Jersey. The characters are completely fictitious, and most of the towns mentioned, if not wholly invented, have long since ceased to exist.

THE PINES

I am he that walks with the tender and growing night,
I call to the earth and sea half-held by the night.
Press close bare-bosom'd night—press close magnetic
  nourishing night!
Night of south winds—night of the large few stars!
Still nodding night—mad naked summer night.

—Walt Whitman

PART ONE

THE BARRENS

It is a region aboriginal in savagery.

Atlantic Magazine, 1858

I have been shocked at the conditions I have found. Evidently these people are a serious menace to the state of New Jersey. They have inbred . . . till they have become a race of imbeciles, criminals and defectives.

James T. Fielder
Governor of New Jersey (1914–17)

Sunday, July 5

Here, rancid air hangs heavily in a void, its texture thick, liquid, clinging, in a night full of the hot smells of decay.

This humid oppression strangely amplifies the dripping, clicking noises: the moldy rasp of dead leaves stirred by tiny animals, the constant murmur of a brook threading the loamy ground, the oozing splash of something that moves heavily through water.

There is no moon, and clouds screen the light from the stars.

Gradually now, sunk in the still and viscous murk, the trees become vague shapes. Silent. Waiting. The ragged leaves of swamp elms hang motionless as insects in a web.

Slowly, the trees begin to glow.

Through the pines, the headlights were baleful eyes, lost and searching. They glanced off trees as the car first skidded around a turn in the soft sand, then veered from side to side on the narrow road. Keeping one hand on the steering wheel, the driver grabbed at the girl's T-shirt, while the car bounced wildly.

"Come on, just let 'em out a little. Come on, just let me see 'em." The old man's face glistened with sweat. "Come on, honey. Wouldn't ya like a few bucks? I won't tell nobody."

"Terrific." With her shoulder already pressed against the door, she couldn't slide any farther away from him. "What are you, crazy? You seemed like such a nice person. God, all of a sudden, you're an obscene phone call! Now, would you quit it?" She smacked at his groping hand. "I think you just better let me out of this car."

He was undoing his pants, fumbling with one hand. "You don't have to do nothing. Just play with it a little."

"Oh shit, would you look at what you're doing?" She made a sound halfway between a scream and hysterical laughter. "I don't believe this is happening. Why me? Would you stop that, please? Stop it!"

"Well, I can make you do it, you know," he rasped. "Come on, it'll only take a minute."

"I've got news for you. It's not even gonna take that long. Just who do you think you are?" Clutching her string bag, she considered jumping out of the car. "Just because . . ." Frightened laughter burst out. "You mean that's it?"

"What the fuck?" His face registered disbelief, then blood flushed darkly into his cheeks. Enraged, he grabbed her left breast. She punched him on the nose.

Brakes squealing, the car skidded to a halt.

"I'm bleeding! Get the fuck out of my car, you bitch! My nose is bleeding! Get the hell out!"

"With pleasure!" As she started to open the door, he gave her a hard shove, and the door burst outward. She fell, her knees and elbows making deep depressions in the sand. "Oww! You little shit! Who do you think you're pushing?" Gears grinding, the car lurched forward as she scrambled furiously to her feet. "Hey! Wait a minute, you can't . . . !"

"Whore!" he screamed, repeating the word as he gunned the motor.

"Asshole!" she yelled back. "You're only about two inches!"

Red taillights pulled away, disappearing around a bend, and droning cicadas drowned out the sound of the motor. She scanned the pressing tangle of vines and fir trees: a motionless horde of pines surrounded her, dwarf shapes with twisted and broken limbs, those along the edge of the road now showing gray beneath the rising moon.

Picking up the string bag, she brushed grit off her skinned elbows and knees and saw that one elbow bled slightly. "Shit."

The hot scent of blood drifted on the night air.

She could see tire tracks in the sand, but not many. *That creep must have come this way because he knew it'd be deserted.* Dark and deserted. *That's the last time I hitchhike.*

"I can't believe this is happening." Half expecting to see headlights coming back, she rummaged through her bag. Wet bathing suit, makeup, half a candy bar. To calm herself, she ate the candy, licking the melting chocolate off her fingers.

Even the beach wasn't this dark at night.

Though plump, Mary Bradley had fine bones and delicate hands, possessing a limp quality that approached gracefulness. Just now, the creamy skin she generally took such care of was sunburned as well as scraped, and her breast was sore where the old man had squeezed it. Yet she managed to grin at the way she'd told him off. At the office, she was famous for her shrill little rages.

The weekend at the shore had as usual been one long party. Too much sun, too much loud music and liquor. She had a regular ride home with her girlfriends, but she'd met this cute guy last night . . . and this morning discovered that the other girls had left without her. *At least they took my suitcase with them.* It had already been getting dark when she'd started hitchhiking. *Bad move.* She shook her head. *Never again.*

Should of made him let me out sooner. But the old creep seemed so normal. Some of her girlfriends told horror stories about their "dates from hell." She couldn't wait to tell them this one. *Stranded in the frigging woods.*

She peered up the road. Nothing. God only knew what time she'd get back to Philly. And she had to work in the morning. Not that she worried about losing sleep: enough amphetamines coursed through her system to keep her going. Diet pills didn't really curb her appetite any, but they sure were great for partying. Maybe one of the girls at work would have some Xanax or Valium or something to help her crash. Otherwise, she'd be a mess tomorrow.

It's too hot to breathe. And I still need to pee. She had the jumpy, thirsty feeling she always got after a couple of days on speed, and the crickets set up an echoing vibration in her nervous system. *God, these bugs.* A breeze stirred now, and it seemed the pines themselves began to resemble giant insects, prickly feelers twitching. *I hope I don't have to wait here forever.*

Soon she became aware of a sound besides the insects, faintly hollow above the constant whir. Cars on the highway? It seemed to come from all around her, and she strained to listen. On second thought, it was almost like the roar in a seashell. Could she be close to a beach? Then she recognized the sound for what it was.

Trees. Hot night air stirring in the trees.

She felt very strange and queasy, isolated. *Even the air doesn't smell right.* No soot, no gasoline fumes.

"Shit!" The mosquitoes had found her, and they whirred in her ears and eyes. *Mosquitoes and God only knows what else.* One flew in her mouth. She slapped at her neck, slapped at her bare legs, squashing something bloated and wet. *Terrific.* Dressed in cutoffs and a T-shirt, she'd be covered with welts soon. She really began to worry how long it would be before another car came along. An hour maybe? She could be sucked dry by then. And what if there wasn't another car tonight?

I almost wish the old guy would come back.

She tried to guess how far she was from the larger road they'd been on and, as she started to walk back that way, wished she hadn't been so chatty and had paid more attention. *This is weird.* Spotted with weeds, the white sand glowed in the moonlight, making her feel unreal, as though she floated through deep darkness on fluid silver. A swarm of mosquitoes followed, swimming through the humid air, and she imagined that in the shadows of the trees, the crickets followed as well.

Her footsteps made no sound. It was like walking on the beach—her calf and thigh muscles began to ache, and the straps of her new sandals cut into her feet. When she took them off, the sand felt soothing between her toes.

Suddenly, she panicked. *I'm lost!* The patch of white trailed on into the woods, twisting onward into nothingness. *Where's the road?* As she got her bearings and moved back, she shivered in spite of the heat, knowing she'd be in real trouble if she strayed far from this path. Something crawled down the back of her damp T-shirt, and she clawed it out, squashing it, wiping her hand on her cutoffs. She was pretty sure there were things in her hair.

Ahead, something glinted dimly. Just able to make out the shape, she raced for it, aching muscles forgotten.

Bullet holes riddled the sign, the red lettering black by moonlight.

> WARNING
> DO NOT PICK UP HITCHHIKERS
> HARRISVILLE STATE PSYCHIATRIC HOSPITAL
> 4 MILES

The needles of the nearer pines might have been thin talons, stretched out straight and clutching.

> WARNING

She took a deep breath then giggled shrilly. "Swell." The sound of crickets receded. "If they find me laughing in the woods, that's where they're gonna put me." The sound of her own voice made her feel better, and she giggled again. "Anyway, I bet they don't really give weekend passes to the ax murderers."

As it wove through massed darkness, the road seemed to narrow again, and she panted, glancing back the way she'd come. Just for a moment, it seemed the pines themselves moved, that they shifted almost imperceptibly, inching onto the road. The crickets resumed. She glanced back and wondered how far she'd walked, but there was nothing by which to judge, no landmarks, only her footprints in the sand. Plodding forward again, she told herself the main road couldn't be much farther.

She carried only one sandal.

"Wouldn't you just know? And I only wore them the once." Reluctantly, she started to backtrack.

Just a few yards away, beside the imprint of her bare feet, the sandal lay on its side in the sand . . . another set of prints trailing next to it.

Some sort of animal must've made them, she guessed. A deer, maybe. But didn't deer have pointed feet or hooves or whatever? These tracks looked flat and broad.

She turned. The tracks were all around her now.

Clearly etched in moon shadow, the prints crossed her own, sometimes running parallel. She couldn't have missed them if they'd been there seconds before.

The night breathed around her, and her teeth clicked together.

A mosquito hummed in her ear, and something rustled in the woods.

She ran. The main road had to be just up ahead, just beyond this bend or the next. She sprinted heavily, fleshy arms jouncing, and one foot came down hard on something sharp. She cried out, hobbling, her full bladder feeling as though it would burst with every jolt.

At last she slowed to check the road behind her. The itch of insect bites was maddening, and her clothes clung tightly.

Nothing. Beginning to feeling silly, she balanced on one foot and pulled something thorny from the sole of the other. "What's the matter with me?" Out of breath and trembling, she wiped sweat out of her eyes and gazed down at the imprints her feet had made in the sand. "Talk about being scared of your own shadow." The pounding of her heart slowed, and she examined the sticky mixture of sand and blood on her foot.

A rumbling vibration startled her. Blinding lights jerked through the night as a truck shuddered past.

The highway lay right there. Not twenty yards away in the dark, this dirt track emptied onto it. She went limp with relief and put her sandals back on. The shadows of the pines had shifted heavily, and she decided it was lucky a car hadn't come along on this narrow road—she could easily have been run down.

The pressure in her bladder still throbbed.

More approaching lights. As another car passed, she smiled at the prospect of bending the ear of whoever picked her up. *What a story!*

Oh well, last chance to use the facilities. She considered crouching where she stood but figured—just her luck—a car would come along and spotlight her. It wasn't fair, she thought, scanning the area to her right: men had it so much easier.

Spotting a clump of pines that might do, she took a few steps toward it. One foot sank deep in muck, and the ground oozed. Her foot made a squishy suck coming out, and she almost lost the sandal. "I don't believe this." Fouled with slime to the ankle, she began picking her way back across the marshy ground.

There came a hideous stench. Behind her, something moved heavily in the underbrush.

Her legs and arms ached with the sudden pressure of blood, and her bladder voided as, with agonizing slowness, she turned.

The darkness moved.

Unaware of the sudden hot tears on her face, she groped her way backward toward the road.

A shape lurched toward her from the shadows.

Branches slashed at her plump bare thighs as she ran. Something exploded out of the thicket behind her. Propelled by terror, she ran faster than she'd ever thought she could, her brain screaming too loudly to register sights or sounds. Only her bones felt the pounding that gained on the road behind her.

Lights! A car ahead—she cried out, but the sandals, plowing through soft dirt, slowed her so that . . .

Slammed into from behind, she was spun around with incredible force.

Distantly, strangely dislocated from herself, from this body whirling through the dark, she wondered if she'd been hit by a car after all. Had the old man come back? It was her last coherent thought.

She lay, pain humming through her in the night, then felt herself being lifted.

A large bat scurried across the sky as a car flashed past the side road, red taillights retreating. The thrashing in the thicket gradually diminished, and soon there remained only the droning of insects.

*   *   *

"You can slow down now, Jack. I told you, there's no hurry—this one's DOA. I'd rather we didn't all wind up that way, if you don't mind."

"Are you saying my driving ain't all it should be, Doris?"

"You mean to tell me you didn't finish filling that out yet?" Ignoring him, she sat down next to the woman in back. "What's taking so long, kid?"

The narrow stretcher creaked. Perched on one of the cushioned seats of worn orange vinyl, Athena looked up. "The first one got a little messed up," she responded, trying to keep dark arterial blood from getting on the report.

"Big surprise. Darn, would you look at my jeans? I throw away more clothes! You should've seen it coming out of my hair last night in the shower." Doris Compson was a short, solid woman. Steel gray hair, steel gray eyes. The patch on her sleeve read CAPTAIN. Originally from the Tampa Bay area, she'd been living in these woods for almost twenty-five years but still spoke with a slight Southern twang. She'd once avowed, "Jersey's the crookedest state in the Union—Mafia runs the whole damn place, like Mexico," but she'd said it with pride, swearing in the next breath that she'd never want to live anywhere else: it was the local style.

With a loud rattle, the ambulance shuddered, spattered ceiling lights faltering. Tires shrieked, leaving twin streaks of acrid rubber on the road.

"What in hell was that?" yelled Doris, jumping to her feet.

The ambulance regained speed.

"I hit a dog." Shirtsleeves rolled on his muscular arms, Jack Buzby wrestled the wheel, steering the rig around a series of sharp turns.

"You what?"

"You heard me, Doris," he said, glancing over his shoulder. The thick glasses he pushed back on his nose gave him an incongruously studious air. He was twenty years old, good-looking and normally easygoing, though just now trying hard not to look upset. "It ran outta the woods in front of me. That headlight's so outta whack, I didn't even see it till too late."

"Kill it?"

"Prob'ly."

"You think it might've been one of those wild dogs, kid? The ones Barry and Steve were talking about?"

Athena glanced up. She felt light-headed, nauseated by the heat.

"We had that happen around here once before, couple years back," Doris went on. "Remember, Jack? A gang of dogs got to running wild in the woods, raiding farms and the like. Hmm, dog days," she muttered, wiping her face. "That's what they call it when it's thick like this. Damn air feels like a dog's breath."

"Feral dogs." Athena stared at the small puddle of blood sloshing around her shoes. The disposable blankets they'd used to sop up some of the liquid lay wadded and soaking. "

"You say something, honey?" Doris peered at her.

"Feral dogs, they're called." Absently, she massaged her leg. "Like feral children."

"Leg bothering you again, hon?"

"No." Scowling, she tried to ignore the ache in her knee while she completed the accident report.

The corpse that sprawled across the stretcher was immensely fat and mangled. The accident had taken place barely a mile from the ambulance hall, and blood had still been spouting from him when they'd arrived. Despite his wife's protests, the drunken idiot had gone up a rickety ladder to prune a tree at night. He'd landed beer belly–first on the chainsaw.

Athena shook her head, writing up the particulars. Her faded work shirt was drenched and sticky, her hair pulled back in a tight bun.

"Hey, Athena, why don't you come up here and keep the driver company?"

"Just ignore him, honey. What's the matter, stud? Need some help with your stick shift?" Doris waved at the air around her face; in truth, it was an old, familiar odor. Before an early retirement, she'd been the local coroner. The appointment had been political, and her professional survival through a succession of graft-ridden administrations had been no accident. She was tough, an expert at cronyism. The fact that Mullica Emergency Rescue, with its small volunteer crew, kept operating at all was due entirely to her fund-raising activities, the shambling wreck of an ambulance itself having been donated by a neighboring township at her instigation. "Christ, this job is a bitch during the summer," she muttered, resisting the impulse to hold her nose.

The bald head of the dead man was splattered and darkening, and he stank of booze and other things, his abdomen a shredded pile that slopped through lacy layers of fat. When the ambulance rattled through a series of rapid lurches, the ruined organs quivered, slipping farther down, and fleshy tendrils vibrated toward the floor. Doris mumbled something about the damn road, and Jack replied with something about a tune-up and new shocks.

Athena tossed a blanket over the body. They were still a good twenty miles away from the nearest hospital.

. . . and Mary Bradley knelt in black water. The marsh was a darkly flooded vision of hell, and the nightmare landscape revolved, rushing with the blood that streamed down her left side.

"No! Please!"

Circling, the thing lunged. It tore at her, ripped her soft breasts, and the force of the attack sent her rolling in the morass. Now glimpsed in scattered moonlight, now invisible in shadow, the thing backed off, moving through dark water with incredible speed, again circling.

"Stay away from—!" A mouthful of warm, stagnant water stopped her screams as something spurted from beneath her rent T-shirt. She staggered to her feet, slipped in slimy muck and went down in a sitting position. Half submerged, she watched the red spot on her shirt spread, watched the water around her darken. "Don't hurt me."

It surged toward her. She was jerked upright. Struggling, she beat wildly, beads of blood flying as it lashed at her. She was thrown against a dead sapling, and the pine toppled, easily uprooted in the muck.

She came down on one knee in shallow water. Splashing,

slapping noises surrounded her in the dark. She slid backward, falling across a mound of hard earth. If she could only rise . . .

Scrambling on all fours, she heaved out of the ooze, tried to get to her feet.

With a leap, it was on her back, wet and heavy. "Help me!" It pounded her to the ground with hammering blows. "Oh God!"

Again, it backed away.

Face in the mud, she listened, struggling to stay conscious. Her skull felt as though it had been crushed. Distantly, she heard it snarl with obscene ferocity.

Then it closed again and flipped her onto her back.

Weakly now, she flailed, as cloth and flesh ripped away. Belly exposed and white, she lay quivering, throbbing with pain. The thing leaned over her—huge, hot, dripping—and she trembled convulsively, closing her eyes hard, her body rigid, as the thing pressed against her, reeking breath in her face.

And then the forcing . . . enormous pressure . . . her screams emerging as mangled chokes.

"No!" *it hurts* "Don't!" *oh dear God oh it hurts* "Please!"

It gripped her, plunging, clawing.

"don't"

Her body arched in spasms, legs jerking as the bloody remnants of her urine-soaked cutoffs bunched at her knees, bound her stiffened limbs. She heard her own flesh ripping, as a sound emerged from deep within the thing—a groan of pleasure. Her mind retreated.

As it pounded and clutched, her bare back jerked from the mud again and again, her skin grinding against the coarse sand with each thrust. Her eyes opened: flesh hung from her left arm in a flap, veins laid open and pumping fluid, bone exposed to the moonlight.

It pushed hard, harder, until something swelled and burst within her. Numb, she rocked with pressure, the flap of skin swaying, dripping, as dark rivulets ran along the folds of her stomach and trickled over her side, making thick black coils in the sand.

The crickets sang.

my string bag . . . I've lost my . . . Her hands twitched feebly on the ground, nothing but wet sand in the flesh between her fingers.

"Hey, we got company." Jack leaned out the window.

Outside, swirling lights and a siren gained on them, the siren switching off suddenly. Somebody yelled, and Jack laughed. "What's that? Yeah, she's in here."

"Watch what you're . . . !" Doris sputtered. "What the hell you slowing down for?"

Athena stood up, wobbling. "Is that Barry?"

"What?" Outside, the siren screamed on again, cutting Jack off in midshout, and the police car swiftly pulled away from them. "They must of got a call," said Jack over his shoulder.

"Barry's going to hear about this! He can't be holding us up like that—we could've had a patient in here for all he knows. For crying out loud, you'd think Steve at least would have better sense."

"Come on, Doris," Jack said. "They got a radio. They must of heard us call the hospital—Steve knows we got a dead 'un. Hey, before I forget, you know you got to drop me back at my car, don't you?"

"I know it."

"Just so's I don't get stuck like last time. I can't believe I was the first one on the scene again. That's three times in a row."

Athena limped toward the front of the rig. Doris stood aside to let her pass, watching her walk, feeling the familiar tug, deep inside.

"Can you raise them?"

"You want to try?" asked Jack, not looking up.

Athena sat next to him and impatiently fiddled with the radio. "I can't get anything. What did he yell?"

He navigated a series of rough turns. "Something about meeting you at the diner."

"Real discreet," Doris muttered. Slipping in blood, she lost her footing for a moment and steadied herself against the soft pile on the stretcher. "Shit. You'd think by now I'd at least know how to ride in an ambulance without falling over." She wiped her hands on her jeans and reached behind the oxygen cylinder. "This tank's almost empty. I'd like to know how in hell I'm supposed to run a rescue team without O_2." She found the thermos bottle. " 'Kill for a cigarette."

"What're you grumbling about back there?" yelled Jack. "You know you ain't allowed to smoke in here, Doris."

"Yeah, yeah," she muttered and concentrated on sipping coffee without spilling it. "Just shut up and drive."

"Forget it," said Jack, noticing Athena's attempt to roll down a window. "Stuck again."

"Great." As pines rushed past on either side, Athena felt the ground drumming beneath her, lulling her. Yet she sat very stiff, very straight. "In this heat."

They all lapsed into a hot, weary silence. The right headlight, pointing upward at a crazy angle, raked across roadside trees.

Athena tried to concentrate on the radio but could only get static. "One more thing that needs fixing." Hypnotic, the woods rolled endlessly past the window, formless as storm clouds. Suddenly, she leaned forward. For an instant, she thought she'd seen a beast trotting at the edge of the road.

"The woods still bother you, don't they, kid?"

She started. Doris had come up behind her.

"Doris, don't you know by now our 'Thena ain't afraid of nothing?" Jack laughed. "Hey, you found the coffee? Gimme some."

Athena looked away from the window. "What happened to his wife?"

"Whose wife, honey?"

She jerked a thumb toward the back of the rig. "I thought she wanted to ride with us."

"I wasn't going to let her in here. You kidding? The way he looks? I don't know where she is though. Jack?"

"Neighbors had her when we pulled out."

He switched on the siren, and it drowned his words, washing them away from Athena. Headlights gleamed off orange reflective disks by the roadside, and she watched as—faintly lit—they sank, dissolved in darkness one by one.

"No, they don't bother me," she began. "As a kid, I used to have nightmares about being lost in the woods. When you consider it, that shows rather a lot of imagination for a child in Queens." She tried to laugh. "Don't you think?"

"That all there was to the dream? Just the woods? Go on."

But the younger woman stayed silent, lost in memories of lying awake, of the crutches by the bed, of her dream closing on her. Knowing that she couldn't run had always made it worse. She'd always known that her grandmother would come if she cried out. But she hadn't cried. Not ever. Too proud, even then. And throughout her childhood, through her adolescent spells of sleepwalking, every night the dark had swallowed her.

The mouth of a side road rushed past, opening deep into the woods.

"Yeah, honey, dreams can sure be rough on a little kid." Even as she spoke, Doris felt the inadequacy of her words, and when Jack snorted in derision, she turned on him gratefully. "So what's your problem? I suppose you never had a bad dream?"

"Who me? I never had no kind of dream in my whole life."

"That's not the way your mother tells it."

"Shut up, Doris. What happened to that coffee anyways? Don't I get any?"

"Not from what I hear. Watch your driving. Besides, it's against the rules to have coffee in here anyways."

"You're drinking it!"

"I'm the squad captain."

Athena only half-listened to them. The night overwhelmed her. Swelling like a huge black wave, it could flood across the highway, crush their tiny particle of light and movement, drown them all in darkness. She forced herself to look away, then leaned over to check Jack's watch. "Did Barry say anything else?"

The thing in the back had stopped dripping, and as the ambulance barreled through the night, streetlights began to emerge, beacons of order in the chaos of the dark.

★   ★   ★

A thought stirred. *ohgodohgod it hurts* The amphetamines coursing through what remained of Mary Bradley's blood system inexorably forced her toward something near consciousness.

She had no body, no localized perceptions. Enclosed by silence, she knew only the shape and size of absolute blackness, hot and suffocating.

Memory leaked—a nightmare of herself whirled and slashed through bleeding skeletons of trees. Awareness seeped back. She lay inside . . . a cave? A pit? A grave? And she seemed to be soaking in a puddle, could feel it on her shoulders and buttocks, thick and sticky like paint, crusty around the edges.

where It seemed she should have arms, and she recalled things done in the mind to move an arm. *ohgod what* She wondered if her eyes were open. *dead*

A hand fell upon herself, and memory flooded. *swamp and* Her fingers slipped along her gouged and oozing stomach, slid to wet and softly mangled places. She shook with nausea, and the movement created searing pain.

An oval area of lighter darkness was eclipsed, then reappeared, like an entrance momentarily blocked. She realized her eyes were open, and through the dampening field of pain, she heard sounds: straining breath, slavering growl.

It scrambled closer. She barely felt its damp breath on her thigh, barely felt the teeth.

The old Plymouth rushed along the paved road, headlights lancing the haze. Telephone poles loomed past repetitiously. Even dead tired, Athena Lee Monroe drove extremely well. *But then this girl is good at everything.* She grinned humorlessly at the thought. She'd been stood up again.

The Chamong Diner was shabby and none too clean. This evening, Doris and Jack and some buddy of Jack's named Larry had all stopped in, and the talk had been loud and cheery, what with the guys bullshitting about scuba diving and backpacking and all the women they were screwing, and Doris regaling them with hair-raising anecdotes from her days as coroner. Drinking coffee and watching the door, Athena had sat at the booth for hours, barely joining in the conversation, just toying restlessly with little packets of sugar and choking on the smoke from Doris's cigarettes.

When she'd finally given up hope of seeing Barry, the others had tried to keep her with them, but she'd resisted, knowing they'd be there till dawn or until old man Sims chased them out. Passing the phone booth in the parking lot, she'd longed to call Barry . . . but Cathy would have gotten suspicious.

She smiled sourly. *Now why should calling at two A.M. make his wife suspicious?* Shaking her head, she recalled the contempt she'd always felt for her aunt's sordid little intrigues. How Aunt Jeanie would crow to see her now. *Not that she would see me.* She understood too well how completely her family had disowned her after her marriage.

The car lost speed, drifting to a stop at the mouth of a sand road. The way home. Just beyond the bright haze of her head-lights, the side road plunged deep into the forest.

Dashboard dials gleamed a pale, plastic green, and her hands looked ghostly in the glow as she touched the radio scanner beside her on the seat, drew her fingertips across its tiny red light. Bracing herself, she fought down the familiar moment of panic. *The way home.* Mindful of the bogs on either side of the road, she drove carefully, fervently wishing she had somewhere else to go.

Home. She thought of her grandmother's house and smiled. On Athena's ninth birthday, Granny Lee had given her a collection of children's stories and poems. Vaguely, she wondered what had become of that book. Did she still have it somewhere, packed away with the rest of her past? She could still recall one of those stories, about a hag who lived along a dismal swamp. She tried to convince herself that it amused her to have become that woman.

Jagged darkness pressed around as the old automobile jounced over the uneven road. Downshifting, she slowed the Plymouth to a crawl . . . and the headlights found strange patches in the sand.

It could almost be blood. "Only children are afraid of the

dark," she said aloud. After that, she drove with deliberate slow-ness, fighting the urge to floor the gas pedal. *Nothing is watching me.* Mosquitoes roiled in her headlight beams. They swarmed along the road, teemed in and out of the windows in this muggy heat. A road sign, riddled with bullets, crawled past, warning motorists about the proximity of the state hospital. *The insane asylum.* She brushed away thoughts of her mother and resolutely searched for something on which to fix her mind.

Once, she'd seen an aerial photo of the barrens, the highways like razor-thin incisions. The photograph had trembled in her hands. She thought of pictures she'd seen of Canada's Great North Woods—giant and majestic—but here, in the forests that stretched through most of southern central New Jersey, the bar-ren sands could produce no such growth.

No. She tightened her grip on the steering wheel. The sands were not truly barren. They produced the stunted, twisted pines . . . as her body had produced her son.

Furious with herself for the thought, she jerked the wheel, and a dwarf pine rasped against the car. Cursing, she concen-trated on driving. There were so many things to avoid.

She switched on the radio—a garbled voice. She twisted the dial but could find nothing clear, the distant signals a cacophony of chopped and liquid sound. She turned it off, and the car crept along. Nailed to a tree, a weathered plank indicated the fork to Munro's Furnace.

The road narrowed until it became a sandy rut walled by brush, and now pine boughs crushed against both sides of the car. Around a turn, the brush thinned, and another winding branch diverted from the main trunk of the road. Dark shells of ruined houses passed.

Soon, her own home loomed, dark and ugly in the windshield. It was her late husband's house really, the house he'd been born in, last surviving structure of an old mill town. The present-day town of Munro's Furnace, such as remained, lay another three-quarters of a mile down the road.

As the car crunched to a halt on gravel, she stared unblinking. No matter how long she lived here, it always proved something of a shock, this reality. Funny, but in her mind she always pictured the place the way it had been when they'd first begun fixing it up—scaffolding and ladders, cans of paint and bags of cement everywhere. A royal mess, but she hadn't cared because they'd been happy, working together until . . .

Glaring headlights held the cobbled-together structure in cruel scrutiny: clapboard walls beneath phantom paint; boarded first-floor windows she couldn't afford to repair; collapsing front porch propped up with old bed slats and cinder blocks. She switched off the engine, got out, and night fell on her.

Her grandmother's home in Queens—no matter how miserable she'd been there as a child—had at least held life. This house lay black and silent. Looking up, she strained to make out the blind diamond panes of her son's bedroom window. *He's been asleep for hours.* She allowed her gaze to drift across the hanging eaves, along the tilting gabled roof . . . missing shingles . . . crumbling chimneys.

While she limped around to the back, shoulders straight, she forced herself to walk closer to the bristling shadows, farther from the house than necessary. She mounted the wobbling steps to the porch and stood, fumbling her key into the kitchen door. Why couldn't Pamela ever remember to switch on the porch light before she left? Something wet and warm pressed against the back of her hand, and she jumped. "Stupid dog!"

From the darkness of the porch came a yawning whine and the scratching of claws on wood. "Get away, Dooley." When she got the door open, the moldy smell of the house met her like an invisible wall. "Go back to sleep. You can't come in." She heard the dog yawn again and flop back down on the porch with a deflating sigh.

Pulling the door closed behind her, she could see nothing, and she stumbled across the rough wooden floor, feeling along the wall for the switch. She flinched when yellowish light flooded the kitchen.

A three-inch millipede tapped along the stove, waving its antennae in blinded confusion. Darkness bulged at the door. Pamela's note lay on the crumb-littered tablecloth.

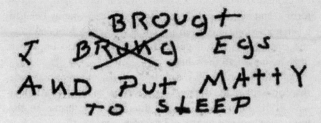

I BROUGT ~~BRIKg~~ EGS
AND Put MATTY
TO SLEEP

Granny Lee once had a dog put to sleep. Her thoughts grew fuzzy and, yawning, she crumpled the note. The cellar door stood slightly ajar. She closed it, turned the old key, remembering how they'd used to tease her about being afraid of the basement at her grandmother's house, and how Aunt Jeanie had always been inventing errands to take her down there. *Such a night for reminiscences.*

The house returned to absolute darkness as she switched off the kitchen light, and a cricket began to throb beneath a floorboard. Groping her way into the living room, she walked into a chair and cursed, then felt her way toward the stairs. The other rooms on the first floor had been closed off. From outside, the voices of the night—the insects and the whispering trees— sounded low and indistinct.

As she started up the stairs, her hand rode along the smooth banister, smearing the dust. She turned left at the landing. Boards creaked under her footsteps along the hall—a loud thump followed by the weaker, softer sound. She went straight to her room.

Without turning on a light, she put the scanner on the dresser, then pulled bobby pins and elastic bands out of her hair. A hair band knotted, and she yanked it out, tossed it on the dresser. Feeling sweaty and dirty, but too tired to do anything about it, she fell across the too-soft, untidy bed. Mounds of laundry lay heaped around her, and her leg ached.

From the scanner, police calls muttered distantly. She listened to them drone and thought about getting undressed, knowing her reflexes would alert her if the tone that preceded ambulance calls sounded. The scanner's small red light was somehow comforting, and her mind drifted to the night-light Granny Lee had given her so long ago. Even as a child, she'd thought it cowardly and every night had dragged herself out of bed to unplug it, loathing herself all the while.

Something rattled overhead. It could have been another tile that had worked loose, clattering across the roof . . . or it might have come from the attic. She listened to the house, to the beams that groaned like an old wooden ship.

She seldom truly slept anymore. Habitually, she'd push herself to exhaustion, then lie twitching on the edge of wakefulness, only to be active at dawn. The hours stretched long before her. Lying in the dark, eyes open, she always ran out of the distractions and evasions. *In the woods.* Whenever she was motionless, questions seemed to whirl around her. She'd expected so much from herself, but what had she done with her life? She was thirty-two years old now and trapped in the pines—ten years almost. It seemed so much longer than that . . . and so much shorter. All the things she'd wanted . . .

Too late.

But her work on the ambulance was important. She tried to hold to that thought as the redness of the scanner grew hazy. Her scalp still smarted from the hair band, and her thoughts drifted to how Aunt Jeanie, jealous of her light skin, had always teased her about her kinky hair, and how Granny Lee had always tried to straighten it with chemicals that stank and burned. *No . . . I don't want . . .* Her hair would come out in fistfuls, and always there would be scabs on her scalp for weeks afterward. *No.*

She closed her eyes, and the darkness was complete.

The bedroom window was open but with the shade drawn against the night. Ten yards from the house, beyond the waving grasses, pines swayed, making a noise like the sea, like a still-boiling primeval element.

And the dream began.

Always, it was the same: torturous fragments raced through her mind, baffling glimpses of frenzy, the savage joy of forest revels, the crazed pursuit of those that fled, blood gushing hot, the rending of fawn's flesh and the splattering of trees in infantile desecration, mad decoration, alone and not alone. She writhed on the bed.

A different noise filtered into her nightmare—a rhythmic groaning, full of the creak of bedsprings.

Half awake, she got up and made her way along the hall. At its end, steep narrow stairs were set in a closetlike alcove, and she went up them practically on all fours, feeling her way in the dark.

The attic room had a sour, baby smell. She felt in the air for the string, and the naked, insect-encrusted bulb blazed, dancing. The attic was a mad jumble of chairs, boxes, broken and unwanted objects from all over the house. *Oh Christ . . . I have to clear out this mess.* Maybe tomorrow she would get to it.

The cot shook, creaking with the boy's efforts. Naked and sweaty, his ten-year-old body twisted into serpentine knots on the bedding, and his teeth locked in the rumpled pillow he ripped with convulsive jerks of his head. The boy was asleep.

She stared. His hair was curly like hers, coppery like his father's, and in the leprous bulb light, his damp skin had an unwholesome yellow sheen. He was the source of the sour smell. She wanted to turn away, obliquely wondering what wordless images comprised his dreams. *He needs a bath.* His sleep-swollen face remained buried in the pillow.

He growled.

"Matthew."

She simply spoke his name, and though his body remained tensed, all movement ceased.

Her son. For perhaps the thousandth time, she wondered about herself, about why she felt no tenderness when she gazed on this child. She would not pretend to herself. Her mind slid to her late husband: she'd let Wallace down in so many ways. The house. The boy. *And the awful thing is I don't really feel sorry, can't even feel guilt anymore. Can't feel anything.* Like hot water scalding dead flesh, her thoughts brought only an echo of pain. *I'm paralyzed.*

There were long scratches on the boy's legs.

He'd been in the woods again, she thought uneasily. *In spite of everything I've said to Pamela, he's been out in the woods.*

She stared another moment. The sheet was a graying tangle, tucked between his legs, and she thought he might have wet the bed again. *If I try to change the bedding now, I'll only wake him.* She switched off the light. *Pamela can do it in the morning.*

As on so many other nights, she groped her way back down into the narrow darkness.

Tuesday, July 14

The sky between dissolving stars grew colorless.

Thick and brown with tannic acid, the sluggish waters of the creek flowed noiselessly over their sandy bed. The fish—the stunted sunfish and carp of the barrens—began to drift up from their murky holes to feed on insects caught on the surface. Occasionally, a young perch would clear the water, landing with a splash, explosive in the prevailing hush. Then broadly circling ripples would spread across the width of the stream, lap softly against the crumbling banks, and vanish.

At the water's edge, a large shape grew gradually more distinct—a man on the bank. Unmoving, he'd stood thus for some time, staring at something lodged upon the rocks.

The dawn light began to glint off tangled yellow hair that stuck out beneath his soiled hunting cap. Al Spencer was a big man, six and a half feet tall. Grizzled face too large, watery eyes too far apart. His whiskey belly bulged under a plaid jacket. Shoulders hunched, he studied the thing in the water; then he peered back into the still-dark pines. Good. Wes was nowhere in sight.

The stream threw off a grayish light that sloshed across the bank. He took off his jacket, folded it and laid it carefully on the sand; then he kicked off his shoes and slipped off his suspenders. The rest of his clothes made a neat pile.

Naked except for his cap, he waded into the stream, slipping on rocks slimy with green moss. The corpse was rigid, shifting almost imperceptibly in the vague current. Al grabbed it by one arm and yanked it around.

The boy's face had become a bloated abomination. Dark hair floated, soft as seaweed, spreading around the head, and gelid eyes had swelled from their sockets, yet clung, opaque as jelly-fish. A huge tongue engulfed blue lips. Even the neck had ex-panded, become a puffy, waterlogged trunk slashed with purple wounds that leaked thin fluid. The green T-shirt, too tight now, rode up and exposed the round white stomach.

There was a watch on the left wrist.

Al crouched low in the shallows, the water warmish on his genitals, and with furtive gentleness, pried the watchband off the swollen wrist, over the stiffened fingers. Barely glancing at it, he slipped it onto his own wrist. Then he stuck his hands in the dead boy's pockets but found nothing. He giggled—other things had swollen too. With a quick heave, he flipped the body over onto his stomach and fished out the wallet.

It contained twelve dollars, some pulped identification, and a graduation photo of a girl. He squeezed the money in his palm and tossed the wallet into the creek. It floated for a second be-fore it opened and spun downward.

Splashing back to the bank, he climbed out, dripping, stuffed the loot in his jacket and picked up his pants. Then he stopped, thoughtful. It was wrong to just leave the body there. He took the pocketknife out of his pants and with long strides sloshed back into the creek.

He flipped the corpse onto its back and launched it into the center of the stream. Flies kept trying to settle. Snicking open the jackknife, he waded after it.

The blade was thick with rust.

Slowly, the woods took on color, pinkish light blazing first at the tips of the pines, then shimmering along the trunks.

He plunged the blade deep into the distended stomach, and the corpse splashed under. It bobbed, and a stiffened arm struck his thigh. Foul gases escaped as he stuck the knife in again, neatly slitting the belly. The gash burbled, and he gagged on the stench. Immediately, the body began to sink, trailing fat bubbles, fluid spreading like smoke through the brown water.

He waded back to the shallows and clawed up a slime-haired rock, breaking a thumbnail in the process. "Shit." Grunting with the weight, he returned to where the body hung just below the surface. It drifted slightly, eyes trailing. He positioned the rock and dropped it on the chest.

The birds were beginning to make a racket as he clambered back onto the bank and shook himself like a dog. Dressing, he smiled the mild smile of a man who has completed some trivial yet satisfying task. Finally, he put the jacket back on and patted the pocket, feeling the damply wadded money.

Already, the sky was so bright it hurt his eyes. Hiking back toward camp, he sucked on his broken nail, tasting blood and foulness.

With the morning sun slanting across the corrugated roof, the heat in the ambulance hall soon reached oven proportions, even with the garage door up. A few feet beyond the blindly staring ambulance, Doris sat at a card table with Larry Jenkins, a trainee.

"This one's from a call we had a couple weeks back." Doris raised her voice to be heard above an old window fan that stood on the cement floor. "We picked up this guy down at that new construction site. You know the one? That development out by Batsto?" Steam swirled from a Styrofoam cup and mingled with the smoke from her cigarette.

Yawning, Larry reached for the report. "Bad?"

She checked the card. "Just a metal sliver in his hand. Lots of blood though. You should have heard him yelling. We took it out for him, bandaged him up, took him over to the clinic at Mount Misery for stitches."

Considering what to show him next, she flipped through reports, found the one about the man who'd fallen on the chainsaw—over a week old now.

"Is this everybody?" Sounding disappointed, Larry glanced down the list of volunteers.

"And, oh yeah, whenever you pick anybody up from the construction site, you got to make sure somebody there follows you to bring the guy back."

"I thought you had more women working this thing."

Walking through the hatch, Jack Buzby sauntered over to the table. It had been his idea to get his buddy Larry involved. They did everything together, almost. Both were volunteer forest-fire wardens, and both worked for a roofing company owned by Larry's uncle. "How's little Larry doin', teach?"

"Man, would you quit it with that 'little' crap?" All five foot six, one hundred and fifteen pounds of him bridled. When angry, his nineteen-year-old face vividly displayed the thick cloud of freckles that covered it.

"He's doing all right, I guess. Let's see now. You know calls are in clear speech, right?" She shuffled through blank forms and looked up at Jack. "Christ, it's hot. Who am I running with today anyhow?"

"Athena and Siggy."

"Sig?" She groaned. "Oh shit, the fate worse than sex. It's not bad enough they bleed all over me, I have to be in a close space with that smell? What's the matter, don't I live right?" As Jack walked away chuckling, she called after him. "Forget I said any of that."

"Said what?" He got a Coke out of the refrigerator and strolled back outside to the hot blue morning.

Larry picked up an accident card, and Doris glanced at it. "Athena filled that one out." She took it from him, holding it gingerly between fingers brown with nicotine.

Watching her read it over, he felt she expected him to say something. "Uh, I hear she's real good."

"Clear head that woman's got. Not like some."

"She really black?"

She raked him with a look.

"I only ask because she sure don't, uh, look like no . . . I mean, do they, uh, have a lot of accidents out at that site?"

Her gaze relaxed. "Almost every day, seems like, and they always call us. One of the foremen is a buddy of mine." She crushed out her cigarette. "Tell you the truth, I don't know why they haven't had a fatality out there yet. They're all a bunch of alcoholics anyway." Leaning closer, she added, "They're claiming there's been a lot of sabotage by locals. Ropes cut halfway through, that sort of thing. Pineys jealous over the jobs, I guess."

Larry nodded, thinking she had a real nice build for an old broad. He breathed in her perfume. Strong and pungent. And oddly familiar. Old Spice? He fanned himself with an accident report.

Outside, Jack shaded his eyes and swigged Coke from the can as a car pulled up. The Plymouth looked cancerous with rust, midnight blue paint flaking off the sides.

"Athena, when you gonna clean out this car?"

Surprised, she peered up through the smeary windshield. "What?" She'd been rifling the glove compartment for a candy bar, her breakfast, only to find a runny lump. "Damn." The vinyl seat next to her was heaped with what looked like a year's worth of junk mail and outdated ambulance paperwork. "Why?" Crumpled paper cups and hamburger wrappings covered the backseat. "You want to do it for me?"

"I'll betchya I could do it for ya, 'Thena." He gave her his best sexy smile. "Given half a chance." Behind the thick lenses of his glasses, his eyes were pale blurs. Staring, he tried to figure out what it was about this woman that excited him. He supposed she was attractive enough in her own way, though not especially pretty, not with her hair pulled back that way and the shirt buttoned all the way up. Then there was the leg, too. Maybe it was just this feeling that she'd be so grateful if a guy could only get her to loosen up a little. Flashing his teeth at her again, he leaned against the car and wondered whether she wore the same blue work shirt every day or if she had a warehouse full of them at home.

She smiled thinly and shoved the door open, almost knocking him over. "You didn't pull duty today, did you?"

"Nope, I came over with Larry—he's inside with Doris." Sweat soaked the front of his T-shirt, and he gulped more soda.

"So how's things in 'Ro's Furnace?" He took his glasses off, wiped perspiration out of his eyes with a muscular forearm.

"How should I know?" Marching around the side of the car, she checked a tire that was low on air. "So it's me, Doris and a trainee?"

"Nope," he answered, grinning. "Sig the Stink's running with you." The face she made almost choked him. "Better not let Doris see you making fun a him."

Larry looked up from what Doris was showing him. "Athena's here. Hey, I been meaning to ask you, how come she limps like that?"

"When she was a little girl, they told her she'd never walk again." The words came out rapidly. "Obviously, they didn't know her very well." Without glancing at him, she lit another cigarette. "Poor kid had a rough time. No parents. Then the grandmother died." She exhaled heavily, then cleared her throat. "Most of the calls in these parts are from the highways. Like I told you, we don't do those except in special cases, like if there's a big pileup, and the hospital ambulances can't handle it all. I'll tell you frankly, since you're going to be working with us, we have an agreement with certain friends of mine. The state won't go out of its way to inspect our operation so long as we keep to the pines. People have a real funny attitude towards us. Nobody gives much of a shit what goes on out here. They just want to stick us with all the prisons and loony bins and forget about them. Before we started, a lot of pineys never even got to a hospital. Now, of course, the hospitals don't even want them half the time." She sighed. "We're underequipped. So you'll just have to make do with what we've got. We'll take anything you can beg, borrow and/or steal from the area clinics. They don't like us much." Suddenly, she smiled. "Hiya, honey. How are you this morning?"

Athena picked up the duty roster. "Who's driving today?"

"Sig's not here yet. If anything comes in, you take it out."

Athena nodded. "So what do you think, Larry? Are you going to be running with us from now on?"

He grinned at her. "I hope so."

Jack stepped forward, a keen competitive gleam in his eyes.

". . . even studied the manual already," Doris was saying. "We'll just have to see how he makes out when—"

Jack horned in. "These cards are a gas, ain't they? Pineys have the weirdest damn accidents. 'Thena, you remember that time when—?"

Larry interrupted, "Man, since when ain't you a piney?"

"Since he took a bath," supplied Doris, "and started wearing tight jeans."

"Is there any more coffee?"

"Athena, you're not really gonna drink Doris's coffee, are you?" Very casually, Jack pressed up close to her. "Look at this stuff—it's like motor oil."

"Don't worry, I don't drink it. Look out." She poured a cup of scalding liquid. "I fill one of the syringes and mainline it."

"Jack, this is your captain speaking. You want to give Sig a call and see whether he's planning on joining us sometime today?"

The phone rang, and Doris shouted. Moving with surprising speed, Athena leaped into the rig. She started the engine and swung the ambulance out of the bay. Doors banged open, Jack hanging on. He hopped off, tugging the bay door down behind them.

Doris jumped in next to Athena. "You want to come, Jack? We're still a man short. Get that side door shut. Make sure it's locked. Come on, Larry! Get your skinny ass in here!"

Heart pounding, Larry clambered through the hatch.

Wes Shourds looked up from the dead animals. He wore his sand-colored hair pasted down flat, which enhanced the vaguely frog-gish look of his broad face and bulging eyes. Just below his left eye, he bore a large inflamed birthmark, and something was wrong with his mouth, a sort of crimping to the upper lip. Though still young, he was already going to beery fat. "Find anything?"

"Nope," muttered Al.

"Sure gone a long time."

"Yeah?" Al picked at his long, dirty fingernails. "So? Didn't find nuthin' 'cept some funny sorta tracks."

Wes knew the tone of voice well enough not to push it. Spencer was a good man to go off deer-jacking with, but you had to be careful with him—he got nuts sometimes. Especially when he had the shakes. Wes swatted away a blackfly that was trying to bite his lip. "Coffee's 'bout ready."

Al's habitual look of hostility lessened somewhat, and he sat on the log. "I got sumthin' here lots better'n coffee fer takin' the chill off." Rummaging through the gear in the bag, he produced a large-mouthed jar of pale fluid and took a deep slug. Golden liquid dribbled down his stubbled chin. As he wiped the hairy back of one hand across his mouth, he silently passed the jar to Wes.

Wes figured Al probably wasn't kidding about being cold—he never took that damn hunting jacket off. Made a man sweat just to look at him. He gulped the burning fluid, wondering if Al slept in that jacket, if he screwed in it. "Shit," he said, eyes watering. "This ain't from the same batch as t'other stuff, is it?" He glanced at the shards of broken glass that littered the clearing.

"Fuck you! What's the matter with it, asshole?" Al snatched the jar back. Some of it spilled, and he started cursing good, then. Wes flinched.

Strange, but he never liked to hear Al cuss. Something about the way Al said certain words made his flesh creep, sort of. "Damn shame about that blast catchin' this one in the gut."

In response, Spencer only muttered blackly and knuckled at his runny nose.

Wes looked him over cautiously, noting the huge pores of Al's face, his rotting teeth, even the straggly sideburns: he had to be about the ugliest man he'd ever seen. Al still fumed over the whiskey, and Wes continued his efforts to change the subject. "Sure ruined a lotta good meat." Beside him, a buck and a doe stained the sand and lichen. Flies swarmed.

The night's hunting had been easy—a lucky thing, Wes considered, since they'd been so drunk—a simple matter of freezing the small herd with powerful flashlights, then blasting away. Because they could get into big trouble if caught out here with rifles, they always used shotguns, the buckshot strung together with wire so it wouldn't scatter. But sometimes the wire came apart. Last night, a peripheral blast had torn open the neck of a second doe, and though spouting blood, she'd managed to bound away. Following by flashlight, they'd lost the blood trail near the creek. Al went looking this morning but . . .

Wes's eyes narrowed. That's why Al had been gone so long— he'd found the doe and hidden her, meaning to come back and get her for himself later. Come to think of it, the bastard was looking pretty pleased with himself.

"You know, Al, we still gotta haul them kills back to the truck." Disgusted, Wes knew better than to say anything about the second doe. "Your son shoulda come. Coulda used the extra man." They'd hidden the truck off an unused road, covered it with branches so the troopers wouldn't spot it.

"Marl don't like goin' jackin'." Al spat on the ground, a curious note of pride entering his voice. "My boy Marl, he hates the woods." He grinned at the pines.

Wes had heard all about Marl Spencer's hatred of the woods. Local gossip was full of it. Wes clenched his fists. He figured anybody that would set fires would do anything. His fists ached— somebody ought to take that loony kid out in the woods and shoot him. He gritted his teeth, flexed his hands. "So what happened to ole Lonny? I thought he's s'posed to be yer helper." He kept his eyes on the dry woods as he spoke. "Jus' one match 'ud do it," he whispered to himself.

"That drunken bastard Lonny don't do shit," said Al amiably. "I been good ta him too. Lettin' him share a room wi' my boy an all. He jus' better be watchin' that still, s'all I can say. Can't even find 'im half the time. Sniffin' after that Pam." Al started talking about sex again.

His sudden anger fading, Wes went back to cleaning out the buck's leaking intestines, a noxious mess shot with black. He didn't pay much attention to the other man's talk. Al was always going on about sex. Specifically, he was always going on about sex with old lady Stewart. In spite of having been past her prime and exceedingly obese for as long as anyone could remember, Lizzie Stewart had been covered by every man and, if there were any truth to rumor, half the farm animals in four counties.

"She come over to the gin mill t'other day, while I was checkin' the still. I really let her have it." He thought a minute, scratched at his stubble of gray-blond beard. "You wouldn't believe the sorta thing she likes, boy."

Though he'd had plenty of opportunities to discover the proclivities of the lady in question, Wes dutifully responded, "You dog."

"Marl stuck 'is head in the door while I was goin' at 'er, an you shoulda seen the eyes bug outta his head." Al guffawed. "That boy took off like the Leeds Devil was after 'im. Couldn't find 'im fer a hour."

Wes finished trussing the buck. He put the jacklights away in the rucksack and hefted his shotgun. "We best get started 'fore it gets any later." He rubbed at his eyes. "All that rum we drunk last night. Meat's gonna spoil in this heat. We shoulda been long gone as is." He saw that Al hadn't moved. "'Less you want 'em to catch us outlawin'."

"You always worryin', boy." Al reached for the tin cup. "I ain't even had no coffee yet."

She took the rig down an infrequently used expanse of old highway—the call hadn't given an exact location. The sun felt blisteringly hot on Athena's left arm and shoulder, and she glanced to the side: a burned-out section of forest, all scorched earth and blackened stumps. Flame red flowers dotted the charred earth though, and glimpsing them, she smiled a little. The ride seemed almost smooth, save for a new knocking in the engine.

Behind her, Doris still lectured. "Then a lot of the time victims refuse treatment, or have left the scene, then what you do is—"

Athena interrupted, "There it is." Her pulse quickened in anticipation.

"That siren sounds like it's dying," said Doris, as she climbed up front. "It'll be the next thing to break down, I guess. Wouldn't you know the first call we get would make a liar out of me? I just got done telling the kid we don't get car accidents."

"Well, that ain't true anyways, Doris." Jack turned to Larry.

"We got this tractor-trailer wreck once where we had to scrape the guy up with a fish knife."

"Cut it out, Jack," demanded Doris.

A blue and white state police car, just parking on the shoulder of the road, honked a greeting. The highway shimmered in waves of heat, and two shattered vehicles hissed, angled on opposite sides of the road. Pulling the ambulance over by the nearer car, Athena turned off the siren as Doris jumped out into the white haze. Larry clambered down behind her, blinded after the dimness of the rig's interior.

A uniformed trooper called over. "You handle this, Doris?"

Crowbar in hand, Athena climbed down, mumbling to herself. "One of these days we're going to have to deal with someone she doesn't know. Bound to happen."

"I'll tell ya whether or not we can handle it after I see what it is," Doris muttered. "Jack, Athena, take this one. You come with me, Larry." She called back to the trooper. "What happened here, Fred?"

"Header, looks like."

Doris sprinted to the car on the far side of the hot asphalt. Nervous and eager, Larry followed.

Halfway out onto the buckled, shining hood, a woman sprawled in a welter of blood and glass, and while Doris checked for vital signs, Larry squinted at the burning glare. The woman's hair was red now. One side of her face was laid open in the sunlight, her back teeth grinning blue and yellow.

The empty road ran parallel to the highway, down which flowed a steady stream of traffic, placid and so close.

The tar was soft and blistered. No air stirred. Larry felt an internal doubling of the heat. His shadow turned black, and the road seemed to be burning through the bottoms of his sneakers, while the sun glinted around the blood on the car. Bits of steering wheel lay all around him.

"Fred? Call the coroner's wagon to come get this one."

The trooper stood by the police car. "Will do, Doris. Sure is a scorcher today." He stooped to the window and said something to his partner.

"How you doin' anyway, Fred?" Abruptly, Doris squeezed Larry's arm. "Go sit over there and put your head down. You'll be all right in a minute."

"Just fine, Doris," the trooper replied. "How's yourself?"

"Can't complain." She peered into the police car. "Don't say hello, Jim."

The trooper in the car shook his head and muttered. "Goddamn wreck shouldn't even be allowed on the road."

"What's that, Jim? You talking about me or the ambulance?"

"How are you, Doris?" he said louder. "Still running that outlaw rig, I see."

"Don't do me any favors. You don't want to talk to me? Go ahead. Be ignorant."

Across the highway, Athena and Jack leaned into the windows of the other vehicle. Gunmetal gray, it was ancient, back doors tied with clothesline, hot vapor still squirting from the radiator.

The smell of voided bowels filled the overheated car. Athena judged the old man to be about seventy; the boy looked fifteen at most. Glass fragments glittered like some impossible frost in the boy's hair, and across his forehead a deep gash oozed, slowly, steadily. One of them groaned. The old man clutched feebly at his chest, and the sunlight, slanting onto his face, revealed an awful pallor.

"He's the one—get the old guy," directed Athena.

"Christ," Jack said. "You could cook in here." He tugged at the smashed door on the driver's side, throwing all his weight into it.

"Just take it easy." Athena reached through the passenger window. "You'll be all right now." She felt pieces of bone moving under the flesh of the boy's arm, and he trembled violently. "Easy."

"Fuck, I don't believe it."

"What's the matter, Jack?"

"You see the way these back doors are tied shut? Take us a hour to cut through all this. Hey, Doris!"

The boy's eyes focused on Athena. "My daddy . . . my

daddy's hurt. Please help my daddy, lady." The voice was that of a very small child.

She realized her mistake: this wasn't a teenager. She'd been misled by the unlined face and the subtly wrong shape of the head. This was a grown man, perhaps twenty-five years old. She watched as one of his overlarge ears slowly filled with blood. "You're okay now. Take it easy." In that moment, the young man's eyes shone with complete trust, and she backed out of the car, attacking the stripping around the crack-rayed windshield with the crowbar. "I could use a little help here, Jack," she grunted. The chrome came off easily, and in seconds they were tugging off the glass. It came out in pieces, and they tossed the chunks to the side of the road. Brushing fragments out of the way, she climbed over the hood.

The old man's mouth moved.

"No, don't try to talk."

He shook, lips working.

"Okay, I'm coming. Take it easy." She leaned her head to him. "What is it? Where do you hurt?"

His voice hissed in her ear. "My boy's slow." His eyes watered. "You unnerstand? You take care a my Joey first." He croaked the words, his chest heaving in strange fluid wobbles. "He don' unnerstand." Breath came in liquid gulps.

"Doris!"

"Let's get moving here!" Doris trotted over with the kit. "What've you got?"

"Flailed chest." Athena crouched over the dashboard. "Little bit harder and he'd be pinned on the steering column. We've got to get to him—now."

Doris grabbed the crowbar. "How's the kid, Jack?"

"Head injuries—broken arm, lacerations," he announced, fixing a splint. His glasses kept slipping down his nose because of the way he was sweating.

Still crouching, Athena bound the old man's arms across his chest. As the sun pounded on her back, she felt flooded with sweat, cramping, and the heat seemed to boil away her strength. "How're we going to get this old guy out of here? Oh."

"That's got it." With a loud ripping, Doris pried the door open and snapped the hinges, letting it fall in the road. "Larry, come over here and watch this. Jack, where's the board?"

Sweat got in their eyes, a stinging blur, as they strapped the old man to the board, lifting him out the side. Jack wheeled over the rattling litter, and the troopers lent a hand. While windshield glass fell from their clothes to tinkle and crunch on the ground, the older man and the younger steadily pleaded that the other be looked after first.

"Christ, these two are going to break my heart," Doris muttered, running alongside the litter. "Fred? You guys hanging around to wait for the coroner's wagon?" They slid the stretcher into the rig.

"Yeah, Doris. Catch ya later."

As they pulled out, Athena grabbed the radio, letting the hospital know what to expect. Doris set Larry to bandaging Joey's head, while Jack checked out the old man.

Still pale, Larry moved slowly, clumsily. Blood seeped through the bandages faster than he could wrap them, and Joey just stared doe-eyed at his father, so white and still.

Every time he bleated for his "Daddy," Athena squirmed in the driver's seat. She couldn't understand why it should bother her so much. She knew little enough about fathers. Few men had hung around while she was growing up, certainly no paternal ones. The family history held that her mother had been raped. Whatever the case, after her mother's breakdowns and suicide attempts began, Athena had been carted from Alabama to her grandmother's house in New York. "Fathers yet," she muttered to herself. "I may be starting to crack up myself." She tried not to listen to the boy.

"How're you making out, Larry?"

"Okay." Joey's eyes seemed to float in murky liquid as Larry wrapped the bandages around and around his head, the red flower blooming through the white gauze. "You get a lot of retards out here, don't you?"

Joey's face quivered.

"Shut up, you idiot," hissed Athena.

Doris helped Jack with the old man. "Inbreeding—woods are full of them," she told him dispassionately. "There used to be a whole sort of village for defectives around here." She glanced up. "I'm not shitting you. The state built a colony for them out in the woods. Make it a little tighter. That's it. You're doing fine."

The woods are full of them. Athena's grip on the wheel tightened. It was what she'd always maintained: there was nothing wrong with her son, he was just a normal piney. The very word still froze her. *Piney.* Siren wailing, the ambulance joined the stream of traffic on the highway, and she swerved the rig in and out, expertly passing cars on both sides.

Frightened by the blaring siren, Joey wept. With a casual gesture, Doris reached to brush glass chips out of his hair. "There's another roll of bandages in there," she said. Then Joey screamed as vomit erupted from the old man, splashing across Doris's leg. "He's choking! Help me get him on his side!"

Larry stared.

"Come on, damn it!"

Jack leaped to assist her while she stuck two fingers down the old man's throat, clearing the air passage. "Shit! He's coding. Jack, mouth-to-mouth, move it!"

Jack looked at the vomit smearing the old man's mouth. "Oh Christ." He grimaced, then went to work.

"I want to go home. Daddy? What's the matter, Daddy?"

Larry just kept wrapping bandages until Joey's head looked huge. The ambulance slammed to a halt.

"Receiving," Athena announced, and they all scrambled to unload.

Confused and panicked, Joey was wheeled through the emergency ward toward X-ray. He kept calling for his father, while men in white wheeled the old man in the opposite direction.

Alone, Larry sat on a bench. The sound of slow typing drizzled from somewhere down the corridor.

"How you feeling now? You still look a little green." Doris slapped him on the shoulder. "We've just got to hang around until somebody signs for them." She jerked a thumb at Athena, arguing at the admitting desk.

Larry nodded weakly. "It's just it was a chick, you know? If it was a guy, I coulda stood it."

"What? Oh, the dead one." Doris looked at him closely, then sat. "Try not to think about it. Most of the calls we get are stuff like, oh, bleeders with minor cuts—there's lots of hemophiliacs out here—allergic reactions to insect bites, that kind of thing."

He smiled weakly.

"That's better." She punched him lightly on the arm. "You'll survive."

"The water fountain ain't working." Jack approached, rubbing his hand across his mouth. "Christ, I hate mouth-to-mouth. You hear anything about the old guy?"

A plume of dust stretched behind the battered panel truck as it bounced and grunted over the sand. The exhaust snorted smoke, and Wes fought the steering wheel. "You know, there's niggers workin' the construction over ta Batsto," he said with shocked grievance in his voice.

"Yeah, I heard, I heard."

"Sure is hard to believe." Both men shook their heads.

Al hurled a jar against a tree.

"I thought you was gonna save that ta put booze in?"

His side of the truck lacked a door, and Al had to grip the frame to keep from being thrown out. "Shit." With each bump, his head felt as though it would burst. He needed a drink. "Knew I shoulda brung more." He shut his eyes for a minute, tried to pretend they were already back at Munro's Furnace, at his place, dipping into the whiskey barrel. He could almost feel it in his parched mouth.

Their gear and guns lay hidden in back under a sticky tarp and some chicken wire. They'd gotten twenty cents a pound for the venison at the Chamong Diner. Al had wanted fifty cents, and in the parking lot he'd roared and blustered, but nobody got the better of old man Sims. The meat was bad, and Sims

knew it, which—while it would not prevent his serving it—
disinclined him toward paying top dollar.

The truck shuddered and bucked, while Al returned to his
favorite topic. "You know what that is?"

"I am acquainted wi' it."

"No, you ain't. But, hell, once they get the taste a it, they don't
want nothin' else." His mien grew serious. "We can't let that
happen. No, sir, none a that."

A shack appeared on the right, then a hundred yards farther,
two more, obviously abandoned. The roof of the Monroe place
became visible over the pines. "Damn shame 'bout the way that
nigger bitch pushed ole Lonny outta his own house," Wes muttered as they passed. "Damn shame."

Al nodded in solemn agreement.

"Somebody oughtta take that gimp out inna woods an shoot
'er," continued Wes. "Her an at retard kid a hers." The truck
thundered across a pine-log bridge, the water of Hobbs Creek
still and muddy around the pilings. "What's 'at over there?" He
pointed into the brush and stamped on the brake.

"What's the matter with you?" Al yelled, holding his forehead. "What the fuck you stopping for? You made me bang my
fuckin' head!"

"That's my old man's truck," Wes said, already climbing out.
"What's it doing just sittin' there?"

"He's prob'ly off jackin' or something. Where you going,
asshole?"

"Not here he ain't jacking." Wes ran back, trampling through
the thicket. "Looks like he just rolled off the road," he mumbled to himself as he approached the truck; it rested against a
small cluster of pines.

Al clambered down. "Get back over here! I need a goddamn
drink an yer—" He saw the sudden tension in Wes's shoulders.
"What the fuck?" Al approached, muttering. He glanced first at
Wes, then gazed into the truck and let loose a low whistle.
"What in hell . . . ?"

Wes stared, the cords of his neck bulging. Then he yanked
the door open, and out billowed the flies. The truck was empty,

cabin torn apart, cushion stuffing ripped out in great fistfuls, all of it spattered with brown. Dripping ropes of a thick, dark substance hung from beneath the door, and dried gobs lay on the ground in places where wetness had been absorbed into the earth, leaving only scum at the top, crusted bits gleaming in the sunlight.

Bloated flies buzzed drowsily in the heat. Some swarmed on a damp patch, covering it with their shining bodies.

"Can't we get the damned windows fixed?"

"Cigarettes bothering you?"

Coughing, Athena kept her eyes on the road. "Your perfume."

Doris laughed. "I overdo it again? Sorry, kid. Just a habit I got into back when I . . ."

"Don't say it."

". . . used to work in the morgue. Like I always say, you can take the girl out of the icebox, but you can't take the—"

"I'd settle for taking the icebox out of the conversation, thank you."

Doris laughed again, then her face went hard. "Was that bitch at the desk giving you a bad time? What's her problem now?"

"Said we should have taken them to the infirmary in Chatsworth."

"Injuries that serious?"

The younger woman shrugged, steered the rig up to the bay door. They found Sig the Stink out in front of the hall, grinning shyly. Siggy Applegate was fat and bald, slow moving and unwashed, but the rest of the crew were under strict instructions to be nice to him. He was a Quaker—there were a lot of them in the area—and through him Doris hoped to gain some measure of community support. They needed it.

Blinking small moist eyes at them, Sig blocked the driveway, and his little arm shot up as though holding back the rig. There was something spastic about the gesture; the arm seemed to have moved of its own accord. "Uh, Athena, uh, don't put the rig away. We had another call, Doris. It just come in. Uh, kid playing with firecrackers out by Ong's Hat."

"Jackpot," said Doris. "I hope you appreciate this training, Larry. Sometimes we go days without a call. Take us out, honey. We'll see you tonight, Jack. Siggy, get in the rig!"

Peeling tar paper covered the few cedar wood shacks. In the center of the clearing, a dog sniffed around a huge mound of discarded clothing and tin cans, and everywhere rotted abandoned cars and pieces of cars.

Munro's Furnace.

With a clattering roar, the truck aimed for the main cluster of buildings. Al yelled as the truck slammed to a halt, spraying sand, just in front of his gin mill.

"You start knockin' on doors!" Wes swung down. "Find out if anybody's seen Pa! I'm gonna round up guys wi' shotguns. An dogs!"

"Count on me, buddy." Al jumped down. "We'll find 'im." Any gathering of the residents of Munro's Furnace would be sure to occasion the selling of whiskey, and as he started toward a neighboring shack, a grin seeped through his mask of concern.

Behind him, Wes cursed. Al whirled around.

A brown and white cat rubbing against his leg, Marl stood on the crumbling cement steps of the gin mill. Unkempt blond hair framed his face, pale and dappled with acne, and his short body looked well padded with baby fat. Half in the shadowed doorway, he blinked at the daylight, his cotton shirt and the lower part of his slack face glistening with wet blood.

A few yards away, Wes faced him, his mouth working silently.

"No, Wes!" Racing toward them, Al yelled, "Leave 'im alone! He jus' gits nosebleeds allatime!"

The cat vanished, and the boy stared after it. By the time his vacant eyes widened, it was too late to run.

Wes slammed into him, shook the boy viciously, Marl's head snapping back and forth. "My pa! You fuckin' loony! Where's my pa? Whad you do to 'im?" He kept screaming while the boy's head knocked against the wall.

Al jumped in as Wes turned, shouting and swinging, and the

pine wall made a buckling sound as the two men hit the side of the building.

Released, Marl sank to the ground, his expression puzzled as blood slowly branched, trickling from his white nostrils.

Under a graying sky, a small group of women hurried out of one of the nearby houses, and from somewhere men came running with eager shouts of "There's a fight down Spencer's!"

"But he's got blood all over 'im!" Wes slumped against the wall, choking with rage and surrender as the blood dripped from his mouth and down his chin.

"I told ya, ya asshole—he gits nosebleeds!" Face white and rigid, Al stood astride Wes, shaking his big fists. "He don't know nuthin' 'bout yer friggin' father."

The gathering crowd made disappointed sounds—it was over.

Panting heavily, Al took a step back and looked for his son. "Where da fuck . . . ?"

Random bullet holes pocked the wood of the doorway like tiny black tunnels. From within the darkened gin mill came a whimpering sob.

Storm clouds massed.

The highway to the shore cut straight and clean through the forest, and Athena drove mechanically through the flat sameness of the countryside.

Doris pointed out a yellow call box. "That's got to be where the call came from."

When Athena pumped the brakes, the ambulance took the turn sharply. As always, her breath caught at the instantaneous transition from highway to wilderness, and her palms began sweating slightly as she tried to imagine what this road must be like at night.

Navigating the choppy sand, she recalled the first stories she'd ever heard about "pineys," so long ago, old tales told mostly as shuddery jokes. Everyone snickered about the pineys, about their being weird and dangerous—seven feet tall, some of them, supposedly; whole families with six fingers on each hand; cannibals, degenerates and worse. She shook her head and half-grinned to herself, remembering the first self-professed pineys she'd actually met: a well-dressed couple, both of whom spoke with a slight country twang. That had been almost a disappointment, and later, upon meeting so many others just like them, she'd dismissed the fables as just that.

She hadn't known then about the shantytowns.

The road became a rut through desolate runty trees, and they passed a shack that looked as though it might collapse at any moment, flowered curtain trailing out a lopsided window. A few minutes later, similarly primitive structures appeared at a crossroads. Ong's Hat, population twenty-three. Sagging beneath a blueberry-dark sky, these dwellings leaned at awkward and unlikely angles, as if built by children out of cards, as if any strong wind might knock them down.

Athena tightened her grip on the slickness of the wheel. All these sand-road hamlets looked the same. Yet something hung in the air. A feeling. A sense that those who lived like this had no hope . . . couldn't help but be brutal. Bestial. Never would she get used to it.

A small knot of people in the road refused to budge, so Athena switched off the siren, and straining at the wheel, swerved the ambulance toward the runty trees. It lumbered off the road between saplings; then it rattled to a stop, and she backed it up.

Pines pressed the crumbling little town, and through them, the wind carried a faint scent of rain. The sky brooded, barely suppressing thunder.

Mumbling and sweating, Siggy peered through the hatch window. Doris tried to look over his few long wisps of sweaty hair, got a whiff of breath like dead mice and drew back hastily.

"It's all right, Sig." She inhaled thinly. "We can handle these folks."

Trembling, he tried to grin. His teeth were yellow and ground to nubs, as though his diet consisted entirely of birdseed. "They, uh, a couple of them have got guns." His voice seemed to come from somewhere around his knees.

"You can wait in the rig." She pushed him aside and shoved the hatch open. Vaulting down, she moved toward the crowd, Larry and Athena close behind her. Athena lugged the first-aid kit.

The cluster of pineys fell silent, still refusing to make way, and several glared openly at Athena's limp. Doris shouldered her way in.

Larry stared. These people had to be the worst he'd ever seen— some of the men held shotguns, muzzles low to the ground, and two sharp-ribbed dogs skirted the group. He followed Athena's slender form as it wended fearlessly through the small crowd.

A woman in a filthy black dress got in front of him, and mumbling an apology, he tried to ease past her, unable to keep from staring at her plastic brooch: a Christmas tree, sparkles mostly gone. Her hollowed face pressed toward him, glaring with rheumy eyes, and he found himself holding his breath.

An adolescent boy lay stretched out in the bloody sand, the crowd poking and prodding.

"Don't touch him!" shouted Doris. "Siggy! Where's that stretcher?"

Larry glanced back to where Siggy cowered in the rig. "I'll get it, Doris," he said and plunged back into the crowd.

Thunder rumbled, and the wind blew harder. The crowd made a murmuring noise, and as Doris and Athena knelt on either side of the injured boy, one of the dogs began to howl.

The boy's right hand had been shattered into burned fragments.

"Very shocky." Athena checked his pulse. "Lost a lot of blood."

"More than he should have."

The crowd grew louder with angry mutterings.

A shotgun leveled. "Whatchyou doin' to that boy?"

"Throw the kid in the rig," Doris whispered. "Be ready to run." She stood up, smiling. "Are you the father?"

"Whatchyou doin'?" he slurred. "Whatsat frizzy-haired bitch doin' to him?"

Her smile never wavered. "Are you the boy's father?" she repeated, making eye contact.

"I might be. Maybe. I could be." Alcohol fumes belched from the toothless face. "No."

Doris spotted a car about thirty yards away, another shotgun sticking out of it. She squared her shoulders.

Larry ran back with the collapsed stretcher under his arm, then stood gaping at the guns.

Athena beckoned him over. While they lifted the boy, she kept one eye on the crowd. *The mark of the barrens.* She'd have recognized the meanness in these faces anywhere. *No.* She noted the threadbare, old-fashioned clothing, that several of the children went barefoot. *Not pointy-eared monsters.* The unconscious boy didn't weigh much. *Not like the stories.* They hefted the stretcher, and the crowd parted, grudgingly. *Human refuse.* As they marched toward the rig, Doris's voice followed them.

"Isn't anyone here related to him?"

Siggy clucked in fussy circles around the stretcher. "They could kill us all and bury us out here and nobody'd ever know."

"Get to work, Sig," Athena told him. The glowering sky made her nervous. "Anyway, what makes you think they'd bury us? They look more like they'd eat us."

Larry barked a laugh.

She glanced back—their squad captain still spoke to the man with the shotgun, pacifying, politicking. *There's nothing like watching a pro in action.* She'd be getting a donation out of him in a minute.

Larry wrapped bandages around the boy's hand, and Siggy had begun fiddling with an IV unit.

"Sig, I heard Doris tell you about that twice already. You set up that IV, and the hospital won't even want to admit him." She turned away in disgust. "We're going to have trouble enough if she can't find a relative."

With a movement both clumsy and graceful, she jumped down from the back of the rig and stood in the road. Sand blowing in her face, she craned her neck to watch gray violence gather in the sky. "Doris, we've got to move," she called. Shielding her eyes from flying grit, she climbed back into the driver's seat. From one of the sagging structures, an infant wailed, but none of the people in the road responded, and the ocean sound of wind in the pines pooled and eddied around the clearing.

The motor idled.

Doris clambered into the back of the rig, slamming the doors. "Take us out, honey." Siggy sighed loudly as they lurched away, bouncing over a rut with a jarring thud.

"Nobody admits to being the boy's family," Doris told them. "Or to making the call. Christ. Guess they're all afraid of getting stuck with a hospital bill. How you making out, Sig? I looked all over the place but couldn't find the fingers." She laughed. "Maybe one of the dogs ate them." Siggy held sterile compresses over the mangled stumps where the boy's index and middle fingers had been, and she passed him more bandages. "It's still coming out. Here, Larry," she said, "push down hard on the wrist, try to slow the flow."

Siggy wrapped another triangular bandage around the hand, and they all swayed as the rig swerved onto the highway. Struggling to keep his balance, Larry pressed his palm on the boy's wrist.

"Harder."

He could feel the pulse as liquid tried to squirt through.

"Hell." Doris went after the brachial artery in the upper arm with her fingers.

Siggy wrapped the pressure bandage tighter. "Uh . . . Doris . . . it's still not clotting." The fresh gauze was already saturated, and their fingers were wet with the warm fluid.

"Christ, this kid's a regular fire hose, got to be a bleeder. You know how to do a tourniquet?"

Larry hesitated. "I thought I wasn't supposed to . . . Could lose the arm that way, couldn't he?"

"Look at it this way—it'll sure cure him of sucking his thumb."

To show he wasn't shocked, he laughed and with trembling fingers felt around in the kit for a length of rubber tubing. Wrapping the cord around the boy's forearm, he jerked it tight, tighter, crushing blood vessels and tissue. The blood gave a strong spurt and then slowed to a darker ooze, finally stopping. The skin of the arm turned waxy, and the boy grunted in agony. His breathing evened out slightly.

"What do you think, Sig?" Doris winked. "I for one think

he's going to work out fine." She beamed at Larry, now almost as white as the boy. "We get lots of fingers blown off around this time of year," she went on. "Goddamn homemade fireworks. Usually they can be reattached—we put them in saline solution. See these? We had a couple of kids in here on the Fourth—half a dozen little jars."

Larry shook a bit, the aftermath of the adrenaline rush. "H-How can you tell whose finger is whose?"

She gave him a big smile. "It helps if they wear signet rings."

"Shut up, Doris," groaned Athena. "You'll be making him sick in a minute."

She snickered. "How we doing, 'Thena-honey?"

"May beat the storm."

"Which way we heading?"

"Out the pike to the Med Center," Athena called over her shoulder. "Probably the fastest."

"Right."

Siggy made a clucking sound. "Uh, I thought you told me they, uh, didn't want us there . . . anymore."

No one paid any attention to him, and the knocking in the engine grew louder.

Lumbering on the highway ahead, an overloaded vegetable truck emitted smoke as black as the sky. Two children ran along the side of the road, and Athena switched on the siren, put the headlights on low. She glanced up uneasily. If this storm came on as hard as they sometimes did out here, there'd be no choice but to pull over.

"Christ, that siren's really on its way out. Turn it off, honey—we're clear." Doris climbed up front. "Listen, are you meeting Barry-boy tonight? I only ask because . . ."

As the first fat drops splattered against the windshield, Athena switched on the wipers, and the blades began a halting, squeaky movement, pushing sharp grit. Rain glittered in the headlights.

Lightning, a single bolt, speared the ground. Line squalls swept the woods, their noise drowning out the snapping of thin trees that splintered in the lashing winds.

Deep within the woods, a broad shallow marsh heaved and shuddered like a miniature sea, and long-bladed grasses flattened under a wind that churned thick water into brown waves with caps of foam. The waves licked and bit at a peninsula of firm soil that reached to the center of the marsh, eating away clumps of grass.

But here the earth supported more than grass: a dozen dwarf firs surrounded a dark, squat box of a hut. Soft and pulpy, pocked with wormholes, the windowless timber walls stood firm against the assaulting wind, and the attacking rain bounced off the clapboard roof.

Reflected lightning shimmered in the water. Through the marsh there struggled a hunching form. Slushing, half-submerged, its quavering body blurred by the moving shafts of rain, it towed a limp burden, something that bobbed easily though water but had to be wrestled over humps of harsh grass.

Reaching the shack, the crude shape disappeared down a burrow under the wall, and for a long moment its discarded burden—the headless, limbless corpse of a child—seeped red. Thick fluid mingled with the rain. Then the torso jerked. It moved again. Then it disappeared down the hole, while the muddy walls of the burrow gave off a sucking sound—deep and obscene.

Rain beat on the walls of the shack.

Wednesday, July 22

Over the woods, an airplane boomed, invisible, the snarl muted, fading through the white haze of the sky. The hikers looked around in stunned disorientation. The pines, here unmixed with any other species, grew to an even height of four feet. "This makes me feel exactly like a giant!" Sandra's voice went shrill.

"It's as though we're the first ones on an alien planet." Alan sounded awe-struck.

"Are you people crazy?" Jenny had just about decided she hated backpacking. "I am not walking through this!" Everything seemed backward—the trees reached only to her shoulders, but some of the ragged weeds stretched above her head. Just trying to maintain perspective gave her a headache. She sighed loudly. This was only their second day out, but the frictions inherent in the group had already begun to spark and smolder, and the summer day stretched long ahead of them. "Couldn't we rest for a while? This might be fun if it wasn't so much like a forced march." The playful whine in Jenny's voice went sour as she tried to brush grit off her neck. She'd also about had it with these group vacations—the mountains last year had been bad enough, but Casey kept insisting it was a tradition. Now here they were in this awful place. "Something's bitten me! Look how it's swollen up already." She ignored the look the others exchanged. "Aren't you tired, Amelia?" Jenny peered at her daughter. "Don't you want to rest?"

The child shuffled her feet.

"She's all right." Casey smiled at the little girl. "Aren't you, babe?" He adored Amelia, although she was Jenny's by an ex-husband.

"Man, this is nothing," Sandra put in, trying to keep the peace. Before Jenny could contradict her, she added, "I could walk like this for hours yet."

Trying to sound downright jaunty, Alan voiced his (strained) agreement.

"That's exactly what I'm afraid of," Jenny snapped.

"I notice she never asks Amelia if she's tired unless she wants to rest herself," Sandra whispered. Shiny with perspiration, she pushed stray blonde hair out of her eyes. The two couples had been friends for years, but Jenny's temperament had always been a problem. Sandra put up with her for the sake of the guys, who'd been close since college.

Sweat glistened even in the black hairs of Alan's mustache. He started to say something to Sandra, then noticed Jenny glaring at them, that martyred look on her face again. "You! Case! Wait up, will you?"

Reluctantly, Casey stopped and stood with his back to the rest of the group.

Waiting, he stared at the stunted pines, at trunks that writhed and twisted in serpentine knots. When the others had almost reached him, he started walking again, his boots silently crushing the mat of needles and twigs.

Amelia picked up one of the pine twigs, but when she tried to snap it, the stick bent like rubber. She dropped it and hurried to catch up to the others as they stepped one at a time over a black fallen tree.

"Then why does she stay?" Sitting in the car, Steve slurped beer from the can while sweat trickled down the sides of his face. He winced—his headache renewed its series of stabbing attacks. He was just tired, he told himself, rubbing at blood-veined eyes. He didn't sleep so well anymore. Running a hand through his hair—and suddenly remembering how badly he needed a haircut—he tried again to organize his thoughts.

If not for the puffy weariness around his eyes and the beginnings of a slight paunch, Officer Steven Donnelly would still have resembled a recruiting poster: the evenly formed features, the blue eyes, the blond crewcut. But even his hair was scruffy now. And his crumpled shirt, like all his shirts, sported the faint outlines of ancient coffee stains. "Why?" he repeated. "I mean, if she hates it so much."

Ignoring the question, his partner exhaled a cloud of cigarette smoke that filled the car. "Yes sir, Athena's got it all out over my wife."

Another twinge of pain shot through Steve's head. Not listening, he felt nauseated, and beer dribbled down the front of his uniform. No, he didn't sleep so well anymore, not since . . . He winced, trying not to complete the thought, and he tossed the beer can and watched it skid, rolling lightly over the sand. There hadn't been enough time, he thought. His eyes, always pale and watery, brimmed now, and turning from his partner, he gazed into the parched woods.

Just off a dirt road, their car rested in shadows. Letters on the side of the vehicle proclaimed TRI-BOROUGH POLICE in red on white. Tri-Borough was an independent operation—just two cars—serving the Marston-Chamong-Hobbston area. Duties were simple enough: patrol the little towns, don't disturb property owners, hustle out undesirable transients—mostly kids traveling to and from the shore—and stay alert for the invasions of African-Americans and Hispanics that their boss, Barry's father-in-law, assured them was coming.

Barry's yawn slowly molded itself into a smirk. "I had a rough night last night." He flicked his cigarette out the window. "Athena wanted me to—"

"I got to take a piss. You should check in with Frank." Steve started to get out the passenger side but banged his head. Hard. The pain staggered him. Knees buckling, he feared he might black out and leaned heavily on the car.

"You all right?"

He mumbled a reply. Face averted, he moved unsteadily away, recoiling from the blinding heat, a heat that seemed to melt the lines of thought, send them blurring one into the next, blotting into memory.

"Watch out for snakes," Barry called after him, laughing.

Swaying on his big feet, he stumbled, and a sober corner of his mind churned with self-loathing. He needed to walk, to find some air, to find . . . He knew Barry was watching him stagger. Only the middle of the day, and the worst part was that he badly wanted another drink. As he stumbled farther into the trees, he could still hear Barry's laughter.

He'd loved Barry once. Really loved the guy. Looked up to him, seeing his faults but rakishly grinning at them. Barry could do no wrong. When Steve and his wife had first come out here, Barry had instantly become his anchor. Only his heavyset partner had made life bearable, providing his sole link to past realities. So he'd buried himself in police work and this new friendship while his wife slowly . . .

Perhaps it was her death that changed the way he perceived the older man. Whatever the cause, Barry sensed it. More than sensed it. Knew and resented it. Yet the outward signs of the relationship had not altered. Only intent changed. Barry's boorishness had become malicious. Steve's silent admiration had become a numbed tolerance, beneath which lay the certainty that somehow he had failed Barry, that this too was his fault.

He stepped over a dead pine that lay rotting in the sand.

Lost somewhere in his cramped house was an old photograph. The officer in that photo smiled broadly, his uniform creased and spotless, the young man muscular and lean. He'd only been married a short time then. So short a time. It seemed to him he'd seen this photo recently, glass cracked, gold paint flaking off the frame. It lay somewhere amid the sad clutter, the debris of a life with Anna that filled his house, preserved in a perfect state of disorder, like a museum collection waiting to be cataloged.

Dark spots spread under his arms. He drew the dusky smell of the pines deep into his lungs, and his head cleared a little. He had to cut down on the drinking. Then he snorted in self-derision and looked around at the emptiness, feeling he'd been deposited here by an outgoing tide of booze.

When they'd known for sure that his wife was dying, he'd resigned from the Trenton Police Department and brought her out here . . . because they'd always said they would retire to the country. A hideous mistake, and from the start, she'd known it, keeping silent for his sake. In a desperate flurry of activity, he'd uprooted her, dragged her away from her family and friends. Trapped her in that awful little house with only her disease for company. And the house was awful, tight as a coffin, hardly the rambling country place they'd dreamed of. She'd accepted the arrangement, as she'd accepted everything. In all their time together, she'd never complained, not even at the end when the pain must have been . . .

A branch snagged his pant leg, and he bent to free it, rancor welling up in him like bile, his clenched eyes stinging with per-spiration. There hadn't been enough time. Straightening, he unzipped his fly and relieved himself against a sapling, then headed back toward the car. Though still in his early thirties, he'd lately come to think of himself as an old milk horse, the sort that made its rounds until it dropped. He thought of his wife as he plodded on, of how little she'd weighed near the end, of how he'd smothered her with petting attentions, both of them knowing the pain he tried to assuage wasn't hers, touching her constantly, as though somehow . . .

Something squelched under his shoes. Coagulated leaves al-most covered the patch of bog, and blueberry bushes grew sparsely in the soggy ground. Sodden branches lay scattered, some laddered with shelf growth, the fungus flowing over them in weird, garish colors. He stared down blankly. He must have walked in the wrong direction. Stooping, he picked up a hunk of cedar wood, his vision clouding as he smelled the dampness. He held the log to his face, feeling sick with the heat as he squeezed. Wet and rotten inside, it crumbled in his hand and dribbled back into the mud.

He stared at his soiled hands—rough and callused, creased

and cut with lines like tooled leather. Not moving away, he wiped them on himself, leaving smears of bark rot on his pants.

"Is that a buzzard circling up there?"

"We're doomed!"

The heavy pack caused sweat to gather in the small of Jenny's back, and her hot T-shirt clung. A thorny, tentacular vine caught at a sneaker and tore her ankle, and every step stirred swarms of gnats from the undergrowth. The terrain never varied. "Some vacation. It wouldn't be so bad if I felt like I was getting some-place." She sighed. "Whose idea was this again?"

Casey plodded ahead, his heavy hiking boots clunking along the trail. Above white socks, rolled fat at the ankles, his hairy legs were thickly muscular, and above the frayed belt loops of his cutoffs protruded the graying waistband of his jockey shorts. Sweat streamed down his back and sides. A T-shirt, bunched up and stuck in his backpack, trailed out, waving to the others like a white banner.

"I see some more deer tracks," announced Amelia. No one responded to the child—they'd all gotten pretty bored with deer tracks. "They look sort of funny though."

Incredibly, the heat increased. Soon they passed a stand of scrub cedars, a welcome break from the pines, but the gnarled trees looked drained, blighted. Webbed with vines, they seemed to huddle together against the surrounding conifers. "Oh my God."

Casey turned back. "What is it?"

Stretched between two cedars was a huge cobweb, a small bird lodged firmly in its center. There came the barest hint of a breeze, and the desiccated creature swayed in a sad parody of flight.

Alan leaned closer to the web. "Is anybody home? You know, I bet there could be spiders out here as big as a house." The laugh didn't quite come off. "What's that noise?"

"Catalpa." Casey pointed to a twisted tree among the pines, the source of a whispering rattle. "The bean pods are dried out from the heat."

"They're not the only ones," muttered Jenny as she moved away from the web. The straps chafed her shoulders, so she slipped the pack off and sat on it. "Who's got water?"

"You know, if that spider is really big, he's liable to creep down and . . . carry off Amelia!" Alan pounced on the child and tickled, and she collapsed in laughter and squeals.

"Stop it, Alan. You're scaring her."

"She doesn't look scared to me, Jenny."

"Look, Sandy, you're not the one that has to sit up with her when she has nightmares."

"Well, if she has one tonight, I'd be only too—"

"Say, Casey," Alan interrupted loudly. "I meant to ask you before—I see a lot of these trees are all black at the bottom. They burnt or something?" He smiled to himself. Casey, a sort of perpetual grad student, could usually be cued to provide a safe, distracting lecture, and they clearly needed one.

Nodding, Casey turned away from the cobweb and, with a motion that seemed almost a caress, drew his large hand across a pine trunk. "Dwarfism might have something to do with fire," he said, fingering a bit of scabrous bark. "Or it may be the soil." His voice stayed calm and measured as he knelt in the sand. "Here—take a look." Pinching out a piece of turf, he held it up.

As he dutifully inspected the plant, Alan saw that it grew everywhere around them—he even stood upon it—and he'd never noticed. Leave it to Casey.

"You could scour pots with this stuff." Jenny kicked at a loose patch of lichen.

"The glands—the red spots—are sticky," Casey pointed out, "for trapping insects."

"I wish they'd trap some of these."

He gave her an indulgent look. "There's an almost complete lack of nitrogen in the soil." Pausing for them to appreciate that, he smiled his slow smile down at Amelia as the child fearfully examined the pale bit of mossy green. At nine years old, she seemed a nut-brown miniature of Jenny, the dark eyes, now lined and nervous in the mother, adding an unusual depth to the child's face. "That means the plants have to eat bugs to live," he explained.

Jenny sighed laboriously at the lecturing drone.

"It's going to be a long week," Sandy muttered.

"This place . . ." A note of awe entered Casey's voice, and he stood up, brushing damp sand from his sweating legs. "Think about it. A forest this size in the middle of the most heavily industrialized state in the Union!" He shook his head in wonder.

Grinning to see his taciturn friend so animated, Alan nudged Sandy.

"What's really incredible is that nobody even realizes it's out here. What do people see from their cars? Trees on the side of the road—just the tip of the iceberg! Most people have to think, a few yards in, there's another road or some houses. They can't grasp it! Can't conceive of—"

"Ugly. Ugly little trees." Jenny stood up and pinched sullenly at the sides of her binding jeans, while Alan helped her struggle back into her pack. "Trees should be pretty. You look at these, and all you're aware of is their miserable little struggles to survive."

"Yeah, it's like they're alive or something."

"They are alive, Sandy," Jenny sighed.

After passing around the canteen, they started moving again, at first plodding along in a tight clump, but quickly resuming the old formation with Casey pulling ahead. For the first time, the air began to stir noticeably about them. As he walked, Casey scuffed at the sand with his boots, the gesture oddly proprietary.

The things he could tell them. For instance, they were crossing the bed of a vanished ocean, an ocean sixty million years gone. The breeze had grown, and he savored the fleeting coolness. He listened as the gentle current of air stirred a strange whirring out of the pines, a low moan like the ghost of a lost sea, and it swept his memories to all those distant Sunday afternoons when, shin deep in collapsing mud shoals, he'd dug for fossils not all that far from here. The mud banks would crumble with soft splashings, and icy waters would ooze, bubbling up around his ankles, trickling down to join the creek, washing away the sediment of shell particles, millions of years steadily melting away beneath his feet. Innumerable generations of monsters had hunted these waters, and the denizens of the ancient seas had left their bones and shells and marks.

The rest of the group pumped along behind him, chattering among themselves, and he moved still farther ahead of them, the familiar thrill of wonder, almost of reverence, coursing through him. He discovered, somewhat giddily, that if he squeezed his eyes half shut the blurring pines resembled a prehistoric landscape. A hairy tentacle clung to a nearby tree, the dark rootlets of the parasite vine, biting deep into the bark, coiling like some obscene, furred serpent up and around the cedar.

Unnoticed, a moth the size of his hand settled weightless on his shoulder.

". . . had to work, and I sweat to God that's the truth. Athena?" Barry depressed the speak button with his thumb. "Athena?" He glanced up as Steve returned to the car. "Damn, that radio of theirs is a real piece of shit."

"Watch yourself. You're broadcasting."

"Huh? Yeah, sure." At forty-three years old, Officer Barry Hobbs was a large man, almost burly. Though the scar that slashed the bridge of his nose was the sort that fossilized a wound and kept it perpetually on display, the lines of his face, the wide, square jaw, still showed firm and handsome. Until a few years ago, he'd been a state trooper—discharged for reasons he never cared to discuss.

"You were gone a long time. You sick or something?" While critically eyeing Steve, he continued trying to raise the ambulance. "What in hell did you do? Fall down and roll in the mud?" His own tailored uniform was immaculate. His wife pressed it every morning.

Steve slumped brooding in his seat while static and the ghost of Athena's voice drifted from the radio: ". . . and profuse bleeding . . ."

"Goddamn, she's on a call." Barry lit another cigarette, and Steve watched, envying his steady hand. Noting the attention,

Barry yawned ostentatiously. "Yes sir, real heavy night last night." He smirked, waiting.

Steve turned his head away, killed another warm beer and stared resolutely into the woods. A slight breeze stirred the pines. Still smiling, Barry tapped cigarette ash on the windowsill.

Steve crumpled the empty can. "So, uh . . . you were with Athena last night?" he asked, trying his best to pretend only casual interest. The attempt was pathetic.

Barry sneered in triumph. He took a drag on the cigarette, slowly exhaled, and finally started to talk. Steve gazed into the pines, letting his eyes drift out of focus.

". . . then she sort of turns on her hip and wets her fingers and . . ." Barry's words drilled into his skull, stuck there and festered.

". . . holds on to it, you know, and puts her leg around . . ."

Steve's headache intensified in direct proportion to the straining against the front of his pants. He sank farther into his seat, banging his knee against the dashboard.

". . . and then she sort of reaches behind to . . ."

Stop. He breathed heavily, sweat trickling down his neck. *Make him stop.* He glanced at his watch. Incredibly, only minutes had passed, but the pressure grew unbearable. "Did you check in?" he blurted.

Barry's big face split in a victorious grin, and he eased off. "Say, I was running a little late this morning." He grinned again, and for a moment, Steve thought he might wink at him. "Did you get a chance to . . . ?"

Another ritual—keeping Barry informed about reports and directives he never bothered reading. It was a small thing. Steve shrugged. Back in Trenton, he'd always been so conscientious, so eager—a real pushover for this sort of maneuver. "Mister Nice Cop," Anna used to call him. Always doing favors. He'd been an honest cop too, and remained one still, save for occasionally covering up for his partner's philandering. He lied to Barry's wife about night duty, lied to the boss, sometimes even patrolling by himself while Barry screwed around. And there were other things. Small things. "They found that little girl's clothes—the one disappeared from Marston's Corner. All bloody and shredded. No body yet, though." He mopped his neck and face with a crumpled handkerchief.

"Sex maniac, got to be," Barry pronounced.

"They're talking about putting dogs on it. You remember that bulletin a couple weeks ago? About that guy escaping?"

Barry looked surprised. "From the penitentiary?"

"From the asylum at Harrisville. Anyway, turns out he's a killer—took his whole family out in Camden. Hospital tried to keep it quiet."

"Well, then there's your sex maniac. I bet somebody's gonna lose a cushy job over that."

"I doubt it." The throbbing in Steve's brain receded. Talking shop like this, they almost sounded professional, and he sat up straighter, his vision even clearing a little. This was as close as he ever got to the way he used to feel, back in the days before his most important duty all week might involve a broken garage window. "We should make our rounds." He took out his pipe, then felt his other pocket and muttered, "Stop at Brower's, I want to get some tobacco."

Barry emitted another loud yawn.

"You want me to drive?"

The expression on Barry's face spoke volumes about his opinion of his partner's driving. He put on his sunglasses and checked himself in the rearview mirror.

"Those shades make you look like some kind of giant bug."

Barry switched on the ignition, and they lurched forward, slamming Steve against the seat. As the car swung onto hot dirt, Barry kept his foot on the gas. Scrub pines flashed past as the car accelerated, and the sand road emptied onto asphalt.

"Wait a minute! Slow down!" Steve twisted around in his seat. "Did you see that?"

"See what?"

"Back there."

"Not that kid with the bandages on his head again?" he asked, not slowing.

Steve peered out the back window. "You know him?"

"Billy Mills picked him up a couple times last week. He's a retard. Just goes wandering the woods. Father died in a car crash. Athena was telling me. Lives with an old aunt or something. She don't want him. If he gets picked up again, probably going to wind up in Harrisville."

Already, they'd left the boy far behind them.

Steve mulled it over. In one flashing glance, he'd observed the dirty bandages, the outstanding ears, the lost look. Yes, probably a defective. Certainly, there was no shortage of them around here. "You're driving too fast," he said with considerable force. "Have you ever seen inside of Harrisville? Poor harmless half-wits they lock up, but murdering lunatics walk." With the wind in his face, he just stared out the window: the pines, a house, another, a half-plowed field. The homes looked like converted farms now. Up ahead, a pregnant woman in a halter top reclined in a beach chair. She glanced up without interest and then continued smearing her arms with suntan lotion. Barry slowed slightly and muttered a comment.

"I hear Larry Jenkins is working with the ambulance now," mentioned Steve. "He's good friends with your buddy Jack, isn't he?"

"Jack Buzby ain't no friend of mine. Damn!"

"What's the matter?"

He drove one-handed. "A splinter or something."

"How you do that?"

Barry sucked noisily on his finger.

"It's a good thing Athena's not here." Steve grinned. "She'd have wrestled you to the ground by now, been giving you heart massage, maybe mouth-to-mouth respiration."

A sly look came into his partner's eyes. "Yeah," he slurped. "You'd like that, wouldn't you?" He took his finger out of his mouth. "You'd like to see that."

Steve went rigid. Suddenly, his back felt soaked against the seat, and he looked away, tried to pretend he hadn't heard. "Christ, it's hot."

Watching him out of the corner of his eye, Barry cleared his throat. "They'll catch him."

"What?"

"The escaped loony. They'll catch him."

"Maybe."

"Come off it, Steve. Soon as they put the dogs on him, they'll get him."

Steve popped open the last beer. "If he makes it to the northern quarter . . ."

"You'd better hide that. We'll be in town in a second."

A distant look on his face, he didn't respond. "I hear there's stretches out there, forty thousand acres, some of them, without a living soul. If he wanted to, seems to me a fellow could stay lost for a long, long time."

"Yeah?" Sunlight glinted off Barry's dark lenses. "And what's he gonna eat?"

Periodic cicadas had commenced their high-pitched, twitching whine, and the sound filled the woods, making them resonate, until the whole tangled structure of pine and cedar around the stream seemed to throb. And the air—the heavy liquid atmosphere of the summer afternoon—seemed to pulse as well.

Jenny floated. Though the creek's level seemed low, such sunlight as filtered through the swath of red-brown liquid failed to reach the bottom, revealing only the tops of shattered tree trunks, ghostly in the murk.

"Isn't this great?" Kicking sideways, Sandra swam over. "It's deep over here!" Her tiny gold earrings flashed dully in the water as she sank to her chin, then bobbed up, large breasts just breaking the surface as she splashed. "Did you see the snake?"

"Snake?!"

"Alan said this great big copperhead went swimming by. I didn't see it, thank God." Turning from Jenny, she giggled and splashed back upstream, her pale buttocks visible through the dark water but the rest of her vanishing in the murk.

Diving from a rock, Casey splashed down heavily, drenching everything around. Everyone yelled. He surfaced, blowing like a whale, then tossed his head violently to clear his eyes. He'd finally put on his T-shirt, and it billowed up around him, holding air, his muscles knotting beneath it as he thrashed about.

Though she laughed with the others, Jenny remained tense. She sensed a . . . wrongness in making noise here. This place held silence, almost like a church. Wondering that the others didn't feel it, she allowed herself to drift farther away from them, toward a bend downstream.

They were an intrusion. No question about it. She treaded water, and the murky warmth felt wonderful, soothing. Yet she kept peering up at the bank. The sun's rays slanted low through the scrub above her, and deep shadows fell on the stream. Small insects flew drowsily, quietly, and the humid air seemed to press on the water.

A thick-bodied dragonfly hovered, iridescent wings glistening; then it thrummed heavily on, following the current. It made her think of jade. Emeralds. She watched it go. Green fire. She bobbed low. The current was sluggish but undeniably there, deep down, cool and heavy. She turned over to float on her back, and water dribbled out of her mouth, trickled shining down her chin and throat. Again she glanced up at the bank. Nothing moved, and she wondered what she kept expecting to see. All day, she'd thought these woods unutterably dreary and drab, but now in the lengthening shadows . . .

Sand and pebbles, late afternoon sun full upon it, the bank shelved steeply down to the murky current. Light striped the water but couldn't penetrate. Bright bands of sediment eddied.

They kept clutching at her ankles—the black and twisted roots that grew out of the banks and deep into the water. And suddenly she recalled that Casey had mentioned giant snapping turtles. The voices of her friends drifted to her as she paddled against the stream toward them, her toes instinctively curled.

". . . weird . . . no beer tabs or broken bottles."

"Only because the water's so dark, you know," said Alan, lazing on the edge of the current. "Anything might be down there."

". . . use to think cedar water was just like weak tea, but this looks more like coffee."

"Amelia, don't you think you should get out soon?" Jenny stroked smoothly. "Before you're permanently stained?"

"Oh, Mom!"

"While there's still sun to dry off."

"I'll watch her, Jenny." Sandra scissored past.

Turning her shining back to her mother, Amelia plunged at Casey, and he yelped as she wrapped her arms and legs around him, commanding him to carry her after Sandra. Watching their glistening limbs, Jenny suddenly felt drained, her leg muscles aching, feet throbbing from the day's hike. Still, the warm water soothed; she wanted only to rest. Then an odd suspicion formed: the stream was attempting to lull her. Goose bumps rose on her arms and legs, and she wanted out.

She kicked toward the spot where they'd left their packs. A clenched mass of roots gripped the shore, and below her, the streambed sloped away sharply, sliding grittily underfoot. To steady herself, she caught at a root, and her hand slipped down it. Slimy as a water snake, it left a wet sheath of green in her palm. She floundered, with one leg sunk to the calf in clammy silt, the streambed tilting farther beneath her. Hardly able to stand upright, she felt herself being dragged back into the middle of the creek and again tried to haul herself out. Clutching, she got a foot up on the bank, but it crumbled under her, sliding into the water. Panic gave her strength, and with a springing leap, she cleared the side.

She clambered onto the sand as a big hunk of the bank fell away. "Oh!" She crawled faster. At last, breathing rapidly, she sat on a flat rock, well away from the edge. The sun slanted down on her, and a column of midges whirled in the light over the water. "Amelia?" Anxiously, she watched the others, as moisture spread around her on the rock. "Aren't you tired yet?"

Long-shadowed birches crowded near the creek, and tufts of pointed grass covered the sand hills. Beyond the bank, scrub merged with unbroken dwarf forest.

She dried quickly. As she rubbed her naked body, beads of water rolled off, leaving a smooth residue, like a fine powdering of rust. Slowly, her muscles relaxed, yielding to the sunlight.

Something fat and black glistened like a garden slug on the back of her ankle.

Behind her, somebody spoke. "There's a leech on you, girl."

They were making their final rounds of the day. The road between Chamong and Hobbston bent around a cranberry bog, where red and green mats of vegetation lay thickly on the water. They rounded another curve, and dogs filled the road.

"Jesus Christ!"

More than a dozen mongrels scrambled madly as Barry gunned the engine, whipping the wheel hard over. The car barely clipped a collie mutt, knocked it tumbling over the sand. Barry hit the brakes, and the police car scudded, plowing deep furrows in the road. Revolver drawn, he leaped from the car.

Frozen, Steve gaped in disbelief.

Most of the dogs had already scurried off, disappearing into the pines. Except for the straggler—a runty shepherd mongrel, tail between its legs. A moment before, it had been secure in the midst of the pack. Now, looking around in confusion, it just stood in the middle of the road.

Flushed with excitement, Barry fired three shots, two of the bullets whipping harmlessly into the pines. One caught the animal at the base of the spine.

The dog screamed. It bounded, then sprawled in the sand, blood bubbling from its rump when it tried to get up and run. The oversize paws splayed all over the road, and the dog tumbled in panic, collapsed, kicking spasmodically.

Barry approached. The beast tried to crawl away from him, eyes rolling in terror, but its hind legs wouldn't move at all. By desperately wriggling and clawing at the sand, it managed to writhe from side to side, feebly inching toward the woods.

Steve got out of the car, stood watching.

The dog bared its fangs, whined and then growled again as Barry stood over it, taking careful aim for the head.

Steve caught a flash of yellow movement in the trees.

"Behind you!"

A thick-furred pregnant bitch tensed to leap.

Barry whirled around, firing several shots. The animal bolted for the woods. A bullet buzzed past Steve as he ducked behind the car. Knocked sideways, the bitch never slowed but vanished into the trees, leaving only a smear of blood on the ground.

Barry looked around, then walked back to the wounded cur. His long shadow densely black before him, he took aim again. He pulled the trigger, and the revolver clicked. "Shit." He stared in disbelief for a moment, then his booted foot lashed out again and again.

As he walked back toward the car, he wiped his boots in the sand as best he could. Behind him, the dog looked like road kill.

Steve closed his eyes. "It was just a puppy. You can tell by the size of the paws." A headache gnawed his brain.

"I winged the other one." Barry sounded pleased with himself as they got back in the car.

Steve nodded with a whiny grunt. He needed a drink.

"What do you think? Should we go after it?"

"We'd never find her." Steve turned away and gazed toward the woods. "Not out there."

Sunset was a lava flow along the horizon.

Ancient, rusted tin cans lay scattered about the clearing. As the last redness drained from the sky, the sand grayed, and colors shifted to darker hues. Shrilling with cicadas, the slender trunks of the surrounding trees grew indistinct.

"Was this really the bottom of the ocean?" Amelia's eyes held a fearful wonder. "Is that why it sort of looks like the beach with trees?"

"That's why"—rolling the last of several logs into a rough circle, Casey spoke between grunts—"everything's so flat."

From the clearing's edge, he was closely watched.

Sitting on a log, Jenny randomly traced mystic-looking symbols in the sand . . . and sneaked a glance at the stranger.

Pallid and handsome with coarse red hair, he couldn't be more than nineteen or twenty. The bright hair accentuated his unhealthy paleness; sharp cheekbones showed like ivory through white skin. He hardly spoke, as though a long illness had left him sullen and shy, wasted. Yet there was a furtive sex-uality about him, the powerful shoulders seeming out of place on his emaciated frame. He wore a soiled shirt, and dirt had worked deeply into the folds of his neck and arms. He'd told them his name was Ernie and that he was a camper, out here alone. Periodically, his body would heave with a tubercular-sounding cough.

Jenny didn't care for the way he never took his eyes off Casey. She didn't care for the way he just sat there, indistinct in the fading twilight. A childhood memory scratched elusively at the back of her mind, and then she had it: he reminded her of a stable hand she used to see during summer vacations. She re-membered there'd been some problem, something the adults whispered about, some reason she hadn't been allowed to talk to the unwashed boy. As though aware of her attention, Ernie looked over, and she caught another glimpse of those sickly, bloodshot eyes before quickly turning away.

"Somebody gather some wood," Casey called to the group. "You ever . . . Ernie?" He sat on a log and mopped sweat from his forehead. "You ever catch any fish in that stream?"

After their swim, they'd hiked another hour before making camp, partly pressed on by Casey's timetable, mostly in hopes of shaking their new acquaintance.

Ernie choked on phlegm, spat thickly. "Can't eat the fish." Raising his shoulder, he wiped his mouth on the shirt.

"Why's that?"

"Full of worms."

Jenny grimaced. Almost the first thing he'd said to them was that someone had recently drowned in a canoe accident right about where they'd been swimming.

"There must still be wet ground nearby," said Casey, waving at insects, "a pond or something."

Ernie nodded.

"Maybe we ought to move."

"But it's almost dark," Jenny objected. "Besides, I'm awfully tired." She immediately regretted her words—if they moved they might finally get rid of Ernie, who presumably was only hanging around in hopes of being fed. After all, he wouldn't even speak to anyone but Casey, and then only to exchange boring wilderness lore.

"Could somebody help me?" called Sandy, gathering firewood in the scrub. "Alan? Jenny, are you doing anything?" she asked in loud, sugary tones. "Shit!" The log in her hand had released a cloud of flying insects.

"Must we have a big fire?" Jenny sighed again, her vision already blurry with perspiration and humidity. "I'm smothering as it is. How come it gets hotter at night? We should have stayed by the stream. Amelia, don't go too far."

Chasing lightning bugs, the little girl paused to watch a bat, wings pinkish and translucent against the evening sky as it darted after moths. "Eww!"

"What is it?"

"Something flew up my nose!"

Having scooped out sand in the middle of the circle of logs, Casey meticulously finished stacking branches, using small twigs and dried pine needles for kindling. "Where are the matches? Oh." Once lit, the fire only served to make the woods darker. Only the nearer trees remained visible, and they seemed to waver as the firelight now caught them, now let them go.

Casey dug out the supplies—plastic forks, fruitcake remnants, half a loaf of bread, smoked hot dogs, canned corn. "Who the hell packed this?" he muttered under his breath. Canned goods, no less—no wonder it weighed a ton. He wished his friends could grasp the difference between backpacking and picnicking. "We'll need more wood," he called, sharpening sticks with a pocketknife with a mother-of-pearl handle.

"Nice knife."

Casey looked up to find Ernie standing right beside him.

"You'll stay and eat with us, won't you?" Alan asked, smoothing his mustache with a comb.

Insects descended in a vampiric swarm. The mosquitoes, wet and bloated but still feeding, surrounded them. Conversations in the clearing became peppered with slaps and curses.

Flames licked up around the pine chunks. Because the smoke

kept away some of the bugs, they all sat close to the fire, in spite of the heat. When Alan passed around insect repellant, Ernie declined wordlessly. Jenny rubbed some into Amelia's small back, already covered with bites, and the oily scent mingled with the odor of smoke. Smelling the food, they sat in relative silence, while corn slowly heated in a pot perched among the coals, and hot dogs sizzled and blackened on sticks.

Ernie drooled. Jenny stared—she'd never seen anything like it before. Shocked, she turned away. Finished with Amelia, she rubbed repellant on her own legs and arms. It stung a spot on the back of her ankle, the spot where Casey had burned off the leech.

Scorching their fingers and mouths, all ate ravenously, jaws and throats working rapidly.

Amelia turned to her mother. "I don't like him. He smells bad."

"Amelia!"

Ernie froze. A hunk of bread halfway to his mouth, he peered through slitted eyes as though afraid someone might try to take the food. Jenny stared at the grease around his mouth.

"Uh . . . good food," said Alan. "I'm hungry as a wolf."

Ernie resumed eating.

Sandy licked her fingers and moved away from the fire. "You think it's going to rain?" Leaning back on one elbow, she gazed upward.

"It wouldn't help," Alan said around a mouthful. "The mosquitoes probably use Aqua-Lungs."

"I mean, it's just so hot." She fanned herself with a paper plate. "Next time, can we bring an air conditioner?"

"What do you mean? What next time?"

Casey distributed the evening rations of cigarettes, and somebody rolled a joint. They all felt pretty good—full bellies, a campfire to stare into. Alan stretched out on the ground.

"What happens if it does rain?" wondered Sandy, sitting back. Last night there'd been more stars than she'd ever known existed, but tonight the sky was blank.

"We get wet." Alan rolled onto his stomach and rested his chin on his arms. "That is what's known as going camping.

Hey, what's that over there? See it above the trees?" Suddenly, he was on his feet. "Is it the moon coming up?" Ernie laughed and Casey joined him. Alan turned to them in bewilderment.

"That's a city," said Casey. "It'll reflect off a haze like this sometimes."

Far to the north, the cold whitish glow hung low in the sky.

"What city?"

"It looks almost radioactive," said Alan. "Tell me, you suppose a war started, and we're the only ones who don't know about it?" He giggled. "Maybe the only ones left alive?"

They all stood, staring over the conifers at the distant wash of brightness. "So faraway."

The sands whispered, faint as thought.

"These crickets sound like they're big as a house."

"Back in high school, I used to borrow my brother's ID and catch the labor bus at dawn, come out her to pick blueberries for the day." Casey's voice droned intensely. "You wouldn't believe the ways they used to get people onto that bus—practically dragged them off the street. These old guys would come staggering out of a bar in North Philly. Next thing they know, they're out here in the fields, throwing up, passing out, sun blazing down."

"Tell me, is that how they caught you?" Alan asked, as he sat down by the fire. "Staggering out of a bar?"

"Why'd they do that, Case? Bring people in from the city, I mean? Aren't there little towns and stuff out here?"

"Well," he began, "there probably just aren't enough pineys to—"

"Pineys! Oh, I know about them!" announced Sandy gleefully. "They're the crazy people who live out here! Man, I'd forgotten all about them. We used to hear all kinds of stories."

"What crazy people?" Jenny edged closer to Amelia, closer to the fire. "What are you talking about?"

Casey looked disgruntled.

"Yeah," Sandy continued. "This friend of mine was telling me. He was driving and he runs out of gas, right? Shit. Something stung me. Shit. Anyway, he said he saw these men in the woods, right, and he gets out of the car, only now the men are gone." She looked around the campfire. "But he feels like he's being watched. Anyway, he starts walking. Finally, he makes it back to the main road. So he finds this broken-down old gas station, and this weird guy sells him some. So he starts lugging gas, right? But when he makes it back to the car, the windows are all smashed. And there's all these weird marks on the side of the car."

The others continued to lean forward expectantly.

"I remember seeing a newspaper article once." All heads turned toward Alan, now perched on a rolled-up sleeping bag. "A couple years back—they found this old house out in the woods, you know, log cabin sort of thing. Inside, they found this ten-year-old girl in a crib. First they thought she was retarded, but then they found out her brain was normal, but mentally she was still, let's say, an infant." He buried a cigarette butt in the sand. "Turned out her mother lived about a mile away with her new family. Once a day, she'd walk over, feed and change the girl and then leave. The girl would just lay in the crib all day, every day. All alone. Never learning to speak."

"But that story's not really true, is it?" In obvious dismay, Sandy tried to make out Alan's expression.

"Honest to God."

"But that's so sad!"

"How come she stayed in the crib?" Amelia demanded impatiently. "How come she didn't just—"

"'S true."

No one knew where the voice had come from. They all looked around, finally locating the stranger's dark form. Back beyond the shifting perimeter of light, Ernie spoke nothing further.

"Tales like that come out of the barrens all the time," Casey told them finally. "The pines seem to breed that kind of—"

"I was just thinking. You suppose our cars are all right?"

"Huh? Oh yeah. Sure."

Firelight flickered over them.

"Mom, are there really . . . ?"

Alan leaned forward. "What are you grinning about, Casey?"

The mood was set. Conscious of everyone watching, Casey took out his pipe and tobacco pouch and, with slow deliberation, filled the bowl, then took a light from a blazing twig. Which would it be? The walking tree monster? The man-eating grizzly? He fed wood to the fire, and waves of sudden heat pressed them all back a bit, smarting their eyes. "I'm going to tell you a story," he said at last.

There was giggling and whispering as they shifted and settled themselves. Jenny glanced in Ernie's direction. If he'd sat closer, they might have done their best to include him, but . . .

Casey's face glowed orange, like a jack-o'-lantern, firelight glinting from his eyes. "This story takes place in the Pine Barrens."

("So where else?" "Ssh!")

"There was a young couple out driving." And so began the old tale. His voice held them. Sometimes he would pause in the telling to look around in a marked manner, and the others would find themselves searching the fleeting lights and shadows as well.

("And then the car broke down, right?" "Be quiet.")

He told them how the boy decided to go for help, leaving the girl alone. "Roll up the windows, and make sure you lock the doors. And stay in the car. Remember that—whatever you hear, stay in the car."

("Uh oh.")

The burning shadows flickered and leaped, swept over them.

Casey sucked on the stem of his pipe. "She heard it go tap, tap, tap."

From beyond the dome of brightness, the crickets seemed to pulse louder.

("Amelia, are you scared?")

"She thought about trying to run for it."

("No!" "Stay in the car, stupid.")

Sandy yelled and smacked at Alan, and he snickered, drawing back. Casey spoke faster now, racing through the part where the state trooper arrives and tells her to get out of the car and walk straight toward him, and not to look back whatever she does.

The soft sound of burning filled the clearing, as did the sharp smell of smoke. Patches of redder darkness erratically circled the flame, revealing first one person, then another.

"Slowly, she walked toward him. Just at the last second, she turned around."

("No, don't!")

He finished the story, explaining that her boyfriend was hanging from a branch above the car and that as he swayed in the breeze, his foot tapped the roof. After the briefest of pauses, the group giggled, groaned and chattered in unison. ("Wait a minute, I don't understand what happened." "You left out the part about the escaped lunatic." "Hey, does anybody know the one about the babysitter who gets the phone calls?" "Do you know any of the Hookman stories?" "Oh, that one's great!" "Who-man?" "You know, the escaped homicidal maniac with the hook instead of a hand." "That's enough. No more scary stories." "Get out! They don't let maniacs have hooks." "I said, that's enough. You're all going to give Amelia nightmares." "Forget Amelia, I'm the one's going to have nightmares!") And Casey sat back, pleased with himself and smiling because of the goose bumps on his arms.

Jenny watched for any motion in the dark that might suggest that Ernie intended to leave. The haze had thinned so that the lunar disk showed, featureless, washing the pines in dull light.

From outside the rim of brightness, came a rasping voice. "Know about the Leeds Devil?"

Everyone stopped talking.

Ernie's thin face emerged from the darkness. "Long time ago." Flame glinted from the eyes of the others, but in his eyes light sank, became deep embers in a face that seemed pointed and hollowed by moving shadows. "Mother Leeds was in labor." He coughed, spat, and his mouth twitched with a smile. "Found a hut, not far from here. Maybe I'll take you there."

They shifted uneasily.

"Mother Leeds had twelve other kids. She cursed it." He coughed again, a horrible rattling. "Didn't do nothing. Wasn't even born yet. It was hers!" He spoke haltingly and with effort, rage and shyness in his manner. "Understand? It had nobody else!" He shouted but looked directly at no one. "Cursed it!"

Isolated in the dark, they tried to find one another's faces for reassurance.

"Unborn. Cursed. Torn from her. It clawed, fought its way out of her stinking, bloody hole."

"Hey!" Jenny's arm circled little Amelia's shoulders, as though to shield her from his words. Strange to feel so vulnerable—sophisticated Jenny and her so-grownup-seeming daughter, their eyes big with fear.

"Said its father was a devil."

"I wonder how she meant that." Sandy attempted a snicker.

"Little baby. Looked normal. That showed what it might have been, if only she'd fucking loved it!" His voice grated. "Her fault . . . twisted . . . grew up, grew . . . became a fiend." A tremor ran through him, and he looked as though he were about to laugh or scream. "Ashamed of it, ashamed of her own. Afraid of it, too. Shut it away . . . locked up. That's what they wanted. They all wanted." He breathed deeply, spat again. "The old whore used to pass food through a crack in the floor. Years. Had to live in his own piss and shit. She got old. Stunk—the basement—enough to make you puke. She didn't know how big he was growing. Never knew." He stabbed a twig into the embers. "One night, the twelve brothers and sisters heard something, the cellar door splintering. They heard him coming closer. Down the hall. Closer. Fucked and ate them all in their beds."

Jenny watched him. Pacing now, he moved in front of the fire. Amelia sat very still.

"Ran out . . . in the dark. Door shut behind. Hung around the yard, cold and hungry. Couldn't get back in the house. Night after night . . . call his mother. Begging. She wouldn't let him in. Stayed in bed. Pretended to be sick, the bitch." His voice dropped to a hoarse whisper. "She starved to death. The monster wandered off into the woods. These woods."

Casey cleared his throat. "Good story."

"Yeah, real good story," said Alan, and as he spoke, he fed twig after twig into the embers. They all threw on wood, bringing the fire back to blazing life. The crickets seemed to pulse louder.

"You know, it sure was a long day. I sure am tired. Hey, where'd that flashlight get to? I, uh, can't see to untie the cords on my sleeping bag."

They all began talking a bit too fast. "What's that over there?" Sandy pointed. "It's like two little eyes!"

"Oh my God!" screamed Alan. "It's the Leeds Bunny!"

Casey produced a flask of bourbon and passed it around. Ernie had already backed away. As a wind pushed heavy clouds across the night, the moon disappeared for long intervals. They started unrolling their sleeping mats. "What's that smell?"

"What smell?" But gradually it filtered to all of them, and one after another, they wrinkled their noses in disgust. The odor of putrefaction seemed to come from several directions, as though something corrupt moved through the pines. Then it diminished and, within moments, had faded away, leaving only a thin, nauseating trace.

Jenny listened. Nothing. Crickets. She scrutinized the woods and strained her eyes to find Ernie. The fire flared for an instant, and she saw him, stiffly facing away from them.

"Where you going, Ernie?" Casey yawned.

"Yo, leave him alone," muttered Alan. "He's probably just going to piss."

"Ernie?"

"Back my own camp." Ernie paused, barely turning.

"What?" Casey stood up. "You can't leave. It's pitch dark. Stay here. I mean, we'll find an extra ground cloth or . . ."

Jenny held her breath.

But Ernie slipped into the trees. "Not far," he mumbled over his shoulder. "Rather sleep there."

Insects whined. For a moment, they all stared at the spot where he'd been absorbed by the woods. Alan broke the silence. "Well, I never."

This provoked giggles. "I'm glad he went finally. What a creep."

Untying his boots, Casey looked about to object.

"Ssh, not so loud," said Jenny. "He may still be out there, listening."

Sandy shivered. "Don't say things like that!"

"Mom, he's not coming back, is he?"

They joked and talked, voices growing steadily lower. Snickering loudly, Sandy teased Casey, poking him in the ribs while he fended her off with one hand. "C'mon, gang. Sleep." Alan unrolled the twin bags he shared with Sandy, zipped them together. "Fearless Leader will most likely have us up at dawn again."

"Damn right." Casey slurred his words, feeling the sugary bourbon a bit.

"Where's that bug stuff? Next time can we hike north, say, to Alaska?"

"Don't give him any ideas for tomorrow."

"I don't even want to think about tomorrow." Sandy unbuttoned her blouse. "Ssh, everybody. Look at Amelia. She's out already."

They dragged their sleeping bags to various parts of the clearing, and soon all save Casey were bedded down. "Aren't you going to bed, Case?"

Everything got quiet. Under their pup tent, Sandy and Alan whispered and giggled softly, and later there came a small, brief cry.

In the dimness, Casey sat, yawning and refilling his pipe. He nipped at the bourbon, decided to finish it before climbing into the sleeping bag that lay beside Jenny. Finally tapping his pipe out on a log, he watched the fire die through half-shut eyes.

And blackness closed on the diminishing sphere of light.

Sounds of the night crowded in, louder, nearer. The insects chirped in unison, and overhead the air thrummed as a horned owl dropped down and sank sharp talons into the squirming back of a field mouse that had been nibbling garbage at the edge of the camp. Long feathers flashed again in the moonlight as the great bird regained altitude with a noise like the shaking of cloth.

The stench had returned, stronger than before.

Catching the heavy scent, the owl screeched its terror and rushed off on flailing wings. The forgotten mouse, already stiff with death, landed on the sand with an almost imperceptible plop.

The woods grew hushed. Soon there remained only small

noises, tiny clicks made by the insects that spent their lives foraging on the bleak forest floor. They had moved in toward the campers, toward this unexpected source of food, but now even the crickets ceased. Small black beetles sang out with rattles and dry rasps. Yet, one by one, those too dropped off, leaving only the muffled thump of clumsy feet against the sand.

. . . mad shouts . . . screams of pain . . .

Conscious only of the others running in different directions, Casey blinked awake. He hopped up, cocooned in his sleeping bag, then pitched forward on his face. Despairing howls and wild activity surrounded him as he struggled with his bound legs. The zipper stuck. He fumbled with it, and someone tripped over him, crying out. Kicking free, he stood, the bag still tangled around one leg.

A snarl ripped the night.

He was slammed against with fury—something slicing through the flesh of his arm—and thrown, rolling in the black sand. As he groped about him, agony raged, throbbing in his arm, and his hand struck something that rolled.

He grabbed the flashlight, switched it on, swung it wildly about the clearing. His eyes took in too much, too many awful images for his brain to sort: the liquid spilling from his lacerated arm, the wreckage of the campsite, the rent and mangled corpse in the sand. His eyes fixed idiotically on the dark-soaked remnants of a double sleeping bag—the blood appeared crimson only in the bright center of the beam.

The throb of the crickets. Everywhere. The throb of blood rushing in his ears. Deafening. The mistiness was not his vision—thin fog curled through the clearing. He realized someone had been shrieking the same thing over and over, but he couldn't make out the words. There was movement. "Jenny, where are you?" Swinging the tiny arc of light, he stumbled bleeding into the pines, and they closed around him. Crickets rose to a dense pitch. He could hear running. Cries came from all around him. But, near fainting with shock and pain, he could see no one, the flashlight providing only fleeting, distorted glimpses.

Now he heard something else, a growling, a thrashing. The child's white face, blank with fear, flashed at him, then vanished, lost in the blackness.

"Amelia!" Sickened with dread, he held the flashlight out in front of him. The beam thrust forward, the shaft of light striking . . .

. . . a visage out of a nightmare.

All thought of fighting, of trying to help the others fled his mind. Casey screamed once, an ugly chopped-off sound; then he dropped the flashlight and plunged into the night.

They all ran, scattered, screaming. They blundered onto trails and off again, losing them where the pines grew thickest. "Alan, where are you?" They ran in winding circles. "Help me! Please, Alan! It's near me, oh God!"

Casey wore only jockey shorts, and branches whipped his legs. Long grasses stung hotly. Behind him, Sandy's screams became gurgles. As his mind whirled in nausea and panic, the pines sped past him, sometimes striking him hard. His heart thundered, and blood pumped from the ruptured flesh of his arm.

He crashed into a tree, and front teeth broke with a sharp crunch. Pain hammered in his brain, and he staggered back, whimpering, then stumbled heavily onward. Darkness came in denser waves, shadows more solid than the night, black pulsations he suspected were internal. He knew he had to get farther away before he lost consciousness, and he clutched at his arm, tried to squeeze off the bleeding, feeling the thick, slow warmth ooze over his fingers.

He sucked burning gouts of air into his lungs. The pines spun, and they made noise, but the noises lay behind him, and he plowed through bushes that clawed the flesh of his chest and legs. Where they fell on dried leaves, beads of blood made a rapid pattering, but when they dropped on parched sand or pine needles, they were silent as soft rain. Mists spiraled across the face of the moon. In the pale light, invisible birds skittered from tree to tree.

Behind him, the haze broke, and from the deep shadows something glowed, cold and green with phosphorescence. The flashlight? Had he run in a circle?

As the ground dropped away beneath him, he shouted word-lessly, clawing at air.

Moonlight glinted off the black surface of the water.

Splashing, choking, he thrashed in panic, then found the soft bottom. The water was chest deep, and he plowed through it, mouth filled. Dead reeds snapped under his clutching hands as he fell across a submerged sandbar.

In a swirl of fog, he fought his way, gasping, through mats of water plants, thoughts of poisonous snakes slithering through his mind. Gases bubbled up around him, and mosquitoes clouded in a suffocating swarm—they covered his bare chest and back. Sinking, he tried to run, but his legs barely moved through the mire, pushing through rushes. Blood clouded the water behind him, coiling and swirling.

Something rose ahead, where whitish vapor tangled through long reeds, something black as the withered pines surrounding it. Dark and squat. A shed of some sort. Shelter. Nearing the end of the marsh, he staggered through deep foulness. All around him, talons of stunted trees clawed into the slippery ground. He fell on his face, plowing a furrow in the fetid muck with his chin. Strug-gling to his feet, he fell again, knees sinking. As he yanked himself loose, something clicked agonizingly in his ankle. He slid, crawled, slithered. When he tried to listen for the sounds of pur-suit, he could hear only the sucking mire and his choking breath.

The hut stood windowless and abandoned in the moonlight. At last, stumbling across hardened mud, he cried out and beat at the walls with black-caked arms. Limping painfully, he pressed between the crowding pines and groped along the walls for the door.

It stuck. Weak and dizzy, he put his shoulder to it, heaved, and the door gave slightly with a moldering crunch. With a grind-ing, the door, ancient hinges rusted through, tottered, shower-ing him with dirt. It struck him on the head—dull agony—and he tasted fresh blood once more, as the door lodged, leaning against the bending pines, revealing an angled opening of less than a foot in width, a passage into absolute darkness.

With his shoulder and chest halfway through the crack, he

nearly recoiled—a sour stench emanated from the hot interior. Pulling himself in, he scraped his legs on the doorframe. With a squelch, his foot went through something on the floor, and instantly the smell rose. He gagged on vomit. Rankness choked the air from his lungs. Dark forms swelled in his brain. Beyond knowing or caring what he shared the hut with, he clung, sobbing, to the walls, their roughness slick with mold.

The moon sank into the pines.

Waves of blackness swept over him, but he didn't fall: he was back in his sleeping bag, and then he was home in bed, but there was something, something squishing, and why did his arm hurt so much? Foulness. Squishing?

A wet slithering moved along the outside wall.

He opened his eyes.

He was peering through the door opening when it came under the wall behind him. Powerful arms went around him, gripping.

Hot and dripping at his back, it drooled on his cheek, pressing him. His own screams seemed to draw inward and penetrate his guts as his ears were torn away, and the smooth flesh at the back of his neck was assaulted by sharp teeth and rough tongue.

Tuesday, July 28

"We should keep the lights like this all the time." Raising his voice above the siren shriek, Larry fumbled about in the half-light. "It seems to have a real good calming effect."

"On you, maybe," Athena said as she gazed down at a blood-streaked face. The child had finally stopped gulping and sobbing, had lapsed into a terrible, staring quiet. She checked the pulse. Very faint. When she let go of the wrist, a film of liquid remained on her fingertips. Slowly, she resumed helping Larry to bind the seeping redness.

Outside, the light failed, and inside the rig, one of the fluorescent tubes flickered.

"Did you see those tracks?" He wound bandages around the girl's arm. "Boy, there must've been maybe eight, nine dogs, at least. You see the way her dog's body was tore up? What probably happened was the wild ones went after her mutt, and the kid tried to save it and got in the middle. Was that about what happened, sweetheart?" The girl just stared up at him, and by the time her mouth began to move, he had already turned away. "You think that sounds right, 'Thena?"

She shrugged, dropping a roll of bandages.

Everything she did today was off the beat, he noticed, watching her grope around on the floor. He supposed it had something to do with the injured child, though he sure wouldn't have figured her for that type.

She stood up, looking pale and sweaty. "The wounds aren't

too bad," she muttered. "She'll need stitches." One arm was chewed, though not deeply, but the torn flap of the cheek would probably leave a scar. She found herself staring at the velvet blood that spotted the floor around the litter. "There's worse things than scars."

"How's it going back there?"

"Just a second, Doris." Setting down the bandages, she met Larry's eyes. "Can you do the rest of this yourself?" Her voice sounded unsteady, but the sympathy in his face only irritated her. "I don't know what's the matter with me today."

"'Thena-honey?"

Siren faltering, the rig moved down the highway at a good clip. "I said, just a second."

"You know, if you wanted to, Mrs. Sims," Doris suggested, "you could go back and sit with your daughter now." Slumped in the seat beside her, the woman looked up, wordlessly pathetic as Athena approached. She stood, absently smoothing her shapeless and wrinkled dress, then wobbled with tiny steps toward the rear.

"She's a prize."

"You don't know the half of it, kid. Least she's quiet now." Doris spoke softly. "You heard all that screaming a while back? Halfway to the highway, the stupid bitch wants me to turn around."

"Some people shouldn't be allowed to have kids." With an angry sigh, Athena plopped down into the seat. Behind them, the woman's weepy mumbles drowned out Larry's low-voiced reassurances.

"You look tired."

"I'm fine." She peered through the window into the gathering darkness.

Doris raised an eyebrow. So something had finally gotten to her, she thought. It didn't take much to figure out what—the kid had to be about the right age. "So how's Matty doing?"

Her voice was ice. "Matthew's as well as can be expected."

Shaking her head, Doris returned her full attention to the road.

"I'm sorry," Athena said after a long moment. "I didn't mean to snap at you."

"I understand, honey." She nodded toward the rear. "This woman—what makes it almost comical is I had her in here once before. She has another kid that got hurt a couple months ago. She carried on just the same as now. Take him to the hospital. Don't take him to the hospital."

"People don't learn from the past. They live in it." Her eyes never wavered from the window. "Doris, would you do me a favor? Are you going to the diner tonight? If you see Barry, would you tell him I had to go home?"

"Sure thing. Listen, honey, why don't you take it easy for a couple days? I'll cover for you. The leg bothering you? I'm telling you, the way you been pushing yourself . . ."

Athena clenched both hands into tight fists and held them in her lap.

Despairing of ever learning to keep her mouth shut, Doris turned down the high beams and drove quietly a moment. Then something occurred to her. "Matty was bit by a dog once, wasn't he?"

Finally alone, Athena drove like a madwoman. *What's wrong with me?* Everyone had noticed, she felt sure. She wondered why she'd become so agitated, couldn't even understand her own decision not to meet Barry. She hadn't been home this early in months. *Too early to go right to bed.*

Through the dark blue lens of the sky, the stars looked enormous. No traffic tonight. Ahead, a few red taillights, small and faraway, kept distant company, smugly hurrying home. *Back to the city, probably. Home from the shore.* For one aching moment, she longed to be going with them. *They don't even know I'm here.* Her headlights flashed off a discarded beer can. *They drive through the wilderness and don't realize it.* It seemed she'd almost spoken aloud, and her mother's face rose in her mind. *Me, my whole life, I don't exist for them.* She gripped the wheel tighter—it grew slippery with sweat.

She reached her turnoff. At the mouth of the dirt road, the night seemed to thicken. Tree shapes flowed on either side, and she imagined herself to be piloting a one-woman submarine.

Headlights sank only a little ways, twin bars of cold white, swirling across thick bracken.

Her house stood solid, an ugly thing in the night, but bright points leaked through a hundred chinks in the lower story. *Pamela's still here.* Quickly, she suppressed the wave of gratitude.

The car rattled to a stop. Picking up the scanner, she pushed open the door, and the car's interior light surprised her. *That hasn't worked in months.* The dim glow spilled onto the ground. Crickets surrounded the house. Her footsteps on the gravel— first the proud, crunching step, then the grating hiss of the lame foot—sounded humiliatingly loud.

As she climbed the steps to the porch, she felt the boards sag beneath her. A yellow brightness seeped under the back door, and she could hear the prattling domestic buzz of the voices inside. They sounded happy. She stood outside for a long time, listening, somehow hearing how her aunt and cousins had always sounded from the room next to hers, voices that had always become just whispers if she'd approached.

The door swung open before she could reach it. The glare from the kitchen caught her eavesdropping, and she flushed.

"You're home early!" Pamela sounded breathless and guilty, her plump face dark with concern. "Matty's not in bed yet."

"That's all right." A small object lay in a cloth lump on the porch, and Athena stooped to pick it up, examining it curiously as she entered, keeping her eyes averted as she pushed past her sister-in-law. She blinked at the brightness of the kitchen, at the peeling walls and fractured chairs. "You're letting mosquitoes in, Pamela," she said, neither turning to her nor moving any farther into the room. "Do you want me to drive you home?" She stared at the mottled yellow walls, at the pebbled mold where they met the low ceiling. She looked down. Tongue lolling, the dog sprawled on the floor planks.

"Now, you know the road to my place is all overgrowed, 'Thena." Giggling, Pam closed the door. "You can't get a car through there."

"I could drive you partway."

"Why? I mean, don't be silly. I'll tell you, first thing I'm gonna make that man do when he gets back is clear out them damn little pines. Well," she sniggered, "maybe the second thing."

Athena looked away in embarrassment.

"Least it's a little cooler," Pam went on. "Did you have your dinner? I never expected to see you this early. Soon as I heard the car, I said to Matty, 'That can't be your mother,' I said." She paused. "Where'd he get to, anyways? He was just here a second ago. He was sitting right at . . ."

"It's all right." She stepped over the unflinching dog.

Pam blushed. "I don't know how that dog got in here. I know he's s'posed to stay in the yard. I'll put him out now." She took a few steps forward. "Come on, Dooley, you big ugly thing." The dog barely rolled an eye in her direction. "Come on now." She stood there, not knowing what to do with her hands. "I guess I'll just go on home now."

"No." Athena spun on her, really looking at her at last. A dishwater blonde, Pamela missed being pretty by a wide margin— nose too broad, eyes too small. The thick makeup with which she tried to cover a large strawberry birthmark on her cheek did not enhance her doughy complexion; yet the overall effect managed to be not unpleasant. She smiled a lot. Athena forced a smile of her own. "Why don't you stay a little while?" Appalled by her own desperation, she turned away quickly when Pamela beamed. "Is there any coffee?"

"I just made some fresh." Pam bustled over to the butane stove, lit it and began to reheat the cold mud left over from breakfast. "I'll rinse out some cups. What's that you got there?"

"I found it on the back stoop." Athena held it up. "Is it yours?"

The other woman took a closer look. "Matty musta found it."

"Matthew was out?"

"Just . . . for a minute." Pam shuffled her big feet. "I brung over some more fresh eggs," she added. "They're in the icebox."

Pushing aside a Ouija board, Athena cleared a spot amid the dirty dishes on the table. When she dumped out the contents of the string bag, bobby pins spilled, scattering like insects, and out tumbled a hairbrush, makeup, a bathing suit. "No name," she said. "Must've been dropped from a car."

"Can I have it?"

"Matthew couldn't have gone all the way to the highway? Could he? Where is he?"

Pam shrugged. "In the other room, I guess."

Gathering things up, Athena stuffed them back in the bag. *Come on, girl.* She tossed the bag aside and slowly crossed the kitchen. As a loose board bounced under her, exaggerating her limp, she gritted her teeth. "Matthew?" She stood in the living-room doorway and looked around at the battered furniture and the crumbling holes in the carpet. "Matthew?" Behind her in the kitchen, she heard the dog get up with a yawning stretch, and a mumbling whisper came from behind the stairway. "Matthew, what are you doing over there?"

Hidden in the shadowed corner, the boy refused to look up when she walked over to him. He kept his face down, his back pressed against the locked door that led into the closed-off section of the house. "Nn–nnooo . . ." Matty hunched into himself. ". . . ammy?" He began a gasping mumble down into his chest that worked toward a clogged weeping. "Sn–no t-time . . . don-wanna . . . go'way . . ." His words emerged as bubbles of sound.

Helpless before such obvious misery, his mother had no idea what to do. "Stop that." She noted the drool that ran along the boy's chin and averted her eyes. *And I was going to ask him about that bag.* She repressed a painful desire to laugh. *What point could there be in questioning a . . . in questioning him?* She made her voice pleasant. "Matthew, it's time for you to go to bed." Placing her hands on his bony shoulders, she attempted to point him toward the stairs. The boy struggled, sniveling, and she tightened her grip. His shoulders were damp with spittle and sweat. She recoiled, and Matthew shrieked.

Pamela rushed out of the bright kitchen. "Oh, what's the matter with my boy?" Matty flew to her, burying his face in her dress. "I'll take care of it, 'Thena," she said. "What's the matter with my big boy now? Is he crying? Is my big boy crying? You know what I think, don't you? I think somebody's tired. That's what I think." The boy's arms stayed clenched about her thick waist, while her words—consoling and cooing and caressing—flowed over him, and she petted his head, wiping at his face with her dress. Gradually, he stopped trembling. As Dooley clawed lazily at the living-room carpet, Pam steered the boy up the steps. "Look at him, crying like a little baby—you should be ashamed. 'Thena? Does he feel hot to you?"

Athena just stood there.

"Are you a big boy or not? Huh? Aren't you a big boy?" Pam called over her shoulder, "He is getting real big, ain't he? Hard to believe he was only nine last Christmas."

Athena followed them slowly up the stairs. *I could never do that.* She listened to her sister-in-law, to the warm, moronic flow of her words. *Never.*

"Now are you going to be a good boy for Pammy and stop crying and get undressed by yourself tonight, like a good boy, like you did the other night? Huh? Are you gonna be a good boy?"

The child's mumbled reply seemed almost inaudible, incomprehensible, but Pamela kissed the top of his tousled blond head as though she'd caught every word. *Perhaps she does understand him.* She watched their backs. Pam's flowered dress looked homemade, Matty's T-shirt had small holes in it. *Perhaps it's some private language they speak. Just the two of them.* Seeing the way Matty clung to Pam's soft roundness, she ran a tentative hand over her own sides and sharp hips.

All the way up the stairs, Pamela blabbered to Matty and Athena in turn. When he looked at his mother, the boy wailed and became so much dead weight. She would have gone back down, but Pamela never stopped talking to her.

Somehow they managed to carry him, squeezed bodily between them, up the narrow attic steps.

The cot springs creaked. "There you go now." The light came on, and Pamela undid the boy's belt. "Don't you want to stop crying now?" Pam got his pants off, clucked over the scabs and bramble cuts. She left the dirty T-shirt on.

Pretending to watch, Athena stood back. "We have to clear out this room." She surveyed the disorder. A second cot, folded and grimy, leaned against the wall.

"Gimme your other foot now. That's a boy. You don't want

to sleep with your socks on, do you?" She struggled with his clothes. "You know, it's sort of funny to think Lonny and Wallace used to sleep in this room, when they was little, I mean, and now Matty sleeps here. You know? Look how dirty you are!" The boy looked almost black in places. "You get a bath tomorrow, that's for sure. Oh, your poor legs, that scab's bleeding again. What were you doing today anyhow?"

Matty lay down and then shot up again. ". . . st-stones . . . my p-pock . . ." He whined miserably, beginning to sob again. ". . . dd-d-don . . . st-st . . . don lose . . ." He rubbed at his runny nose and eyes with dirty hands.

"What's the matter, baby? What is it? Something in your pants pocket?" She lifted the jeans from where she'd tossed them. They were stiff with sweaty dirt and strangely heavy, and she turned them inside out. "Oh, your stones!" She turned to Athena. "He was playing with these stones before. No, I won't lose them. They'll be right here in your pocket for tomorrow. Do you want them? You want to sleep with them? How 'bout just one?" She gave him a smooth white pebble, and he clutched it tightly in his hand, smiled and lay back down. "What a little pack rat you are." Smiling, she got him under the graying sheet. "That's it, go to sleep now. You and Chabwok can have a good game with the stones tomorrow."

Chabwok. Athena shook her head. Pamela always insisted that "Chabwok" was the name of Matthew's invisible friend, but Athena had her doubts. God knows the boy must be lonely enough to have invented an imaginary playmate, but those few times she'd heard him use the word, surprising him at solitary play, it had been too slurred to properly understand. It might have been a name. It might have been anything.

Pamela cooed and Matthew jabbered, a mindless recitation. Athena stood close by the doorway, looking at the junk, trying not to listen. *My son.* As always, she found herself dispassionately examining her responses. Why was she so numb with him? What was she afraid of feeling? Pity? Shame? The light bulb swayed slightly on its cord, and the string, tied to a short, broken chain, danced back and forth.

Shadows swayed.

When Wallace Monroe first brought her to this house, she'd had such enthusiasm. She'd even thought there might be something consequential hidden amid the clutter of this attic, something valuable, antiques perhaps . . . but hadn't needed to examine things too closely before discarding that notion. It was all what Granny Lee used to call "cracker furniture." The pieces looked old enough, certainly, but in an advanced state of disrepair and poorly made in the first place. *Early American trash heap.*

Still fussing, Pamela kissed Matty one last time, loud and moist. "You go to sleep now." She gave the light cord a tug, and the doorway became a gray rectangle surrounded by brown darkness.

The two women started down, Pamela whispering. "I wonder how come he just won't never talk around you hardly. You should just see the way he talks around me all the time. Sometimes I can't even get him to shut up."

Athena nodded, half listening, not believing. *Strange, the way she won't accept the truth about him.* Ignoring Pamela's further prattling, she cursed the thin slats of the attic stairs with each twinge of her leg. *I'm his mother and I've accepted it. Long since.* The other woman's murmurings seemed very far from her, empty and shrill as the creaking of the stairs.

"He threw another one today," Pamela confessed reluctantly while she clumped down the hall. "Oh! But not one of the bad ones!" Pamela Stewart Monroe lived in perpetual fear of Athena's deciding to put Matty away. With no children of her own—and her husband in the penitentiary—her entire life centered on the boy. "No, not one of the bad ones. Just one of the ones where he gets all kind of glassy-eyed." At the end of the corridor, she continued down the stairs with slow, heavy movements.

During the first eight years of Pam's marriage to Lonny Monroe, four babies had been stillborn. At last one child, badly deformed, had survived, and "the lump"—as her husband fondly referred to it—survived still, in a state institution. As far as Athena had ever been able to tell, Pam had blocked all memory of her sole offspring.

Dooley lay at the foot of the staircase, groaning in his sleep, and they had to step over him. The acrid smell of burning coffee filled the kitchen.

The large-bodied woman shrieked across the room. "I forgot!" Black foam spewed out of the pot and over the burners.

"It's all right," Athena muttered. Clearing the table, she stacked plates, piling some on the iron stove, dumping others in the overloaded sink.

Pamela poured the coffee, sloshing dark liquid over the tablecloth, and the wet spots steamed while she fetched spoons from the drainboard. Athena pulled up a chair, and both women shoveled sugar into their cups. Thin crack lines traced the heavy white porcelain of the sugar bowl. The coffee smelled terrible.

Athena scalded her tongue. *Foul.* She blew on the cup, and steam swirled away, her glance following it. "I remember the day Wallace papered this ceiling. How many years ago? All coming down now. Ruined." Oily residue collected thickly on the surface of her coffee, and she found herself idly examining the chipped opalescent cup. *All the old things.* A fine thing once, the cup had come from her grandmother's house. *Broken. Or worn out. Everything. That house . . . the way it smelled toward the end . . .* When Granny Lee had lost her strength, everything had just fallen apart. *That's the way it'll happen with me. Not that I'm doing so well as it is.* She wondered how the cup had escaped being packed away, hidden with the rest of her grandmother's things . . . as though they shamed her somehow. "Why does everything in this house have to be so . . . so dismal?"

"I never did understand why you would even want to live here," said Pam. She waited for a response, then resumed, made bold by her sister-in-law's uncustomary familiarity. "You ain't, I mean, you're not one of . . . of . . ." Agitated, she halted. "I mean, you're not like a piney. You're too good for . . ."

"Oh yes. I have fine qualities."

Pamela faltered, confused by the bitterness of the brief laugh. "I mean, it just don't seem right that you"—she gulped coffee and blushed—"that you . . . you . . ." Her voice became a pleading whine. "You know, I was thinking tonight, Lonny and

Wallace was so different, for brothers, I mean. I mean, Lonny's so dark, not like Wallace was. I guess there must really be some Indian blood in the family, like they say. And Lonny's got them eyes."

Athena took a deep breath, deciding she might as well make conversation. "Have you had a letter from Lonny recently?"

"Not in a long time." Pam relaxed into the subject. "I told you, the last one said that guy who was writin' them for him was gettin' out. I sure miss him. Those eyes." She gave a small, dramatic shiver. "The way he looks at me sometimes—sort of like an animal."

The other woman stirred her coffee . . . around and around . . . and concentrated on the rattle of the spoon in the cup. It embarrassed her to hear Pamela talk this way. She knew Lonny Monroe neglected his wife, even during those rare intervals when he wasn't doing time.

"Course most a those guys in prison is black. I, uh, you think . . . I mean, I always meant to ask you if it was true what they say about black guys having . . . I mean, the reason I ask is just . . ."

Athena didn't know where to look. Resembling nothing so much as a transistor radio, the scanner lay on the table in front of her. Idly, she adjusted a control, and faint grumbling sounds issued forth.

"So, what happened today?" Pam giggled, leaning forward and fairly quivering with anticipation. "Go on any calls?"

Athena glanced at her eager face, then got up and limped to the door. "Out, Dooley." She held the door open. "Go on out." The shaggy brute of a dog rolled its head in her direction and exhaled heavily. Athena advanced purposefully, raising one foot as though to kick, and with vast reluctance, the dog struggled, yawning, to its feet, shook itself, then shambled with infinite slowness out the door and across the dark porch. She slammed the door.

"So what happened? Was it bloody?"

Tight-lipped with annoyance, Athena briefly sketched the events of the day, while Pam visibly savored every word. Finally, she described the last call and the woman who'd been so difficult. Ordinarily, she found Pamela's company barely tolerable, but tonight the alternative seemed worse.

"Them damn pineys," Pam interrupted. "They just don't know when they're well-off." Pamela had once worked a civilian munitions job at Fort Dix, and in her own eyes this forever exempted her from piney status. Weak static crackled from the scanner. "Wasn't there no other calls today?"

She almost snapped but caught herself. "Actually . . . I don't know how much longer I can afford to work on the rig."

"What? You're kidding!"

"The money's almost gone." Athena shrugged. The money—the few thousands that Granny Lee had left her. Every penny of Wallace's had gone into the house before he died. "I can't even pay you much longer. Not that I've even been very good about that."

"I keep telling you, you don't have to pay me."

She stirred her coffee again. "I used to be so sure of myself." She laughed. "God, I've made such a mess of things."

Puzzlement spread over Pam's face. "So, what are you gonna do? Get on welfare?"

"Like every other piney?" Grimly—as though it were the most important thing in the world—Athena examined her chewed and broken fingernails. "I hear there's going to be an opening at the state hospital."

Pam gasped. "But Matty's . . . !"

"A job opening," she explained hastily as she turned her gaze to the horrible coffee and mused on a future of spoon feedings and bedpans.

"Harrisville? But you can't even stand to be around one. . . ." Pamela blinked and set her cup down. "That'd be a real shame," she continued carefully. "I mean, if you had to quit the ambulance and all. I know how much you like it."

Athena waved a fly away from the sugar.

"Uh, you know, 'Thena, about welfare," she explained with an audible gush of sympathy. "You could probably get some. I mean, since you got Matty and all."

The other woman glanced up and then averted her eyes again.

Pam searched her face. Panicked by the conjunction of subjects—the boy and the asylum—she cast her eyes about wildly. The Ouija board had been pushed to one side of the table, and she pounced on it with desperate enthusiasm. "You want to play? You should of seen all the fun me and Matty had tonight. Chabwok just wouldn't shut up for some reason. You should of seen all the stuff he was saying. 'Danger' and 'death' and stuff." She slid the board between them. "You want to play?" Pointed stars and moons with faces decorated the chipped and peeling board. An empty water glass rested upside down over the letters. "Come on," she coaxed. "We can ask it about the ambulance!"

"I don't think so."

"Come on, I bet it says you're gonna get money from somewheres."

"My grandmother had one of these." She rested her hand lightly on the board. "She was so religious. Did I ever tell you? Something of an amateur spiritualist. All the neighbors and church folk always used to come in for advice."

"Yeah? Like old Mother Jenks?"

"They used to try to give her money." Athena's voice stayed low and soft. "She'd never take it. 'It's a gift.' That's what she'd say. A gift."

"You went to live with her after your mom died?"

"Did you hear something outside?"

"Prob'ly just the dog."

"Shall we make the trip to Mount Holly this week?" Changing the subject, Athena cleared her throat. "We must be out of nearly everything. I know we need sugar."

"Yeah, all we really got is cans a soup. Remember, 'Thena, I bought all that stuff, and then I forgot and bought more?"

The red light on the scanner wavered, and Athena went absolutely still.

Pam could just make out what sounded like garbled numbers in the static. "What . . . ?"

"Police dispatcher, out by Atsion." She listened. "That's an accident."

"Will you have to go?"

She shushed her. "At this hour, usually they'll call Burlington County." For another moment, she strained to hear voices. "My mother's not dead. She's in a . . . a sort of a home."

Outside was blackness, and the crickets raged. The two women sat in the grimy kitchen and listened to the scanner and planned a trip to a distant supermarket, the Ouija board untouched between them. "You hungry?" Pamela scrounged stale cookies out of a canister.

Small wonder they were running low, Athena reflected—her sister-in-law ate everything in sight. Setting down the pencil stub, she twisted dials on the scanner, trying to recapture fading words. Finally giving up with a sigh, she continued writing up a shopping list on a bit of brown paper.

". . . an' as long as we're gonna be in Mount Holly, I'll be needing some more bug spray, because them damn bees are eating up my flowers again. I swear, you can just sit there an see them going right after my flowers."

Athena almost choked on her coffee.

"Oh, an' I used your last light bulb. Didn't you notice how nice an bright it is in here?" She waited for a response, but Athena had stopped paying attention again. "I guess it must be getting late." Noisily draining the last of the liquid, Pam plunked her cup down on the tablecloth and stood up. "I guess I better be—"

"I'll walk out with you. I want to get rid of this garbage before the ants find it."

"Can't that wait till morning, 'Thena? I know you don't want to go out there."

Ignoring her, Athena maneuvered around the crowded kitchen and scraped plates into a leaking bag.

"Here, why don't you let me help you with that?" But she just leaned against the cellar door and watched.

"You want to get the back door, Pamela? Don't forget your board."

"I'm gonna leave it here. We're supposed to play again tomorrow." She held the door open while Athena carried the garbage onto the porch. "Oh, I meant to carry up that . . ."

Pam hesitated. "You know that bag of clothes down the cellar? Matty needs . . . never mind, I'll get them tomorrow."

"I'll do it," said Athena. It took a few seconds for her eyes to adjust. The open doorway lit the porch floor; it seemed to silence the crickets. "No." The light began to swing away. "Leave the door open."

"But, 'Thena, the mosquitoes . . ."

"Leave it." The night sounded like a rustling curtain. Holding the bag away from herself, she moved down the porch steps as a brown form emerged from the yard.

"Why don't you just give that to me to dump?" Pamela trudged along behind her. "You go back to the house."

Athena kept walking, her shadow, framed in the kitchen light, spreading across the yard, while the dog frisked around, sniffing at the garbage.

"Well then," suggested Pam, "why don't you just dump it here for now and . . . Oh well. Sure is dark tonight. Get outta my way, Dooley." Reluctantly, she took the path that led around to the front of the house. "Well then, see ya tomorrow then, I guess. You walkin' me home, dog?"

Athena stopped walking. "Do you want the flashlight?" she called. "It's in the car."

"I can see. G'night. I'm takin' Dooley."

"Are you sure?"

A faint voice drifted back through the darkness. "I sure hope them wild dogs ain't nowheres round here!"

"Pamela?"

An insect trilled.

Beginning to sweat, Athena forced one foot in front of the other, quickly passing beyond the farthest perimeter of light, her footsteps making almost no noise in the sand and clumped weeds. She skirted the unused shed as a skittering sound issued from within its indefinite shape. Maybe rats, she thought. The weeds grew higher this far from the house, and they rustled dryly as she moved through them. Behind the shed, well beyond the yard, the trash heap was a formless hump, and tonight the smell seemed especially bad. It would have to be burned soon. Trusting her nose for sense of direction, she chucked the garbage, and a tin can rattled.

Pines circled everywhere, beyond the mound, around the shed.

Another cricket called to the first now, softer, subdued, fading. *I'm an intelligent adult.* Then a third began. *It's irrational to be afraid of the dark.* Heading back toward the porch, she tripped over something invisible, almost falling. *I will not run.* The yellowish light of the doorway seemed faraway. *Never make it.* The dark began a hollow roaring in her ears; like a swimmer swept out to sea, she foundered, the lighted doorway providing her only lifeline.

As she climbed the porch steps, she could feel the darkness sucking at her. *Heartbeat a little faster.* She slammed the door and leaned against it. *Respiration a bit more rapid—that's all.* All around her, the house lay still.

Alone. Clearing the coffee cups, she stacked them with the rest of the week's dirty dishes. *Alone in the house.* She picked up the scanner. All the downstairs lights were on, yet shadowed corners filled the rooms. *Except for Matthew, of course.* Her hand hesitated before switching off the kitchen light. Quietly, almost stealthily, she checked the living-room windows. Most were boarded, but through one intact pane the strumming night showed solid: iron nothingness. She tried to cover it by pulling and poking the skimpy curtains closed, but it was as though the window glass had been coated with black paint that seeped through the fabric.

At the center of the room, an armchair stood on scrolled claw feet, and she perched on one of the massive arms. She'd always liked this chair. The frayed material, scratchy with the ghost of a raised pattern, had long ago faded to some indeterminate and dusty shade of gray. It was ugly, really, but so solid, so protective.

She wound the rubber band out of her hair, smoothing back the dark curls with one hand, holding the scanner lightly in the other. She knew she should go to bed now. The armchair faced a tight, grimy fireplace, and blackness lay in the cracks of the floor. Dimness around the lamp transformed the room into something smaller, more personal. She crossed her arms in front of her breasts, hugged herself, breathing against the pressure, then letting go, allowing her arms to fall away and fade in her lap. She thought about bed again, but it seemed an impossible distance. She'd have to climb the stairs to her airless room, all that way. So far. Crickets sounded dimly through the walls, an empty nighttime noise, like the voice of faucets leaking at the edge of her awareness.

Darkness pressed the house.

Pamela picked her way across the bridge. *Just my luck to fall in some night.* She grinned to herself. *They'll hear me yelling from here to Leeds Point.* One of the planks was missing, and she could smell the brown water below.

Far ahead, she heard Dooley bark, the sound deep in his barrel chest. *Chasing a possum or something.* The dog often escorted her home, always ranging far into the night around her. She stepped up the pace. Her trailer lay just down the road toward town, making her Athena's nearest neighbor.

She heard loud breathing and the soft sound of running, then Dooley charged past her. "Good dog." Panting, the dog padded around, licking at her. "Yuck." She petted his head, wiping her hand on his fur. "Good boy now." He trotted alongside a moment, then launched off into the darkness again.

That pig. Following, Pam frowned. *That piney bitch.* Her mother also lived along this road. *Always flauntin' all them men in my face, even when I was little.*

As she walked on, the memory of one afternoon in Athena's kitchen came to her. She'd been boasting about how important her job at the army base had been. Becoming excited, she'd babbled about her "double life," dropping exaggerated hints about the night she'd managed to get herself used by a group of drunken GIs. Maybe she'd been trying to shock Athena, or perhaps she'd wanted some sympathetic response. Whatever she'd been looking for, she hadn't found it: Athena's face had twisted with disgust. *I don't see what she got so high and mighty about anyhow. It ain't like everybody don't know about her and that cop.* Immediately, she felt ashamed. *I shouldn't think that way about 'Thena. Why she's . . . she's the most . . .*

Her landmark towered over her—a dead cypress the locals called "Hanging Tree." *They say she hung there till she was just a skeleton.* The cypress loomed about the pines, one thick limb stretching over the road. *Till the bones just dropped off one by one.* By daylight, the rotted remnants of rope fibers could still be seen clinging to the bark. Athena always said it was probably just an old tire swing, but Pam believed, even cherished, the tale of the hanged witch.

A branch of the road, just a fading trace, lay behind the thick cypress. Saplings and tall weeds had begun to cover it. *Lonny'll take care of things when he comes home.* But some inner part of her understood that Lonny would approve of the overgrown road, that he'd like the way to the trailer being hidden, impassable, because the state police would never find it now. She was fairly certain their trailer was stolen and hoped Athena never found out. *She gets so funny about that sort of thing.* Sighing, she walked on. *Such a shame, Wallace dropping dead like that. They was so happy.*

A breeze stirred in the smaller trees.

Lonny's been gone almost two years this time. Leaving the road to town behind her, she wended between the little pines. *Lord, I miss him.* Even as she thought it, she knew it wasn't really true. What she missed was what she'd never had.

Something rustled in the bushes.

"Dooley?" She stopped moving, stopped breathing. "Is there somebody?" She heard the dog bark somewhere far behind her. "Who is that?" Her voice trembled.

A match scratched and flared, and she flinched from the sudden light. "You scared me all to death!" she screeched, beginning to giggle.

Framed by tangled white-blond hair, a bloodless face floated in the dark. Marl Spencer stared stupidly, the flame glowing purple in his eyes. "Skeared ya?" The match twitched away.

Pam heard sucking. "You burn yourself, Marl?" Suddenly maternal, she moved toward him. Another match flared, and she paused, blinking.

Marl held the flame high with the other hand as he blew on

his wet fingers. He had a crumpled paper sack under his arm, heavy shapes inside it.

"Is that my stuff?" she asked, not reaching for the bag. "Al Spencer shouldn't be makin' you deliver that so late at night," her voice scolded. "An you can tell him I said so, too."

"Gotta do it a'night," the boy answered in a voice both shrill and husky.

"This-here purse is brand-new," she told him proudly. "So I don't have no money on me, but if you'll walk me home I can . . . What's that you sayin', boy? Your pa said I can have credit, did he?" The match went out, and the paper sack rustled. She guessed he was holding it out to her. "I don't want no credit. Now, you just come on to my place." The bag rustled again. "It won't take a minute, now. It's just over here. Sides, I want to get you something for that burn."

The boy mumbled.

"Oh, you got to put something on it right away! It'll get all pus if you don't. Now, you just come with me." She started forward along the choked path. "You was on your way to the trailer anyways, right?" After a moment, she sensed his fleshy presence following.

The boy hung back when they reached the dark and littered clearing. The woman hurried past the black hulks of two automobiles, one on blocks, one on its side. "Well, here we are now." She stamped up the metal steps of the trailer.

The door opened with a squeak, and lights came on inside. She stuck her head out the open door. The gleam revealed the clearing: a chicken-wire and plywood enclosure dominated the bare earth, and white petunias were bedded up against the trailer's cinder-block foundations. Sagging from the roof, thick cable looped into the trees. "Ain't you coming in?" The boy had his back to her. "What's the matter? What do you keep looking over your shoulder for? You hear something? That's right. You scared a dogs, ain't you?" Still peering at him, she laughed. "Hell, the things people is scared of." She liked the way the back of his head was shaped, she decided—he was growing up real nice. Of course everybody knew he was a retard, and he was still sort of pudgy. "Well, don't just stand there then. Come on in the place."

Reluctantly approaching the steps, he removed three large jars from the sack. Electric light gleamed yellow in the liquid as he handed them up to her. "Pop wants da jars back."

She disappeared. "Can I git you some?" she called. "Oh, c'mon, have some. Maybe I'll have a little. Not that I really drink or anything, you know. I just think it's good to have some around. In case anybody should visit. You know, like a relative or something."

He lingered on the stoop. "Uh . . ."

Something banged within, then glasses clicked. "Marl? What are we? Like cousins sort of?"

Backing away from the trailer, he folded the paper bag and stuck it in his pants as the woman's voice faded behind him.

"I bet everybody in town thinks I'm real snotty, like I think I'm better than them or something, right? Marl? Marl?"

He'd already crossed the clearing.

Suddenly, she stood, tapping her foot in the doorway. "You don't got no more deliveries to make tonight, do you? Well then, come on in here and let me see that finger."

Through the trees, there came distant, lonely barking. He froze. Slowly, he walked back toward the trailer. One foot on the stairs, he turned to the woods—the barking sounded again. He entered.

The night breathed through the empty clearing. Trees whispered. A slight breeze pressed through, muttering and sighing, and the pines moved, barely swaying. Moths danced in the arc of pale light from the doorway through which the woman's voice drifted. "That's a boy. Come on in here. You know, my sister-in-law was telling me just tonight about this bunch a wild dogs that's running around. Now, hold it out while I put some of this on it—won't hurt. Yeah, that's right. They're still out there somewhere, so you got to be careful going home, you know, and me all alone cause a Lonny's still being away. Don't move. Still away. It gets real lonely out here. Course 'Thena and me is real good friends. Hold still now. They talk about me in town? They tell jokes about me? Hold still. That's it. Don't that feel good? Don't it? You're really growing, really getting big now, ain't you? Such nice big hands. You know, Marl, you ain't like them other pineys in town. You're more like me and 'Thena. Yeah, you got . . . fine qualities. I never believed none a them stories about you starting fires. Does that feel good? Come on. Yeah now. That's it. Does it feel good now?"

Disturbed by the light, crickets chirruped erratically. In the coops, the chickens stirred and complained.

"Don't move away now. This is nice, boy. Just let me . . . feels so . . . No!"

The boy burst out of the doorway, leaped the three steps and hit the clearing a good yard away. Tripping in the darkness, he picked himself up running.

"Hey, what's the matter with you?"

He glanced back once.

"Boy, you're really weird!" She stood framed in the doorway. "Where you going? I won't tell nobody. You coming back?" As he tore along the darkly tangled trail, her voice followed. "You gonna tell? Weird! What's the matter with you?"

Reaching the road, he raced toward town, her words festering in his brain. Something clicked in his face, and his hand came away wet. He sucked in his breath. The barking seemed closer now, and he ran, his temples pounding. A pulse throbbed in his neck, and he panted, stumbling in the sand. Thoughts of wild dogs pursued him, raging in his mind: hounds smelling his blood. Howling surrounded him. He fled through the night in panic, blackness dripping onto his shirt.

The woods were not silent.

She'd lain awake, clenched and sweating, but sleep had finally rolled over her in thick, smoky waves. Athena's mouth made tiny whistlings like a child's as she breathed in the damp, moldy smell of the mattress. The liquid sigh of the pines seemed slower, more somber tonight, only sometimes peaking with a rush. Crickets called weakly, and her breathing droned. The house itself creaked. Some deep recess of her sleeping mind still listened, as gradually the wooden groans grew rhythmic. Soon she could hear the slapping of waves on the outside walls. Rising. Receding. Darkness seemed to lap around her, and the mattress floated. On her spinning bed, she tensed, squirming as the nightmare began.

Dark . . . drowning . . . black choking . . . and suddenly eyes. At first many. Burning red. Malignant. Then only two.

Something hungry, watching from the dark.

Starting, she came fully awake and sat up, her body wet with perspiration. She kicked a tangled sheet and some clothes away from her legs, felt a wave of coolness. With one hand, she forced herself back down, felt the pounding in her chest.

Through the open window drifted the distant howling of the town's dogs.

Well, that's a new twist. Eyes wide-open, she lay, seeing nothing. *Not just the dark this time, but something in it.* Beads of sweat rolled down her face, and she inhaled deeply. *After all these years, why should it change?* The scanner's tiny red light winked from the dresser. *There's my red eyes.* The recognition brought no comfort—why should something so familiar, so positive, seem threatening? Her heart still hammered against the heel of her hand, and the sense of menace failed to dissipate.

It was reaching a peak. She knew it. This sense of dread—the nameless premonition that kept her paralyzed and waiting—grew each day more intense.

Reflexively, her hand reached across the bed, finding only the old depression beside her in the mattress. *There's someone in this room.* Abruptly, she sensed it. Every cell of her body recognized a presence, as though the dream continued. "Matthew?" Again, she sat up in bed, her pillow sliding softly off the edge.

The house made its night sounds.

"Matthew?" Though growing weaker, the impression remained: the boy was here in the room, or had just been. She rose quickly, a twinge of pain in her leg as she felt about. *Am I still dreaming?* She groped her way along the bureau toward the deep opening of the doorway.

"Matthew?" She took a few blind steps into the hall—a mineshaft. She retreated, her right hand sliding along the must-furred bedroom wallpaper for the light switch. The dingy litter of her bedroom flared. Waiting for violet blotches to melt from her vision, she turned her back on the room, stared downward, her shadow spreading gigantically across the hall floor. The peeling green linoleum depicted leaves, impossibly huge and curling, now all but worn away.

Shuddering with a yawn, she snatched a frayed terrycloth robe from the bedroom floor, shook the dust balls free and wrapped it around her shoulders. The bedroom light almost penetrated to the end of the hallway, creating a faint haze. Again, she stood and listened. *Nothing.* She started down the hall. *What if he's not in his room?* Feeling the steps above her with her hands, she limped heavily up the attic stairs.

The bedclothes rustled. In the charred darkness, a creak of cot springs fused with the hissing rhythm of his breath, and she heard him roll over, muttering wetly. The chain, when she reached for it, rattled against the bulb.

The boy didn't flinch from the light. She bent over him. His sweat-slick body sprawled across the cot, and his hands stayed clenched into small fists, damp and sticky. *Pamela has to bathe him.* His T-shirt had balled up around his armpits, and the lump of stone was still clutched in one tight hand. She straightened, staring. He sweated, inert on the mattress.

The light rattled again.

She went back down toward the dull glow of her room. *He really is asleep.* She moved down the brightened hall. *I'm tired. Doris said . . . working so hard.* Switching off the overhead light, she thought of the boy. *Dreamed it.* She sat on the edge of her bed and pulled off her robe. *Matthew is squeezing a stone.* Through the window, a slight breeze carried faint sounds of the night. It felt cool on her still-damp body, and she lay down, partially covering herself with the rumpled sheet, thinking about her son who gripped a cold stone. *No.* Her mind grew heavy and hazy. *That's not the way it is. It's not.* Her eyes closed. *not like that not*

When he was sure the sliding footsteps had returned to her room, Matty opened his eyes and sat up.

For a while, he played with the stone, pretended it was a giant boulder that rolled end over end across the pillow landscape, but soon the sounds of barking reached him, and he listened, staring at the beams. And the wind brushed across the eaves, so close, and the barking swept through the pines with a rustling as of things long dead.

He looked around his dark attic, his kingdom: the old pieces of furniture, some covered, some trailing cobwebs in the dust, loomed all around the bed. On the far side of the room, the diamond panes of the window gleamed pale black. He listened again to the dogs in the woods, and to something else, something that called to him by name.

He hid the stone under his pillow.

Slowly, he brought his upper arm to his face and mouthed it, licked the hot, salty flesh. Then he bit down—hard, harder, small teeth sinking in. And at last it came. The taste . . . the wet meat. His mouth filled with drooling warmth, hot wetness at his crotch. He felt dizzy. Sweat trickled down his body while the dark room swayed around him, warmth spreading between his legs as he flooded the bed.

From the woods, from faraway, from far below, the howling of the dogs grew muted, and there drifted to his ears a thin yapping that held something of a human quality, leaving in his mind an echo like the cries of many voices. There was hysteria in those voices . . . and abject sadness. The boy sucked at his wound, and the dark room swayed about him.

PART TWO

MUNRO'S FURNACE

Scattered over widely separated huts . . . exists today a group of human beings as distinct . . . as to excite curiosity in the mind of any outsider brought into contact with them.

Elizabeth Kite, psychologist, 1913
"The Pineys"

They have come to form a race by themselves, with the well-defined mental and physical stigmata of degeneracy and inbreeding. . . . Their annals reek of overt viciousness and of half-hidden murders, incests, and deeds of almost unnamable violence and perversity.

H. P. Lovecraft

Friday, July 31

The faint drone gradually swelled as a fly jerked through the room. One hand in a shallow depression, she lay on her side in the rutted center of the mattress—it seemed the furrow alongside her grew fainter with each solitary night. There had been a dream . . . drifting away now: her grandmother's worn, warm face, a feeling of safety fading into a memory of the infant Matthew and the sweet breath of his warmth in her arms. Such a shame he never knew his grandmother, she reflected, easing her legs over the side of the bed. Great-grandmother, she corrected herself. *My mother is his . . .*

By the dimness that pried under the window shade, she read the alarm clock on the bureau. *Damn.* She got up too quickly and felt a sharp twinge in her knee as she hobbled across the room to raise the shade. *I'm always up before this.* Thin morning drizzle fell, and the casement framed a drab square on which water spots made swerving patterns. *Always.* She felt bloated with sleep, and her eyes burned as though she'd been crying. *Am I about to begin spending my life in bed?* Fighting the stupor, she rubbed at gritty eyes. *Is that the next phase, girl?*

She pulled on a robe and padded down the hall, then smoothed the sleep from her face with a washcloth at a sink stained blue and orange. Putrid noises emanated from the plumbing. The towel smelled of mildew, and the odor mingled strongly with that of soap. While the faucet pattered, and the runneled pane of the window rattled in a breeze, vines over the back of the house rustled like the wings of startled pigeons.

Leaning on the sink, she looked at her arms—browned from sun and wind—and remembered a time when they'd been pale and soft. *Well, maybe never pale, exactly.* She gazed at her dark eyes in the mirror, at the curve of her cheek. Stray curls hung about her face, catching the light, glowing softly. She grabbed an elastic band from the pile on the washstand.

The mirror held shadows. The bathroom walls curled, peeling like lizard skin, and in the corners lay hair and dust and flakes of plaster. The drain choked and growled.

Returning to her room, she began the exercises intended to strengthen her leg. Afterward, she rummaged through her clothes, looking for things lately worn only once.

In the hallway, a new spot leaked from a dark ring on the ceiling, and drops plunked rhythmically on the linoleum, slid off around the edges. She threw a towel on the puddle. Was Matthew awake yet? From the top of the stairs, the living room still looked mostly dark with streamers of watery light flowing through chinks in the boarded windows, giving the room an air of drowsy desolation. Dust floated. Muffled silence told her she was alone in the house. Only rain on the walls and her uneven tread on the stairs broke the quiet.

A glow soaked through the parlor curtains, brightness mottling the floorboards. She pulled a curtain aside, and the drizzle twisted the soft light, sent it spinning in slow torrents along the glass. Outside, a single strand of vine had found its way across the pane, leafy course erratic as that of any caterpillar.

She rummaged around the kitchen. Coffee wasn't made, and as usual there was nothing much to eat. Where the hell was Pam? Where was Matthew? The mug held concentric black rings, and congealing bacon grease filled the iron skillet. The previous night's dishes covered the table, and the floor needed to be swept. She glanced out the back door at a fine mist blowing. Coffee, she remembered groggily, then searched for matches to light the burner.

* * *

Door banging, the shed slouched in gusts of damp wind. Within, boy and dog played in determined silence.

The interior was thick with the woody smell of wet leaves. While the dog frisked about the dirt floor, the boy clambered over stacks of soggy cardboard boxes. Gray spiders dropped off the boxes, their fat bodies making audible plops as they fell on newspapers in the loamy shadows.

Waiting for the coffee to brew, she stood in the doorway and stared at gray-veined trees. "Oh hell." Laundry sagged heavily from the clothesline, making her recall her grandmother's house, festooned with washing. *It's just a sort of rural ghetto, after all. Even the setting for my life doesn't seem to change much . . . just the same situations over and over.* Again, she struggled with the sense of being held here, frozen in place, waiting for something to happen. *As though I'll never be free to move on until . . .*

Winds that wetly snapped the sheets carried to her the smells of the rotting pine forest. Beneath the ashen sky, Dooley barked at the flapping linen, and Matthew ran around the shed. About to call out, she hesitated and sadly watched him play. *He hasn't even got sense enough to come in out of . . .*

While they scampered around each other and wrestled for sticks, the boy talked to the dog, constant and low, his voice a hum, sometimes a chatter, part of the wind that brought it to her. And a name reached her from across the yard, clearly, twice.

"Chabwok."

A name—she felt certain now. He was playing with Chabwok. Listening, she marveled at how much more verbal he was when alone. The rest of what he said eluded her, vague as the words of a song being played in a passing car. Again, Pamela had been right. *I'm his mother, and I know nothing.* Despite herself, she listened as the louder parts drifted to her with the rain that had become little more than haze, so fine she scarcely felt it.

If I went back to the city, it might be the best thing all around. She could leave him with Pam. *She'd take good care of him, even if she's not exactly the most reliable person in the world.* She shut her eyes against a dizzying sorrow that surprised her, and for a second, she tried to imagine Matthew in some apartment with her, walled in by cement. *He'd die.* He'd die if she took him away from here.

"Muther-fucken . . . muther-fucken . . ."

What?

"Fucken loony . . . shit-fuck, man."

They played harder now, the dog beginning to bark with excitement, the boy yelling and running. He hadn't seen her yet. *Where could he have learned those words?* Pamela would never use them around him. Frowning slightly, she stared at the boy's back . . . as he began a clever mockery of her limp.

The dog barked steadily now, a new sharpness to the sound, and from the shadowed kitchen, she watched them, stricken. They ran in and out of the shed, the dog snapping at air, teeth meeting in a click audible even at this distance. The boy twisted with strange movements, lifting his feet exaggeratedly high, as though something blocked the doorway. Bewildered, she moved onto the fading, whitewashed porch and watched him repeat the pantomime, over and over, in and out. A steady spattering noise drowned his rapid words. The leaky spout from the roof had gouged a pool along the wall, and water still dribbled to the deep puddle. *Basement will be flooded again.* She looked away.

There came a yell. Suddenly the boy seemed to have been jerked back, away from the shed. Tearing through the yard, he began to race in narrowing circles, panicked confusion on his face as he made breathless clawing motions at the air.

"Matthew!"

Dooley barked furiously, then slunk away, back hunched. Ugly animal sound in his throat, the boy gyrated wildly. Words mingled.

"Matthew? Matthew, stop it!"

Head thrown back, the boy ran and shouted, drunk with his own wildness. "Bite 'em an Chabwokchabwok get Ah! Ah! 'em an chab chab . . . !" His eyes reeled at the watery gray of the sky, all confusion in his face replaced by madness. Rain-laden wind soughed through the trees.

"Matthew." She stepped down the rotted boards of the porch

stairs, and a long, pointed splinter broke off. *He's calling . . . calling to . . . his playmate.* She strode toward the boy, her eyes raking the pines as she tried to fight down the growing conviction that someone or something was present, lurking just out of sight. Behind her, somebody coughed.

"Did I scare ya?" She whipped around, and the man grinned at her. "Sure is spooky, ain't he?"

She faced a living death's head, a macabre caricature of her handsome husband. Unable to speak, she stared at the man in the dark gray work clothes. *They age so quickly, these people.* The thought ran inanely through her mind, almost provoking a giggle. Lonny's face was a Technicolor marvel—red nose, bloodshot eyes, hollowed cheeks mottled with purple where small veins had broken under the sallow skin. Yet the resemblance to Wallace lay in every taunting feature.

"What are you doing here?"

"Wa' da ya mean? I come to see my sister-in-law an' nephew. Ain't a man allowed ta come see family when he wants ta?" Dirt had tangled in the dark hair that swayed as he nodded. "My only nephew. My only brother's son. Sometimes I feel like that boy's my own."

She turned away, watched Matthew run silently around the shed. The drizzle had trickled to nothing, and sunlight began to bleed through the overcast.

"I used ta play in this yard. Me an' Wallace."

A tremor deep inside, she kept her back to him. Wisps of remembered conversations drifted, memories of how close he'd been to Wallace—a closeness inexplicable to her. Wallace had been such a good man, while Lonny . . .

Their mother had been a teacher, and the two boys had gotten more education than most locals, for all the good it had done Lonny. After their parents' accident, Wallace and his brother had lived like ghosts in their ruined house, by their ruined town. Sometimes they'd drifted. She knew there'd been farm jobs, even a government work project down South. But always they'd been drawn back here.

"An we always had dogs too. 'Thena? I gotta talk to you."

Almost before he spoke, she recognized the pleading sorrow in his voice and felt herself draw away.

Seeing the way her face hardened, he twitched, then pointed at the boy. "Poor li'l half-wit." Suddenly, he leered. "An' you hate him for it, don't ya? 'Cause he ain't perfick. An' you s'posed to be his mother."

"What do you want?"

"Who was it wanted to have 'im put away?" His eyes seemed to tighten as he watched the boy. "Huh? Answer me that. You ain't no kinda mother."

"Do you want money? Is it that again?"

"Ah, 'Thena. You used ta like me once. What do we gotta fight for? We're family." He leaned into her face, his breath reeking of booze.

The condition of his teeth shocked her, and she grimaced with disgust.

"Ya think you care 'bout him? You don't care for shit!"

"When did you get out?" She tried to look bored. "Does Pamela even know? Have you been home yet, or just to Spencer's?"

"What's 'at s'posed ta mean? You think I'm drunk or something? I'm sick. Shit. You runnin' round in that fuckin' ambulance. Makes me laugh. You don't even care 'bout your own kid," he'd begun to shout. "You just provin' how s'perior you are wi' all them hurt people. That's disgustin' if you ask me. Fuckin' nigger wonder woman gonna save the day, huh? You just a cripple, 'at's what you are. 'At's all you are!" He pointed. "It's your fault he's like 'at! My brother's kid!"

Though she tried not to flinch, her lips went thin.

"That's right, 'Thena," he gloated. "Don't lose control. Gotta stay s'perior. Matty! Matty, c'mere. Your uncle's here, boy—c'mon over here."

As she looked at the boy, all her germinating suspicions to the contrary melted away. Rooted to the spot, he stood with his fingers in his mouth, staring as though about to flee. While the boy drooled, Lonny began ranting at her again, and she felt enraged, wanting to laugh and scream with shame . . . and sorrow.

Matt didn't run away.

His concentration excluded the adults. He brought the inch-worm that crawled on his hand closer to his face and watched the pale green movement. The insect bowed its body, feeling blindly in the air before making contact with his flesh—the barest tickling sensation. Gently, the boy crouched and held his finger to the ground, watched the tiny life crawl away.

"Why don't ya go back to the city then? If ya hate us here so much? Shit. Go on—go live in slum housing. Go ask your black aunt ta take you back! You'd die before ya did that, wouldn't ya? Does your wonderful family even know ya got a retard kid?" Suddenly, his voice slurred even more. "Never should've stopped the chains. You'll find out. They used to know how to treat 'em." He kept rubbing at the back of his gray neck. "Look at 'im. Oh Jesus, look at 'im. You ever know 'bout my father's brother? No, Wally wouldn't tell that, would he? I'm so damn tired of hearin' how wonderful ole Wally was. Don't look like he's doin' you much good now though, do it?" He sneered. "That boy. He's a real member of this family, he is. It's gonna take 'im." Shouting again, he moved closer to her, his hands spasmodically clenching into fists.

She braced herself. The subject of his rant might switch from moment to moment, but the momentum built steadily.

"You're the one with the crazy mother. Don't even know who the hell yer father was. You didn't think Wally told me that, did ya? Coulda been any animal retard."

She wanted to retort with something about his own children, dead or deformed, but couldn't. For Pam's sake. Couldn't. Moving away from him, she trod on one of the scattered iron flagstones, splashes of rust red on the sodden earth. Once—how long ago?—Wallace had hauled topsoil from well beyond the barrens, dumped it here so she might have a garden, but the rain had leached it away, until now only heroic clusters of crabgrass grew in the darker earth around the flagstones. The erratic trail of a slug glistened wetly on starved weeds.

"I don't know as how a cripple should even be allowed to have a kid!" Then the voice turned soft and wheedling. "'Thena? 'Thena?"

"I'd appreciate it if you'd leave now. I'm already running late. By the way, welcome home. Hope you can stay longer this trip. Matthew," she called, refusing to look back at the man who followed her across the yard. "Come here."

Matty stared at them. His hand had found its way back to his mouth, and drool ran down his arm. She pulled him to her and tried to take his other hand—sweaty, sticky. With a wail, the boy pulled away from her, cringing where he stood.

Lonny approached. "He knows ya don't like 'im." Tall and stoop shouldered, he looked odd walking, almost unbalanced, as though his joints all pointed at subtly wrong angles. "Never could stand nothin' weak, could she, boy?" He grabbed at Matty, hugging him against his legs, the boy at first unresisting. "Looks like he's gonna be a big 'un, all right. She's ruinin' it for everybody, huh, boy?" He crouched beside him, tousled wet hair. "She drove poor Wally till 'e dropped, froze me outta my own house 'cause I was sick." Suddenly, he was all over the boy, holding and patting him. "You're a good kid, ain't ya?"

The child twisted to pull away, redoubling his efforts and crying in panic when the whiskered face pressed to kiss him.

"Leave him alone."

"Look at dis—he's filthy! Don't ya never give him no bath?"

"He's been playing in the mud," she told him, annoyed by the defensiveness in her voice.

Noises choked from the boy. Lonny stood up, and the boy hunched over, the contents of his stomach gushing out onto the dirt. She said nothing—not even permitting herself a small victorious smile—just put a hand on Matthew's shoulder.

"I wanna move back in. Me an' Pam."

She looked up at him, her face caught with an incredulous grin. "Well, you can forget that." The boy coughed and held his stomach, pouring out the scalding misery.

"I just wanna come home." Lonny's face twisted with pain. "It's my house."

"No," she spoke slowly, staring him down, "it is not."

"All ya did was pay the fuckin' back taxes! Ya don't even wanna be here. We built this place! My family. Ya hate it here." He drew himself up and began to walk toward the house. "Not fair. It's my parents' house, my goddamn brother gets it, he dies and you keep it? 'S not fair! Ya don't even belong here. We're gonna move back in whether ya want us to or not."

"Don't even try this."

"I was born here! In this house!" Trembling with rage now, he swung back toward her. She saw his hands shake and knew what they suppressed. " 'Thena, please—I won't never bother you. And I'll even fix the place up, you'll see. I jus' wanna come home. I'll die if I don't. Wallace, he woulda wanted me ta be here. I'll die. It ain't like I won't have money. Me an this friend a mine—he just got out too—we're gonna start a mink-trappin' business an' . . ."

"Of course you are." She guided the boy back toward the house.

"You better let me! I'll make you! I swear to God, you'll be sorry. 'Thena, you listen a me! It's 'at cop, ain't it? You think that cop you're screwin' can keep me out?"

"Yes." She whipped around to face him. "That's it, if that's what it takes. He's done a lot more than that for me already. He's had to, thanks to you and your buddies in town. Do you imagine I don't know who's responsible for all my windows being broken? Do you think I don't know who tore the fence down and drew those things on the walls?" She almost spat. "Thank God for Barry. We wouldn't have been able to live here, if it weren't for him. He can keep you out all right. Or put you away. How'd you get out anyway? You weren't due for a while yet. Maybe I should have him look into that. How'd you like to be back inside? I should do it anyway, for Pam's sake. I could, you know. So don't start threatening me again. You think I'd let you back in this house? For even a minute?"

A weird appreciation on his face, he laughed. "Ain't so cool now, 'Thena. Huh? Not so calm and collected."

She grabbed the struggling boy and resumed dragging him toward the house.

"Ain't nuthin' wrong wi' my family!"

Only in the last instant did she hear the footsteps running up behind her.

"You . . . !" He grabbed her in a clumsy, flailing lunge. "You hear me?" He shook her.

"Stop it!"

"Ain't gonna stop, and there ain't nuthin' you can do 'bout it neither. Where's your fuckin' cop now?"

She pushed at him with her fists as his grip tightened. "Take your hands off me."

He met her eyes and backed away. "You think there's sumthin' amatter wi' me? You're the one's sick. Don't gimme that look."

"Matthew, come back here." The boy had fled around the side of the house.

"I can see your face, bitch. I know that look, that 'you're disgusting' look. That's your opinion. Wally didn't think so. An' I ain't stupid, neither. You're the one. Too goddamn good for my family. Oughtta be too good ta live in our house then." His voice rose as he worked himself toward frenzy again. "I'm a bum or what? Is that what you think? Oh God. I oughtta punch your face in. What do you think a that? Like ya think you're some fuckin' saint with . . ."

From the corner of her eye, she caught a blur of brown movement.

". . . that ambulance crap, I—"

"No!"

The dog seemed to explode at him, paws striking his chest. Lonny careened backward.

"No, Dooley! Down! Down, I said! No!" She got hold of the old leather collar and pulled back as the snarling dog lunged again, jerking her forward.

Cloth ripped. Half crouched, Lonny held one arm protectively at his throat while the other beat the air as though still fending off the dog. "Hold 'im! Don't let go!" He recoiled slowly, reflexes off.

Only now, watching him, did she realize just how drunk he really was.

He scuttled backward, almost falling. "Oughtta fuckin' shoot that dog! Looka the size of 'im!"

Again, Dooley tried to go after him, dragging Athena. She yelled, planted her feet and held on to the collar with both hands. "I think you'd better get out of here." She staggered forward, barely restraining the animal. "Down, Dooley! Down!"

Lonny stumbled near the edge of the yard. "Le' me tell ya something," he yelled, his voice horrible with fear, an aggressive whine.

Dooley barked furiously, front paws rising off the ground. "No!" Standing almost straight, the dog was as tall as the woman, and it took all her strength just to slow him down. Lonny's shouts sounded incoherently obscene. Both arms wrapped around the dog now, she considered just releasing him. "Good boy," she soothed. "Good old Dooley, take it easy, boy." His barks—this close—hurt her eardrums.

The man's voice slurred even more as he staggered into the trees. Even from this distance, she could see that his eyes had unfocused. The effect was one of gradual disintegration, as though he'd been held together only by purpose. " 'S my house." Only the rage remained, though grown confused and diffuse. "Oh Jesus, it's my fuckin' house."

Saturated air hung over the pines like a heavy blanket. Dooley pulled away, raced to the edge of the dripping trees and stood baying at the departing figure.

"Shut up, Dooley!" Suddenly, she moved toward a sapling that had edged its way into the yard. She grabbed it with both hands and tugged. The roots gripped deeply, but thin branches stripped off, became whips that cut into her palms, leaving her hands full of wet needles. The green wood bled. Inhaling the acid wetness of the sap, she grunted, twisting the black bow of the trunk, pulling it apart. "Oh God." She let go of the ruined sapling, wondering if she should go get the ax and put it out of its misery. The tree swayed, and she stepped back. She had to go find Matthew.

Hurrying along, she brushed her smarting hands on her work shirt, and gravel oozed underfoot like mud.

"Look what I found!" Waving, Pamela came along the road

with the boy in tow. He weaved behind her like a balloon and seemed fine now, though his cheeks were still damp with the brine of tears and sweat.

"Sorry I'm so late, 'Thena." Pam sped up her shuffling walk. She waded barefoot through the damp, loose earth, carrying her good shoes. Her best blouse—red—seemed to burn against the sodden grayness. "How come you're still home? I mean, I thought you'd be down at the hall already. The reason I'm late is I was over at . . . Oh, 'Thena! Your poor hands!"

The palms bled. She held them out of sight. "Oh," she said, noticing the tightness of Pam's skirt. "So you do know he's out."

"What? I just thought maybe . . ." Pam clutched the boy, feeling his shirt. "Oh, c'mere now, baby. You're all wet. Let's go in the house and get you changed."

Of course, she thought, looking away: Lonny could never have walked all the way from town in that condition. Nice of him to stop with his wife. She tried to put a hand on her son's shoulder—he felt bony as a colt as he dodged past her and followed Pamela toward the house.

"Let me get you buttoned right, leastways, baby. Did you dress yourself this morning, huh?"

"Pamela? The roof leaked upstairs during the night. Could you mop it up?" She felt the pockets of her jeans. No car keys. But she couldn't go back in the house. Not right now. She needed air.

"Aren't you going down the hall? 'Thena?" Her voice sad and childlike, Pam called after her. She wanted so much to talk to Athena about Lonny, to brag and dream, but now . . . Miserable, she watched her retreating back.

Then Matthew stood at her side, rain-battered weeds clutched in his fist.

"No . . . don' be sad, Pammy. Look . . ."

"Oh, Matty!" She brushed them to her face. "Black-eyed Susan! Oh, baby." She kissed him. "How'd you know they was my favorites now, huh?"

The weeds around the town dump began to straighten and bristle, exuding their noxious perfume.

Marl Spencer scavenged for jars in the refuse. He lifted one specimen, inspected it, then chucked it. The impact made a damp thud. He saw another, partially buried, and began rooting it out. The jar held a black lump of ants. Then he jerked back with a cry, swatting at his head, and slipped on something rotten.

Flying slowly—and always lower—the huge insect whirred on darkly veined wings, and from where he lay in the rubbish, the boy followed it with his eyes. It struck a tree, clung.

Marl stared into the pines. All around him in the hard shadows lay the tracks of dogs.

Once out of sight of the house, Athena felt bigger somehow, more vital, as though she'd left behind a great pressure. Long strides carried her over rain-packed sand. Rapidly shrinking puddles reflected hot gray, and the air felt like a wet sweater. She veered away from the road and followed a nearly invisible trail across the springy turf.

With aimless determination, she passed a stream and breathed in the almost-pleasant smell of fecund water. The current made only the smallest hushed lappings. As she moved on, she examined the shallow cuts on her hands and decided it looked as though she'd been picking roses. Green scum lapped at the mud, and in the soft bank were pressed dozens of tiny tracks, no bigger than a housecat's, with long fingerlike claws. A willow stooped low over the creek, casting shade thinner than the sunlight, and when she paused to lean against the trunk, a bird flustered in the branches. The trailing strings of the willow brushed her face as she turned away, and the bird began a faint trilling call.

Walk it off, she told herself. *Clear your head, girl.* A fitful wind stirred, and the pines smelled cool now. *Keep your head above water.* She inhaled the deep green scent. *Put your thoughts in order.*

The trail soon became no more than a gully, sides sloping to a rut in the center. Was it a dry stream run? Vines and dense wet growth tangled, harsh and green, on one side of the path, but the brambles and thorns on the other looked brown in the spray of sunshine. Of course, she realized—a fire ditch. Off the path, a teeming mound of ants seethed over a small dead animal, and she glimpsed white fur. *Albino, whatever it was.*

She ducked half-bare branches as the trail narrowed, needles and twigs crunching briskly underfoot. The ditch became choked with stiff waist-high weeds, and her long legs swished wetly through the undergrowth. A sweet smell grew cloying as she waded farther.

She passed a rusting bale of barbed wire. Hornets crawled over the rotting apples that littered the ground now, and among the gnarled trees of the old orchard stood the ruined fragments of a brick wall, pitted, weathered almost to the color of sand. A bullfrog—large enough to eat mice and birds—squatted on the wall, fearless as she passed. Incredibly, even here lay the empty husk of a car, surrounded by the broken glass and trash that lay scattered around fragmented bricks.

Everywhere, walls had tumbled in huge sections and a fine dust had settled like volcanic ash.

The old town.

Sunlight streamed through the small stands of pine, white places shimmering with flies and gnats. A black-dirty cast entombed one arm, the other wrist and both ankles bound to tent pegs. Filthy head bandages had come unraveled in the sand, the earth around them, cratered by the rain, scaled with a pocked crust.

"Joey?" Ernie's voice cooed gently as he leaned over him. "Do you want water?" Ernie smiled. A thread of saliva fell from the corner of his mouth, beading Joey's cheek. "Do you see it? Do you want this again?"

But milky opalescence had covered the boy's eyes.

"You see it, don't you?" Ernie held a pocketknife with a gray mother-of-pearl handle. Smiling, he touched the sharpened point to the boy's flesh and slowly pressed. A dot formed, and the tip entered slowly. He cut down.

Not much blood now. Instead, a yellowish fluid leaked out, flowing easily over the thicker, slower stuff that puddled around his body. It accumulated around the blood, thinly circling it before soaking into the sand.

A warm breeze stirred the woods, and a butterfly flitted past.

Fierce heat beat down on Ernie. Pushing orange hair and sweat out of his eyes, he straightened and stared into the pines.

He was tanned dark from living in the open. For a time he'd survived on foodstuffs scavenged from the torn litter of the campsite. But now he was hungry.

He waited for the woods to give him a sign.

Nothing.

Why?

Sighing, he crouched, pulled away the rest of the bandages and tenderly caressed the stubbled head. Then he stood and faced the trees again. "I offer you this!" Clenching his eyes shut, he spread wide his arms, opening himself to the sentient woods. *Accept it!* His teeth gritted with concentration. *My gift!* A chattering hum came from his mouth. *Accept my offering.* Beginning to go into a coughing fit, he opened his eyes to the sun, and the pines seemed to shiver. *Please!* On the verge of once more falling to his knees and prostrating himself, he let his vision stray to the boy.

Sunlight fell softly now, and the purple wounds looked almost pretty. *There!* Startled and jubilant, he stared at the incision across the chest. *I didn't do that! I'm sure I didn't make that one! I didn't!* He began to laugh. The woods! The pines! In a pool of motionless white light, he reveled. *They did it! A sign!*

From the trees, the crows were calling.

Often, she found herself drawn here, here to this island of peace, this sanctuary where the stones lay deep and quiet. Silently, she skirted the mounded rubble of ore slag, lumps of refuse from the extinct forge. Stalky weeds sprang from the piles, reclaiming them. She stumbled over an old shoe, cast off in the yellow earth.

Finally sitting down, she flexed her leg. The shattered wall, already sun warmed, felt almost dry, and drowsily, the hornets buzzed. She'd always found a peculiar solace in this place. Heavy with age, it had long since surrendered its fight against the pines.

Vines grew over sun-soaked bricks. She sighed, glad she'd decided to come here, then laughed, because she hadn't decided, not consciously. Rising, she stretched and approached the foundation hole of the old furnace itself.

The stones here weren't soft and crumbling, but black and fused together as though spewed forth by an eruption. The hole . . .

Bottomless.

Something like coldness breathed out from it, coldness and a permeating silence. Everything wooden had rotted away, leaving only this dim brick outline. It was the grave of a town. Black leaves oozed beneath her feet.

Balancing like a child, she walked along the bridge wall between two cellar holes, the only sound the murmur of the sides crumbling into stagnant water as she passed. She gazed into one shuddering pool. Something plunked. A frog? The weaving patterns of water-strider spiders stirred a patch of iridescence, and rippling crescents spun. Disks interlocked and overlapped, trembling at the edges of the granulating bricks, turning them to sediment. At last, her anger seemed a distant thing—the sun had steamed away the breeze, but what remained of it caressed her hair. She glanced up at the rough ring of the clearing, now bathed in sunlight, clear and fresh.

Flowing, the morning's dream came back to her, not in fragments, but slow and thick as honey: herself straining, here, in this place, screaming on a slab of stone, and the baby's head, enclosed in a bluish caul, squeezing through the redness. The features looked . . . not normal. She squirmed from that vision, from the burning agony and tearing. The dream shifted, and she was once again a child, facing the image of Granny Lee's lined face, explaining about the blood, the old lady embarrassed, the little girl deep in shame. They walked through this empty town, her leg brace chiming against the stones as she tried to avoid places where blood had pooled. Suddenly alone, she flew down the road with mystifying speed, lame no longer. And she walked in the new town, empty as these ruins. Doors flew open to show tables set with drying dinners. But she saw no people. Only caked blood everywhere. In the streets, like a crushed-brick paste. On her legs. She passed a truck with its motor running. And everywhere the crusting wetness, as if it had rained blood. And the moaning of the truck became the droning of a fly, became the buzzing of the hornets.

Shrugging away the images, she blinked at her surroundings. Though still saturated with sunlight, they no longer seemed calm. She heard the agitated voices of birds.

Standing straight, she looked beyond the clearing to the circle of pines. *Why did I come here?* More than anywhere else, this place made her realize how self-enclosed the barrens were, how cut off from the outside world.

God, I've made such a mess of things. Tension pulsed in her stomach. *I was only trying to make a life for my husband . . . for my son.* She clenched her teeth. *Liar!* She struck her thigh with her fist. *For yourself!* She wanted to laugh at her own ineptitude—her being alone seemed so inevitable, so inescapable. She thought of Granny Lee and wanted to cry. *How could you leave me? There's no one for me. I'm all alone. Oh, Wallace, how could you leave me here?* Suddenly blinded by tears that almost came, surprising and frightening her, she put her hands to her face. *But I never cry. And they won't make me leave. I won't let them. He loved that house. We worked so hard. Someday, I'll . . .*

He'd been working on the fence when the catastrophic heart attack had come. She'd found him in the yard, his face already gray.

Someday I'll finish fixing up the place, and then . . .

The locals had hated her from the first day—an outsider who thought herself too good for them. Once they learned about her African-American background—and she knew she could thank Lonny for this—they'd been implacable. But their respect for Wallace, for his strength and his position in the community, had kept their resentments at bay at least to a certain extent. After his death, it hadn't taken them long to assert their bigotry. Then she'd found Barry, or he'd found her. She knew he was nothing like Wallace, except in strength. A powerful cop, he had clout around here, and the townspeople, living as they did on the fringes of the law, feared him. Besides, she'd been so lonely.

She drew away from these thoughts, loathing her self-pity. *I have to stay strong. Have to.* Squeezing her hands to tight fists, she cleared her eyes with the pain of scratched palms.

No, no magic lingered here, and no nightmares either. It was just a town that like so many others had been swallowed by the pines. No ghosts. Crumbling bricks and a sense of vast age yawned all around her. Yet the pines were older still. They'd ruled here before the colonials had come, even before the Indians. Only small remnants of the Leni Lanape nation lingered; only fragments of the works of the settlers remained.

She considered those people who had mysteriously stayed, pictured their huddled encampments after the collapse of the bog-iron industry. Nearly starving in the woods, they'd survived on almost nothing, becoming ever more primitive, slipping in time until their children became like the descendants of castaways. Alcoholism, illiteracy and incest constituted social norms. *The South Bronx with pine trees.* This was what she'd escaped to, the legacy into which she had married.

But Wallace wasn't like that. With a smile and a shake of her head, she recalled their first meeting. She'd been a sophomore at City College, a stack of books in her arms as she hurried through the park, and this tall soldier had walked right into her, scattering her books all over the grass. He'd been so embarrassed as he helped gather them, stuttering and stumbling all over himself. He'd been perhaps the handsomest man she'd ever seen in her life. So sweet. So shy. And he couldn't take his eyes off her.

She stared again into the flooded basement holes, and a weight settled on her, the lead of great age and of sadness and failure. She thought of the pineys and hated them, hated the limited gene pool, the inbreeding that resulted in all the deficiency and deformity. She'd heard that in the old days, whole decades would go by with the only new blood coming from escaped lunatics and convicts. *And now my genes are floundering in that pool.* She kicked sand into water, watched circles gently widen. *Cripple genes, at that.* She cringed at the thought. What if Lonny were right? What if Matthew's problems were her fault? No, she wouldn't consider this. If she were to blame, she could never face the boy.

And do I face him? Slowly, she retraced her steps, moving back toward the woods. If only her grandmother hadn't died before Matthew was born. She would have known how to love him. *After all, she even loved me.*

She looked back at the once-prosperous community of Munro's Furnace. Generations ago, her husband's family had owned this town, building their own house just close enough so they could sit on their front porch in the evenings and watch the bustling activity. Only this remained. *And if you try to sit on the front porch today, you'll probably go through the floor.*

The heat increased by the moment. As she walked, she resisted scratching her mosquito bites. If there were ever a war, she reflected, and the big cities were destroyed, it would be as though a dam had burst. Someday the pines would pour out, flooding into New York and Pennsylvania, and the barrens would cover this part of the world.

Someday.

The heat weighed on her, and she dragged her feet, feeling lashed to the earth. The trees around her stood ragged and stark, tortured looking, like the people who lived among them.

Monday, August 3

Three hot days had passed since the rain, and again the parched ground crunched underfoot.

His hair gleaming, bronzed by the sloping sun, Matthew stooped to the wildflowers, their small heads bobbing like insects. As he picked more blooms from the clump of weeds, he sang to himself, a soft, wordless tune of his own creation. Taking a bite of the crab apple in his other hand, he imbibed the sweet-acid flavor, then chucked the core. All around him, tall grasses lay down before the wind.

From the pines, a man watched through narrowed eyes. He inched forward. "Hey, you. Boy. C'mere." He stepped suddenly onto the path. "I wanna talk to ya."

Only the boy's eyes could actually be seen to change; yet his body tensed with a movement like the shifting of light.

"It's allkay, I jus' wanna ast you 'bout sumthin'. Don't be 'fraid."

The boy stood poised, ready to dart like an animal through the trees. Only curiosity held him.

"It's awright, honest." Wes edged closer, holding out his hand and smiling. "Your ma said I could talk to ya. You know what I wanna ast 'bout, don't ya? Yeah, you know." The smile twisted, became something else. "You know sumthin'. Fuckin' loony."

The flowers fell to the ground.

Wes lunged and grabbed the boy's arm. "In a hurry?" They tussled. "You ain't goin' nowheres. You go runnin' round in the woods a lot, don't ya, retard? Yer out here allatime, I hear. Ya ever see a old man?"

"You! What're you doin' ta him?" The blonde woman charged down the path. "You leave him alone!"

"Ah, Pam, I was just . . ."

She crashed into him, shoving his chest with one hand and pulling Matty away. She pushed the boy behind her. "You stay the hell away from him! You hear?" She looked ready to fly at him with her nails, her face suddenly red and swollen with anger, the birthmark standing out vividly.

"I wasn't gonna hurt the little squirt," said Wes. The blotch on his face matched hers exactly.

"You shut up! I don't want you round here!"

Snickering, he slouched away from her. "Yer mother don't mind me comin' round."

"You think that bothers me, Wes Shourds? That don't bother me. I don't care what that whore does. Matty, you go back inna house now."

"I just wanna ast the moron a couple a questions. Ain't gonna hurt 'im. Thought he might a seen sumthin' is all."

"I don't want you bothering him!"

" 'Bout a month ago," he yelled after the running boy. "Old man with a truck. You see him?"

"Shut up! You stay away from here! Dooley!" Quickly, she stooped and grabbed a small rock, made as if to throw it at Wes. "Dooley! Come on, boy. Where are ya? Dooley!" The dog was nowhere in sight, but sharp barks came from the direction of the house.

"Whose turn is it?"

"So anyway, between us and the cops, we bust down the door."

"Yours." In the ambulance hall, the crew sat around the card table.

"And there's this fat guy laying there, and you could see he'd been cold awhile. You know how you can tell, right? He's on his face with all the liquid pooled in his gut. You know, all sort of blue the way it gets, and the rest of him gray-like." Showing off, Larry talked too fast, alternately smiling at Cathy Hobbs and blushing. "So anyway, I knew soon as we tried to move him that skin was gonna split and it'd come spilling out, so . . ."

"Listen to him, couple weeks on the rig and he sounds like a pro," interrupted Jack. "Come on. You gonna play or what?" He leaned toward Cathy with an astonishingly intimate grin. "More coffee?"

Cathy was kind of cute, Athena supposed, looking her over. Little on the plump side, too much blue eye shadow. But why were the guys giving her the treatment?

Both Larry and Jack reached for the coffeepot. Jack won.

"Yuck," observed Cathy, getting a whiff of the blackness he slopped into her cup.

"I keep telling everybody not to let Doris make the coffee."

"So anyway," Larry went on, "what we did was, we slid a sheet under him and lifted from the corners."

Experimentally, Cathy brought the cup to her lips, grimaced. "This is awful strong. I'm surprised it doesn't melt through."

Before Jack had a chance to think of it, Larry tossed her a couple packets of sugar, then fumbled with a bag of plastic spoons.

"Now those will dissolve," said Athena, breaking the silence she'd slipped into half an hour before. Cathy glanced at her, and Athena returned her eyes to her cards. She'd never been sure about how much Cathy guessed about Athena and her husband.

"No, thanks"—Cathy waved away the spoons—"I'll drink it black. So, anything else been happening?"

Matthew waited around a turn in the road, and Pam caught up to him.

"Tha' sonafabitch." Her hands shook. "That bad man, did he bother you, baby? What was you doing over here all by yourself? Just playing like a good boy? Don't you let him bother you. If he ever comes round here again, you just come get me. You hear? I'll show him."

"Says . . . he says . . . sumthin' 'bout a old man." Dark bars of shadow leaned across the road, and the boy couldn't look away from them. "Inna woods. I seen . . ."

"Now, don't you pay no attention a him. I don't know what he's talking about anyways. Don't even know hisself. Everbody knows his father just run off." Seeing how he stared down the road toward town, she stopped.

"Sumthin' might be . . . gonna happen a him." The empty brilliance of his eyes held a dark wonder. "Sumthin' bad."

"Nothing much," Jack was saying. "Couple cases of heat-stroke."

"Looks like you're in for more of those." Cathy fanned at the neck of her blouse, then sighed and looked around the hall. "It's been so long since I've been over here. Oh, is it my turn? Rummy."

"Shit." Larry tossed his cards down. "I quit. Look at this hand," he laughed. "Cathy? Look at what I've got."

"Yeah, Cath, it's been a while since you came by. You should stop around more often." From behind his glasses, Jack's eyes studied the thin material of her blouse.

"Oh, you know." She shrugged, adding up her score. "Doris doesn't like it. I sure wish she'd let me run again. I go crazy in that house."

Athena laughed, a small explosive noise that cut off when they all looked at her. "I was only . . . trying to imagine sitting around the house."

"How many points you got stuck with, man?"

"You saying that house of yours is still standing, 'Thena?" Jack winked at Cathy as she gathered up the cards and began to shuffle. "I'm telling you, you should get in touch with the historical society." Taking off his glasses, he massaged the bridge of his nose. "Besides, ain't you scared of that dog pack way out where you are? I heard they killed somebody." With an elaborate gesture, he got up and flexed his muscles. "Sitting so long makes me all stiff." He smiled at Cathy.

"Who's winning?"

The bay door, shut against the mosquitoes, trapped the heat

and boxed in the steady drone of the fan. Picking up her cards, Athena played mechanically, trying to ignore the conversation, only occasionally glancing up at the other woman. From time to time, she caught Cathy looking back at her.

"You guys still running to fires with those old Indian pumps?" Cathy snickered. "You're going to get your asses fried."

"We had a couple good ones last month." Jack nodded. "Couldn't figure out what started them. Turned out Fort Dix was using the woods for artillery practice."

They all laughed. Then the back door banged, and everyone tensed. Invisible from the table, the rear exit was behind the refrigerator. "Christ, another hot night. I swear to God, I'm not going to live through this summer." Shirtsleeves rolled up, Doris stopped in front of the table. "What are you doing here?"

"I came over to see my friends, Doris." Cathy sat up straighter. "I do still have friends here, you know."

"Yeah? Well, I guess stranger things have happened." Turning her back on them, Doris stomped toward the lockers, silence trailing after her. "You do those reports yet, Jack?" she barked. Everyone just looked at their cards while she grabbed some cleaning rags and headed for the exit.

The door banged shut behind her, and Cathy slapped her cards down.

"Hey, Cath." Jack put his arm around her shoulders. "You shouldn't let her upset you that way."

"What gets me is the way she acts mad—like I did something to her. It's the other way around. I was always her friend."

Athena gave Larry a small smile and put her cards down. "Well," she said softly, "so much for rummy."

"The call came in real routine, you know, that last one I went on?" Cathy's voice droned almost too low to hear, a self-absorbed monotone. "Household accident, supposed to be. Nobody else was on, just me and Doris, and this guy answers the door, standing there with a beer in his hand. 'All right.' That's all he kept saying. 'She'll be all right. Just needs a little rest.' We found her under the kitchen sink with a drill bit broke off and sticking out of her head. While we were getting her out, he asked me if I wanted a beer."

Athena watched her closely.

"In the rig, it started coming out again. All over the place. I didn't know which hole to plug first." She laughed with a sound like tearing cloth. "At the hospital, they counted seventy-one of them. And Doris kept yelling at me."

"Didn't you call the cops?" Jack asked. "Did your husband come?"

"Yeah, Barry was there." She nodded, expressionless. "Me she fires, but that goddamn useless Siggy she keeps on. I know I freaked, but Doris didn't have to be so goddamn mean."

No one spoke. Athena wiped an arm across her forehead and got up. "I just want to see if she needs any help back there." As she left the table, the group stayed silent.

She reached the back door, pulled it open and heard the hiss of the hose, then decided Doris would probably appreciate something cold. Letting the door slam, she turned back to get a couple of Cokes from the refrigerator.

"She gets on my nerves, that's all." Cathy's voice had risen sharply. "She's so stuck up, and it's a joke. She thinks she's so smart. What did she ever do? Tell me that. Far as I can see, she's never done anything."

Athena froze. She felt the anger harden within her, then fade again as quickly. In the shadows, she leaned against the bulletin board. Then a thin crust of sand particles whispered beneath her shoes as she moved back to the door. She closed it quietly behind her.

All the rig's doors stood open, and the hose played across and through them. Floodlights glared from the garage roof, throwing the words "Mullica Emergency Rescue" into stark relief.

"She must know."

"What? Oh, hiya, honey." Doris looked up and smiled. "What did you say? Grab a rag."

"That time of the month again so soon?"

"Christ, you've been hanging out with me too long."

Things from the rig, stacked along the wall, tilted precariously, and a radio, perched on a window ledge, muttered and squawked about sending money "to help develop mental defectives in south Jersey."

"Is that really necessary?" Doris stepped back to snap it off, then gestured toward the rig. "The old girl washes up pretty good, doesn't she?"

"You look lovely tonight, yes."

"Oh jeez, I walked right into that. I repeat—you're definitely spending too much time around me."

Athena hefted a bucket of water. "You were a little hard on Cathy just now, weren't you?"

"I don't want her hanging around here." She twisted the nozzle on the hose, squeezing off the water. "Besides, it's not like I fired her. She quit on me when I needed her." Taking the bucket, she heaved soapy water onto the floor of the rig. "She wants to come back, doesn't she? Well, she can forget it."

"We need runners."

"Not like her, we don't. What the hell good is she if she's going to get hysterical on calls?" Doris snorted. "Got to run home and spend a week in bed."

"Some people just aren't strong enough to . . ."

"Then they don't belong here! Strong! Oh Christ, I've heard that before. Like it's a curse. Does that mean we've got to spend our lives mopping up after people that aren't?"

"Isn't that what we do?"

Doris shrugged. "Never thought of it that way." She opened a first-aid kit and sorted through it. "Let me ask you something. Don't you ever, I don't know, kind of resent all the people who expect something from you just because you're supposed to be strong? Don't answer that. Where the hell are the BP cuffs? Oh."

Athena took the hose, started rinsing down the tires. "Lonny came over the other day."

"What?"

She turned off the water. "I said . . ."

"What did he want?"

"To move back in." She dropped the hose, and it slithered, spitting on the ground.

"So the son of a bitch is out again, is he?"

"He was drunk. He looked . . . terrible."

"He didn't hurt you or anything, did he? I know he tried to get rough with you once before."

"Doris, I know it's weird, but I feel so sorry for him. All of a sudden. Him and Pamela. They can't turn their lives around any more than I can."

"Is that what you're trying to do, honey?"

She didn't answer.

"That's so hard for me to understand," Doris resumed. "I mean, I guess it just seems to me there'd be all kinds of things you could be doing. You're so bright and all. If you were someplace else, there's no telling how far you might go. Don't look at me like that, you know it's the truth. Christ, I mean, I'm glad you're here. It'd be pretty stale for me if you weren't. You know that, don't you?"

Again, no answer.

Doris turned on the hose and played it into the rig. With a sudden smell of old blood, water washed brown from the metal to gurgle down the drain. "There was a little bit of a breeze before," Doris muttered. She saw the look on Athena's face and followed her gaze into the dusk. "It just keeps on getting darker, doesn't it?" She shut off the water, and for a moment, they listened to the evening noises, to the katydids, to the hissing leak of the hose. "Just look at that big romantic moon. You know, honey, I remember stories from back home. I don't know what's been making me think of them lately. Stories us kids used to tell. Especially ones about a lost tribe of Indians, supposed to live way out in the Everglades. Right out of the Stone Age. Where's my cigarettes? Great stories. Scary as hell." Doris chuckled. "Then I got to college and found out it's all true." She turned toward a hint of movement. "You leaving?"

"I'm going to the diner." She forced a smile. "Will you be around later?"

Doris tried not to sound disappointed. "Later."

Not wanting to go back inside, Athena walked around the outside of the hall. She heard the soft whoosh as the hose came on behind her; she heard crickets in the grass and the distant clatter and whir of cicadas in the trees.

Larry and Cathy stood together in the front doorway. Really together. They jumped apart when they saw her.

Skinny little Larry and Barry's wife? She hurried to her car, pretending not to have noticed. *What's the matter, girl?* Her hand shook as she stuck the key in the ignition. *Does this make it worse? Better?* She felt shocked at the intensity of her own reaction. *What is it?* She wanted to put her head down on the wheel. *You all of a sudden afraid you might end up stuck with Barry? Isn't that what you want?*

Moonlight spotted the sand: jagged shards of white. Silent as cloud shadows through the trees, the beasts prowled. The humid air churned with insects from which even thick fur offered no respite.

Lean and hideous, held together with sinews and scar tissue, the bitch had learned to move efficiently on three legs, the fourth held stiffly to her ribs at an unnatural crook. The bullet wound had crusted over.

She led the pack. They moved when she moved, paused when she paused. They had to eat soon, especially the small ones that trailed behind. The dense forest offered concealment but little else. Her milk had almost dried, and though instinct told her this litter would not long survive, the imperatives of caring for them drove her forward nonetheless. The runty wild pups followed, even the one with legs that splayed at almost useless angles. Another, barely remembered, had disappeared two days ago.

She sniffed the air and made a low, whining grunt. Agitated with hunger, the brood came loping through the pines, black swift shapes converging.

Food.

Yet, she bristled and growled. There on the changing, scent-charged breeze, she found a trace of . . . them. And with that recognition, her crippled leg began to burn, and her bared fangs dripped saliva.

The bitch hesitated, wanting to turn back. But now the pack had caught the scent of the garbage heap, and they pressed forward, viciously jostling for position.

Sky through trees: fragments of thinner blackness. Beneath the branches, shattered moonlight flickered over the running beasts.

Pulling off the wide road, Athena parked by the police car. Throughout the drive, she had tried to convince herself that she had nothing to worry about, that Barry would never marry her anyway, but she wasn't sure whether she found the thought comforting or more disturbing. Though grimy and mud splattered, the diner offered glass and aluminum brightness in the night. As she hurried through the lot, she could see them at the window.

Behind her—a growl. With one hand on her throat, she spun and faced into the bellowing snarl. Claws raking the flatbed truck, a mean bull of a farm dog strained its chain. She stood close enough to be struck by the foul breath, and deep-pitched barks went through her like hammer blows.

As her paralysis eased, she moved away and tried to imagine being savaged by a pack of such animals, brutes like this one, gone feral, the way that poor little girl had been. She glanced back.

The drip and hum of the air conditioner filled the lot with noise, and in the spill of light, the dog's eyes glowed with utter malevolence.

Watching from across the table, Steve noted the way they greeted each other. No hint of romance. Not even warmth. As though they prided themselves on how cold-blooded they could be. Shuddering inwardly, he glanced around the diner. Fairly good crowd for a weeknight, and if anyone should happen to look over, they'd detect nothing about these two. Cold.

Smug. And yet her eyes seemed neither cold nor smug. Always, he found something in her face, something brave and lovely, a quality that suffused the body she held so erect. Yet again, he studied her. The way she moved could scarcely be described as graceful. The limp remained too distinct, even her smallest gestures too defiant. Yet he felt she possessed a certain elegance, like that of a wounded cat.

"Did you hear we picked up a couple of poachers today?" A cigarette dangled from Barry's lip, and he still wore his dark glasses.

"Really?" Clammy in the air-conditioning, she kept plucking at her damp shirt.

"Yeah, city people. I'll tell you, I can't wait for hunting season to come around. All them businessmen come out here with their brand-new thousand-dollar rifles and start having heart attacks. Then the stateys gotta go in after them. Yessir, can't wait." A weird pride rang through his heavy sarcasm, akin to that of a new recruit complaining about the difficulty of being a marine. "Gotta haul their fat asses out of there, and let me tell you, some of those guys weigh a ton."

"That's something to be grateful for anyway," put in Steve. "At least you're not a trooper anymore."

"Well, it's all the same." She changed the subject fast. "You should know. You've been a cop a long time, haven't you, Steve?"

"Him? All his fucking life." Barry's glare couldn't disguise the envy in his voice. "Used to be a fucking police dick up in Trenton."

Old man Sims dragged over. "What's it gonna be?" He wiped beads of sweat from his pale forehead, wiped his hands on the wretched apron.

"About time," Barry growled at him. "We been sitting here for twenty minutes."

"Shit," commented Sims.

"Heaven forbid you should have to wait," she said.

Shifting around, Barry stared at her in astonishment. "Look, I'm tired of telling you. I couldn't make it that night. All right?"

"What'll it be?"

"Barry, I was only kidding."

"What're you having? I ain't got all night."

"It ain't my fault you can't get your goddamn messages straight."

When they ordered, Sims grouched. "How come nobody never orders nuthin' but friggin' hamburgers?"

"Yeah," said Barry. "It ain't like anybody's ever proved nothing about the claws in your rabbit stew."

Steve laughed, but Sims walked away muttering, "Friggin' cops."

"Barry? Just ignore him." She sounded worried. "Anything else interesting happen today? Barry?"

"Yeah, real exciting." He still glowered at the old man's back. "Some old biddy in White's Bog got her groceries snatched by some guy came out of the woods."

"White's Bog? Since when is that your jurisdiction?"

"We just heard about it," Steve answered. He peered into her eyes for just a moment too long, then stared down at the table.

"Was that true, Steve? About your being a detective?"

"Ten years." He nodded. "In the heart of the Cancer Belt."

Back behind the counter, Sims dropped a plate and cursed, kicking at the pieces. There came the dancing sizzle of hot grease, the smell pervasive and too sweet.

"So what was that like?" When he didn't answer, she added, "Was it rough?"

"She wants to know about procedures, Stevey-boy. She digs that stuff."

Steve shook his head as though coming out of a dream. "In a big case," he began, leaning back, "first I always liked to find out the background. A lot of guys complain about paperwork, but you'd be surprised how much you can pick up from the files, questioning the neighbors, that sort of thing."

"What kind of big cases?"

"Shit." Barry blew smoke in their faces. "You know what the Pine Barrens is famous for?" His voice rumbled over them. "Swear to God, the number of unsolved murders. You look in any of the famous crime books, and alls you're gonna find is Pine Barrens, Pine Barrens, Pine Barrens—none of them ever solved."

"That's because they mostly weren't discovered for twenty years," explained Steve. "And then all you've got is some bones."

"Only reason anybody even remembers Hog Wallow is they had one there once." Barry continued, ignoring the interruption. "Remember the Cleaver Murders? Listen to this, 'Thena. There was this woman . . ."

"Hog Wallow?" she asked. "Isn't that where they found the biker in the trash bag last month?"

"That was Dead Forge."

"Would you both shut up and listen to me for a minute? This woman just disappeared, then later on they found a skull in the woods. Never found the rest of her."

"Never found her husband either," appended Steve. "Not very mysterious."

"Yeah, but don't gimme that shit like you don't know what I mean. And it goes way back, too. Too many of the shack people just turn up missing. And it's not like they just wander off into the woods neither, so don't say that, 'cause sometimes they find pieces out in the swamps."

Athena tried to look away from Barry. She found something in his childishly gloating expression both fascinating and repellent. "So, Steve," she said after a pause, "after all those years in the city, I guess this must be a big change for you. Right?"

"Chain of command is the biggest difference." His laugh graveled pleasantly. "There isn't one here. I always had trouble with the higher-ups. Always. They'd hand out commendations with one hand and reprimands with the other." He laughed again, but more tightly. "What's really funny is—now that I've got the freedom on the job I always wanted—I don't care anymore."

She never knew how to react when Steve said things like that. Fortunately, Barry started telling them the latest gossip about the sheriff of a neighboring township, who apparently had blown away his son in a sexual conflict over his daughter-in-law. But Barry soon launched into his usual complaint about how these "lowlife pineys" gave a bad name to the decent hard-working sort like himself. She'd heard it all before and listened until the contours of his words melted into an indistinguishable lump. Nodding in an interested fashion at regular intervals, she allowed her gaze to wander over the diner.

Several of the men wore fancy cowboy boots, and a fat woman had thick braids to her waist. Most were dressed with some degree of odd formality, but she found it difficult to pin down exactly what made it peculiar. A few of the customers began returning her stares, so she looked around, as though suddenly fascinated by the institutional-green walls. The fluorescent tube above the dusty moose head blinked, orange and unnatural, and she studied the bristling head. With an idle nausea, she wondered if she'd ever eaten any of the huge creature. One never knew about these hamburgers. Following its glass gaze, her eyes came to rest on the painting above the counter.

Applied too thickly, lurid colors turned the image almost three-dimensional, a crude mass of swirls and ridges. She couldn't make out the words on the brass plate from here but recalled the title as something like *Devil in the Swamp*.

"Nothing but miles of wetland, quicksand, poison snakes," Barry's voice droned on. "Don't go in. That's the first thing they teach you on the force, practically. Let them settle it themselves."

She nodded again, her attention not straying from the painting. Fat, crusted strokes formed hills and lumps, and out of the trees twisted a wraithlike mist, on top of which drifted a malformed skull. She squinted. There appeared to be words scrawled in ghostly letters in the background, lines of doggerel under the greasy dust.

From across the table, Steve watched her, wondering what fascinated her so. Barry kept talking, and Steve groaned quietly. Inevitably at this point, in terms all the more irritating for being arch and vague, his partner would begin to brag about his underworld connections and about mob activity in the pines in general.

Barry winked at him, oozing confidentiality. "Better than dumping them in the Hudson where they're only gonna swell and float. Am I right?" Suddenly, he stood up. "Gotta go visit the little boys' room."

She slipped out to let him pass, and with a familiar gesture, he allowed his hand to slide along her thigh. Steve reddened.

"All that crap about the mob. The most he's maybe involved in is that stolen-car racket with his father-in-law and his damn biker friends. And I'm not too sure about that even."

"Then you shouldn't talk about it." She gritted her teeth.

The food arrived. Smelling like old sweat, Sims bent over them, hairy stomach visible through holes in his rotting T-shirt.

"It's a shame about Barry's wife not being able to have kids." Steve hurried through the words as a grease-sodden hamburger landed in front of him. "Hey, when you going to hire yourself some help in here?"

"Shit," Sims replied, turning away.

She prodded at the steaming meat.

"Watch out for buckshot," he kidded. "Yeah, it's a shame about Cathy. I know that bothers him. Talks about it all the time. Still, what kind of a father would he make? Always running around." Despising himself, he spoke with strained casualness, his eyes fixed on the table. "Of course, if they had kids, maybe he wouldn't run around. So much." He looked up when she laughed at him.

"Thanks for reminding me. That's right. I'm going out with a married man. A married cop no less. That's why you're here, Steven. You're my red herring."

"So what's he with that gut? A blowfish?"

"My, we're witty this evening, aren't we?" She looked away.

"He's what my wife used to call a lady-killer. You don't know how he talks, the things he says about you."

"You don't often mention your wife." Bored with this, she wanted the conversation to at least seem normal. "No children?"

He shook his head.

"Family?" She found herself avoiding the wounded intensity in his eyes.

"Up in Newark."

"See them much?"

He shook his head again.

"I guess you get used to being alone." She sugared her coffee.

"You can get used to hanging if you have to. Another of my wife's expressions." He picked up his hamburger and stared intently at the lumpy meat. "Seems to me I've heard a person can get diseases from eating venison with ticks in it." He took a bite and chewed slowly. "He was from around here, wasn't he?" he asked, swallowing. "Your husband? So how come you're still out in the pines?"

"My grandmother passed away." She glared at him a moment, then sighed. "Where could I go? And there was the boy. And the house."

He nodded, studying her face. "You think there's any future in this? With a guy like Barry, I mean?"

"Couldn't we have a friendly conversation, Steven? Just once?"

"The way you act around him"—his words came out with a surge of harshness—"makes me sick. The two of you, like you've got ice water in your veins. I know you're not like that. What are you trying to prove, for crissakes?"

"I'm sick of hearing that!"

Startled by the furious hiss of her voice, he knocked over a water glass. At first he just stared at it; then with ever clumsier gestures, he tried to blot it up, pulling wads of paper napkins out of the holder and knocking over the ketchup in the process. Water slipped off the table onto his lap.

She wouldn't look at him. She understood her anger only too well: he thought they belonged together, that they were two of a kind, the walking wounded.

"I'm drowning over here." He tried to laugh.

She pushed at the spreading puddle with her napkin. She'd always known why she resented him so, and every glance confirmed it. The broad shoulders, the muscular chest and arms, the blond good looks. But the resemblance never extended beyond the merely physical. Everything else was wrong. Wallace would never have been a failure, no matter what. He'd never have allowed himself to be beaten by life. Never.

"I'm sorry," he said. "I get clumsy like this when I'm worked up. I break a lot of things." Grimacing, he continued his attempts to clean up the mess, rapidly making it worse. "I guess I do the same thing with my life. I drink too much and . . ."

"I see he struck out again." Grinning, Barry stood over them.

"Thought I'd give the kid time to put the make on you." He sat down and put his arm around her. "What the hell happened here?"

"I spilled something."

"Again?" Barry held Athena with an ostentatiously casual possessiveness.

Steve got up suddenly. "I guess I'll head on out." Without another word, he walked away.

"Pick me up here at midnight," Barry called after him. "And stay sober!"

Everyone in the place heard. She saw him flinch as he went out the door, all eyes upon him. People often watched him, she'd noticed that before—the tall blond cop with the handsome face. And she knew him to be oblivious to it, just as Wallace had never been aware of his physical impact either. Through the smeared window, she watched Steve cross the lot toward the police car, and she noticed that the truck with the dog had gone.

"Don't start. He's all right." Barry counted money and grumbled about Steve not leaving enough. "He's always doing favors for me."

"Oh, yes, just terrific." She blotted water with more napkins. "So full of the milk of human kindness he slops over. Are we going to talk about your partner all night? Let's go. I'm not hungry anymore."

Ernie crumpled shut the end of the bag and scraped a shallow hole in the sand. He buried the wrappers, a little worried about animals scenting the food.

A lot of stuff he'd had to throw away, things that needed to be cooked, like rice and instant mashed potatoes. Useless. But the ground meat had been devoured raw, the potato chips reserved for breakfast. The rest would be rationed, because he didn't like exposing himself the way he'd had to in getting this.

He sloshed the carton of milk around in his hand. He drank deep, though it was hot, already souring. Then he lay back and rubbed his stomach, full now for the first time in days. Gazing up at the stars, he wondered anew at their hugeness. He had trouble getting comfortable, his clothes stiff with sweat and dirt and other things. Tomorrow he'd rinse them in the creek, maybe. But soon he began to drift off, hazing, the weariness in his body flowing out his arms and legs, running off into the dry earth and carving a channel, until the depression of sand in which he lay became a burrow in the mountain of the night.

The outpost was a tiny structure, and dust made the shuttered window hard to see through. A single candle barely lit the room within.

The face of the man inside wasn't clear. Did he glance at the window while getting his pants off? The watcher drew back slightly. But the man turned away and peeled off his undershirt, the faint light glinting from the sweaty hairs of his back.

Beyond him, the woman stood almost out of sight. She lifted something from a small table, held it to her ear with a childlike gesture. The window glass muted her words.

". . . never like that . . ."

"Never liked what sound?" The man's voice carried. "Ticking?" Folding his pants, he laid them over the only chair, then pried loose his wallet and removed a small packet. "That why you never wear one?"

She put down the watch and stepped forward into the light.

Breath stalled in the watcher's throat. Her body—molded with warm shadows—took on a slender grace that clothing usually denied it.

"I keep telling you, you don't have to use those. After Matthew, I had my . . . you don't have to use that."

Looking downward, her companion only smirked.

". . . guess the reason I don't like . . . hear the time going like that . . . ticking away so you can't ever get it back . . . can't ever catch up . . ." Dreamily, she seemed to speak more to herself than to the man, though her eyes never left the heavy, sweat-oiled body. Did she wonder briefly when he glanced at the window again? Probably not. She just sat on the narrow cot, waiting. At last, the man came close to her, pressed himself against her with soft, shadowed movements.

". . . hear something just then?" She rose abruptly. "Out there?"

But he knew she could have seen only a smoky reflection of her own nakedness against the perfect void.

Breathing hard, he made it back to where he'd left the car, having rolled it, lights off, as close to the squat fire-brick structure as he dared. Pulling the door closed carefully, almost silently, he sat at the wheel and squirmed in sweat, his erection almost painful. *She shouldn't be doing this.* Her car was parked beneath the window, and unclear forms moved beyond the pane. *She's too good for this.* He swigged from the bottle. *Besides, somebody might see.* He bit the back of his hand to keep from laughing.

Light flickered at the window. Naked, the man moved back and forth, slowing for a moment with his back to the glass.

Needing air, Steve rolled down the car window and listened to the gentle rasp of the night, to the endlessly ticking throb of the crickets, to the faint rustle of black foliage. He wondered if he dared creep back to his hiding place. He knew that soon Barry would begin the noises, and if he listened closely, he might even hear her, hear the gasping sob of her breath. It could be worth the risk.

Heat lightning flickered on the sky, and he was drenched with sweat. *I've got a fever. For weeks now, been so sick.*

Nothing moved in the station now, and he knew they lay on the cot against the wall. *Why do I do this?* He squeezed his eyes shut and the tears burned like acid. *I don't want . . . sweet Jesus, help me . . . always been a decent man.* His left hand went to work, and the furious mechanical movements caused the seat to squeak slightly. *Why do I do this?* Blood pounded into his face. His neck muscles tightened, cramping until he thought they must burst. His teeth clenched. His face turned upward, beseeching, a silent howl.

Crickets surrounded the car, and soft-bodied things battered at the window of the outpost.

His movements became spastic, wild. Hurting himself, he grunted, and finally fluid warmth spurted in slow beats as from a severed artery.

Shuddering and damp, he reeled with nausea. The foul thickness of the air choked him, and tears burned down his face. His stomach lurched again.

He barely got the door open in time. Always, it was like this, and dimly he realized—wet and trembling as bile splashed the sand—that the sickness came mostly from his straining to resist, from his efforts to fight this fierce longing.

All around him, the night breathed.

Wednesday, August 5

Here, beyond the outskirts of town, shacks were few and mean.

Early in the day, the little girl had been set outside to get some sun . . . and forgotten.

When little Molly Leek stroked it, the cat in her lap stirred, purring fitfully before curling back to sleep, and Molly smiled, the late afternoon sun warm on her small, blind face. She loved her cat.

She bent to kiss it. The cat smelled wonderful, and it gurgled in token protest when she hugged it.

"Don't go gettin' all rambunctious, fella. Your old man's prob'ly just run off with some hooch girl."

Though still early, the gin mill had already begun filling up with men, old men with grayish skin, some with front teeth missing, young men with scabs on their faces, their arms smeared with grease and motor oil. Through the open door came the choke of a dying car. Sometimes the engine would turn over. Banging followed, then deep-voiced advice, then the noise of a wrench applied to metal with more determination than skill.

"Ain't that the damnest thing, the way we jus' never found no trace a him?" muttered a younger man to no one in particular. "Shot a dog though."

Periodically, Wes would grumble about his father in tones both aggrieved and resigned. The rest of the men had grown pretty bored with it by now.

"Them damn dogs was up at my place t'other night," one of them said. "I let 'em have it wi' some birdshot. My ole lady was cookin' dinner. She says they was tryin' to come right inna door!"

"Mamma?"

The air felt damp, and Molly shivered slightly in the growing dusk. Behind her, she could hear her mother screaming at the other kids in the shack. She sounded drunk again. Obediently, Molly stayed on the crate, some distance from the smell of her home.

She missed her cat. It had left her as the sun faded, and it wouldn't come back, no matter how she called. Her stomach felt like a yawning ache in her middle now, so long past dinner. She'd never been left out this long before. She considered trying to make her way back to the shack, but she'd been told to stay put and her mother might beat her again if . . .

A wave of foulness swept toward her with a sudden breeze, and the child went rigid. She heard a rustling sound, deep in the underbrush.

Something crunched, circling her.

"Mamma!"

The warped grain of the wire-spool table resembled a coastal map, swollen lines edging ocean-dark stains, the continents pocked with burn craters. His cigarette smoldering, old Dan Jenkins glowered into the flame of a kerosene lamp, feeling the hot, sweet drifting of his mind as it floated on the booze, feeling all solid thought dissolve with the blurring of his vision.

"So anyhow, we left 'im there wi' his guts in both hands." Al threw back his head and roared, showing off rotting back teeth. "Cryin' like a baby into his innards."

Old Dan craned his corded neck to listen as he leaned forward, getting the sleeve of his long undershirt wet with spilled rum. As he sucked on the cigarette he'd just rolled, his single discolored eye focused on the yellowed nudie calendar—a decade old at least, tacked above the planks that served as a bar—and on the meat cleaver that hung from a nail alongside the calendar. He glanced around at the men who sat on the barrels and crates scattered about the dirt floor. Most were locals, the rest from neighboring shantytowns with names like Collier's Mill, Tom's Grave, Slabtown. Shotguns leaned against the walls, even more than usual.

Seemed no one went out without a gun these days.

She fell from the crate.

A deep-throated roar exploded in front of her. From behind, a growl ripped.

Whatever they were, there were two of them.

The child cringed, not knowing which way to crawl. Her hands pushed at the air all around her.

From behind came a snarled challenge.

The heavy breathing passed very close, and her fearfully questing hand found rough softness. With a sob of recognition, she threw her arms around the animal's neck. The shaggy hulk pulled away from her, hackles up. Planted firmly in front of the child, the dog barked furiously into the woods. The barks sounded like cannon fire, and the girl fell back.

Finally, the rumble grew fainter.

Something brushed her. The wide tongue covered her face. Small grubby hands clung fiercely to the fur, while Dooley carefully licked every exposed part of her.

"Maybe it was the Devil."

Smoke from the noxious local tobacco stained the air blue, and the room stank of urine and ashes. As always, the lamps had been turned way down to conserve fuel, and the room stayed dark and quiet. When some of the men did speak, it was either to argue the finer points of wire snares or to plan deer-jacking trips, but always silence lapped at the room, ready to seep back like the shadows before which their words became gruff noises, then faded altogether.

"Maybe the Devil got him," Dan continued. "Hey, Al, ain't there no more applejack? Dry Squad giving you trouble?"

"Nobody gives me trouble. Shit. Why don't you get the hell outta here wi' them stinkin' shoes? Look at 'is! It's all over 'is shoes! Go on. Get out!"

"Where's your boy tonight?" Dan kept his voice pleasant to the point of servility.

"What're you talking about?" demanded Wes. "He's right here."

Dan blinked back the haziness. "Where da hell'd you come from?"

Slow shadows shifted in the corner, and Marl's face glowed softly.

"Startin' many fires lately?" muttered Wes.

There came the muffled thump of a whiskey jar set down carefully. A couple of regulars glanced at Al, then at Wes. The boy could be heard breathing. "Don't you go botherin' that boy," Dan said in a low growl. "Don't let his father hear ya." A match flared as someone lit a cigarette, and the shadows jumped.

Old Dan nodded and gave the boy an encouraging if bleary smile, while reflecting on how funny it was that most of the regulars had such protective attitudes toward the kid, almost as though he were their own kin. Maybe it was the way people just naturally got around half-wits, feeling sorry for them and all. But that didn't ring true. For instance, the Stewart loony took a lot of abuse, especially around here when he came cadging drinks. So maybe it was just that . . . He lost the thought when a farmer, already undoing his belt buckle, got up and swayed toward the door, leaving a good half inch of whiskey still in his glass. Dan looked around, then his gnarled hand shot out with the speed of a cobra. He bolted it, just a taste of burning sweetness.

Silence dripped through the room like something molten. The lean brown and white cat skulked through, belly low to the floor, tail twitching like a snake with a broken spine.

"You know what's out there, boy?" Dan had already sidled up to the boy and begun his usual teasing. "There's storks out there, four feet tall, that's what." Foul gasses bubbled in his damp breath. "They see a man, they fly right at him, spear him through the eyes, eat his brains out." He made a stabbing motion at Marl's yes, and the boy jumped back, as much from the smell as from alarm.

"D–Dey ain't real."

"Sure is real. How you think I got this?" The old man fingered the pocket of hardened scar tissue where his left eye should have been. "That ain't all, neither." He leaned forward. "If'n the storks don't get you, the Devil will."

"Leave 'im alone," another man muttered. "He's liable ta throw one."

"You know how big the Devil is? He's big as a house, boy! An' he got wings like a bat!"

Marl tried to pull away, but Dan had him by the arm, gnarled fingers digging hard into the tender flesh about the elbow.

"All you'll hear'll be flappin' like sheets on a line. Soon's you hear that, you know you gonna die." As he spoke, Dan leaned in and out of the sphere of light, eclipsed face, gesticulating hands, appearing and disappearing in fragments. "He'll come right down behind you, he will. An' first thing he'll do is just swallow your head, just put your whole head in his mouth and bite it off. Then while he's chewin' he . . ."

With a startled cry, the boy leaped back, almost pulling the old man off his perch.

"Don't bring that in here!" A general tumult erupted. "Put it outside!"

While the newcomer stood in the doorway, blinking and trying to identify the problem, his dog frisked to the end of its chain and sniffed at the room.

"You get that fuckin' mutt outta here! You hear me? Or I'll get down 'at meat cleaver and chop it up!" Al bellowed. "What did you say?"

Still shuffling his feet in confusion, the man faintly grumbled something like "Oh yeah?"

Al went berserk. "Good, an' I'll chop you up too, motherfucker!" Some of the regulars tried to calm him as he reached for the cleaver.

"What's the matter wi' him?" The man backed up, pulling

the now growling dog. "Jest a hound dog." He kicked the animal and dragged it outside.

"Who da hell's he think he is?" Al started slamming things around. "Comin' in my place with a dog? Ain't no dogs allowed in here. I own the fuckin' place, don't I?"

"Sure thing, Al."

"You're right, Al. You're right."

Something crashed on the stairs.

Everyone looked while Lonny picked himself up and seemed to get his joints going in the right direction again. Eyes still rimmed with sleep, he headed straight for the whiskey barrel.

"'At's it. Drink up my profits, shithead." Al saw him freeze. "Good for nuthin' rummy."

Lonny blinked at him. "I jus' want one, Al."

"No."

"But, Al," he began, the trace of a whine already in his voice, "gotta have one. Al?"

"No."

Lonny stood with his mouth open. He started to shake, and Al watched, smiling with satisfaction. The door opened and the guy who'd taken the dog out came in again, looking wary. Al shoved an open jug at Lonny.

"You tie up tha' dog?" demanded Al.

The man looked up warily. "He's outside."

Spit ran down Lonny's chin while he drank. It hit him fast. The almost painful warmth spread from the pit of his stomach and poured into his chest, flushed up his neck and face, melting his eyes.

Watching, Dan shook his head sadly, dirty gray hair flopping over the back of his collar. Lonny looked even worse than usual, yet for a moment, the old man recalled him as a boy, full of hell and haunting the pines.

"Well, then sit down and buy yaself a drink." Al smiled expansively. "I ain't seen ya in here before, buddy." He pointed at Lonny. "Look at 'im. He don't think I knew 'bout that jug he had upstairs. I knew. Yeah, I knew. Asshole."

"Usually, I go out Bear Swamp Hill way." He was a thin, gray sort of man, and as he moved into the light, Dan guessed him to be part Indian. So many around here were.

"It's my boy, y'see," Al explained, chuckling. "He's scared a dogs. Like to have a fit when he saw ya bringin' that one in here."

Dan glanced at Marl—the stocky youth sat by himself, watching everything as usual. No, not so stocky, he decided, looking closer, not anymore leastways, and taller too, really starting to shoot up. "Hey, there ain't been no ghosts tonight," Dan announced, peering around at the shadows and making sure the stranger noticed.

"How's at?"

"This here gin mill's haunted," replied Dan. "I thought everybody knew that. You should see it sometimes when the spooks is out—things flyin' around by themselves. You wanna hear about it?" He toyed with the cracked fruit jar he'd been drinking from, letting the guy see it was empty.

Jagged laughter exploded from the corner.

"Way I heard it, Lonny went after his brother's wife one night, but she grabbed a shotgun and just 'bout blew ole Lonny's head off."

"How's about it, Lonny? Can the black bitch take you in a fair fight?"

"Them ghosts—Hessian mercenaries they was." Sooty lanterns flickered, and Dan's eyes glinted as the words spun out. "Shot 'em against a wall in the old town. Back during the Revolution."

"You pullin' my leg, ole man?"

"Come to think on it, there ain't been no ghosts in here fer a while. I remember once . . ." But the newcomer's eyes had strayed to Lonny.

"I know wha' tha' bitch really wants." Muttering to himself, Lonny began to get loud.

"I told you to lay off the stuff."

"Ah, let 'im alone, Al," somebody yelled. "It's just getting good. What you saying, Lon?"

Lonny kept drinking. All around him voices blurred with the smoke, fogging into an uneven buzz.

"Yeah, tell us 'bout it, Lonny. Whatchya gonna do to 'er?"

". . . what tha bitch . . . she ain't takin' nuthin' . . .'smy house, Jesus, 'Thena . . . what she really wants, my . . ."

"At's a boy, Lonny!"

"You tell 'er!"

"Tha' bitch!" He pounded his fist on the bar. Voices splashed around him. Words whirled about his ears, piercing his head. Hands slapped his back. Many hands. His friends—a flickering blur. Al laughed, and Wes kept pushing him, pushing him and yelling things. Someone—old Dan?—tried to take his arm, but he shook free like a dog throwing off water. And suddenly he was sailing toward the door, riding a crescendo of goading that seemed to carry him out into the night. The hollow roar of the gin mill burst behind him, then trundled away.

He couldn't feel his feet, couldn't see the ground, but he kept walking, somehow never falling, and one of the hounds that lay in the shadow of a truck got up to follow.

So strange to be outside. Such relief. No lights to hurt his eyes. But even here the air felt dense, stirring with damp heat, like the breath of a beast. His thoughts churned: it was his house, but he had nothing because of her. Choking, he loosened his shirt. He was a grown man, and they all laughed at him, because he had nothing, no home even, and all he wanted was to go home. He stumbled down the road. He was going home, and nothing could stop him.

His thoughts grew even more muddied. Had he lost his bearings? The house lay . . . that way. Ahead of him, pines swayed, and the breeze carried away the stink of the town dump.

The hound that followed idly, stopped and sniffed the air. It sat back on its haunches to watch the man's progress into the woods. The dog stiffened. The beginnings of a growl stirred in its chest, then it twisted around with a wrenching movement and ran away as fast as it could.

As the sky began to flicker, the wind blew stronger.

Pine detritus crunched under the tires. Raindrops plopped randomly across the roof of the car, and dust billowed around the house. In the woods, a dog was howling. As Athena pushed the car door open, sudden wetness splattered over the windshield. *Couldn't wait two more minutes, could it?* She sprinted toward the dry shadow of the house while all around her hot sand hissed and sighed.

Lightning illuminated the kitchen as she pulled open the back door. She slapped at the wall, groped for the switch. Thunder sounded distantly. The house creaked under the rising wind, and fitful rain tapped like moths at the windows. She moved swiftly through the first floor, switching on lights. Another clap of thunder detonated, the loudest so far, and through the rumblings came ragged shrieks.

"Matthew?" She raced to the foot of the stairs. "Matthew, what's the matter?"

Shrill cries grew louder. She caught a flash of movement.

"Pammy! Where Pammy an' Chabwok got in his m-mouth and red . . . all red?" Crashing down the stairs, the boy charged at her. No time to get out of the way—she clutched at the banister as he slammed into her, tumbling her backward.

The house lights went out.

Toppling in sudden darkness, she landed on her hip with the boy on top of her, pain and panic searing through.

"Pammy . . . d-dark now . . . Pammy red and the rain! Go and . . . got to!" They grappled furiously in the blackness, Athena struggling to get up, the boy screaming and shaking her, desperation in his voice.

"Matthew, it's all right." She got hold of his arms, tried wriggling free. "Everything's going to be all right." A glancing blow caught her on the side of the jaw.

"Pammy! Chabwok, the dogs! Save Pammy. Save!"

Somehow, she pushed him back, warded off beating fists. She tried to pull herself to her feet, but again he flung himself at her. He grabbed her around the waist and hung on, wailing with fear and need.

"Matthew, stop this, please. Let me up!" She managed to free herself from one clinging hand. "What's wrong? Can you tell me?" Prying herself loose, she stumbled into the darkened kitchen to lean against the table.

Lightning probed at boarded windows. The boy hadn't followed her. The flash showed him still lying on the floor, weeping as he hadn't since infancy. Pam was in danger—his hysteria convinced her. "It's all right now, Matthew." She felt along the wall for the cellar door. The key grated, and the doorway opened deeply. An ammoniacal smell flooded the room: a damp musk, full of the stench of mouse droppings and dust-laden cobwebs. Steadying herself against the door, she reached for the shelf, groped among the cans and jars. Finding the flashlight, she turned it toward the choked sobs. "Everything's going to be fine now."

"Pammy . . . n-n-no no don . . . Chabwok!" The boy stood at the kitchen threshold, face running with tears. "Pammy, no, don wanna . . ." The glare of the flashlight made his tear-swollen features appear even more distorted.

She directed the beam back toward the shelf, then lifted down the kerosene lantern and took the rattling box of matches from the stove.

". . . dogs . . . the dogs inna woods . . ." He dropped to his knees, then slid to his side, moaning. ". . . gonna get Pammy! Pammy!" An explosion of wind brought a cracking noise from the walls.

A quivering puddle of lantern light covered the table and overflowed into the rest of the kitchen. While the boy wept, she stood searching for her strength. She had to do something. Could the feral dogs really be near Pam's trailer? And how could the boy know? How could he?

Something scraped the back door. "Pamela?" Hurrying, she pulled it open—a burst of coolness. Rain gushed in. A dark shape heaved up from the porch. "No!" She tried to slam the door, but the shape struck against it with a yelp, shoving the door out of her hands and knocking her aside as it plowed through. Claws skittered loudly across the floorboards. "Oh." She clutched at her throat, feeling her pulse hammer while the door flailed in rainy wind.

Black and soaking, the dog ran twice around the kitchen, then stopped to lap at Matthew's face before shaking, spattering her jeans and the room with mud.

Drifting mist surrounded her, and she breathed in the scent of the rain. Then she heard fiercely chaotic barking, murky through the storm, definitely coming from the direction of Pamela's.

The boy grabbed her, startling her. When she put her hand on his head, he whined and shook all over. The words wouldn't come out through his chattering teeth, and he pressed shut his eyes, his whole face clenching. The veins on his face swelled as though they'd burst at the temples if the choked-down sobs did not emerge.

She knew what she had to do. Freeing herself, she moved quickly to the cellar door, reached again for the shelf. "Matthew, you're to stay in the house with Dooley." Her voice sounded odd, and she tried to imagine the expression on her face. "The lights should come back on soon. You're not to touch the lantern. Understand?"

The boy watched as she grabbed down first the shotgun, then the box of shells.

"Do you understand?" With a steady hand, she loaded two shells into the gun, then picked up the flashlight. The boy tried to follow her out onto the porch.

"I said stay in the house!"

The boy hadn't moved in long moments. He stood rooted to the spot, staring at the back door. It had already swelled from the rain, and she'd had to shove it several times before it had closed properly. He'd watched it jerk and tremble, listened to her grunt against it. Then the lock had clicked. Since then all had been silent save the storm.

It rattled at the walls. He lifted the lantern from the table and carefully carried it into the living room, the dog barking and following. Shadows lurched and fled before him, swinging wide across the floor and walls. Matty set the lamp down on the little table and ran to the window. He stood there, his face pressed to the glass. Silent incandescence showed only the running pane, as though the world slipped away, pattering. The curtain of water glittered . . . and when the night-voice found him, he'd already begun to shake. Cries of distant hounds drummed through the window glass with the thunder.

Reflected light gleamed dimly from the glass. Reversed, the room wavered on the pane. He stepped back, saw a face against the liquid night, a face like his, in a room such as this, framed by hair that held the lamplight like glowing coils, with eyes that seemed those of the night itself. "No! You! No, I won't!" He screamed and the face screamed with him. He raced into the dark kitchen, struck a chair that overturned. Sand grated on the windows, trying to get in. "No, Pammy! Not again! I don't want it to be! Save!" The dog growled once, then whimpered and began scratching frantically at the door while the boy yelled.

"Gotta get out!" Froth clung to his lips, and he clutched his abdomen. His eyes rolled back in his head, and gasping shrieks tore in agony from his stomach.

He lunged for the door. The dog scrambled away, whining, to slink into the living room. "Chabwok! Chabwok!" The boy screamed, and the door shook as he beat on it.

Squeezing beneath the sofa, the dog lay very still.

She'd been soaked through in seconds, yet she slogged on determinedly.

Wet sand blew full in her face, then slackened somewhat. The flashlight broke the storm apart, reduced it to dazzling fragments. She tilted the light downward, and it threw a wavering patch on the yellow ground. She was glad the dog had come home, because she couldn't have left the boy alone otherwise. Pamela must have had sense enough to lock her door and stay inside, she decided. *She must have.* Dashing for the road, she listened. *She wouldn't try to make it over here, would she?* Muffled, the barking seemed to have moved away. *If she were frightened?*

She was already running for the bridge when she realized she could have driven part of the way. *Damn.* She splashed through a puddle. The shotgun weighed so much, it interfered with her balance, its shaft so dense the lightning scratched no reflection on it. For just an instant, she considered going back for the car, then realized the road might well flood anyway. Ahead of her, the flashlight's beam created a wraith of luminous vapor that darted from tree to tree and melted into the battering water, a pale and shimmering extension of herself.

The rain picked up to gale force again, sweeping the road in thick, rapid sheets. *Oh damn.* Half drowned out, her footsteps drummed across the bridge. Below, water churned. She paused for a moment, breathing heavily, then ran forward. Her foot found nothing, empty air, then caught, wrenching beneath her. She thudded hard against the wooden bridge and rolled.

She fell into blackness, one with the storm.

Lightning flickered through missing planks.

She splashed on her back, and water rushed up her nose. She reached blindly for the surface, and the flashlight swirled away from her, a blob of luminous churning. By instinct alone, she kept hold of the shotgun as the current pushed and spun her. The gun dragged her down. A thick root hit her thigh.

Rolling, she fought her way up the streaming bank and lay panting in the mud. She hunched over, gasping and choking, wiping at her eyes, her body heat bleeding away with the water that poured from her. *That was nearly it, girl.* She coughed uncontrollably. *Nearly it.*

She thought about hiding under the bridge until the storm lessened, but the stream swelled and twisted at her feet, growing wilder by the moment. And where was the bridge anyway? Grunting, she staggered up the embankment.

Will the gun even work, now it's wet? She considered abandoning it, but howls twisted all around her in the wind. Pines hissed with the rain. They seemed to dance in a shimmer of light. She listened, not sure of anything now. Trying to get her bearings, she pushed on.

Those red eyes in my dreams. Again, her thoughts turned to the child who had been bitten. *Please, Pamela, please be all right.* Hurrying, she thought of the hound that had frightened her the other night. *You have to be. If only for Matthew's sake.* She shivered. *I'm almost there, Pamela. Don't be afraid.* Gripping the shotgun, she tried to keep it pointing straight ahead.

In a burst of brilliance, the road seemed wrong somehow, unfamiliar. Thunder seemed to grow louder, to follow closer on the flash. She couldn't spot the turnoff or the hanging tree or any other landmark, though she should have by now. A branch struck her shoulder. Forked lightning cracked the sky overhead, revealed a road grown narrower than it should have been.

Behind her, something moved. With a harsh cry catching in her throat, she spun. A solitary tree swayed wildly. Saplings seemed to leap at her with each bright glare, and thunder left her too deafened to listen for dogs.

Is that it? Is it Pam's place? Ahead lay a low structure. *I must've come around from the other side somehow.* She trotted forward, realizing even as she ran that the dark form couldn't be the trailer. "Pamela! It's me!" The shape was all wrong, somehow flattened and broken, and beside it rose a black obelisk.

Dark pillars surrounded her, and she stood absolutely still. The chill she'd been fighting went through her, forcing her teeth together with a sharp click. She blinked at the thing she'd mistaken for the trailer: one wall only, cut through with window holes that opened to nothingness. Lightning slanted behind it.

Thunder staggered her. *The creek.* She must have gotten turned around in the water. *I'm lost.* This had to be the old town, but a part she'd never seen before. Motionless in the ruins, she stared, her teeth chattering.

Through the pines floated an agonized, choking scream.

There was no way of telling if it came from a man or a woman, but there was no mistaking that it was a cry of terror and pain. And close.

Isolated in the downpour, she listened. There was no way of knowing even from what direction the cry had come. While the gale whipped through the pines, they seemed at last to have merged—this force and this terrain—to have become a single unit, a rippling universal shadow.

And something bulky moved with a heavy sound, crouching

through the blurring trees. And a horrible stench sifted up through the rain.

Numb with terror, she backed away. She heard it moving again, could almost see it now, there in the underbrush.

Backing away, backing farther, she felt it, felt it slowly emerge. *No, it's not.* Dimly, she glimpsed it—a form. *Not there.* A shape, all wrong. *It's . . . not.*

Squat and heavy, it hunched on four legs in the flattened brush.

It's a patch of mud or a tree trunk or . . .

It scrambled toward her.

Shoot! The gun shook wildly in her hands. *Shoot it!* She tried to aim. *Why don't you shoot?!*

The gun exploded, rearing upward, striking her shoulder. The shot went high. The muted tearing of the pellets through the trees mingled with the soft battering of raindrops. After the flash, she could see nothing. The storm had become a steady drizzle, and the water pressed down her body like a hand. Wishing she had more than one shell remaining, she took a step backward, aiming at first one dark area, then another.

Flames sprang in the air, heat and a crackling shock that sent her staggering backward, stunned and reeling.

Don't look!

Lightning slithered on the ground, and a lump of ore fused in blinding brilliance.

Its eyes! As a red afterimage, she saw it standing erect now, scant yards away. *Oh my God looking into mine its eyes.* Returning to black, the ground seemed to shake, and her weaker leg gave out. *The mouth God I can't run the snarl with its lips drawn back.* She fell to one knee. *Teeth in the red mouth.*

Rain already beat down the flames that crept across the cloven earth between them.

Now, she ran with no knowledge of how she'd risen. Tripping, she slid on her face, the gun discharging on the ground beneath her. She was slow to get up, sure some part of her had been ripped away. Again, the full force of rainfall hammered from the sky.

Crashing sounds surged toward her.

No. She lunged through the woods, shotgun left behind. *You won't get me!* The tearing pain in her side jolted. *Not this easy!* Branches clawed. *I won't let you!* Then the ground was gone in sliding mud, and rushing black water knocked the breath from her, filling her mouth. Cold and powerful now, the creek boiled, tumbling her like a leaf.

Narrow here. Lightning glowed off the water, freezing her as she crawled up the sand.

Doubled over, she hobbled on, shivering and limping. *I won't look back. I won't.* Then she staggered into the clearing.

"Pamela!" She launched herself at the trailer. "Pamela, it's Athena!" She pounded and yelled, her voice lost in the shriek of wind that buffeted and pulled at her. "Open the door! Let me in! Hurry!" Bubbling up through the downpour, the screams emptied out of her. "I think I hear it coming! God damn you! Open up!"

"Go away!" There came faint, frightened squeals. "I can't unlock the door. They're out there. I can't now!"

"Let me in, Pamela!" Her words swept away before the growing howl and the roaring pound of terror in her ears. "Please, oh God." The baying of dogs surrounded her.

The door popped open, and Pam collapsed out of it. Falling, she struck Athena, knocked her off the trailer steps. They rolled on top of one another, both struggling in the mud. "The lights went out!" Pam sobbed. "Oh, 'Thena, the lights went out and I didn't know what to do. I hear it! Oh, what is it? I hear it!"

Athena jerked her head toward the thrashing in the trees, caught a glimpse of rapid motion. She heaved herself up, dragged Pam back inside.

Small lights glinted, and something slipped, smashing under her feet as she latched the door. Thin white candles stuck to the collapsible table, and their box lay open, contents scattered about the floor. Thunder rattled the window. The storm drummed on metal walls.

With a tinny sound, the door moved. Pam pulled Athena closer. The latch clattered.

The whole trailer shuddered. The door leaped. It banged and shook with impact after battering impact. Pamela cowered, sobbing in Athena's arms.

The pounding stopped abruptly. Something tore at the walls.

"Pamela!" Athena took her by the shoulders. "Is there a gun here? Pamela?" She shook her. "Is there a gun?"

A terrible screaming roar ripped through them.

"What is it? Oh Lord!! There ain't no gun. Oh Lord oh 'Thena."

Metal wrenched loudly. The whole trailer jolted, tilting, and Athena threw out her arms to block her fall. Some of the candles toppled, went out.

In the gloom, the wall began to bow inward, groaning. "It's gonna get in! Sweet Jesus, 'Thena, what is it? It's gonna bend down the wall."

The window vent shattered. Spinning around, Pamela screeched as a particle of glass struck her cheek. The remaining candles went out with a rainy gust.

Lightning—something like a hand at the window—then blackness.

Pam fell on her face and screamed in static terror with every breath.

Athena groped her way around the other woman, found the small cabinet and clawed through the drawers. Paper, rags, flatware. From the broken vent came scrabbling and a rasping breath. *There's a face pressed at the window.* She clutched a paring knife. *Please, don't let there be lightning. Please, don't make me see it.*

But when brightness flared again, only rain showed at the window.

"Where's . . . ?" From the floor, Pam made a noise like gagging. "Where is . . . it?"

A tremor ran through the walls.

Something rattled overhead. The trailer rocked wildly on its foundation. Athena hit the wall, slid sideways, the knife clattering away from her. Her knee struck the floor. Pamela grabbed at her and hung on as they rolled.

The pounding on the roof merged with the sound of the

storm—giant hailstones, beating one after another. Rapid light flashed at the ruined window, and they watched the low ceiling bend, sagging toward them. Athena knelt beside Pam and held her hand. There came a small tearing sound and a splashing, sudden trickle of wetness.

"Oh no, oh no my baby, oh no, no." Pam wept.

Athena stroked her hair, so long and soft. Pam clutched her, her breath very hot on Athena's face.

"Maybe if we don't say nothing, maybe it'll go away if it don't think we're in here. 'Thena?"

Athena raised her head. It had all changed, the one roaring replaced by many growls and snarls. Was the forest alive with them?

Rain muddled the sounds from outside. Something scrabbled overhead, and scufflings blended with ferocious baying in the wind. Barking became shrill yelping, then reverted to snarls.

Moving with numbed calm, she worked herself painfully to her feet and limped to the broken vent.

" 'Thena, what?"

She stood quietly at the window while the storm and something else raged outside.

" 'Thena?" Pamela peered from between her fingers. A double flicker of lightning showed her an impassive face beneath the dark mass of hair.

"It's gone."

"What?" Pam whispered in a voice like a child's. "What's the matter, 'Thena?" She crept to the window.

They peered through the twisted metal slats. Intermittent glare afforded them glimpses of the dogs in the clearing, starved and diseased looking beneath wet fur, insane from fresh blood. The chicken coop lay in twisted fragments, and all the mongrels had drenched hens in their jaws, shaking them, crushing them with gushes of black fluid.

"No!" A white hen tried to flee, and Pam made a small wretched sound as she watched.

In silence, the two women stood, now in darkness, now in sudden radiance. They stared. Small rent bodies were tugged apart, and white feathers were flung about in the downpour. Small legs kicked amid the mangled flappings. In burning glimpses, through hanging shards of glass, they watched the miserable gray slaughter of the hens.

Thursday, August 6

They watched night fade to shades of dawn, watched the fragmented glass slowly brighten. Outside, it still drizzled.

Athena shifted about, uncomfortable in damp clothes. A blue glimmer came through ruffled chintz, a drowned sort of daylight that made the flowers on the curtains seem to crawl. Knowing she approached nervous collapse, she blinked at the acid-gray horror of the morning. Without comprehension, she watched Pam cheat at solitaire, then glanced at the broken window again. Her eyes felt tight.

Pam put the two of spades on the ace. She'd been playing at that table since before there'd been light enough to see the blunted deck. Her hair had dried plastered to her face, and her movements seemed both jerky and slow, like an old film run in a faulty projector. Every so often she'd mumble something about the rain being a good thing for the woods and all.

"It's light enough to leave."

"There sure ain't no gun here." Pam kept playing.

"When we get home, I can take care of your cut cheek better."

"I told Lonny, I said to him, 'What happened to that gun?' an' he asks me what do I want with a gun anyhow, but I told him, 'I'm scared out here by myself an' you not home alla time.' So then he gets mad an' says . . ." No ripple of emotion disturbed the perfect calm of her voice.

"We have to go, Pamela."

"Not yet." Black queen on red king. "I don't wanna."

"We've got to make sure Matthew's all right." She got up, wobbly with fatigue.

" 'Thena?"

"I'm all right. My leg's asleep." She saw the knife on the floor, set it on the table in front of Pam. "You take that."

Pam's eyes looked bruised. She didn't touch the knife.

The floor was wet, and cracks in the dented ceiling still dribbled moisture. In the tight closet, Athena found a broomstick and screwed off the mop attachment. Heading for the door, she stumbled. Rug remnants lay several layers thick in places, a quilt of damp, faded colors in the haze. Red rectangle. Blue square. Her own muddy footprints. Maddening hints of pattern. The toe of her shoe slipped under a green L-shaped piece, and she almost pitched forward again, feeling even clumsier, even more disoriented.

"I know it's still out there." Pam's voice sounded listless and flat. "You better not open the door now." She didn't glance up from the cards, but her face twisted when she heard the squeak of the latch.

The door stuck, dented into the frame. Athena yanked. A heavy mist of rain blew in. Outside, it was still a little dark. The front of the mobile home seemed to have been repeatedly struck by a car. "Come on, or I'll leave you." She stared: beyond the clearing, the woods looked vacant and pure.

"Watch out for these steps. They're sort of ripped loose. Are you coming, Pamela? I swear, I'll leave you here by yourself. Are you listening to me?" She took a deep breath. "How long do you think this door will hold if it comes back?"

Once outside, Pam wept again at the sodden piles of bones and feathers, at the petunias flattened in the mud. Looking wildly about, she clutched the little knife with both hands.

The rain fell lightly, so gentle they barely felt it as they moved in silence through the fog-soaked trees. The sand looked churned and lumpy, and the pines possessed a frightening, crawly clarity.

Pam kept looking back, her eyes showing white all around. Suddenly, she began to run.

"Come back! Pamela!" Yelling, Athena pursued her. As she caught up, she saw her dive and make a wild grab.

Pam stood up, a bedraggled hen in her arms and mud on her dress. "Oh poor baby, Pammy's got you now you don't have to be afraid of those bad dogs no more there."

"You've got me all turned around." Athena shook her head, scanning the dreary stretches of pine growth. "Where's the road?"

"This way," Pam called. Carrying the chicken, she virtually skipped along. "The sky looks sorta like pancake batter, don't it?"

"What?"

"All kind of yellow-gray and lumpy."

"Oh." The rain had gone, leaving the sky overcast and quiet. They hurried, Athena leaning heavily on the broomstick. Letting Pam pull farther ahead, she stopped and stared, her mind straining to make sense of what she was seeing. Was it some sort of carving or statue?

A broken figure sprawled on the ground. She blinked. It focused, became a prostrate human form, caked with sand. Focus sharpened.

"Oh dear God."

The familiar face seemed to gaze back at her. Darkly stained, the clothing lay in shreds, and the contents of the pockets had leaked in a pathetic ring of meaningless objects. The thing twitched. She rubbed her eyes. It seemed to keep moving in tiny jerks, until she realized that crickets crawled all over it.

" 'Thena?"

"Stay back." The belly had been torn out, and cracked ribs protruded from the flesh. Intestines trailed in twisted loops.

"Whatchya lookin' at?"

"Don't come over here." She looked away. The sands were endless, sodden nothingness, veined with rivulet marks, the pines a fatty gray. Hoping her tired eyes would blur, she took a step, then another.

"What is it? What is that over there? What?"

She heard a dull roaring, more substantial than the wind in the pines, and she hustled Pam toward the sound. They found the road and started across the bridge while the swollen creek thundered against the planks. "My fault. All my fault." Athena peered down through missing timbers at black water. A leafy branch twisted madly, disappeared in the dark churning.

"What? Hurry up, 'Thena. What was that back there anyways? I mean, we gotta go see if Matty's all right."

Damp wind made a hollow whining at the walls.

The boy lay collapsed against the back door. He hadn't moved in hours. Pammy was dead. He knew it. Face screwed tight in misery and exhaustion, he held his body in a rigid fetal position.

The blood . . . Pammy . . .

He'd heard it, heard Chabwok kill, felt it.

The taste.

She was dead. He had no strength left even to cry.

The dog ran barking at them. Pam shrieked once, a reflex of abject terror, then kept her arms held tightly around the chicken, while Dooley circled and leaped. "Now you get out of here now! Go on!"

Something wasn't right. Athena shook her head as the dog bounded back to greet her. Then she had it. The dog shouldn't be outside. She had locked him in the house with Matthew. Suddenly and deeply frightened, she stood in the gentle mist and stared up at the house.

The porch had bloated, thickened boards protruding, bursting upward. Pam had her key out, and she yelled to the dog. When the back door opened, the boy tumbled out. Pam dropped the hen, which squawked around them while the boy lay there, blinking.

When his wordless cry rang out, his mother looked away, feeling like an intruder. Numb, she gazed at the morning woods. She didn't see the boy's gratitude, didn't see the light in his face as he turned to her.

Marl brushed a chewed piece of field mouse out of the corner.

"You're a good son, boy. Don' know why she'd wanna run off tha' way. Your mother. You's justa baby." Al stretched out on the wooden bench, and each time it seemed certain he'd finally fallen asleep, he'd raise his head and babble some more. Then he'd grunt, reaching for the jug under the bench. "A good son. But we don' need 'er."

Not listening, Marl swept the floor of the gin mill. Only a dusty sort of light drifted through the open doorway. It made everything seem peaceful. Curled on the counter plank, the cat licked at its paws with a bright pink tongue. And Marl kept sweeping, pushing clumsy-looking homemade cigarette butts ahead of him across the relentless sand, densely packed between the floorboards. Shoulder blades twitching, the cat furrowed its face in the direction of Al's clogged snores. Then it rolled away, exposing all of the sharp teeth in a pythonic yawn. And the broom continued its rhythmic swishing, quiet, soothing.

At last, the boy leaned the broom against the wall and walked softly toward his father. For a moment, he stared down at the large, mottled face. Then he moved to the other end of the bench. He took hold of a boot and pulled, tugged it off. Al muttered wetly in his sleep.

Before he tossed the boots under the bench, Marl stared at the gray flesh of his father's feet, at the long, curving toenails, jutting like black hooks.

The siren stayed silent, and the tires left a damp whisper. Staring out the window, Athena remained mute and unseeing. At the sides of the road, pines bristled and sagged, flowing past.

"Honey, I just feel so bad that I took so long getting here. The roads. I mean, I'm just so sorry," said Doris, her voice raw with cigarettes. "I tried to call Larry. I even tried Siggy but couldn't get hold of anybody. Half the phone lines are still down from the storm. I'm just so sorry." Spray flaring up behind them, they swerved to avoid a downed tree in a sheet of water. All the roads were flooded, many impassable, forcing them onto winding detours that seemed to take them always farther from the highway. "I'm just afraid of getting stuck out here," she muttered between her teeth as she wrestled the wheel. "We'd never get a tow."

Athena shut her eyes. No matter how she tried to unfocus her thoughts, she couldn't blunt her awareness of the sheeted form behind them. "Oh, don't get stuck."

Doris shot her a look. When she'd first picked her up, Athena's words had tumbled out, hysterical and fantastic, but since then she'd retreated into silence. "Will you look at this!" The rig splashed around a turn. "What in hell's going on up there?"

In the half-submerged road, several vehicles had parked haphazardly, and people milled around a bogged car. A uniformed trooper stood in the middle of the road, shaking his head. He looked very young.

"I'm sorry, honey." Swaying, the rig slowed. "I just have to see what this is."

Athena nodded, already jumping down. Though the water rose above her ankles—part of a sudden lake that stretched to cover the floor of the woods—the sands felt solid underfoot. With a dazed expression, she looked around. Pines stuck out from the wash as though caught by an incoming tide.

" 'Thena? What are you guys doing here?"

Searching for a dry place to stand, she looked up to find Steve sloshing toward her.

"We tried to call you," he said. "I didn't think you'd be able to get through."

She saw the confusion on his face as she moved away from him and walked toward the knot of people at the foundered car. Wind in the wet branches made a low whistling moan.

The car windows were crystal webs. It had sunk up to the axles, and through a forest of uniformed legs, she saw the crimson film on the soaked floor. She drew closer. She stared a long time, nodding, as though this were only to be expected. There was very little blood really, but she imagined that most of it must have been washed away. The body had been so badly savaged that it barely looked human anymore. The throat had been mauled out to the neckbone, and whitish segments showed through straggling veins. There was no face left.

"I tried to talk her out of coming along, but you know how stubborn she is."

She recognized Doris's voice. And soon she realized that other people around her were speaking as well, had been all along, but their words sounded as distant and meaningless as the drip of rain from the trees. She couldn't seem to make sense of anything, so she stopped trying. "Doesn't matter," she whispered to herself. "The wind knows." Her shoes began to sink into the watery soil. "The pines know."

"Shit, it's like his stomach was bit out."

Feeling a dim sympathy, she glanced at the young trooper beside her. Vaguely, she became aware of Barry's voice, somewhere off to the side, on the edges of the crowd. Swirling, all the voices drifted away from her again, and there yawned a cathedral quietness, swelling with the rush of wind, punctuated only by damply muffled footsteps and splashings. Sand shifted and yielded underfoot, the earth soft as seaweed, soft as ruptured entrails, and the deep whirlpool of silence broke only upon the sharp, liquid twittering of the birds. She realized that Steve was beside her again, that he was asking her something. "It looked like Wallace," she told him, knowing he wouldn't understand. "Lying there in the mud. I thought it was Wallace again." Dizzy, she leaned on a police car, wondering how she hadn't heard the birds before. "And the crickets on him, moving, like Wallace was still moving when I found him. Only I didn't know what to do. Not then. I would now." Her voice trailed off, and she wondered if he'd heard her, if she'd even been speaking aloud.

She tried to walk away, conscious that the sand made no brisk noise underfoot, just this rotten, mushy sound. The pines whispered. She looked for the birds but couldn't see them any more than she could the toads. She wanted to call out to someone. To Barry, yes, Barry. Always so forceful, he would help her. People milled all around, but her throat felt dry, and the small sounds she made and the sounds made by the other people seemed muffled to the point of muteness. Yet the wind held many voices, gently hissing ghosts among the trees. They pleaded with her, surrounded her with their desperate longings.

Barry appeared to be questioning a bald, muscular man with

a red face. A trooper kept interrupting, while another muttered something.

"We was gonna come back with a tow." Only Athena really listened, heard the words and understood. "It got so dark," the man kept saying. "We couldn't, the rain, it come down so hard we couldn't see." The young trooper she'd first noticed stood by one of the blue-and-whites, trying to radio for instructions, and before long, she'd heard enough to piece together some of the facts: car pool of construction workers; late shift; short cut. "It just, the road, it washed out from under us. We got stuck." It was widely believed that the area was riddled with car thieves who used these back roads, so they'd left one man behind with the car while the others had hiked to a farmhouse. The bald man looked as though he'd been sick. "We just wanted a tow. We tried to come back. We did."

"Are you all right?" Steve stood beside her. "Doris just told me what's, I mean, who's in the rig." He stared at her. Too closely. "Athena, what can I say? Can I do anything? I'm so shocked, so sorry. Doris said something about dogs. Lord, that's awful."

"Hey, 'Thena!" Putting his notebook away, Barry approached. "How'd you get here?"

"Leave her alone," Steve said.

"What's your problem?"

Doris and the trooper wheeled up the litter, and the sound of the invisible surf boomed louder than it ever had in Athena's ears. The night tide. Only it was morning. Mourning. The tips of the pines vibrated, describing circles that grew ever smaller. Athena shut her eyes and knew the sea swirled all around her, knew the breeze that whipped through wet branches carried a faint tang of salt spray.

In erratic bursts, the radio warned that power lines, downed by the storm, remained potentially deadly, and a phone number kept repeating through the static. "Fat lot of good that number's going to do," Doris muttered, switching it off. "Damn phones are down too, lot of places." She kept turning to look at Athena. Through the rearview mirror, Athena watched the police car that followed them; she imagined she could make out the faces behind the windshield, imagined she could hear their voices.

"I handle all emergencies well, don't I? And I don't cry. Did you know this? I never cry. Not even as a child." When finally she began to talk, her words rambled uncontrollably. "And my aunt used to tell me my mother wouldn't nurse me, that she said it hurt too much."

"What, honey?"

They reached the metal bridge, and the tires moaned across the grating, the water high beneath them. Athena glanced down. Black and skeletal, a grove of dead trees rose from the river, and scattered patches of high ground had become islands. She faced front again: distant and engorged, low hills swelled with evergreens.

" 'Thena, I want you to understand this. If you ever need anything, you just have to call me." Singing tires threw water, and the water threw a mist behind them, and a whistling rattle pounded through the rig when she dropped the clutch.

"It's not my fault." The words bolted out. "God help me, I'm relieved he's dead. That's all I feel. Relief. But I didn't want him to die."

"I know you didn't."

"I didn't! It's me. Don't you see? It's me it's after."

"What are you talking about, honey? What's after you?"

"It's just letting me know it sees me, trying to hurt me through them, to get me to stand still and face it. At night. I've always known that. I've felt it." She seemed to be having trouble breathing. "What's wrong with me? I don't even feel sad. My husband's brother. Everything they always said about me is true. I can't even feel. I think I heard him cry out. God, I think I heard him in the storm. Just at the end. When he died." Turning around in the seat, she faced into the rig. "Two of them back there. Right behind us. Look."

"Stop it now."

"Two corpses. Did you see them, Doris? Did you see how they looked?"

"I saw."

"When it didn't get me, it had to go after somebody else. But why . . . if it already had Lonny . . . ?" She watched the road for a moment. "Maybe now it's rained, the murders will stop." Her eyes glittered like jagged bits of glass. "Maybe now it won't need blood."

"Athena."

"I'm going to kill it. Whatever it is. I am."

Doris only nodded. Collapsing barns began to pass in fields, yellowed from the recent heat, now thickened and sodden, and the matted grasses at the sides of the road could have concealed lions, whole prides of them. "You poor kid. Talk it on out, honey. Go on." But Athena had apparently lapsed back into silence. The distant, mournful thump of gunfire drifted across the meadow. They skirted a ragged group of children who stood in the road to gawk at Asian workers laboring in a flooded cranberry bog. "Funny how things change," said Doris. The children turned to stare at the rig, a few even giving chase. "I've been seeing workers get off the farm-labor buses for twenty years now. Used to be all blacks they brought in. Then Puerto Ricans mostly. Now are all you see is Vietnamese or Cambodians. I guess they're right at home out there." She glanced at the woman beside her.

"I wonder what's happened to Barry and Steven. I can't see them anymore." She turned to Doris, shocking her with the sharp emptiness of her eyes. "You have to help me. I know you'll help me. You always do." She pointed back at the strapped and sheeted mounds. "The one from the car. It's the same. The same as Lonny. Everybody is going to blame it on dogs. I'll need evidence. When we get to the hospital, I want you to be the one to examine the bodies. You understand? Will you do this for me?"

The dirt road had emptied onto a paved one, slick and puddled, but Doris drove no faster. "There are a few markers I could call in, I guess. I guess it depends on where I take you. Which hospital. Maybe I could at least observe some preliminaries."

Everything on the road changed; now beautiful homes alternated with hovels. The ambulance crept along, and Athena stared out the window. She watched a slanting shack go by and noted the absurd debris that littered the yard: old washing machine, bits of farm machinery, giant plastic squirrel. And everywhere the rusting cars. Then a mansion with smooth lawns and unbreached walls slid into view. Another hut sagged open, roof flopping, one wall having caved in beneath the weight of garbage that spilled out like entrails. "Isn't that funny?" Two-lane blacktop, recently resurfaced, ran clean and straight. "It's almost like seeing two centuries at once." Her voice gentle and wondering, Athena jerked her head from side to side. "Don't you think? Like different times overlapping. So many layers." She caught her breath, as though from a sudden pain. "I thought it was Wallace, you see. Just for a second. On the ground. Like before. I guess I never noticed how much alike they looked."

They passed another ruined structure. A blank fabric, the sky jealously absorbed all light, suffusing little on the earth, but the burning gray reflected, caught on the splinters of a broken window. "Look, Doris—a blind house. Eyeless." She twisted around to watch it pass. "It could be my house. In a few years."

Saying nothing, Doris increased the pressure on the gas pedal. As the rig went by, a ram in a makeshift corral stared after it impassively. Beneath curving horns, its slitted eyes gleamed yellow.

The face under the mud. The difference in Lonny's coloring had been hidden beneath slick grayness. *How am I going to tell Pamela?* Like Wallace dead all over again, dead and on the ground.

A taper of smoke still rose from the butt of Doris's last cigarette in the ashtray. She'd followed a man in a green surgical gown down the hall just a short time ago. Athena squirmed on a vinyl sofa in the waiting area, her body clenching and unclenching, while she mouthed the paper cup of flat Coke that was supposed to settle her stomach.

The way Doris acts on the rig—sometimes it's easy to forget she was a professional. I guess I make a lot of mistakes about people. They aren't what they seem. Her head hurt. *No, it's that people don't seem to be what they are. Or that . . .* She let the thought go.

It didn't matter. All that mattered was what Doris would tell her. She sat, fighting nausea . . . and waiting.

PART THREE

THE HUNT

The summer woods now, green with gloom . . . where even at noon the sun fell only in windless dappling upon the earth which never completely dried and which crawled with snakes— moccasins and water snakes and rattlers, themselves the color of the dappled gloom. . . .

William Faulkner

Consider the subtleness of the sea; how its most dreaded creatures glide under water, unapparent for the most part, and treacherously hidden. . . .

Herman Melville

Friday, August 7

From deep within its shelter, it called. The cry echoed in the flesh.

No response came.

It waited. It called and waited, an aching monster, sated but alone.

"But these dogs are killers! We can't just sit back and hope they go away."

"Come off it, Steve. They already canceled all the camping permits. Stopped all the canoe rentals, even. Goddamn—just what the fuck else do you want?" The corners of Barry's mouth curled down in sneering exasperation.

Red-faced and sullen, Steve didn't answer, just stared through the windshield. Both sipped from quart bottles of beer. Lazy with the heat, a yellow jacket flew in a side window and buzzed against the glass before finally settling on the dash. Barry's hand shot out, smashing it flat. "Finally got one of the suckers."

"Can't understand you." Steve shook his head in chagrin and bewilderment. "I mean, why you're taking his side. I know I usually don't say anything, but I can't see what's so damn threatening here." Their boss, Frank Buzby, had officially opposed the idea of the stateys launching an all-out hunt for the dogs and even now worked every connection he had in an effort to squash the project.

Barry's face went hard as he coolly threw the bottle at the

trunk of a dead tree. The bottle splintered and fell, leaving a trace of foam on the gray wood. To end the discussion, he started the engine, slammed the car into gear. Worn tires dug, leaving twin furrows. "Just can't figure it out, can you, detective?" he smirked. "Never stopped to think maybe ole Frank and me know some guys who wouldn't be too crazy about a search party. Or maybe we got some stuff of our own hidden we don't want nobody messing with."

"You going to start that crap about your fancy mob connections again?"

Barry snorted contemptuously, and they rode for a time without speaking. Then, casually, he asked if there had been any interesting bulletins lately.

"Yeah, a good one. Maybe you should read them once in a while. I mean, just for entertainment."

Barry stopped humming. "What the hell's the matter with you all of a sudden?"

Determined not to answer, Steve gulped from his beer, but the angry silence couldn't be maintained against the heat and the stale swim of alcohol in his brain. "They brought in some woman, just about dead from exposure—bulletin said—found her deep in the woods. Practically catatonic at first."

Barry watched the road, frankly bored.

"Then she started babbling about how her and her daughter'd been camping with some friends and got attacked by some guy who came out of the woods. They're still trying to figure out when the hell all this is supposed to have happened. Nobody knows how long she'd been out there. Or what direction she came from."

"Shit, Steve, she could've just been on drugs or something and got lost out there." Abruptly, his face took on an uncustomary expression of interest. "Say, did they ever catch that guy? You know, the one got away from the asylum?"

"Putting one and one together like that." His partner nodded. "Dangerous lunatic escapes. Campers get attacked. Might be a connection. Regular steel trap, that mind of yours. Ought to be a cop or something."

"Well, us country boys can't think too good. Shit. Know what I'm talking about? Not like you big city officers. Shit. I suppose you're gonna tell me dogs did this too? Look, Frank's got us working on it, don't he?" He lowered his voice to what he considered a persuasive tone. "What in hell more do you want?"

"Yeah, great job he's got us doing, too." Steve held up the map Buzby had given them, a topographical chart marked with red *X*s and circles. "For crissakes, spreading traps and poisoned meat over half the county."

"Reckon that should do it for the dogs, don't you? Easier than sending a damn army out here." Barry smirked again. "Probably get that loony too."

Steve watched the trees go by. "I hope they catch him soon," he muttered. "Starving—that's no way to die. And this heat. Dying of thirst must be like burning to death, only slow."

"Yeah, well, I guess you'd know all about thirst." He took his hands off the wheel, cracked his knuckles and grinned. The car veered rapidly toward a wall of trees. Smiling broadly at Steve's sharp gasp, he settled his hands back on the wheel and wrenched the car back on course.

Again, Steve tried not to speak. He took a deep breath, imbibing the musty pine smell. "Poor Athena. Must've been quite a shock for her yesterday. Finding him like that."

"Shit, she ain't all that upset."

Matty lay at the rim of a hollow: smooth contours suggesting the foundation of a vanished house, only a smear of white in the lichen to show where the frame structure once had stood. Small cacti grew in the loose soil. He knew of many such places in the woods.

The boy played with some pebbles, rolling them down the sloping sand, his voice a constant gentle murmur. Dooley sniffed about him, then plopped down in the sand and studied a grasshopper that made its way across the turf. Sunlight ran warm across them, and wind rattled in the dry weeds.

Bare arms on heated sand, the boy continued to launch the

stones. They were runners, racing downhill, and he was in the lead, feeling the wind cool his face, feeling courage and grace surge within his body. He was winning the race, and she stood at the bottom, cheering him. And now the rolling shapes became soldiers, like his father in the pictures or the ones Pammy had told him about, racing down a dune to the rescue. His mother was among those camped at the bottom, captive, straining her eyes toward the bright figure at the head of the column.

The pebbles changed again. Now they became other people. Bad people. The ones who pointed at him and laughed. But now they ran before him, ducking through the wild pines, screaming like babies. Like loonies. He'd show them. He was the brave one now, the fierce strong brave one, and try as they might they would not escape as they struggled and slid. Bad people, all of them . . . like the one with the clear bottle of foul stuff.

He shut his eyes and fragments of half-forgotten dreams drifted under the lids: a dusty road . . . himself floating . . . the windowless shack in the swamp.

Dooley whimpered, then howled. Matty looked up to see the dog backing away from him, body low against the ground. "Dooley?"

The animal continued to retreat, but its tail wagged briefly.

"Dooley!"

The dog hesitantly returned. Matty reached out to rough the dusty whorls of fur, and the dog's tail beat his legs. Soon, they rolled together, happy and relaxed again. The boy's breathing steadied, and in another moment the soldiers might have resumed their charging rescue. But the boy's quick eyes caught movement overhead. A hawk circled in the air, searching, wheeling lower. It swept in ever-tighter circles.

It dove, disappeared into the trees. The boy's eyes followed the motion, and he stared into the breeze-swept, kaleidoscopic pines. Patterns altered. Matty's hand ceased to stroke the dog's back and slid forward, coming to a stop on Dooley's neck. Through his light fingers, he could feel the pulse. The hot, infuriating pulse. His body stiffened.

Dooley sprang away, vanishing into the brush.

The voice spoke, clearer this time, more compelling.

Chabwok.

And for five minutes, his face gone dark and fierce, it was as though the boy lived a raging, biting life on the forest floor.

"No! Go away!" He stood, angry and confused, hurtling stone after stone into the woods. "You were gonna hurt Pammy! You were gonna hurt her! Ain't your friend no more. Go 'way!" With a dull thump, the final pebble bounced off a pine trunk and fell noiselessly into the sand.

"Look, Frank, calm down, will you? I'm telling you, it's not gonna be a problem. We're . . . Frank . . . Frank . . . We can handle this ourselves, boss." Barry opened the phone booth, letting some of the heat out of the glass box. "Would you . . . would you listen . . . would you listen to what I'm telling you for just a minute, Frank? What? Yeah. Don't worry. I'm gonna talk to her about it. Yeah. It's that Doris. She's the one might cause trouble. Huh? Yeah, I will."

"Hey, Bar." Looking over the map, Steve sat with the car door open. "Hurry it up, will you?"

"Listen, Frank, I got to go. Yeah, I don't want 'Buford' over here to know I been talking to you. I told him I was calling home. Like I said, we got all the poison placed and everything. It's only cause a the stateys and the reporters that we can't move the cars yet, but soon as the dogs are all dead, everything'll quiet down again."

Steve refolded the map as Barry approached. "You ready?"

"Yeah, let's go in," Barry muttered, shading his eyes against the sun to peer at the diner.

"So how's your father-in-law?" Steve hoisted himself out of the car and slammed the door.

"Huh?"

Steve shook his head, dismissing it. "Got any ideas what this is all about?"

"Doris just called and said Athena needed to see us here at one o'clock. Sounded kind of weird."

"It's one thirty now." A dark puddle spread beneath the clattering air conditioner. They crossed the parking lot, Barry a little in the lead.

"Damn." He sauntered in the door. "Would you look at this reception committee?"

Blind from the sudden change in light, Steve stood in the doorway and relished the coolness. He strained his eyes in the direction of the corner booth. Even from across the room, the group's quiet conveyed a tautness, and only Athena failed to look up as Barry approached. Steve stared a moment, shocked: her face was the color of lead.

"You're late," said Doris, and Steve noticed the worried way she kept sneaking looks at Athena.

Barry stood in front of the table, glaring down. "You got guts, boy. What the fuck you doing here? You didn't tell me he was gonna be here, Doris."

Very red, Jack fidgeted and shot Larry a glance, while Steve appropriated chairs from a nearby table.

"Yessir, you really got balls." Barry sat. "You're lucky to be still breathing."

"Look, Barry," began Jack carefully.

Barry leaned across the table, pushing his face too close to Jack's. "Don't give me that 'look, Barry' crap."

"Hey," Doris interrupted, "what goes on? I thought you guys were supposed to be such good buddies."

"Not no more," Barry growled. "Some buddy." His tone became aggrieved.

Steve relaxed as the violence almost imperceptibly melted from his partner's stance.

"A guy don't want buddies that are hanging around the house while he's out working."

"You got it wrong, Barry. Cathy and me ain't . . ."

"Oh Christ," interrupted Doris. "You two would have to start this now." She kept checking Athena, but the other woman kept her eyes fixed on the table, her face unreadable. Larry, however, had gone dead white.

"And you supposed to be her cousin," Barry went on with a nasty smile. "Let me tell you something, cuz. I ever catch you two at it, I'm gonna blow your head off."

"You're crazy. I never . . ." Jack stopped. His jaw tightened, and he gave Larry a look that clearly said "you owe me big-time, pal."

Steve's gaze never wandered from Athena. Something was going on here. Something bad. There were blotches under her eyes. Her blouse was newly washed, very clean, very wrinkled. She'd been the source of the tension when they'd entered—he felt sure of that. Dread coiled deep in his gut.

Finally, there came a lull in the noise from Barry.

Still gazing down at the table, Athena drew a deep breath. "I asked you two to stop here because, well, really, Doris asked you, but we both thought so, because I wanted to ask you—I mean, tell you—what I've just been telling the others." She paused, gathering strength. Barry stared at her, and the ambulance crew squirmed. "The night my husband, I mean, my brother-in-law died, the night before last when Lonny was killed . . . I saw something in the woods. It came after me. Something like a man."

"What?"

"But I thought"—Steve paused, searching her expression—"I thought it was the dogs." She raised her head for the first time, and with a sinking feeling, he recognized the look in her eyes; he'd seen it often enough in mirrors. But what could she have to feel guilty about? "Are you telling us a man killed Lonny?"

"Like a man."

"What are you saying?" Barry glared at her.

Everyone shifted uneasily. Doris picked up a hamburger. "There's a hair in this. Oh Christ, I think it's from Sims's mustache."

Larry nudged Jack. "Quick, man, get the throw-up pan."

"What exactly did you see, 'Thena?" Steve kept his voice calm.

"You can't expect her to describe it," Doris interrupted, bristling. "Not after everything that's happened, not when—"

Athena put up a hand. "It was dark . . . and the storm . . ." Her voice fell, and she turned her face toward the window. "Barry? I saw its teeth. They were human teeth. And it stood up."

"So what are you saying? It was the Jersey Devil or what?"

Steve asked, "Did anyone else see this . . . this thing?"

Athena looked away from the window. "My sister-in-law was there."

"And did she see it?" he repeated gently.

Doris leaned forward.

She shook her head. The Formica tabletop was scratched and yellowed, and she stared at the worm tracks of cigarette burns.

Steve's voice coaxed. "What did she see?"

"Dogs," she whispered, gazing into her coffee mug as though peering down a well.

With a laugh both exasperated and triumphant, Barry sat back. Before he could speak, Doris added, "I took some scrapings from the bodies of both victims."

"What both?" Barry looked ready to snarl.

"Athena's brother-in-law and the construction worker found in the car."

"Oh for—"

"I took scrapings," she continued, "and left them with a friend of mine at the lab. Unfortunately, the hospital administrator got wind of it. Took sort of a dim view." She sighed. "So we don't exactly have a lab report, but—"

"You support this?" Steve interrupted, watching her face. "You're supporting this story? This claim that there was a man or whatever involved? Do you know something about this?"

"It's like I was saying, I don't exactly have a report. But one of the bodies, the hard hat, I'm pretty sure what the scrapings were. Semen."

"Jesus," Larry breathed.

"You may have noticed this last little fact wasn't in the official account," Doris finished. "No mention of it at all." Exhaling a cloud of smoke, she put a supportive arm around Athena's shoulders.

Barry stared hard at Athena. At the next table, a woman asked loudly for the check.

"Even so." Steve nodded slowly, his voice grim. "It could still have been dogs."

"Oh shit." Larry looked sick.

Unnoticed until now, photographs had been lying facedown on the table. Doris flipped them over.

"Jesus H. Christ!"

The color enlargements revealed each wound in pornographic detail.

"Where the hell'd you get these?" demanded Barry. "Oh. Of course. You and your frigging friends."

"Doris?" A slight tremor marred Steve's attempt at a tone of mere professional interest. "Have you got anything else to go on?"

Some of the anger drained from her face, but her hands remained clenched. "Well, for one thing," Doris began, "there are no animal hairs on this body. And there should be, especially considering the method of attack—the ferocity, the violence. Look at the claw marks." She pointed to a photo, nodded to Steve. "We both saw those. Even on the side of the car." She stubbed out her cigarette. "There should be fur all over, inside the wounds, even."

"And the other? Lonny?" asked Steve. "Was there any fur on him?"

"Well," Doris hesitated. "He may have been killed first and later eviscerated by dogs."

"Shit," Barry grumbled. "So what you're saying is there were dog signs all over Lonny. Am I right?" Again he laughed. "This is fucking ridiculous."

Steve watched Athena. Her fingertips stroked her forehead, one hand shielding her eyes from Barry, screening her face from his words. She seemed so drained, so weary, yet still so strong. He felt as though he were seeing deep inside of her now, as though this quality, this endurance, this purity were something she normally kept hidden from the world.

Hesitantly, Larry turned to the older cop. "But what about

the guy in the car?" he ventured. "I mean, like Doris says, if the dogs did it, why isn't there . . . ?"

"The rain." Barry spoke slowly. "The rain washed the dog fur off him. That's all, twit." He looked at his watch. "Is that it?"

"The stateys may have something," added Doris.

"Yeah, so? What do you want me to do about it?"

"Couldn't you maybe talk to somebody?"

He mumbled an obscenity.

"When I was in the trailer . . ."

Everyone turned toward the flat voice.

"I think I heard . . . whatever it was . . . fighting with the dogs. It . . . the man . . . may be bitten. We could check hospitals."

Barry made a scornful noise.

"Maybe what you heard was your brother-in-law," Steve suggested, "being attacked by the dog pack." His hand inched across the table toward hers, then stopped, fingers curling.

Barry blew smoke. He leaned forward, parodying Steve's position and tone of voice. "Listen, Athena, I understand how bad you feel about poor old Lonny, but you really do know it was dogs tore them men up, don't you?"

Athena clenched the handle of her mug so hard her knuckles stood out like a row of pearls.

Steve cleared his throat. "Barry, I thought you were the one saying these animals weren't dangerous."

"I never said they wasn't dangerous," Barry railed at him, obviously feeling betrayed. "I just said—"

"It wasn't an animal! I told you, it stood on two legs like a man! Why doesn't anybody believe me?"

"And I'm telling you we don't need to stir up no trouble like that!" Barry answered, breathing hard.

"About what time would you say this all happened?" asked Steve. " 'Thena?" When she didn't answer him, he looked around and realized that all over the restaurant, people were staring at them. " 'Thena?" he repeated. "What do you want us to do?"

She looked at him and didn't say anything.

"What?" He furrowed his brow.

"I don't know." She shook her head. "I want you to help me, I guess. I had a chance to shoot it and couldn't do it. I waited too long. I don't know why."

"Could it have been your brother-in-law who chased you?" asked Steve.

"Listen, Doris." Jack started to get up. "Larry and me, we got to get going."

"Yeah, right," said Larry. "We, uh, got things to do."

"Could a couple of scrawny mutts tear a man's arm off?" demanded Doris.

"You saying a man did that?" Barry slammed the photos down in the center of the table. "You said it yourself—look at the claw marks." He sat back, satisfied he'd made his point. In a softer, patronizing tone, he added, "Now, it would be different if you had one shred of evidence."

"That's exactly what we do have." Doris shoved the pictures back at him. "Shred of evidence."

"I'm not crazy. Don't everybody look at me like that!"

"Honey, nobody said that."

"Let's get out of here."

"Wait a minute, Barry," Steve said. "If it is wild dogs, and if they have started attacking people . . ."

"What the frig's going on at this table?" Doris looked up to find Sims glaring down at them, his mustache twitching with outrage. "People comin' in here for lunch, an my customers is complainin' you're takin' their appetites away. Good Christ, what are those?" He snatched the photos off the table before anyone could stop him. "What the hell kinda thing is 'is to bring inna restaurant?"

Larry and Jack took advantage of the diversion to edge away from the table. Hopelessly, Athena watched as they headed for the door.

"If they're your patrons, they don't need us to make them sick," Doris growled, her hand on Athena's shoulder. "They should thank us. We probably saved them from ptomaine." She turned back to Athena. "Excuse me, honey. I have to go to the little girls' room."

"Wait, Doris, please, just . . . Even if the dogs killed Lonny, I tell you I saw what was chasing me. After I got away, the thing must've found the man on the road and . . . Doris?"

"Back in a minute, honey. Yo, Sims, why don't you turn the air-conditioning up?"

"Shit."

Steve watched as Doris took the proprietor aside. They stood by the door, Doris whispering and gesturing rapidly, and Steve knew Sims wouldn't bother them again. When he returned his attention to the table, he saw Barry leaning across it with both his hands on Athena's folded hands. She kept shaking her head. When he caught some of Barry's words, he faced away in embarrassment.

The woman at the next table had impossibly blonde hair sprayed to brittle stiffness. "So she was riding the . . . you remember the old Camden trolley, don't you? And there the Devil was, she said, just sitting right on top the power cable, wings folded up, she told me, just sitting there like a bird or a bat or something." She waggled bright red fingernails. "Anyways, the driver stops the trolley, and they all hanged out the windows to watch until a policeman come along and shoots at it. Then it flaps away. She says it made a awful noise, like something dying."

Steve craned his neck to look around the room and overheard wisps of similar conversations. Some people even kept glancing at the windows, and a few actually started gathering up their things.

"But it's what you said. Remember?" Athena's voice grew louder. "There's always been too many deaths and disappearances out here. There must be a reason. Remember, you said . . . ?"

Movement across the room caught Steve's attention: Sims stood on a chair and, after several wobbling attempts, managed to unhook the painting that hung over the counter. He jumped down heavily, muttering, then stuck the picture of the Devil behind the counter before hobbling back to the stove where things were frying. A dark grease shadow lay where the painting had been; at its center, wormy laths showed through a hole in the crumbling plaster.

"She told me herself she had a big fight with him a couple days before he died. He even hit her, and she had to set that damn big dog of hers on him. Now he's dead, and she finds the body? If she makes a federal case out of this, who the hell's she think the prime suspect's gonna be?"

Pines whipped furiously past the car.

"Slow down. I'll bet Frank won't care much for this development. If they get a manhunt started, it'll really ruin your little business."

"Shit." Barry gritted his teeth, jerked the wheel. "We'll handle it," he said finally, flicking a butt out the window. "Things'll die down after while."

"You hope." He looked hard at his partner and didn't like what he saw. "I doubt the ambulance people will just let it drop."

"Well, then, maybe Frank's got some ideas about that." Barry shook with laughter. "Ideas that'll fix their wagon." The car swerved.

Uneasy, Steve watched him, puzzled.

By the time she'd left Doris—after an evening spent hanging around the hall—it had already grown quite dark.

She wondered what time it was as she slammed the car door and walked around to the back of the house. She only knew that it had to be late. She felt drained by anger and frustration, sick and furious with herself every time she thought of Barry. At least Steve had seemed more receptive. Or perhaps just more polite.

The darkness around the house seemed more solid than usual as she limped heavily up the porch stairs. Every light in the place blazed. She couldn't wait to see this month's electric bill.

A shriek assaulted her ears, and a heavy iron skillet gouged wood from the doorframe. "It's me! Pamela, stop it!" The thrown skillet rolled, thudding on the floor.

Pam cowered against the stove, one hand on her heart. "Oh

God, 'Thena. Oh, I'm so glad, oh God . . . I got so scared. I'm so glad you're home."

"Yeah, me too," she muttered as she locked the door.

"I kept hearing noises. Oh, 'Thena—all night long, I kept hearing noises. All alone here. An' things kept moving by themselves and all, I swear to God. By themselves. 'Thena, I heard footsteps outside. I knew it was them dogs coming to get me, or a monster. I know it was Lonny's ghost. I know it." She blinked red, swollen eyes. She hadn't gotten dressed today. When she'd seen it in the catalog, her nightgown had possessed the glamorous shimmer of a frost-covered window pane. Now it hung like an old curtain. "I asked the Ouija board an' it just kept on saying, 'danger in house danger.' Oh, 'Thena. An' then a rat got in the house, I swear to God, a big black wood rat. I tried to get it with the broom, but it ran behind the stove, an' then I didn't see it no more."

"All right, Pam. I'm home now. It's all right." Standing at the stove, she poured herself yet another cup of coffee and wondered if she'd ever sleep again. She marveled to think that just a few weeks ago she'd been worried about sleeping too much. "Could you do me a favor, Pamela? Could we just sit here and be quiet for a few minutes?"

A moth swung about the light globe on the ceiling.

"Oh, I'm so glad you're back. Oh, and you know what else? Y'know what Matty said while I was feeding him dinner?"

"Where is Matthew?"

"Oh, I put him to bed a while ago now. Anyhow, you know what he said? I said, 'Eat it all up an you'll grow up big and strong now,' an' he said, 'I don't wanna grow up!' Just like that. 'I don't wanna grow up!' Wasn't that a funny thing for him to say? I'm gonna push the table against the door now you're home. You think I should?"

She closed her eyes, shutting Pamela out, shutting herself in with bleak thoughts of Matthew's future. There were times when she didn't want him to grow up, either. If possible, she felt even more weary than before.

"An' look—he hit me today. I mean, he didn't do it on purpose or nothing, but look at that." She displayed a large bruise on her upper arm, already mottling from purple to green. "The dog ain't here. I'd like to know where the hell he goes at night. Matty gets all upset. An' those bad dreams he's been havin'. Why should he be havin' bad dreams about Chabwok all of a sudden? What's that? Oh, what's that?"

"It's just Dooley scratching at the door. Let him in, will you. Oh, never mind. I'll do it. Be quiet, Pam. I'll lock it again. Get in here, dog."

"Why should Matty be havin' bad—?"

"I don't know." She sat at the table. "What have you told him about Lonny?" She put her head in her hands. "No, not now. Please, Pamela, I'm so very tired. Could we talk about this some other . . . ?"

Terrible screams obliterated her words. They came from upstairs. The dog went wild. So did Pam. "Matty! Oh my baby! Oh my Matty! Oh God!"

Athena pushed past her, ignoring a twinge of pain in her leg as she took the stairs two at a time. She could hear Pam lumbering behind her, and the cries poured through her as she sprinted down the hallway.

"Not chains! Chabwok! No!"

Horrified, she paused on the attic stairs.

"Chabwok! Not the chains!"

She stood mesmerized. The voice was Matthew's yet somehow not. With a jarring thud, she was shoved to one side as Pamela thundered past. Picking herself up, she stumbled to the top of the narrow stairs and stood transfixed.

Pam had thrown herself on the boy's cot. "He's having a dream," she sobbed. "Oh, he's having a bad dream now. Oh Matty. Oh my baby." The boy's eyes stared vacantly as the woman rocked him in her fleshy arms. He almost looked dead. Then she saw the way his mouth trembled, the lips drawing back over the teeth, saliva running down his chin and neck.

Pamela wailed. As though an electric current had passed

through his body, he stiffened, limbs flailing. One of his arms struck Pamela across the chest and sent her tumbling in a heap to the floor.

"Grab him! Pamela, help me!" Athena leaped onto the bed. "Get hold of him!" She grappled with the thrashing boy, attempted to pin down his arms. "He's strong! Get up, Pamela, help me! Quick, give me something to put in his mouth. He's biting his tongue."

Blood frothed at the boy's lips, and Pam shrieked. "Oh God oh God oh my God oh Matty oh God oh!"

Athena yelled as his teeth clamped down on her fingers. She struggled with him, forced his mouth open. "That's it! Now quick, hold this arm down! Do it! Here, just sit on him!"

Swaying and trembling with each violent seizure, the two women struggled to control him while the springs of the old cot sang in loud protest.

Night insects fluttered and ticked against the window, and he found himself listening for the leathern beat of giant wings. An open can of beer in front of him, he just sat at the dining-room table and fought the sourness in his stomach. Then he put one hand on the telephone. Ring marks covered the table's dusty surface, and the handmade doily in the center had yellowed. His pipe rested in a cut-glass bowl, the red cinders slowly turning gray.

"Ambulance." She answered on the first ring. "Yeah, this is Doris. Hey, Steve, how you doing?" Her voice sounded odd, and he could picture her cradling the phone with her shoulder while she lit a cigarette. "No, she headed home a while ago, Steve. I'm here by myself, just drawing up the duty roster for next week. Should've done it earlier, but Athena needed to talk. What? Yeah, that's what I figured too. I'm not gonna let her work for a while. She can answer the phone or something. We've got a couple new people starting anyway. Listen, Steve, you didn't call to ask me about the rig. What can I do for you?"

"Right." He took a deep gulp of beer, the foam gurgling down his throat. "Doris?" He smashed the can and tossed it toward the overflowing wastebasket. "You saw Lonny. Right? I

mean, you examined the body and everything? What did it look
like to you? Hello?"

"Dogs," she said at last. "About the other one, the hard hat,
I don't know. But Lonny was all chewed up."

They listened to each other breathe.

"So?" she asked. "What do we do now?"

Saturday, August 8

"Goddamn middle of the night. Ain't even awake yet."

"You want some of this coffee? Duke's wife made it." A uniformed trooper passed around the thermos.

"Not enough sugar." Loosely grouped around the blue and white cars, nine troopers loitered just off the sand road. Nearby, their superior called questions into a radio.

One of the troopers gulped coffee out of the thermos lid, then spoke in a low voice. "How many guys they got out here?"

"Four other groups, I heard," his buddy replied. "Ten guys each." He hefted his special-issue shotgun. "When you think we're gonna get started?"

"Soon's it gets a little lighter, I guess."

He'd passed her mailbox ten minutes down the road. Now he gazed up at the astonishing house. Tunneled by termites, it tilted and sloped. He barely glanced at the green things sprouting through the back steps, barely noticed the patches of raw board warping in the sun. His footsteps, drumming across the porch, were echoed by hammerings from within the house. The screen door was off the hinges and leaning against the porch wall, so he knocked on the frame. The banging continued.

"Hullo?"

Athena stopped pounding and turned around in surprise. "Oh, hello." She smiled a bit awkwardly. "Steven. Almost didn't recognize you in civilian clothes." She set the hammer down on the table and brushed at her clothing. "I didn't hear you drive up."

"I went around to the front of the house." He stood self-consciously in the doorway, finding the kitchen dark after the glare. "I take it you've got some of the rooms shut."

"The floors are rotten. In fact, I'm surprised you didn't fall through the front porch." Brushing off plaster dust, she looked at him in confusion, wondering if she should understand his presence here. "Oh, I'm sorry. Can I get you some coffee? Come on in."

"No. I mean, no coffee, thank you, but I'll come in for a minute, maybe." He took a few hesitant steps into the kitchen. "What were you doing?"

She picked up the hammer again. "Some of the boards over the windows looked a little loose."

"That to keep something out or something in?" Startled by loud giggling, he spun around. A plump blonde with plastic barrettes in her hair loomed in the doorway. She held one hand over her mouth, her face going deep red at the sight of him.

"This is my sister-in-law, Pamela Monroe," said Athena with evident reluctance. "Pamela, this is Barry's partner." She peered out the back door. "Where's Matthew?"

"Well, hello now." Pam still giggled like a five-year-old, though the flesh around her eyes was swollen and bruised looking. "So nice to . . . We sure don't see too many people out here, 'cept for them pineys."

"Pamela, where's Matthew? I thought I told you to stay with him."

"He's over that way somewheres." Pam shrugged. "Playing with Chabwok."

"If you can't watch him, I want him inside. I have to leave soon anyway."

"Oh, but he's just right there." Complaining under her breath, Pam wandered back outside. "I'll get him."

"This is the wife of the man who was killed? She seems to be taking it okay. What did she say? Chabwok? What's that, an Indian name or something?"

" 'Thena, I just want to tell you one thing." Pam stuck her head back in the doorway. "If you want . . . I know you want me to watch Matty and all, but I just want to tell you this. I can't find Dooley anywheres, and he wasn't around for breakfast neither. That's all I wanted to tell you."

When she withdrew, he asked, "Is Dooley your dog?"

"More or less."

"Then you better find him and keep him in the house. That's why I wanted, I mean, the reason I stopped by was to tell you the state troopers are hunting the dogs."

"Oh?" Suddenly, she became aware of the condition of the kitchen. Dirty pots covered the stove, and newspapers were spread on the floor around the sink. To keep him from looking around, she stepped closer to him.

"Yeah." Confused, he backed away from her, out onto the porch. "They're down that direction now." He pointed toward the woods.

"That's something, anyway." Following him as far as the doorway, she raised one hand against the sunlight. "Or don't you believe me either?"

He shuffled his big feet. "Feels like you got another weak spot."

Silence.

"In the floor," he added, avoiding her eyes. "You should do something about it. Place could fall down."

"No such luck."

He let out a sigh. "I'm not sure what I believe anymore. I can't find what could connect those two deaths. Is it possible . . . ? Could your brother-in-law have been involved in an attempt to steal what looked like an abandoned car? An attempt that somehow ended up . . . ?"

She stared at him with sad disbelief.

"How long has this screen door been down like this? House must get full of bugs. Hinges look all right." Moving quickly, he dragged the door loudly across the porch, stood it upright. "Where's that hammer you had? Are there nails?" He pushed past her into the kitchen.

"Uh, yes . . . in that can . . . there. Wait, you don't have to . . ."

Smiling and humming, he started hammering the door back onto the old iron hinges. "Quite a house."

She gave a laugh. "Thanks. It's a little big and pretty ugly, but we hate it. You don't have to do that," she repeated over the banging. "I've been meaning to get to it myself for—"

"You really hate it?"

"I'm a city girl. It's like being buried alive out here. Really, you don't . . ." She stood and watched him. "Why do I get the feeling this is my cue to say how nice it is to have a man around the house?"

"What? Can't hear you."

Red flakes of rust settled from the screens. "You want to fix the shutters next?"

Hammering away, he ignored her. The full heat of summer beat at the edges of the porch. "Good solid cedar," he said between grunts, crouching to work at the lower hinge. "These old houses. Built to endure."

Reeling from the heat and the hypnotic pound of the hammer, she murmured, "Tell me about it."

His hair fell across his forehead like a golden claw, curling at the back where it grew long. Heat stinging his sweat-washed face, Matty stood rapt, one hand cupped about the slender pine. Cloud light, filtering through the trees, conveyed a greenish tinge to everything it bathed.

The insect had to be close to three inches long, and he thought it the fiercest, most evil-looking thing he'd ever beheld: the leering caricature of a face, the crablike pincers that reminded him of a crawdaddy. Especially, he stared at the cruel claws, then reflexively pulled away his hand. Seventeen years ago, years before his own birth, a rattling cloud had swarmed the woods, leaving their grubs beneath the loam, and now again it was their season, the air thick with the beat of transparent wings and with the urgent, rasping love song of the males.

Clinging tightly to the bark, the thing never moved.

He tapped it with one finger, and the carapace crackled like paper. Now he saw the jagged hole in the back, and he put his eye up close. Empty. Hollow. As though something had pecked through and eaten the insides. But, no, that wasn't it. . . .

And suddenly the boy understood.

The bug had climbed out of that hole in its own back. He pictured it, pliant and green, struggling to squirm from the prison of its old dried body. He could almost see that horrid face pressed against the translucent tightness, chewing its way free, giving birth to itself.

"Matty! Matty, where are you?"

"You there! Keep it moving. Spread out. Keep your formation."

"Damn." Out of earshot of their sergeant, one of the troopers kept up a steady stream of complaints. "Ain't seen a damn thing all day. Course there could be elephants out here for all we know, let alone a couple mutts."

"Duke bagged a deer," said his buddy. "Didn't ya hear?"

"Damn, it's hot." He tried to estimate the distance to the green-covered hills. As the horizon wavered, hazing toward invisibility, he strained his eyes, and vision blurred and flattened. One mile? Or five? He squinted from the blinding clouds. The sun looked enormous through the haze, bright hot only at its center. "When are we supposed to get a break anyway?"

Their uniforms darkened under their arms and down their backs.

"Not until we meet up with one of the other squads, I heard."

"Damn." The tiny round burrs that stuck tenaciously to clothing turned cruel where they touched flesh. The thorned seeds held life, waiting only to be carried to richer soil.

Their uniforms a dull gray through the scrub, the men trudged, shotguns held low. "Hey, what's that over there?"

Twenty yards away, the thicket had begun to rattle and shake. They took aim. Another trooper, battling vines that clung to his uniform, broke through the brush. "Don't shoot!" The newcomer saw the barrels pointed at him. "Don't shoot!"

"What the hell's going on over there?"

"Oh shit. Here we go," the first trooper muttered darkly as the sergeant charged toward them. "I wasn't gonna shoot him. What the hell's he coming this way for anyhow? Supposed to be going the other way."

Before anyone could speak, there came the first faint sound of gunshot, a rapid spattering through the trees, followed by a thunderous and sustained volley.

The Plymouth pulled up behind Doris's station wagon. Athena let the motor run. A look of horror and disbelief on her face, she just sat at the wheel, staring.

The rig—diagonally across the middle of the road—was a burned-out hull. It looked like nothing so much as some huge dead insect. Nothing remained of the ambulance hall but so much wreckage. Doris hadn't even looked around when the car pulled up. Her back to Athena, she stood amid the debris.

Slowly, Athena got out of the car and approached. An acrid stench hung heavily in the air. The two women only gazed into the rubble, and a buzzard wheeled high overhead.

The building's shell held thick soft mounds of ash and charred wood, among which rested half-recognizable objects: the blackened metal frame of the card table, a file-cabinet drawer. It looked as though, for a single moment, the summer had intensified. Here.

"No." Doris put out a hand to stop her. "Stay out here, honey. It's still hot, and what's left of the roof could come down easy." She kicked at a bit of wood. "Besides, there's no point in going in anyhow. Ain't this a bitch?"

"You went inside already, didn't you?"

Black with soot in places, she shook her head and smiled slightly. "You can still smell the kerosene."

"Does anybody else know?"

"Yeah, Larry and Jack showed up in the Jeep. They left a while ago, I guess. Larry mentioned something about going down the shore, some kind of a job or something. May as well, I guess."

"The police?" She gazed into the sooty ruins.

"Not yet. Anyway, what's the use? I guess we're out of business all right." She lit a cigarette, curling her hand around the match to shield it. "They didn't take much though, did they? Not that I can see anyway. Not even the tires. You have to wonder."

"Why would . . . ?" Suddenly, Athena raged. "We tried to help them! Why would they do this?"

"Pineys?" Doris shrugged, then tossed a bit of junk back into the rubble. "Don't let it bother you, kid. Sure was fun for a while though." She gave her an odd kind of smile. "Wasn't it?"

What am I going to do? Athena just sat in the car, knowing that at any moment, Pamela might discover she was back and descend with a million questions. She wanted to start the car and drive away again, drive anywhere. *What am I going to do now?* The question echoed in her mind with increased urgency, mingling with thoughts of all the days to come, all the nights when there would be nothing to occupy her, nothing, until finally she became like Pam, until finally . . .

She became aware of someone calling.

"Matty? Maaatty!" It came from the other side of the house. "Maaatty!"

Getting out of the car, she walked around back, the day heavy upon her.

"Matty!" There was no mistaking the alarm in that voice from the woods beyond the shed. "Matty, where are you? You be a good boy for Pammy. Okay? Matty, you come home now!"

Dappled and patterned with shadows, Ernie stood on the edge of the pines and stared at a cluster of dismal shacks. He hesitated.

At his feet, plants with furred leaves sagged against the ground, blasted by heat. Everywhere lay brown patches and fissures in the sand. Late afternoon sun fuzzed through the heat haze, and from the woods came a cicada's rattle, twitching faster and louder into one long, fading rasp. The day burned at the back of his neck, and his head throbbed.

Sweat glued the red hair to his forehead, and his eyes felt dried and crusted. A long smear of blood streaked his left arm.

The not-so-distant sound of gunfire decided him.

Dustily, he plodded toward the ramshackle buildings. The earth began to hum softly as he staggered. Droplets ran down his arm, fell from his curling fingers, leaving a trail of red dots on the sand.

"Yes, I'll hold." Athena held the phone to her ear, while Pam watched her, waiting for her to speak again. Beyond the doorway, the crickets had begun their deafening rattle.

Through the back door, gunfire still sounded, muted and faraway. Violent burning colors streaked the sky, deep purples and reds. Small stars emerged, and bats commenced the evening's hunt for flying insects.

"But where is he? Where could he be then?" Pam had nearly doubled over. "We looked everywhere. Did you get them yet?"

"Could you be still? Hello, operator? I'm trying to reach the state police. That number's busy. Could you—? Yes, it may be an emergency. No, I want the . . ."

Pamela shrieked.

A massive bundle in his arms, Matthew stood at the door. His face ran with grimy tears. Both he and his burden were covered with a mixture of fresh and drying blood.

Athena dropped the phone as the boy stepped unsteadily into the house. He panted, a shining line of bubbles at his mouth. He staggered, and she ran to him. "Matthew, give him to me. Let go. Let me take him. Matthew, give me the dog." She got the animal away from him, grunted and stumbled under the weight. "Jesus! Clear a space! I've got to put him down!" Almost dropping the beast, she marveled at the boy's strength.

"Oh, 'Thena, your blouse," Pam sobbed. "Blood, 'Thena, blood gettin' all over you." Her hysteria unabated, she pointed a trembling finger as she backed away from the dripping, unmoving animal. "No! Get it away! 'Thena, dogs! The dogs! Oh, my baby! Get it away! Get it away 'fore he gets rabies!"

Already, blood coated the floorboards, and almost slipping,

Athena set the dog down carefully. Dooley whined and squirmed feebly, eyes rolling in pain. "Matthew, are you hurt anywhere? Matthew, look at me. Does it hurt?" The bloody boy only stood still, breathing heavily and looking at the dog.

Pam had backed up against the wall. "Oh my baby oh my Matty." She made desperate, clawing grabs at the boy but kept snatching her hands away.

"It's all right. I don't think he's hurt. At least, I can't find anything. Just exhausted, I think." She turned back to the animal while Pamela began to fluster and shriek around the child.

The dog lay with its tongue hanging out, sides heaving.

"Oh, my God. Oh God, it's dead! Oh Matty, poor Dooley's dead!"

Athena got the first-aid kit from under the sink and crouched beside the animal. "Pamela, please, shut up." She poked at the bloody fur, prodding, examining the furry lips of a wound. Taking a bottle of peroxide out of the kit, she uncapped it and poured it over the gash with one hand, groping in the kit for a package of sterile gauze with the other. "Pamela, I need . . . Pamela, would you be quiet and listen? I need more peroxide. This stuff. Run upstairs to the bathroom. In the medicine cabinet there's a brown bottle. Just like this one. Bring it to me." She returned her attention to the dog. "Now, Pamela! I need it now."

Wringing her hands, Pam slowly wandered out of the room.

Something nudged Athena's arm. She turned to find the boy crouched beside her, fresh tears streaking the dirt on his face. He gazed into the eyes of his dog, eyes that had gone all milky.

She mopped blood with a small sponge and snipped away fur with a scissors. "It looks as though the bullet passed right through the shoulder muscle. I don't see any other holes." Soon she was red to the elbows. "It may not be as bad as it looks," she added more gently. "I can't feel any broken bones. He's in shock, Matthew." She watched the boy's face. "How did you find him?"

Matty only stared down at the scarcely moving dog, at the leaking mess of Dooley's back.

"Is this what you wanted, 'Thena?"

She snatched the bottle from Pam, emptied the contents over the animal. "Damn it. I wish we had better light in here."

Pam hovered uncertainly, still trembling a little and looking nauseated. She watched as Athena began to thread a needle. Matty sat on the cracked, worn floor beside his mother, closely observing everything she did, taking it all in.

"Do you want to help?"

"Oh God oh, 'Thena, I—"

"Not you. Matthew? You want to help?"

Gently, the boy reached out his hand and stroked the blood-matted tail.

"Put your finger here. Now push while I . . . no, not like . . . just enough to hold it so . . . That's it." Drawing the edges of the wound together, she pushed the needle through them.

Pam gasped, and Dooley whined a little. Fresh blood glistened in the folds of the boy's knuckles.

Sunday, August 9

The air hummed with flies. Straw covered the floor, and the hot interior held an overpowering stench of old feces. Only a few unshaded bulbs above the corroded cages diluted the gloom, and Steve peered into the shadows. Many of the pens appeared empty, though small shapes might have huddled in the corners. The clearly occupied ones contained a pathetic lot: an ancient raccoon, a turkey vulture, a barnyard goat.

The proprietor followed him into the barn. "Like I said, no charge for seeing the animals, Officer. Not for one of you guys." He smiled nervously at Steve's back. "I bought this place from a guy. Could of made a fortune, they'd only built that damn highway they was all talking about. Used to have a two-headed snake, but it got away."

"Any other animals ever escape from here?"

"Never." The old man's eyes slitted. "Why do you want to know? Somebody say something? You should of seen that snake with them two tongues, one in, other out. Wild."

The man looked scared, and Steve figured he probably had a still hidden somewhere nearby. "This the lot?"

Muttering to himself, the old man beckoned toward an open back door, and Steve strode out of the barn. Once outside the fetid shed, he spat, and some of the thick saliva clung to his lips. Raising his shoulder, he rubbed his mouth against his shirt. The air seemed cooler. Post and wire enclosures tilted against the buildings, and as his eyes adjusted to the sunlight, he spotted some chickens, a few overfed rabbits. And a wolf.

"Officer? Could you tell me exactly what you're looking for? Officer?"

Steve edged closer to the largest pen.

Full in the sunshine and scarcely breathing, the wolf sprawled in its own urine. The stench was primitive, intensely territorial. Steve pressed against the fence. The animal looked diseased. Insects crawled on it. Nose twitching, it unsteadily lifted its head, and the gummed slits of its eyes opened, barely focused on him. Those filmed eyes burned.

Matthew tilted the mug, pouring tepid broth into his cupped hand. Supporting the animal's head with his other hand, he held the broth to Dooley's mouth. The mongrel felt hot to him, even through the fur. With flickering movements no more powerful than the wings of a butterfly, the dog licked the broth. Even the tongue felt hot.

The steady lapping tickled his palm. Pam had made the broth, at his urging, and as he poured more of it into his hand, he could hear her outside, humming to herself as she scattered feed for the remaining hen. Unconsciously, he began to turn in the direction of her voice, and his eyes were drawn to the open back door.

Beyond the porch, beyond the yard, waited the ragged pines. He stared through the screen, and a rippling sensation traveled across his skin. *Chabwok.* The sick dog trembled. The boy tried to look away, but the call sounded in his mind again, forcefully, almost a command. *Chabwok.* Every day more powerful, each day wilder, more fearsome. Crouched on the kitchen floor, the boy resisted, shaking with the silent struggle. The broth trickled through his fingers.

The dog's breath felt damp on his hand, and Dooley whimpered. Turning back, the boy murmured soothingly and poured the last of the liquid into his hand. "Come on now," he coaxed. "Come on now finish it up like a good boy now finish it."

★ ★ ★

As the shadows of the pines grew longer and darker, they left the car on the shaggy road and walked toward the fire tower. "And you're the one's supposed to be so goddamn conscientious, too. I waited over a hour for you."

"Look, I'm sorry," repeated Steve. "I told you. There was something I wanted to check out. Unofficially."

"I'll bet. So, how was it?"

"What do you mean?"

"Come off it." Barry turned away. "And I frigging covered for you with Frank too."

"Barry, I don't know what you're talking about. Where do you think I went?"

Shooting him a suspicious glance, Barry kept griping. "Not bad enough we got to work on Sunday. We got to get started a hour late on top of it." One of the local fire watchers had disappeared, apparently just gone off without notifying anyone. With the heat wave continuing, they'd been instructed to periodically check his tower.

"Quit bitching, Barry."

"From now on, the only thing's gonna be working overtime is this. Sunday's the only time I get to spend with Cathy."

"I never noticed you being anxious to see your wife."

"Yeah? Well, I am now. Especially since that Jack's been sniffing around."

"You sure about that? It doesn't seem likely somehow."

"What, you gonna defend him now? Guess I ought to expect that from you." He glared. "Did you think 'Thena wouldn't tell me about you being over there the other day?"

"You've seen Athena?"

"I called her. Not that it's your goddamn business."

"Barry, I only went over there to—"

"I know what you went over there for. What, do you think I didn't know you was spying on us all them times? You sick bastard. What do you think 'Thena's going to say when I tell her about that?"

Steve turned his back to him, willing himself not to listen. He looked up. The ladder to the fire tower hung just above his head.

"Huh? What's the matter, boy?" Barry stopped ranting, and a sly look came onto his face. "Too high for you? You're the one supposed to be in such great shape. Are you too drunk? Big hero. Too drunk today? Let's see you climb it, boy. Let's see what kind of shape you're really in. After how many years of hitting the bottle? Ever since Anna died, you ain't been nothing but a drunk. So what you covered for me a couple times? You think that makes you a better cop than me? I been carrying this team. About time you remembered it. You don't do shit, just sit in the car and get loaded, and now you're hanging around 'Thena's. Big cop from the big city. You ain't nothing but dead weight. When I tell her about . . ."

Steve threw himself at the base of the ladder and climbed, pulling himself arm over arm, rung by rung away from the voice.

Halfway up, it became excruciating. A drop of sweat tickled his stomach. Barry was right. He was out of shape. Breathing hard, he pulled himself up another rung, his uniform suddenly drenched. The voice rose from below, taunting, ridiculing. The heat grew unbearable, and a nerve throbbed in his temple. Sweat got in his eyes, and it became hard to clutch the wet, slippery rungs. His arms trembled. Barry's voice surrounded him, but he could no longer make out the words, though vaguely he realized the tone had changed to one of alarm. Almost to the top, he heaved himself, and lights flashed in his brain.

The insistent voice seemed to be coming from another planet.

At last—thick breath bursting from his lungs—he muttered, "Yeah, yeah, I'm all right." He lay on his back on the platform. The shouting continued, and he turned on his side. "Quit yelling. I said I was all right." The air he drew seemed filtered through blood. "Just got sick for a minute."

"I'm coming up."

"No. Stay down there." He sat up, ashamed. Of course, Barry was right. All the years, all the drinking—the body in which he'd taken such pride had betrayed him. Or rather he'd betrayed it. Panting heavily, he got to his feet and leaned on the rail until his whirling vision steadied.

Distant pines clawed the horizon. Astonished, he turned around: an ocean of harsh green. A dim corner of his mind tried to estimate the acreage. Endless, it swept to the bristling sky, and except for the police car directly below, nothing man-made could be seen. Gradually, his breathing returned to normal.

"You okay up there? What the hell are you doing? I didn't mean what I said before. About Anna. You gonna make me drag myself up there?"

Steve started down. "Would you shut up already?" He expected to be shaking when he reached the bottom. Instead, with his feet on the ground, he felt strangely calm.

"Asshole! What, were you just goofing off up there? I thought you had a heart attack or something." Barry stomped toward the car.

After a moment, Steve followed, slowly at first, more acutely conscious of the woods than he'd ever been. Every muscle in his body ached. And it felt good. "You know," he said, catching up. "When I went over there, Athena said something about wanting to talk to us again, about what she saw that night." As though suddenly distracted, he stopped and looked away into the pines. "She mention it to you?"

"You ain't gonna start all that crazy shit again, I hope."

Steve didn't flinch from the sudden hate that blazed in his partner's eyes. He drew a deep breath.

"No, shut up," Barry cut off his response. "I don't want to hear about it. Anyway, you know what Frank said. He's the boss, and he told you to lay off—he don't want no more crazy talk."

"I'm pretty hot about that too. Seems to me, somebody must've gone to Frank with a story to get him to jump on the thing the way he did."

"Don't give me that," Barry sneered. "I know what you're hot about."

He only restrained himself with an effort. "Maybe it's true. Maybe you just don't care what happens out here. Some cop. Maybe all you care about is what the troopers might uncover. I got ears, Barry. How many hot cars has Frank Buzby got out here right now? You think I don't know who torched that place?"

"Big fucking deal! I don't see you resigning," he laughed. "What's your goddamn problem, Steve? Wouldn't she give you none when you went over there?"

At the last instant, Steve managed to pull the punch.

Even so, Barry staggered back against the car. His teeth turned red. Instantly, he started swinging. "You fucker!" His knee caught Steve in the groin.

Doubled over, Steve tried to dodge or block the worst of the blows. "Stop it!" Then the muscles of his back bulged and flattened as he struck. Quickly, efficiently, he pinned the heavier man against the car, twisting his arm behind him. "I said, knock it off!"

Barry grunted, seemed to relax, and Steve eased off. Barry drew his gun. Steve hit him in the gut. As Barry crumpled, gasping, Steve disarmed him . . . then just went wild.

Barry clung to Steve, tried to pull himself up as punches hammered into his stomach. His face turned to the sky.

Steve grabbed him by the throat and squeezed. The face clotted to a deep purple. Hands clawed wildly.

Steve threw him to the rough soil, and small infantile noises broke from Barry's open mouth. Steve bent and retrieved his partner's gun from where it had fallen.

Choking, Barry looked up. Their eyes met.

Steve turned away. He tossed the gun through the open window onto the backseat and got in.

Barry knew he'd never been closer to death. He'd seen it in Steve's eyes. The dust cloud from the car still settled, gagging him, as he lay in the dirt and waited for his breath to return. His throat hurt so bad he couldn't swallow. He rolled onto his side and curled up. The pain diminished, though the side of his face continued to throb. Finally able to rise, he brushed away some of the sand and stood, clenching and unclenching his fists. He peered down the road after the car.

That son of a bitch had wanted to kill him, Barry thought with something like admiration. Who would have guessed old Steve had it in him? Wondering how long it would be before

Steve came back, he massaged first his arm, then his throat. He knew Steve would come back soon as he cooled off. In the meantime, he was stuck out here. Nowhere to walk to. Not much chance of a ride. Staggering slightly, he turned and wandered toward the shade of the fire tower.

The cicadas had begun in the surrounding woods. Glinting red along their tops, fir trees began to sink into the gloom. Pacing around the tower, he winced and spat blood on the sand.

The last of the few patrons having left without her noticing, Athena sat alone in the diner. What remained of the daylight failed to penetrate the murky windows, and Sims never turned the lights on this early. To think she'd actually come here to cheer up.

At the grill, old Sims scraped grease into an iron trough with a spatula and glanced over at her. He wiped his hands on the apron.

"Want something else?" She jerked her head up. Sims looked down at her, yellow teeth gleaming in the poor light. His right hand held a steaming coffee server. "Some more?" She nodded, and he poured the stale coffee.

Suddenly, he laid his hand across her arm. "I just want you to know how much I always liked Wally, an how sorry I was to hear 'bout Lonny." His grip was trembling and clammy. "Some folks 'round here, they says things 'bout you, but I always stick up for you. Just the other day, I says to . . ."

He smelled dead, and the T-shirt was a horror. She nodded, trying to endure this politely. He stroked her arm with two fingers.

And then his words seemed to come to her from a long way off. Catching only snatches, hints of sound, she struggled to listen. ". . . nice girl . . . little getting use to is all . . ." The pressure pounded in her ears. *What's happening?* It throbbed behind her eyes. *What's happening to me?* The churning started low in her intestines and burst hotly upward like a flare. As she hunched over in the booth, Sims's voice rose thinly in shock and concern. Through her swirling agony, she sensed the physical world waver and ripple about her. Then the rending of her bowels ceased as suddenly as it had come, leaving behind no trace of nausea.

"Barry?" Steve looked around.

He'd gotten tired of honking the horn and had left the car door open and the motor running.

"Yo, Barry?" He walked around to the other side of the tower. Where could he be? He wondered if someone could have happened along and given him a ride. But he must have known Steve would come back for him.

The last of the twilight faded rapidly, and he stood under the tower, wondering what to do.

Something dark dripped onto his hand. And again. He looked up. He stared a long time, only slowly comprehending what he saw. An unraveled version of Barry dangled from the platform overhead.

Monday, August 10

He had to do something. Impotent and cold, the rage congealed in his gut. When Anna died, he'd been helpless. But he would do something about this. He would.

He had to.

But it wasn't his fault. Earth throbbed beneath the rhythmic beat of his tires, and he squirmed in denial. The pounding headache had returned, and he doubted now that it would ever leave. The woods retreated behind him, and as he drove, he dwelt on his visit to Barry's wife.

Barry's widow. He'd left her not half an hour ago. Poor Cathy. She'd seemed so glad to see him, glad to see anyone. Not that she'd cried—a numbness had claimed both their faces— but she'd kept saying her father would be over later. And she'd kept muttering something that sounded like "be all right—just need a little rest."

Poor Cathy. She shouldn't have been alone in that house. There was time enough to be alone.

"We used to try," she'd said. "But then we found out his— what do you call it?—his count was too low. That really bothered him. I think he would've made a good father. Was that the phone? My dad might call before he comes. Did Barry ever say anything to you? About me and Larry? You can tell me, Steve."

His mind wrenched away from the morning. *What happened?* Gears ground with a chattering whine as he shifted into the next lane. Did Barry climb that ladder trying to escape something? Was he dragged up there? Tires shrilled. *You're a cop—be a cop.* The car yawed. *Find out what killed your partner.* Roadside vegetable stands gave way to suburbs. *Do something about it.*

Houses with small garages and rectangular lawns began to dominate the coarse countryside, and soon these gave way to liquor shops and roadside adult bookstores that advertised LIVE NUDE SEX SHOWS. As opposed to dead, clothed ones, he wondered. There seemed to be a gas station every hundred yards or so. A sign pointed the way to a school for retarded adults. Traffic grew dense as he approached a strip mall, and still the pines ran in thin packs by the highway.

The way she'd carried on. Steve shook his head. Just as though she hadn't known what a two-timing louse Barry had been. He flinched at that—thinking ill of the dead. Thinking ill of someone he'd caused to be dead.

The inside of the battered Volkswagen smelled of beer and old sweat. No, the headache would never leave now.

He supposed at the very least he'd be fired, and he wondered if he'd be officially suspect in Barry's death. Buzby hadn't asked many questions yet, questions about where he'd been, about why Barry had been unarmed. But he would ask . . . and soon.

Flies battered the screen door from both sides, their bodies like black hailstones.

Athena stood in the doorway as an old woman might, one trembling hand against the screen. And dry-eyed, she watched as swallows swooped and darted through the yard.

The phone rang. Probably Doris again. She didn't move. She clutched a filthy cleaning rag in her hand and listened to the gentle stirring of the wind.

Flies pattered.

While his grieving daughter waited for his visit, Frank Buzby swaggered about the clearing in his cowboy boots. His sideburns were untrimmed and whitish, his face and neck sunburned a deep red. As always, he held himself with the self-conscious stance of an aging bodybuilder.

The lieutenant came over to speak to him again, and Frank made an effort to look solemn. The death of one of his officers—and his son-in-law, to boot—had made Frank the focus of a lot of official consideration, and he relished it. Several troopers milled about the fire tower, their voices drowned by the croaking barks of the bloodhounds. The dog handler restrained the beasts only with difficulty. The smallest hound, an ugly, bristling animal, whined loudly.

Suddenly the dogs fell silent. Then—given their head—they belled for the woods.

Shouting a gruff order, the lieutenant beckoned his men toward the pines, and Buzby followed.

The fire tower stood silent and abandoned. The blue-and-whites sat empty on the road. No one heard the call coming in over the car radio.

Through static, the voice of a rookie blabbered about having found a naked corpse staked on the ground. He begged for immediate assistance. ". . . badly decomposed . . . maggoty . . . can't even . . . what sex it . . ." A sound like choking mixed with the static.

"You mean you bought that blouse before you was married and it still fits?" Pam sounded more dismayed than astonished. After all, astonishing things had been happening lately: the kitchen was spotless, and Athena was all dressed up. Pam was getting used to surprises.

Sponging down the table for the third time in half an hour, Athena kept one eye on her sister-in-law. Pam had adjusted so well, so oddly well, to Lonny's death. Perhaps immersing herself in Athena's problems kept her mind off her own. In some ways, she seemed not to realize what had happened. Yet she could speak of it, had conducted herself surprisingly well at the hasty funeral in which her husband had been interred near his parents. But sometimes a look played across her face, almost a smile really, as if she thought all this just some private joke. Athena suspected Pam didn't actually know he was dead, didn't really understand it. It just hadn't hit her yet. After all, she remembered how long it had taken her to grasp it.

WALLACE MONROE. A headstone. BORN. DIED.

"'Thena, I just can't get used to your hair like—" Someone knocked. "What's that?" Pam grabbed the skillet. "Who's there?"

"Would you quit that?" Pausing to switch off the grumbling scanner, Athena went to the door.

"Hiya, honey. Are you all right? I brought doughnuts." Doris entered, carrying a white pastry bag. "You look great."

"I'm glad you could make it."

"Don't be silly." She tried to offer Pamela her condolences, but Pam's eyes remained fixed fearfully on the door. "Hey, 'Thena, what's the matter with the dog?"

In the corner, Dooley lay curled on an old piece of rug.

"No, Pamela. Leave it open. Let's get some air in here."

"Open? You want it open? But . . . but the mosquitoes and all."

"Steve fixed the screen, Pamela. Leave it." Turning, she saw Doris's raised eyebrows. "Troopers."

It took a minute. "Christ, you're kidding. Poor dog."

Athena flustered about the kitchen, self-consciously playing hostess.

"Yeah, thanks. I'd love a cup." Doris settled herself at the table. "I like the hairdo."

"You don't think it's too young for me? All I did was wash it and brush it out. You don't think it's weird of me to do it now?"

Sitting at the table, they listened to Pam slurp her sweet coffee. "Well," Pam said at last, "I got to go up and sit with Matty." Reluctantly, she deposited her cup in the newly scoured sink and left the room. They heard her go heavily up the stairs.

Doris touched Athena's arm. "Okay, honey. What's this about? Why were you so insistent about my coming over here tonight?"

"I should get a plate for the doughnuts."

The screen door opened, and Athena's face froze. Steve entered with a stack of books and papers.

"No, that's all right. I got them." He dropped the books on the table. "What happened here?"

"State troopers shot him," Doris answered. "Ain't that a bitch?"

He crouched by the injured dog and scratched the broad skull. Dooley sighed, tail thumping feebly on the floor.

"Am I allowed to ask what all this stuff is for?" Doris fingered the books, already guessing. "What do you think of her hair?"

"Uh . . . it looks . . . makes your face look . . . I never saw you so . . ."

"Sit down, Steve," Doris growled. "What did you do? Rob a bookstore?"

"Just about." He smiled thinly. "You should've seen me. I had to show my badge and bluster a lot to get so many out. Also, I think I'm involved with the librarian."

Doris laughed too loudly. Shaking her head, she watched him spread the books out in front of him, and suddenly she wanted desperately to avoid dealing with this.

"Well, you're here again, I see." Pam flitted in and made straight for Steve. "It's nice to have a cop around. That Barry always made us feel nice and safe, didn't he, 'Thena?" She played with the ribbons on her dress. "Don't the place look nice? Oh, 'Thena really cleaned in here today. All day long. I'm so glad her friends is here. I just come down to get a doughnut. For Matty." She broke a jelly doughnut in half and put one piece on a plate and the other in her mouth. She turned to leave, smiling at him with her cheeks bulging, then just stood, chewing. "I wanted to ask you something, 'Thena," she began, clearly wracking her brain. "I wanted to ask you . . . Matty's almost asleep. Do you want me to do the sheets tomorrow?"

"Where is your son?" Steve asked. "I never did get to see him."

"Pamela, could you and I talk about this later? We're rather busy just now."

"I didn't think you was busy." Looking skeptical and hurt, she shuffled out of the room. "I thought you was just having coffee."

They stared at the volumes on the table. "Well." Doris exhaled smoke and paged through the first book that came to hand. "Let's see what we've got here. *The Encyclopedia of American Folklore.* Say anything about the barrens? Barrens . . . barrens . . . nope. Wait. 'Barren ground—traditional—ground reserved for Satan's use.'"

Athena spoke. "Look up Jersey Devil."

Steve and Doris exchanged glances.

"Jersey Devil. Let's see now." Doris dragged deeply on her cigarette. "Nope. There's a Devil's River, Texas. Listen to this: 'Lobo, the Wolf Girl.'" She scanned it. "All about this naked chick who used to be seen doing things like devouring freshly killed goats in the company of two large wolves." She let the book fall closed. "Sounds yummy," she added, the facetious tone of her voice not matching the vaguely accusatory look she gave Steve.

"Do you suppose that's what we're dealing with?" asked Athena, her voice clear and fragile. "Someone . . . feral?"

"What?" Doris studied her face. "You mean like the—what do they call them?—the wolf children in India? I saw something about that in the paper once." Suddenly, she smiled. "So that's why we're here. We're monster hunting." Picking up another book, she examined the binding, but the title had worn away. She opened to the title page: *A History of the New Jersey Pine Barrens*, compiled by the Federal Writers Commission, copyright 1933. "This is a real gem." She paged through it. "There's a whole chapter on the barrens in New York and Pennsylvania. What's the matter, honey?"

"I only just remembered something. My grandmother used to talk about the Georgia pine barrens."

"So long as we're talking about the so-called Jersey Devil . . ." Steve cleared his throat, and the women turned to him. "I've got some notes here. I checked out all the different versions of the story. The mother is variously recorded as Jane Leeds

Johnson in 1735, and as a Mrs. Shrouds in 1855. I looked for anything that made sense, anything that might give us a lead." He squinted at the notebook and shrugged. "A lot of it's pretty crazy, and certain things vary with the telling, like about its being born with teeth, drawing blood with milk. I think we can discard that sort of thing as pure folklore. Still, the basics stay pretty much the same."

Doris stared at him. "Before we get too far into this, I'd just like to know why. I mean, you know that feeling you get when you're the only person on the bus who isn't communicating with a UFO? You start to wonder if you're the crazy one. I mean, are we really assuming the actual Jersey Devil is involved here?"

He told them about the starving woman who'd been picked up in the woods, and about the dead body found staked in the sand that morning. "I found myself recalling things Athena said." He kept his eyes on the table. "About there being a history of unsolved murders out here. Seems to me if we're going to find out what happened to—"

"Barry."

"What?"

"It was Barry," Athena told him. "He said that. Not me."

"So?" Doris set down the book she'd been holding. "What's the story? Exactly?"

"You've never heard it?" he asked.

"Let's hear your version."

"Well, let's see, near as I can figure, a deformed child was born to a woman in the pines. She apparently kept it hidden for years, locked up in a shuttered room. After her death, the child went berserk with hunger and took to making raids on the local farms."

"A star is born," muttered Doris.

"That's all really. The stories say he always escaped to the swamps. In time, mysterious raids on livestock, even the deaths of small children, always got attributed to him. Anyway, there's a lot of that sort of thing, stories about the Devil. The creature was even said to mutilate strong men." His face drained white as Doris sucked in her breath. He shuffled through papers.

"Go on," insisted Athena.

He didn't look up from the notes. "Eventually, any freakish child could be labeled another Jersey Devil. And in time, whenever campers disappeared, due to say a boating accident or something, it got blamed on the creature."

"Or the other way around."

"How do you mean?"

Athena's voice seemed to come from a long way off. "Whenever the creature took someone, they blamed it on a boating accident."

"What about Barry?" Doris asked.

"What . . . ?"

"Officially."

"Oh. They're saying it was dogs."

Doris choked out a laugh. "Climbing ladders?"

"This doesn't help. This is crazy." Athena sounded defeated. "Some poor starving goon running around the woods. What's that got to do with . . . with the horrible things that . . . ? First Lonny. Now Barry. It's getting closer. I can feel it. I've always felt it."

"I looked for details common to the different versions." Steve clutched the wad of notes. "You never know what's going to be important." And he stared at the papers with hard-eyed pain. "Most of the variations involve some sort of transformation as a major feature. Depending on who you listen to, Mrs. Leeds's little boy is reported to have grown a long tail, bat wings, hooves, antlers, or—"

"That's a dead end. Athena's right. It doesn't help. Malformed animals—we've all seen things out there, things that shouldn't be."

Athena tried to talk over her. "There's an image I can't get out of my mind. Something on top of Pamela's trailer, dogs all around it in the storm."

He shuffled papers, afraid of the look on Athena's face. "I found something that ties in with what you just said, Doris. Where . . . ? Here it is. A British soldier during the Revolutionary War—the researcher gives him the name of Kallikak—

fathered eight mentally defective children by various women in the barrens, then returned to England and sired three normal children." Putting down the notes, he wondered why Doris kept shaking her head at him.

"Maybe it's the vegetation." Doris stirred her coffee, then stubbed her cigarette out in a saucer. "What are those things?" She pointed to a pile of slick-looking papers.

"Newspaper and magazine articles mostly," he said, "some stuff from books. I must've gone through a hundred of them."

"Looks like you spent a fortune copying this." Doris flicked dismally through the pile. "Do we need to read it all?"

"For some of them, I just underlined a few things. Look, through 1840 and 1841—reports of strange tracks, and of screams heard in the woods. 'Again, posse unsuccessful,'" he read. "'Heavy losses of chickens and sheep.'"

"That could've been a bobcat," said Doris, lighting another cigarette. "Or a bear even."

He pushed the chipped ashtray toward her. "In 1858, near Hanover Iron Works . . ."

"What's wrong, Steve?"

"I don't know—I felt a chill. Maybe I shouldn't go on with this. Maybe we should stop here." He set the notes down on the table, drained his cup with one swallow. "We could still. Stop, I mean." He looked at the two of them, then down at the notes. "Like sane people. I get the feeling there's a border we're about to cross."

Athena got up and put on a fresh pot of coffee.

"Read the rest of it." It was Doris who finally spoke.

"Uh, Hanover Iron Works. 'Management has trouble with workers afraid of Devil and refusing to venture out of their tents.' Then in, let's see . . . I don't have to read all of this. The gist of it—time and again, we've got reports of laborers barricading themselves in their huts."

Athena stood at the stove, seemingly totally involved by the task of making coffee.

"It seems to come in waves. Fifty years later, we hit pay dirt."

Steve read on, his voice deep, without emphasis. "In 1909, between January 16 and January 23, there's literally thousands of sightings and incidents. All over Jersey, we have factories closing, schools closing. A theater in Camden closed. And, uh"—he squinted, trying to make out his own handwriting—"this is sort of confusing. We've got several accounts of local sheriffs emptying their guns into the woods. The mills in Gloucester and Hainsport shut their doors. People in Mount Ephraim refused to leave their homes even in broad daylight. There were full-scale hunts with dogs mounted in Burlington County, Columbus, Dunbarton, Haddonfield, Hedding . . ."

Doris emitted a low whistle.

". . . Kincora and Rancocas. There was a substantial bounty offered, and twice the militia was called out." He turned the page. "In 1927, we have two reports of stranded motorists threatened by 'something that stood upright like a man but without clothing and covered with fur.' Then, let's see now, that same year, following reports of what sounds a lot like a giant German shepherd, posses formed in both Woodston and West Orange. Oh, and this one I especially like, it's dated Thursday, November 22, 1951."

"The date of my birth, how nice," added Doris.

He ignored her. "It's from a Gibbstown paper, *The Chronicle*. A group of youngsters are playing in a tree house, when a ten-year-old points out the window and screams. . . ." He held up the paper and read. " 'The thing! It's staring at me with blood coming out of its face!' " The paper rattled. "Then, let's see . . . 'The boy fell to the floor and his body was wracked by spasms.' " He set the page down on the table. "I checked the files. Two days later, we have an unexplained disappearance in that area. But a search party only began beating the brush after numerous sightings of what's described either as 'a chunky man with a bestial face' or a 'half-man, half-beast.' Good, huh?"

"So what are we dealing with?" asked Doris. "Is it the missing link? Neanderthal man? Tell me. I can take it—I watch old movies."

Athena returned to the table, coffee spilling over the side of her trembling cup. "Oh, I'm sorry. Did anybody else want some?"

"Another bounty was offered," Steve droned on. "A few weeks later in Jackson Mills, several dogs were torn to pieces by 'sort of a wildcat, four feet tall . . . long . . . grayish.' Then things quiet down for a while, until—"

"Oh, that's enough! Let me see this." Doris snatched the notebook from him. "Your handwriting stinks." She glanced at the top page, then passed it to Athena.

She skimmed the list of dates.

1959: Wall Township, St. Trps arrest 30+ rifle-bearing "vigilantes" claim to be on track of creature.

1960: St. Police quell panic in Dorothy, NJ. Set traps & patrol w/rifles. Same in Sims Place, Jenkins Neck.

April 1966: Mullica River. Farm animals mangled and strewn about. Trps follow "humanlike" tracks deep into barrens before lose trail.

"She's right. Your handwriting is terrible. Is that all of it?"

A jumble of papers spread across the table. "That's about it, except for a couple dozen reports a year, mostly by vacationers."

"Reports?"

"Just sightings mostly—of something that sounds a whole lot like Lon Chaney, Jr. Then there's the poem of course."

"What poem?"

He pointed. She flipped the notebook and read the scrawl on the back.

When the moon stands over the cedars,
And the waters are hidden by fog,
Comes the cry of the witch's child,
And the Devil will rise from the bog.

"I couldn't think where I'd seen it before. Then it dawned on me—it's from that damned painting at the diner. Uh"—he looked around—"did you put more coffee on?"

"You say it comes in waves," began Doris. "Does that mean there's really a pattern? Let me see the dates again." She scanned. "You realize there's plenty of secondhand stuff, tracks, dead chickens, that sort of thing—even disappearances—but nothing you could really call evidence."

"You mean like an eyewitness report? Somebody left to talk about it afterwards? No, there isn't. Somehow I don't find that especially reassuring."

"Is it . . . God, I can't even say it." Athena put her cup down. "Is it a werewolf?"

Doris shuffled papers in embarrassment. "Look at the dates. It goes back . . . two and a half centuries. Well," she sighed, "we've certainly got enough books here. Let's see, here's a good one—cannibal clans on the Scottish moors. Check out the pictures. I crave that bearskin."

"I wasn't sure what might be relevant to the case, so I just grabbed everything."

Athena had been holding her fists close to her body. Now she relaxed slightly, comforted by the professional sound of that: relevant to the case. Listening to their voices, she sipped coffee and watched Doris's cigarette smoke fill the room.

"This book's about ghosts."

"Let me see that. I didn't mean to bring that one. Must've picked it up by accident."

"Great chapter headings. Look, honey. 'Haunted Places.' Not houses, mind you. 'Psychic Phenomena in America,' 'Poltergeist Activity and Pubescent Girls.' Is this dirty, I hope?"

Athena paged through volume after volume, her attention only partially focusing. Now that they were actually down to it, it all seemed so foolish, so fantastic. For over an hour, they all leafed through in relative silence, skimming indexes, peering at illustrations.

"Here's a good one," said Doris. "Did you know you could tell a vampire by the smell?"

"Matty's asleep finally." Pam wandered in. "Oh, are you still talking? What are you still talking about? Them pineys, I bet."

Athena opened another book. "Yes, we're still talking."

"Oh well, I'll just get some coffee and go in the other room then." Pam poured herself an inch of coffee, then filled her cup with milk and sugar, stirring it slowly and with some apparent difficulty.

Something thumped. Steve had opened a heavy tome. "I found this." He turned to a marked passage. "The librarian told me the author was supposed to be a famous warlock. He claims that lycanthropy—that's being a werewolf—that it's . . ."

Pam's eyes opened very wide.

". . . kind of a 'malevolent astral projection,' whatever that means." He kept his eyes on the page. "Apparently the person goes into a kind of trance, and his 'animal soul' is free to walk around."

"No mental projection tore those men apart," Doris muttered.

"He did it." Pam dropped her cup. Quickly, milky coffee found its way into the cracks between the worn floorboards.

"Pamela!"

"Oh! Oh, I'll get it, 'Thena." She grabbed a cloth off the sink and began to sop up the mess. "And you just cleaned in here too."

"No, it's all right." She got out of her chair. "Just leave it. Pamela, I'll get it."

Steve hadn't taken any notice of the accident. "I don't see why we're assuming that what we're looking for is a he."

"You saw the bodies," said Doris. "No woman did that."

"I don't know. When I was on the force in the city, I saw some pretty horrendous things."

"You're forgetting the semen on the body. It's a he."

"It's an it," said Athena.

Rag in hand, Pam crouched over the wet spot on the floor, listening with her mouth open.

"Yeah, I guess." Doris nodded. "It. Makes you think of cavemen huddled around a fire, seeing eyes out there in the dark. What?"

"No, it's nothing. Just a dream I had. Pamela, if you don't mind . . ."

"You mean I have to leave? You're kidding!"

"Please." Athena waited for her to exit, then turned back to the others. "Reading all this stuff, I don't know, it's just a feeling I get. I can't explain. Did either of you look through this one? It talks about central Europe and the plague. Think of them— isolated people with death all around, barricading themselves in their huts to keep out disease and wolves and vampires. And then, like what you talked about before, Steve—immigrant workers huddled in the pines. Pretty similar. Whatever it is, couldn't they have brought it with them?"

"You sound like an expert all of a sudden, honey."

"I guess without knowing it, I've been thinking about all this." She stopped. "Without knowing it. But do you think it's possible?"

"You mean something congenital?" Doris considered it. "What's that word again? Here it is—lycanthropy. Something in the genes maybe, waiting for the right combination . . ." They watched her mull it over. "Okay." Taking a drag on her cigarette, she sat up straight. "Okay, I'm starting to put something together, just hypothetical. But how's this sound? See that book there? The Indians of the north country are afraid of the bear men. In Europe in the Middle Ages, they had werewolves. What if it's all the same thing? See what I mean, 'Thena? Steve? Where's that article? Leopard men in Africa? Tiger people in Asia. We get identical legends in, look, China, Brazil, Hungary. Right? Always in blasted countryside, bleak mountains or swamps, barren ground. What if it's the same creature?" They nodded hesitantly, trying to follow. "Not a bear or a tiger anyhow. But something so terrible that the locals always interpret it as the animal they most fear."

"And here?"

"They called it the Devil."

He sighed. "That puts a hell of a dent on the whole idea of shape-shifters. It's what I just read. Have you seen this?"

"I glanced over it," Doris responded.

"It's about people who believe they can be trans . . . trans-mogrified."

"Trans-who?"

"Changed," Athena put in quietly.

"Could I see that?" Doris read in silence for a moment. "Of course, right down the page here, he completely contradicts himself. This bit—a man does something, something so horrid that he blames it on some monster or other he's dreamed up. Right? Because he couldn't have done it, obviously. Not a nice guy like him. Or else, if he did, he must've been changed into a beast somehow." She laughed sourly. "In which case, they'd go out and look for a witch to burn. I tell you, they always find a way to stick it to the woman." She tossed the book down. "Where's that other thing I was looking at a minute ago?"

"What?"

"You know, about certain kinds of psychos who completely block out what they've done from themselves, so they really don't even know they're doing it. Steve? Steve, what's the matter? You looked funny there for a minute."

"You know what? You know what?" From the doorway, Pam's words poured in a rushing babble. "At my ma's house, when my uncle Nim died, when I was just a little girl, one night I woke up, and I was real scared, and there he was, and he was just standing there, standing by my bed, and he had these real big eyes, and he just kept looking at me and looking at me. I was so scared. And his eyes was all strange like."

"How long have you been standing there?"

"And then one time when I was fooling around with the wee-gee board and I asked if anyone was there, remember, 'Thena? You was here. And it spelled out . . ."

The books lay in a disorderly heap. "So, is it a monster all the time?" Athena made her voice very loud, but her words barely got past the forlorn laugh that caught in her throat. "Or is it sometimes normal?"

"C'mon now, honeychile," Doris drawled. "Down home we all know the loup-garou looks human except during the full moon."

"It wasn't a full moon when I saw it," Athena told her.

"And then, child, he's all covered with hair, of course," she went on. "But there's one way to tell. Surefire. You only become a werewolf when one bites you. You catch it like rabies, and the bite never heals." Pam drew closer, and Doris played straight to her. "And the wound is supposed to drip blood in the presence of the next person you're going to kill."

"Do they kill everybody?" asked Pam in a small voice.

Steve went to the sink where he began rinsing out cups.

"Everybody except for witches." Doris crumpled the empty cigarette pack.

"You don't have to do that, Steve."

"There's supposed to be a strong sexual bond between witches and werewolves." Doris winked. "I'll just bet that's a real howl."

After a moment, Pam recognized this as a joke and giggled uncontrollably.

"That's enough of this for one night." Athena started gathering up the books and stacking them. "Pamela! If you could excuse us." Her voice struck like steel, and Pam sulked out of the room.

"So?" Stretching and yawning, Doris pushed away from the table. "How do we begin? Oh Christ, my leg fell asleep. Do we all get silver bullets or what?"

"I figure we'll use this house as a base of operations." He returned to the table. "If that's okay with Athena."

She nodded.

"Of course, we can't expect to find much in the way of evidence lying around in the woods," he continued. "What with the state cops tramping about with dogs, and all that rain."

Doris peered at the map he'd brought. "If those campers you told us about were supposed to be all the way over here . . . and the fire tower is way the hell over this way . . . I don't know but . . . could there be two of them?"

"Why stop at two?" Athena made a grim sort of chuckling noise. "Perhaps the woods are full of them."

"I think it's safe to say that the person or persons we're looking for cover a great deal of ground. I'll want to see the trailer," he added. "After that, we should start questioning all the people around here. Someone may have heard or seen something. As of today, I'm on indefinite leave of absence, so I . . . I'll . . . uh . . . have plenty of time." He stammered at the sight of the gratitude on Athena's face. "I'll call you tomorrow." Rising, he banged his knee on the table. "Both of you," he added hastily, picking up a stack of books. "I want to get started right away. I'm going to take this stuff home and look through it some more. Unless you want them, Athena?"

"I should get going too, honey, and let you get to bed. Big day tomorrow, apparently. Though I sure as hell ain't going to sleep too good tonight. C'mon, sport," she called to Steve as she headed for the door. "You sure you're all right, honey? Call me if you need anything. Have you got all the windows and everything locked? You're sure?" She pushed the screen door open against thick darkness. "Steve? You following me to the highway?"

"Good idea." But he remained with Athena a moment and dropped his voice to a whisper. "About Barry . . ."

"Don't. Please. I don't even know what I feel yet. I just can't believe he's gone. No, please, don't say anything."

He took something out of his pocket and placed it on the table. "Belonged to my wife." Then he hurried out the door.

"Night, honey." Doris's voice drifted back through the dark.

"Steven?" She could hear their footsteps fading on the gravel around the house, and she wanted to run after them but could only stare at the bracelet.

It was an antique, quite lovely really, but not the sort of thing she could ever wear, she thought. Designed of interlocking grape leaves, it lay there on the table like a sprig of some strange, tarnished plant. Puzzled by the gift, she picked it up, wondering what Steve's wife had been like.

Her blood went ice.

It was silver.

He drove slowly, the taillights of Doris's station wagon bright in his windshield.

But his mind was on something faraway. And long ago.

It could only be played at night, he remembered, and it had

been a very popular game, especially with the bigger kids, especially with the boys. All the kids would gather around a lamp-post to chose who'd be "It." Then, talking in hushed whispers, those not chosen would go up a "safe" alleyway where—giggling nervously—they'd count to a hundred, then trickle out in quiet groups.

And the game would begin.

As deep shadows poured across the block, loose, fearful waves of children would sweep along the tree-walled street. At times, the quiet would be broken by a laugh that was almost a scream. They were hunting the "werewolf."

In memory, the maple trees always swayed and whispered, dropping enormous blots of shadow over the sidewalk. A child could enter those blots and vanish. Was it hiding behind that car? On that porch? Sometimes they would disperse in screaming flurries. Sometimes they would search alone. And soon would come the time when the werewolf crept up behind some kid, and that kid would become a werewolf too . . . but no one else would know.

And that had been the beauty of the game.

He took his sweating hands off the wheel, wiped them on his pants. His high beams picked out pines, holding them until they whipped past to merge with other ghostly shapes.

When he was about nine years old, there had come a night when, all unknowing, he'd been the only kid left on the block who wasn't a werewolf, when suddenly all the other children had turned and grinned. . . .

Doris honked her horn at him, the sand road having run out. She honked again, in farewell, then turned her car onto the asphalt. He stared a long time at her diminishing lights. The paved road surged away in front of him, hard and straight.

Pam was finishing the doughnuts. "Anyways, you should see him, he's real handsome," she continued in a possessive whisper. "You know, real dark and tall. So Al rents him Lonny's old room. You know? Overtop the gin mill?" She sucked the sugar off her fingers with smacking sounds. "Course I ain't actually seen him myself yet. But I heard all about him and all. They say he's real strange."

Not listening, Athena sat across the table from her, examining the bracelet, turning it over and over in her hands.

"They say he was a camper, and he had a run-in with the dogs too. And his arm was all bleeding." Her eyes shone. "Like it been bit."

Tuesday, August 11

Wallowing in softness at the turns, the car crept along the shore road, while a radio voice, fuzzy with static, jabbered cheerfully on about the heat. Driving with one hand, Steve checked the map. Barely able to read the directions he'd scrawled in the margins, he decided Doris had been right about his handwriting. The flat sameness of the countryside became hypnotic. Pines drifted in the wind, coasted in the billowing grass.

Finally, after cruising the same stretch of road three times, he stopped the car. This had to be it. The people back at the last general store had been very specific. Getting out, he stepped over a low guardrail and struggled up a sandy hillock. Panting, he stood at the top.

Leeds Point. The name rang in his brain.

Nothing much of the shack remained. Below him, a scruffy line of dunes hemmed the salt marsh. At the far edge of the marsh slumped the remains of a crude structure, just a few charred timbers scattered about the tilting remnant of a corner post.

He stared down at it, the sea air stinging his eyes. Could this really be the original shack? It couldn't be reached without a rowboat, he now saw: floating vegetation had hidden the dark water. It could be the one. Or it could just be some old hut the locals liked pointing out to tourists. Did it really matter? If the Leeds house did still exist somewhere, it would be in similar condition. He hadn't expected to find anything here; yet he'd felt compelled to come.

Below him, beyond the shack, beyond the marsh, sandy hillocks humped down to the sea, a grayly wavering band from which sunlight glinted in liquid fragments.

"You okay, honey? You sound sort of groggy."

"The heat. And I didn't sleep."

"After last night, who did?"

"Hang on a second." Athena set the phone down while she poured another cup of coffee. "No, I haven't heard from him yet either, and I tried calling him again right after I talked to you the last time. I don't understand it. A whole morning wasted."

"Now you listen to me, honey. I'm going to come right over, but you are not to do anything until I get there. You understand me? I don't care how antsy you are to get started. Under no circumstances are you to go anywhere yourself. Especially if you're right about this guy. Hmm? No, I don't think we should call the police until we've talked to Steve."

"All right, Doris. You're probably right. . . . No . . . I'll wait for you. I promise."

Pam was playing with the Ouija board. "You're drinking more coffee, 'Thena? You'll never sleep." Pamela looked frowzier than usual today, and the hot kitchen reeked of bacon grease and unwashed breakfast dishes. "My name! Oh look, 'Thena! It spelled my name! See?"

"I still don't understand, Pamela." She set her cup down. "Why didn't you mention this man last night?"

"I tried to tell you! But you wouldn't listen. Nobody listens to me."

Claws scraped dully across the linoleum. Stiff legged and wobbly, Dooley paced into the room. Following, Matty stumbled into the kitchen.

He watched the dog drink, listened intently to the lapping. Suddenly, the boy jerked his head around. "I . . . d-ddooo you . . . ?" In the sunlight from the back door, his eyes glinted. ". . . know if . . . ?"

Athena cringed away from his stutter, from the unbearably jumbled syllables.

"W-Will it g-get like . . . ?" His face twisted with concentration as he forced himself to hold his mother's gaze. "Like when it gets all yella and thick like . . . will . . . ?"

"No, I don't think so." Amazed, she stared at him. "No, Matthew, I don't think it will get infected. I've been watching him pretty closely." She refilled the dog's water dish, the boy close beside her. "Though I think it's time he had his pill. Would you like to give it to him? Then later we can change the bandages again and put on more salve." She took a small brown bottle from the shelf—antibiotics left over from an illness of Matthew's—uncapped it and broke one of the pills in half. "Just do it the way I showed you. Put it on the back of his tongue and hold his mouth closed."

Taking the pill from her, the boy knelt by the dog. He took the animal's large head in his small hands, and the dog swallowed. "L-Like this?"

She blinked. "Yes, just like that." She watched while he stroked Dooley's head. He didn't look up at her again.

"It went to the *L*. That means love." Starry-eyed and completely absorbed, Pam prattled on about the Ouija board, about the handsome stranger in Lonny's old room.

Athena found herself standing by the door.

"You going out?" Pam asked.

"No." She pushed open the screen. "Perhaps just right outside. For some air. Keep Matthew in here. I don't want him out at all today."

"Matty? C'mere and play, baby. You want to talk to Chabwok?"

Letting the screen door slam behind her, Athena went quickly down the porch steps and stood, blinking at the dazzling afternoon. Behind her, shadows muffled the house, and she heard the murmur of Pam's voice. Even the insects had receded to a dull pitch, reiterative, everywhere and dying, spent. With some notion of watching for Doris, she went around the side of the house.

The headlights of the rust-eaten Plymouth glimmered almost invisibly in the daylight. "Damn!" She ran to the car, switched them off and tried to start the engine. "Damn damn damn."

The car didn't even cough. "Oh, great going!" She slammed the door. Now she was really stuck here. She stamped away from the car and stood by the side of the road, fidgeting. "Okay, Doris," she muttered to herself, "where are you?"

This man in town—he had to be the one. But what if he were gone by the time Doris and Steven got here? It seemed to her he might fade back into the woods as easily as he'd come, and there would be no way to trace him. But what could she do alone? Ask around at least, she thought. Find out if this were more nonsense of Pam's before sending the others involved. Maybe get a look at him at least? No, she had to wait for the others, but she couldn't just stand still.

The sky breathed down. Swatting away biting flies, she paced along the white-powdered road.

"Nobody ever listens to me." Pam sat at the table, her fingers on the old jelly glass that scratched across the board. "*W-I-C . . .*" She stopped, confused about the spelling of "witch." No longer moving from letter to letter, the jar hesitated a moment, then moved resolutely to the YES.

She smiled, remembering what Doris had said about the sex/magic bond between werewolves and witches. She held her arms close to her body, hugging herself. Everything she felt for her husband stirred somewhere deep within, mingling with a generalized misery and resentment that grew worse by the moment. "Them damn pineys. I'll show them. I'm better than they are. It said *L* for 'love.' Didn't I tell you?"

He knew it wasn't really him she was speaking to. Breathing in the deep, warm smell of her, an aroma of sweat and coffee and some indefinable sweetness, the boy sat close, watching her move the glass back and forth across the board.

She told herself she was going for a walk, just as far as the bridge, just to stretch her legs.

The woods looked very different this afternoon. She wasn't far from where she'd found Lonny. *Maybe I should visit the spot, lay a wreath or something.*

The water was low. Standing on the bridge, she gazed down: debris choked the stream. *Or perhaps I should just take a stroll over to Pamela's and check on things at the trailer.* The water looked thick and brown. *No one's been there since that morning.* But she didn't turn aside at Hanging Tree. Instead, she trudged along, fighting the sullen lethargy of the day. *It's stupid of me to come this far without a gun.* She climbed over singed-grass hillocks, and sand flew up dry in her face with the least breeze.

Even from a distance, the raw town had a beleaguered air, as though a great battle had been fought amid the rusting cars and the concentration of low buildings. Some trick of the light distorted everything. Heat seemed to press the shadows, condensing them till they bore no resemblance to the shapes that cast them. And she heard no dogs, unusual in itself. Something smoldered on the central garbage dump, leaving a thin haze through which the shacks and other structures seemed to waver, and the smell that washed across made her think of rancid glue—sweet, corrupt.

Nothing moved. *Where is everybody? And what do I do now?* The air seemed filled with floating particles, scented, invisible dust, which emanated not only from the houses but from the mean yards and rickety fences, an odor held in place by the pressing heat. *Should I go from door to door asking if anyone has seen a monster? I've got to make some move.* Taking a deep breath, she started forward. *We've waited too long.*

Constructed of dark cedar wood along more solid lines than any of its neighbors, the first house scarcely slouched at all. *Somebody has got to do something.* Approaching the mud-spattered door, she knocked solidly and had the impression of movement beyond the curtained windows. "Hello?" But no one came. Turning her back to the house, she looked around. Apparently, unoccupied shacks.

"What d'you want?"

Even as she spun around, she recognized the voice. *I should have remembered the house.*

"I know you. 'At daughter a mine's sended you over here, dinchee?"

Athena didn't believe she'd ever seen anyone so dirty. The dress looked as though it had been used as a cleaning rag. Hair trailed about the shoulders in gray-blonde strings, and the rough complexion lay buried beneath layers of old makeup. "Hello, Mrs. Stewart. I wonder if . . ."

"Miz." Opening the door farther, the woman spat on the step. "Miz Stewart. I ain't married."

"Yes. I wonder if you'd mind talking to me about your son-in-law Lonny. I wanted to ask if you'd seen or heard anything the night he was killed."

"She sended you round here to spy on me, dinchee? She wants my boy, donchee? She tried to get 'im from me before. You can tell 'er she ain't gonna get my kid." Lizzie's chubby eyes slitted as she appraised Athena. "You got a retard kid too, doncha?"

Athena took a step forward. Holding her breath against the rotten-meat smell of the house, she spoke forcefully. "The night Lonny was killed, did you . . . ?"

Lizzie stepped back, correctly assuming she would not be followed. "I don' know nothing. Shit. You seen my boy out dere?"

"No, actually I don't see anyone. Could you tell me where they all are?"

Lizzie just leered.

"I asked you a question." She leaned on the door. "Perhaps you'd rather I had some friends of mine come around and talk to you."

"Home. Behin' locked doors. Where da ya think everbody is?" The woman threw her weight against the door, slamming it. Metal rasped as the bolt slid home, but cursing penetrated the wood. ". . . gonna send 'er friends 'round . . . who da fuck she think she . . ."

A fine start—strong-arming old whores. She walked rapidly away from the house. *Maybe I should go back to the city and get a job with a collection agency.* She peered up the road. Doris was probably at the house by now. *When she sees I'm gone, she'll be after me like a shot. I could probably walk up the road and meet her.* The stench drifted from another direction now.

Let me just see what's burning. She followed the odor, not to the garbage dump, but toward the main cluster of buildings.

A boy sat in thin shade. The fumes from the still house out back surrounded him, thick and overpowering. *He looks like he's been sniffing glue.* She got to within a few feet of him before he so much as blinked.

She didn't recognize him. From beneath a battered fishing hat, fine, light hair trailed almost to the boy's shoulders. His face lacked color. Pale eyebrows and lashes faded into invisibility, and the whites of his eyes nearly matched the color of his flesh, his dilated pupils providing the only hints of darkness, like black specks floating in milk. The hum of flies was all around him.

The flaccid face moved. The boy's mouth twitched in what might have been a smile. Even his lips were nearly white.

"My name is Mrs. Monroe." While her eyes took in every detail of the boy's appearance, she listened to her words flow nervously together. She wasn't sure why she felt so nervous. Clearly, the boy presented no possible threat. Almost pretty, his blankly pubescent features had a waxen delicacy. "My brother-in-law used to live here. Did you know Lonny?" With sudden inspiration, she added, "I've come to get his things."

The boy stared past her. She followed his gaze to a lean cat that was slinking around the side of the house, and she began to wonder if the boy might be deaf. Then he tilted his face toward her.

There was nothing that could really be called an expression. The light seemed to sleep there in his eyes, reflected in bright silence. "L-Lonny?"

"Yes, that's right. Lonny." She waited, smiling encouragingly, but he only blinked. "Do you know where his things are? Are they in his room?" She stepped up onto the porch.

"His stuff?" He looked away from her. "Gone. Took it."

"Who took it?"

He gestured with one hand, vaguely indicating the town. His hand shook, and it troubled her to see an adolescent who trembled, palsied.

She couldn't think what else to say. The boy shyly refused to look up at her again, and his arms and legs seemed to quiver. She sensed his desire to run away. "Do you live here?" He might have nodded slightly in response, but she couldn't be sure. Turning from him, she surveyed the town: still no one around.

Suddenly realizing who he must be, she faced him again. The last time she'd seen the boy, he'd been fat and pimply. Now he looked almost wasted, as though from a long illness. "Is your father around someplace?" She looked about warily. She'd met Al once.

"N–Nobody's here."

She peered around back at the still house, a shed with no windows. Foul whitish vapor flowed steadily from a pipe chimney stuck through the roof. She turned back to the boy, who just kept staring at his feet. She moved closer to the door of the gin mill, peering into the gloom.

"Nobody?"

"J–Jus' Ernie. Sick in bed. Upstairs."

Jackpot. She beamed a smile at the boy, but her eyes went hard. "He's sick? What's wrong with him?" She stepped back to peer at the tiny second-story window. "Maybe I should go check on him?"

The door to the still house burst open. In a swirling cloud of steam, there emerged a pair of lurching forms, and the smoke cascaded about them, rising and suffusing into the bright haze of the sky. The door banged shut. One of the two men giggled, an unnaturally high-pitched sound. "Hey, lookit!"

The steam dissipated enough for her to get a look at them. The gangly one hung back, smiling broadly, but the heavyset blond man strutted toward her.

"Hey, girlie. D'you come out here lookin' fer a man?" He swayed a few feet away from her. "I knows yours's gone." He grinned back at the other one, who giggled again. "So you come lookin' for ole Wes?"

"Is that your name? Wes?" Resisting the impulse to punch him in the throat, she tried questioning him about Lonny, not very successfully. While she talked, the two men fell across the porch, squatting and then jumping up again like apes or drunken gargoyles.

"Yeah, I seen things, girlie." Wes's glance at his cohort elicited an appreciative laugh. "You wouldn't believe some a the things I seen."

She pointed toward the gin mill. "Do you know anything about the man upstairs?" She looked around. The boy had vanished.

"Ain't nobody in there. Who you been talkin' to? Marl? Can't pay no attention a him. Can't you tell he's crazy? You stupid or something?"

"Could you tell me why the town seems so deserted?"

Both men broke up. "Well," Wes gasped out. "When people starts to get et up by the Leeds Devil"—he collapsed with mirth—"everybody jus' naturally runs away!" Wiping at his eyes, and slapping his friend on the back, he sidled closer to her. "You jus' lucky Al ain't here." One leered, and the other smirked. "He'd eat chyou alive."

"Oh? Where is Mr. Spencer?"

The men stopped laughing and looked at each other. "I'm his man now Lonny's gone. 'Smy job takin' care a things 'round here when Al's . . . got business." He swayed, and his mouth twitched. "It don't like me. Tries to get in at night. I hear it. Hey, you was in dat—whazat thing? With the sick people and the rescue stuff, right? Maybe you kin help ole Manny here. Manny, what wuz you telling me 'bout yer little girl?"

"Yeah," said Manny Leek. "She bit by a spider, day 'fore yestiday. Head's all swole. Chile's mother say she got fever." Manny stumbled against her, and she shoved him back. "Wuz gonna get ole Mother Jenks to come, 'cept she ain't been 'round lately, an' 'er shacks all way down to . . ." He pointed off into the pines, and his legs seemed to buckle. She steadied him, grabbing hold of the gray length of rope that served as his belt. "Down that way. 'S far." He belched, smiled at her with toothless gums. The red birthmark all but covered one side of his face.

Brakes squealed as a car whooshed sand at the gin mill. The woman charged out of the car.

"Hi, Doris."

"You okay?"

Hastily, she began trying to explain the situation. When she got as far as the little girl, Doris drew her aside. "So what do you want to do? You want to check on this kid? I've got my first-aid kit in the car."

"The child may need help," she whispered, nodding to the men who slouched a few feet away. "I haven't been able to get anything out of anybody. But if we go to someone's home, I mean really get in, maybe they'll talk more freely."

Manny seemed to go falling-down drunk all at once. Wincing at the smell, they helped him into the backseat while Wes stood watching. "Yeah, the two a you do 'im," Wes said with approval. "That's right." He waved a grease black hand. "You both do 'im."

She slammed the back door and went up front to sit with Doris. A deer rifle leaned across the front seat.

"Is it this way?" Doris looked back at where Manny sprawled. Barely conscious, he smiled, nodding, and Doris turned furiously to Athena. "Do you smell him? Christ, I'm going to have to fumigate. Hey, fella, my upholstery isn't getting your clothes dirty, is it? Damn it, 'Thena! You were supposed to wait for me."

She didn't respond, held silent by the sight of the rifle.

"Why the hell can't you do what I tell you? I specifically . . . Yeah? What the hell are you mousing around about back there? This way? Good, rosebud, you can pass out again now. Oh Christ, what a stink! What did he do, die back there?" She wrestled with the wheel, the car rolling too fast across lumpy sand. "You think you're going to get information from him? Go ahead. Question him. This I've got to hear."

Athena stared at her a moment, then turned around in her seat. "The night Lonny got killed, you remember? The night of the storm? Did you see anything at all unusual?"

By now, his face slack, Manny didn't appear even to realize he was being spoken to.

Doris snorted. "We want to find a monster, so what do we

do? We open a taxi service for the sobriety impaired. Makes perfect sense. You suppose this is the direction he meant? Ask chatterbox. Is this the way?"

Leek snored. The road had become little more than a rough trail, then vanished altogether, and the car bounced across the littered, overgrown field.

"This shit is for the birds." The car took an especially bad bump. "You know that, don't you?"

"Doris . . ."

"That's got to be it." She stopped the car. "No telling what's in those weeds. I'd hate to get stuck out here. Better walk the rest of the way. Or we'll walk. He'll stagger. Christ, look at that place. Hard to believe people live in it."

From the house, Matthew watched as Pam danced around the shed. She'd forgotten about him.

Coarse weeds lashed at her ankles, leaving faint pink lines on her plump flesh, but she didn't seem to notice. The silver bracelet she'd taken from Athena's room clinked with every step. With the plastic barrettes left off for once, her hair blew in a blonde tangle about her face, nearly concealing the angry-looking blemish. She held a short knife.

The dry remnant of a distant storm stirred the heavy summer air, and wildflowers bent before it. She called out, her voice a gentle clucking full of terms of endearment. Soft white feathers ruffling in the wind, the hen fled through the sharp grass.

Pam lunged for it and missed, going down on one knee, clutching earth. The chicken flapped in panic as it weaved toward the gently swaying woods.

Inside, the shack reeked, and ancient, soiled newspapers covered the floor. "Best ins'lation inna world," claimed Manny. The half-dozen children stared at them like silent savages.

The pregnant woman never spoke either, just glared at Manny, and the sight of her stunned Athena. She looked as though she'd never been out in the sun, the knotted lips and grub-colored flesh nearly translucent and shadowed with blue. Her face sported the characteristic Munro's Furnace birthmark, the tissue swollen with blood. In the bad light, her eyes appeared a deep pink.

Even the flies had stopped moving in the heat.

"What do you think?" Doris whispered, nodding toward the children. "Hookworm?"

"Dis Molly over here," said Manny, waving at something in the farthest corner, near a potbellied stove. As he staggered toward a wooden crate, the woman suddenly tried to head him off. Casually, he struck her across the face with his fist, and she clawed at him. Without giving her another look, he got a jar from under the crate and drank from it. Athena couldn't look away, convinced the woman would hurl herself on his back like a wildcat.

" 'Smy booze."

He ignored her.

Doris cursed under her breath, and Athena moved toward her, then recoiled slightly from the stench. Doris waved her away, trying to keep her from the dark corner. "See if you can prop that door open with something. Get some air in here. And some light. That lamp's empty."

The other children still gaped, and the tallest boy bolted out the door as she approached.

She returned to Doris and gasped. The child on the soiled cot had a head bloated to twice normal size. "What . . . ? Oh God. What sort of spider bite . . . ?"

The face turned toward the voice, almost, and she realized the child's deformity: there were no eyes, nor any place for eyes. Sounds came from writhing lips, sounds that formed no words. Quietly, Athena began to tremble, feeling ashamed in front of Doris.

She hacked the head off the still-twitching bird, and crimson spurted down the feathers.

Brown leaves leaped from the pile she'd made and skittered across the yard. With red hands, Pam smeared blood on her forehead and drew marks on the ground.

She chanted in a whining monotone, and the wind blew her words away. She had a hard time lighting the kitchen matches because the striker got sticky, but at last one sputtered into silent flame. Leaves shriveled. Her hair got in her eyes as smoke swirled up. Faster and faster, she swayed, barefoot, loosening her clothing.

". . . witch . . . the man and blood on his hand . . . love, it said . . . hear me . . ."

Bitter smoke rode the wind back to the house, and Dooley sniffed excitedly at the screen, then growled a little. Lying beside the dog, Matty sprawled in the doorway.

The boy's body shook with a seizure. ". . . n . . . nn . . . nnnn . . ." He raised one hand and clawed at the screen. "St-Stop!" He stared with eyes that no longer saw the woman who faced the pines with open arms.

"Your name's Molly? That's a pretty name, that is. My name is Doris. I just want to look at your arm now. That a girl." She turned to Athena. "Watch this cat, honey."

From under the cot came a rabid yowling, and Doris held herself warily, ready to leap away. On the floor by the bed, a pile of unlicked kittens squirmed blindly on an old shirt. Athena's eyes grew accustomed to the gloom. A couple of the kittens looked stiff, but one of them lifted a trembling head to hiss, exposing tiny, sharp milk teeth. From across the room, the Leek woman stared with passive malignity.

Manny approached, gesturing with the whiskey jar. "Cat don't wanna nurse 'em. Born wi' teeth."

"You're blocking the light." Shaking her head, Doris got up from the cot. "Excuse me, honey." She brushed past Athena and approached the child's mother as Manny sprawled into the only intact chair and instantly appeared to become insensible, though his eyes remained open. "Any vomiting? Shortness of breath?"

Her expression full of spite and almost animal shyness, the woman didn't respond.

"I'll try one more time," Doris muttered. "Has the child ever been to a doctor?"

Visibly calculating, the woman watched Doris for a long

moment. "Saw doctor wonst. Said we hadda keep 'er. Kin you
get 'er inna place?"

Athena stood over the cot, one hand outstretched as though
to stroke the drowsing girl.

"That's it. I give up. There's nothing we can do here, honey."

"But . . ."

"Come on now." She took her arm. "Come away." Moments
later, they stood outside in the clean air. "I'd be willing to bet
those two didn't have to get married to share the same last
name." Doris still carried the unopened first-aid kit. "Christ,
what a hellhole."

Athena cast one last glance back into the dim, dirty cave of a
shack. "You've seen worse though, haven't you?" They pushed
through waist-high weeds toward the car.

"Yeah, but never with you. Don't feel bad, honey. There's
nothing anybody could do about what's wrong with that kid."

A breeze sprang up; yet the air grew corrupt.

"Look. Over there." Athena ran a few steps, then pointed.
"What are those red things? See them?" She raced ahead.

"Honey, where you going?" Dismayed, Doris hurried after
her. "Wait up. You got to be careful running around out here."
She pushed through reeds, rounding a small knoll. "'Thena?"

Deep in the undergrowth, Athena stood before a massive lump.

"'Thena, what . . . ?" Dimly, Doris realized they were surrounded by the lumps, rust-red and corroded, sinking in the
earth and vines and burned grasses.

"They're tombstones." Athena's hair caught and held the sun.
"Iron tombstones." Her fingers traced carvings in the crude
block: an angel with a death's-head. "Look, you can just make
out the dates. 'Born 1809 died 1824.' But there's no name left on
this one," she murmured. "No name at all. Doris? Why does that
make me feel like a ghost, Doris?"

She heard a damp thud and violent movement. Behind her,
Doris moaned with sudden fear and agony.

It had her by the feet.

Brambles tore at her legs, and a red furrow oozed from abdomen to ribboned throat. A smear of blood covered her slack face, and the wetness clotted on her trailing hair.

It dragged her deeper into the brush.

Both women grunted. "We make a fine sight." She leaned heavily on Athena's arm. "Both of us . . ."

"Yes," Athena finished for her. "Talk about the blind leading the blind." Helping her up the back steps, she held the screen door open while Doris hopped painfully over the threshold.

"Oh good Christ!" Horrified, Doris grabbed onto the doorframe. "I almost tripped over him."

Staring blankly, the boy lay on the floor planks.

Athena crouched beside him and shouted, "Pamela!"

"What's the matter with him? 'Thena?"

"Matthew, can you hear me? Can't you get up? Pamela! Where are you? No," she said as Doris moved to help, "no, I've got him. Can you make it to a chair?"

The boy blinked, and his throat made gulping motions. The dog limped in from the next room.

"I'm okay. You take care of him. He's all right, isn't he?" She had a sudden insight and asked, "This has happened before? How often does he get like this?" When Athena didn't answer, Doris hobbled across the kitchen and eased herself into a chair. "Christ. Damn stupid thing to do. Running around in the damned woods when we knew there'd been God knows how many troopers out there setting traps just the other day." She grunted with pain as she raised her right foot to examine Athena's field bandaging. "Well, if you've got to injure yourself, I suppose it's just as well to do it with a first-aid kit in your hand. Talk about being prepared." She gritted her teeth against a spasm of pain. "Is he okay?"

Athena started toward the porch to call Pam again, then turned back. She gathered up the boy in her arms and heaved just as the phone began to ring. Breathing hard, she stood there, staring at the wall phone.

"Hell." Doris stretched, reaching for the phone. "Hell." She got out of the chair and dragged herself to it. "Hello? Steve, is that you? About time."

Athena carried the boy out of the kitchen. As she staggered up the stairs, she listened to her friend's voice fade behind her.

"You better get your ass over here, boy. On the double."

She stumbled. The boy was dead weight, his face innocent, helpless. She tried to remember the last time she'd held him in her arms and couldn't. She could, however, remember the first time. Vividly. *Don't go too maternal all at once, girl. There'll be a re-action.* She heaved up against the banister to ease the pressure on her arms. *Besides, who are you kidding? You didn't just carry him out of that kitchen to help him.* She thought about setting him down for a moment. *You just didn't want Doris to see.*

At last, reaching the top, she hugged him closer.

Doris hung up the phone and limped back to her seat. "We both look pretty banged up, kiddo." Bending from the chair, she scratched Dooley between the ears. The dog promptly curled up under the table.

Athena returned. "Let's see the foot."

"How's the boy?"

"I put him on my bed. He's as . . . as well as can be expected." She dragged out her own kit, getting scissors and bandages. "I don't know what to do here. I mean, I should take you to the hospital, but I can't leave Matthew alone and Pamela doesn't seem to be around."

"It's okay. Steve is on his way."

"Not such a bad job of wrapping, if I do say so myself." Her voice strained toward cheerfulness. "I only want to check this dressing." She began to snip away at the bloody gauze. "Get it cleaned up better."

Doris grunted and watched her face. Athena's lips moved as she worked. "Who you talking to, honey?"

"Huh? Oh. I was just wondering how long he was lying on the floor like that." Rebandaging the foot, she looked up. "Did you see me back there? Doesn't it make you laugh? How concerned I was that the little girl wasn't being taken care of properly. Wasn't I funny?" She had to put down the bandages. "I'm no better than my own . . ."

"Yeah, honey. We all grow up like our mothers. Don't let it get to you."

She looked away to stare out the back door. "And now it's my fault that you're hurt." The edge of a red sun just touched the pines.

"Don't be silly."

"It is. All my fault. If I hadn't gone running off like that . . . if I'd only let Lonny and Pam have the house . . ."

"Honey . . ."

"You still can't wiggle the toes, can you? I don't think it's broken, but maybe the tendon . . . Doris? Why don't you come stay here for a while? Now that the rig's gone . . . I mean, just till you're better." She rubbed Doris's leg. "I could use some-body around here. Pam's not much company for me, and she's not very responsible. It would be perfect."

Something happened behind Doris's face.

"What's wrong?"

"I, uh, I don't know, honey, I'll have to think about . . . uh . . ."

"You're afraid of being trapped out here, aren't you? And crippled. You're afraid of being like me now."

"Don't talk crazy. I just, uh, just don't want to be a bother, that's all." She groaned. "Where's that goddamn Steve? My foot's killing me." Hoisting herself up, she hobbled across the kitchen to collapse in another chair. "What's taking him so long? I'm probably going to get tetanus as it is. I think I can feel my jaw tightening already."

"Shut up, Doris."

"That's what I'm afraid of."

They drove away in Steve's car, leaving Doris's station wagon behind.

For a long while after she could no longer hear the car, Athena remained standing by the back door. Finally, she closed it and drew the bolt against the night. There was still no sign of Pam, and the last time she'd checked on Matthew, he'd been in a deep sleep. She moved about the kitchen, mechanically going through the motions of straightening up. Dumping cups in the sink, she spotted a sheet of paper stuck behind the dishes and, pulling it out, shook grains of sugar off it.

It was one of Steve's Xeroxed sheets, an old newspaper article, very old, from before any of them were born, an editorial ridiculing the superstitious pineys. A drawing at the top depicted a faintly kangaroo-like creature, something like an upright jackass with wings. The caption described it as Jabberwocky, and her eyes wandered down the page. In a facetious tone, the article claimed that P. T. Barnum had offered $100,000 for the capture of the Jersey Devil "for exhibition purposes."

A joke. The paper still in her hand, she wandered into the living room. *It's all just a joke.* She pulled aside a curtain and peered between two of the planks she'd nailed up. Warped and pitted window glass distorted the moon's sheen.

Finally acknowledging her exhaustion, she collapsed into the armchair. *Where could Pam be?* The thought caused a crawling apprehension at the back of her neck. *She wouldn't have gone back to the trailer. Not alone.* She rubbed her eyes. *Maybe I should ask the Ouija board.* She yawned, sank deeper into the chair. *I should make more coffee.* The room waved and receded. *What a cliché. On the edge of sleep. And I could, could just tumble off.* Her thoughts whirled to Matthew, to Chabwok. *It's all some horrible farce. Doris hurt. My fault. Everyone dies . . . everyone around me . . . Granny Lee . . . Wallace . . . Lonny . . . Barry . . . Where's Pam?* She sat for a long time, her thoughts increasingly groggy and tortured. *Around me. Circling . . . circling . . . closing in on me.* The paper fell from her hand. *Beware the Jabberwok, my son.* She heard the words as clearly as if they'd been spoken aloud.

And she jerked awake.

Pulling herself out of the armchair, she limped heavily into the kitchen and switched on the light. She stood before the massive basement door and turned the old iron key with a harsh scraping noise. The door creaked open.

She looked up at the clutter of objects on the shelf: ancient paint cans, aerosol sprays with unreadable labels, motor oil. Pocketing the key, she pulled down the dusty kerosene lamp and heard the gurgle of fuel. While she took matches from the stove, a spider sank from the lamp and hurried across the table.

The lamp sputtered and smoked, then began to burn steadily, and she replaced the glass, ignoring the soot that got on her hands. Run through by a curving crack, one side of the lamp's chimney was blackened, marred by greasy fingerprints. *Pamela's fingerprints.* She took a deep breath.

Holding the lantern out before her, she passed slowly down the cellar stairs into the depths of the house. On the crack-veined wall, the rocking light revealed only a thick layer of dust on plaster and slats.

Uneven strands of cobweb melted across her arm as her shoes scuffed at the rough floor. Monstrous shadows swung about her as she moved forward, and the smell of wet coal hung in the dampness. Granny Lee's trunk lay far in the back, boxes stacked all around it. She set the lantern down, and the swirls of the lamp glass made concentric patterns on the floor.

Mice stirred as she shifted boxes. Taking hold of the handles, she heaved the chest forward a bit, clearing the way as she pulled. The hinges stuck at first, then the top opened soundlessly.

She brought the lamp closer and held it above the trunk. Her hand went to the old shawl on top. She sighed and held the fabric close. It smelled of dust and age and lilac. Perching the lamp on a box, she rummaged deeper, while flights of dust rose. One by one, she handled the bits of bric-a-brac, the framed diploma, the family album, a shoe box marked DOCUMENTS. Underneath it all lay the book.

It was a volume of stories and verse for children, and by the dim glow, she leafed through it, scarcely seeing the faded illustrations, truly seeing only her memories of them. Parchment crumbs and clots of dust flaked down. Expanded from the dampness, the rough-cut pages felt thick, the paper fuzzy at her fingertips. The book was yellowed and cracked, but her memories were soft and deep. She paged past stories of treasures and handsome princes, through fairy tales with grotesque drawings of trolls and witches, then past selections from Mother Goose and the Brothers Grimm. At last, she found the Lewis Carroll poem, and her lips softly formed the words.

" 'Beware the Jabberwok, my son.' "

She savored the soothing whisper of her own voice. Almost, she seemed to comprehend the nonsense words, which for the first time appeared to mask some underlying reality.

" 'The claws that catch, the jaws that bite.' "

Irresistibly, an image formed in her mind, an image of something that hovered just out of sight above the pines, something that played with Matthew when he was all alone. As she crouched on the grimy basement floor, she recalled reading this poem to her baby, her bright baby, much too young to understand.

She turned the page, and a sound choked in her throat: the monster—the famous Tenniel illustration. Horrible and bug-eyed, the creature tore at her from the page—the flapping wings, the feeding tendrils, the reptilian tail.

Behind her, the basement door swung shut, and a slithering sound shifted on the stairs. The book dropped. Unsteadily, she stood and slowly raised the lantern. The light didn't quite reach. "Who's there?"

Bare feet padded on the stairs. "Pammy's dead."

Looking at the bloodless face, she felt sickened.

"Chabwok got her . . . blood . . . coming . . ." The boy spoke in a dulled voice. "He's coming."

"No, Matthew, it's all right. Stay there. Don't come down in your bare feet." Going to him, she tried to turn him around and lead him back up the steps.

The floorboards above their heads vibrated as though from an explosion.

"Chabwok . . . killed . . . Pammy."

She froze. Instinctively, she stretched out a hand; the boy's shoulder felt rigid as wood.

Overhead, something growled, breathing down through the boards.

"No!" She tripped, almost dropping the lantern, caught herself on the banister. *The thing! It's in the house. The thing from the woods!*

Her reeling brain tried to interpret what she heard. "Listen . . . it's going upstairs," she hissed. "Don't make a sound."

There came animal cries—more felt in the skull than heard—a snarling, rampaging fury. Groping toward the door, she pressed close, trying to make out exactly where the noise was coming from. *My room?*

Sudden silence.

Doris's rifle is just outside in her car. Her hand touched the doorknob. Listening, she turned the knob slowly. Her muscles tensed with a dull nausea as she opened the door an inch. *If I can move fast enough . . .*

"Don't . . . try. H-He knows . . ." Behind her, Matthew spoke clearly. ". . . hears me, hears in my head, knows where we . . . coming now."

The ceiling rafters shook, and dust sifted.

"Coming down."

Thunder drummed through the walls.

"Down here."

She pulled the door shut. "The key!" A cry of fear spurted from her as she thrust her hand in her pocket. "Where did I . . . ?"

She found it, fumbled it into the lock.

The door thundered and shook, gritty cinders raining down on their heads. The key fell out and rattled down the stairs. She stepped back, grabbing the boy. The door leaped in its frame.

"It won't hold!" she shouted over the roaring. "Oh God, it won't hold!" Letting go of the boy, she scrambled back to the landing and reached for the shelf. *It's gotten stronger!* She stood with her back to the door, and it slammed against her spine. *Stronger than before!* Something screamed in her ear. Clutching the shelf to keep from being thrown down the stairs, she screamed herself as she dragged down the toolbox.

She pulled it open, crouching on the stairs by the lamp. "Don't be frightened, Matthew!" Snarling rage and a stench poured through the battered door. "Don't be afraid!" As she tore the shelf plank off its braces, the entire contents of the shelf crashed down the stairs. The boy watched, his face blank and cold, while she grabbed the hammer and a fistful of nails.

She threw herself against the door. The thing beat at it, and the door struck her head, but she pressed with all her strength, trying to hold it still while she drove a nail through the plank. "Matthew, help me!" The first nail bent, and she struck her finger. Clawing at the wood, she drove in another, slippery with blood, felt it bite deep into the wood. And another. In the dark, her blood dripped down the frame. The boy never moved. Waves of fury beat at the door with hurricane force.

Hammering and shrieking, she drove in all the long nails she could find. But it would not hold, she knew. Already, the wood splintered.

She clutched the hammer to her breast, then dumped out the contents of the toolbox. Screws and nuts and buttons scattered, bouncing down the stairs. No more nails. She dropped the hammer, held up the lamp. *When it gets in, I'll try to break the lantern on it. Burn it.* But the house would catch, and Matthew was behind her on the stairs. *God help us.*

With wild ferocity, it beat against the wood, and the door began lurching apart. She felt the boy's hand on her legs. "Oh Matthew, I'm so sorry." She bent to hold him. Her vision wavered, and her thoughts began to spin. Shock waves pummeled them, rhythmic now, as the thing crashed into the door again and again. Matthew clutched her tightly, and with a blurring of senses, it seemed to her they joined somehow, became for an instant like vines grown thick and strong together in the storm. She shook her head forcefully. "No! Go away! Do you hear me? Leave us alone!"

The door would burst apart in seconds. Dazed, she watched bright cracks radiate across it, kitchen light seeping through. "Matthew! Stay behind me!" She reached back for his hand. Nothing. Empty air.

The boy crouched by the door.

"No! Get back!" Nearly paralyzed, she tried to grab him.

Kneeling, Matty whispered. Through a chink, a shaft of light struck one of his eyes. Ivory. Onyx. He murmured. Instantly, the attack became less violent. Then it stopped.

On hands and knees, the boy continued murmuring under

the door. On the other side, weight slid against the wood. It eased inward again. She sank to her knees and tried to make out the boy's words, but his voice stayed too low. From the other side, something snuffled and snorted around the doorjamb, as though a giant hog rampaged in the kitchen. She heard a padding sound. Foul breath oozed through the cracks. Drawing back from the smell, she touched the boy, listened to the comfort of-fered by his crooning voice—gibberish, baby talk.

And then silence.

"Is it gone? Matthew, did it go away?"

They crouched in silence, and the lantern burned low. She leaned an ear against the wood. The door wobbled. *Anyone could kick it down now. If it comes back . . .* Holding her breath, she groped about for the hammer.

She waited, listening.

"Matthew, we're going to try and make a run for Aunt Doris's car. Matthew? Can you understand what I'm saying?"

But what if—just this once—Doris didn't leave her keys in the ig-nition? Trying to work quietly with the claw end of the ham-mer, she began pulling out nails. They squealed softly. *What if it's outside waiting for us?*

The door pulled away from her, broke from its hinges and heaved to the floor. She blinked at the light. Gripping the ham-mer, she took Matthew's hand and drew him after her. Splin-tered wood crunched underfoot. The kitchen table lay upside down atop two smashed chairs.

The boy stumbling behind her, she crept to the back door.

She stared. The bolt was still in place.

How did it get in? She couldn't tear her eyes away. *How did it get out?*

The door shook, and she screamed.

"Athena! 'Thena, let me in! What's wrong? Athena!"

"Steven? Oh God. Steven." She unlatched the door and swung it open, the hammer falling from her fingers to thud on the loose floorboards.

He grabbed her. "Sweet Jesus, 'Thena, what . . . ?"

"It's here. The thing. In the house."

Reaching for his service revolver, he pushed past her. She hung on to the door.

After a moment, he returned. " 'Thena?" His eyes took in the demolished kitchen.

"It . . ."

"It's okay, 'Thena. I'm here now."

Still shaking and gripping the door, she turned to the outer darkness. "We locked ourselves in the basement." Her voice grated with exhaustion, words barely emerging from her throat.

"We?"

As she looked back, her eyes went wild. "Matthew! Where are you?"

In the living room, the boy knelt by the sofa and crooned.

"There!" Her fingers stabbed. "Behind the sofa!"

He waved her aside, motioned for her to be silent. The boy appeared not to be aware of him. Revolver drawn, he got down on his hands and knees, grunting. "It's okay, boy. It's okay." He got up again. "There's one hell of a frightened dog under there. That's all."

But she only held her head to the side as though listening to things he couldn't hear.

He wondered if he'd ever seen a more terrified human being. " 'Thena, let me look around. Why don't you come and sit here?"

But she moved to the boy. "Matthew? Are you all right?"

When finally the boy looked up, Steve stepped closer. He squirmed as the boy's queer eyes fell upon him. Steve turned away, not knowing where to look. Stuffing had been ripped from the sofa, and an armchair lay on its side in the center of the room. Curtains covered the floor. "I'm going to go upstairs and search."

"No, it's gone." She gave him a trembling smile and tried to smooth back her hair. "I . . . knew it was gone . . . the second we came out of the basement. I could feel it. I don't know why I acted so—"

"You're okay." Again, he surveyed the room. "Everything's all right now." He righted the armchair. "But you can't stay here anymore."

"Where could we go?"

"Neighbors? Family?"

She shook her head.

"The two of you could come to my house." He waited, but she said nothing. "How did it get in?"

Distractedly, she shrugged.

Steve paced the room, examining the windows. "No signs of a break-in." The dog wouldn't come out from beneath the sofa. Matty stopped mumbling and just sat there on the rug, playing with his fingers, walking them about on the floor.

She sat in the armchair. "How's Doris?"

"They were getting set to do X-rays when I left. What's behind this door?"

"The other part of the house. Rooms we don't use."

"Let's take a look."

"It's dangerous. The floors . . ."

There were bolts at the top and bottom of the door, and he drew them with difficulty. Stiff hinges gave only when he threw his weight against them. "Can we get some light in here?" Again, he drew his gun. Behind him, she righted a lamp, removed the shade and brought the bare bulb as close to the doorway as the cord would allow.

Inside lay thick emptiness, the air heavy with moldy dust. Covered by a sheet, a large piece of furniture occupied the center of the room. Steve took a few hesitant steps. "I see what you mean about the floor." He stumbled and cursed.

"What's the matter?" she asked from the doorway.

"Nothing. A soft spot." The lamp didn't illuminate much; only water-damaged walls stood out in the gloom. He heard boards groan as she came toward him. "Better stay out there. Is this the only other door that leads outside?" He moved toward it, feeling the uneven floor sink with each step. "Still bolted." He rattled the bolt and turned to her, his vision adjusting, saw the glitter of her eyes as she approached. "Walk along the edge of the floor, near the wall," he advised. "When I was driving Doris to the hospital, she said something about your going into town to find some guy."

"Pamela told me about him."

"Why didn't you wait for me?" His back to her now, he tested the boards across a tightly shuttered window.

"Pam's still missing," she told him. "Matty says she's . . ."

"Doris also mentioned about some locals having left the area." Again, the unspoken reprimand sounded in his voice. "What's through here?"

"Just another room. Steve, wait."

He ducked through the doorway, and she stood motionless. The amount of dust in the air made it hard to breathe, and wheezing slightly, she looked back at the lamp in the doorway.

"Jesus!" The deep voice went hoarse with fright. "What's that?"

The floor creaked loudly just in front of her. Overhead, blackness squirmed. "It's just a bat, Steve. They get in sometimes."

Breathing heavily, he took her arm and led her back toward the light.

"There's just the one window in the other room." He could see only her face, a pale oval. "Looks intact. No one could have . . ."

"No, no one could have. Look." She tilted the lamp. In the layered dust, her narrow footprints crossed Steve's large, broad ones. There were no others. She closed the door and began struggling with the bolts.

He walked into the kitchen. "And you're sure this back door was locked?"

She followed him. "I only opened it for you."

"Well, I can't figure out how anything could've gotten in here." He gazed down at the gouged and shattered cellar door, at the hammer on the floor. "What did you say happened to this door?" He stared at the claw end of the hammer.

She started to speak, then spun around. Soundlessly, Matty had entered the room behind her. Silent and stone-faced, he kicked a piece of chair out of his way, then pressed himself between the stove and the wall and pointed down.

Steve leaned over the stove. "Crap. That would do it all right."

"What?" She looked. Blackness sank deep in a large hole behind the stove.

"Looks like it goes under the wall and right outside. Look out." He waved her back, and she drew the boy to her. Steve took hold of the stove and, straining, inched it away from the wall. "You have any more of those boards you were using?"

". . . knew there was something wrong the day Lonny was . . . when I found Lonny and we came home and the dog ran up, but he couldn't have been outside because I locked him in the house and the door was still . . ."

He said nothing, just hammered planks across the mouth of the tunnel, while the boy stood back, watching.

For what seemed like a long time, the words poured out of her. ". . . what really bothered me the most, I mean, was the way he talked to it, really talked to it, whispered through the door and it seemed to listen and . . ."

"Okay," he grunted. "This ought to hold." Careful of the gas pipe, he got to his feet and came around, shoving the stove back against the wall.

"Oh God, listen to me. I sound like a crazy woman." And she started to laugh. "Good going, girl. You finally made it." She sat in the sole upright kitchen chair, her head in her hands, as her whole body trembled.

Brushing himself off, he stepped closer, wanting to touch her, to hold her. "You've really been through it." He looked around at the shambles of the kitchen; it was as though their talk of the night before had called something into being, summoned it here.

"I can't remember ever having been hysterical before. God, where's Pamela?"

"Don't you think she could've just gone somewhere?"

"And left Matty alone?" She practically giggled. "And look—there's her handbag. You don't know. She carries it with her everywhere, like a little girl, all around the house even." Suddenly, she grabbed the boy and shook him. "That string bag! Where did it come from? Does Chabwok bring you things? Does he leave presents for you on the stoop?"

" 'Thena, stop it. Think. Isn't there someplace Pam could have gone?"

"No place." She let go, and the boy shrank from her. "Not her mother's. No place."

"You said some of the townspeople left. Couldn't she just have gone with them?" He waited for her to respond, then followed her gaze. On a shelf about the stove, a jelly glass held wilted crabgrass and black-eyed susans. "You say Matty spoke to . . . your visitor? Athena, listen to me. You think the boy might know something? Would you like me to talk to him?"

After a pause, she nodded.

"Come here, son." He put his arm on Matty's shoulder and led him toward the living room. Matthew complied, following easily, yet scarcely seeming aware of Steve. He might as easily have gone in the direction of any gust of wind. Rising, she followed them as far as the doorway and stood, watching.

He seated the boy on a still-intact section of sofa, and scratching noises came from underneath as the dog shifted.

"Your name's Matt, right? Mine's Steve." Smiling, he held his hand out, but the boy never blinked.

She saw the tension grow in Steve's shoulders as he studied the weary pain in the boy's face. Unable to watch, she turned away.

For long minutes, she sat alone in the kitchen, knowing she must resemble one of those women they used to get in the ambulance, hysterical mothers whose children had been injured through negligence. *But nothing has happened to Matthew. Nothing.* Indistinctly, she could hear her son's voice from the next room, jumbled sentences and the word "Chabwok" repeated over and over. *Jabberwok.* Then Steve's deep grumbling sounded again, gentle and too soft for her to make out the coaxing words. When the boy spoke again, his words came lower and slower.

She looked at the broken dishes. *All that cleaning for nothing.* The coffeepot lay on the floor by the stove, soggy grounds beside it like a heap of drowned ants.

" 'Thena! Come quick!"

He had hold of the boy's upper arms and kept shaking him. Oblivious, the boy mumbled with his eyes rolled white. ". . . try run . . . they can't . . . slip, sink inna sand . . . run blood . . . taste . . . Pammy . . ."

"I can't make him stop."

". . . through woods . . . blood . . . running safe place . . . hurt . . ."

As though mesmerized, she stood before the boy, listening. "Who, Matthew? Who's running?"

". . . trees . . . hitting branches . . . tearing . . ." The boy grimaced in pain. ". . . blood-hot . . ." He slurred the words like a drunk. ". . . shed . . ."

"The shed out back?"

"No doors . . . no windows . . . trees in front . . ."

"Matty? Baby?" She took his hot face in her hands. "Is it Chabwok? Is Chabwok moving toward the house or away from us?"

"Oh my God." Steve stared at them.

"Matthew, it's important. We have to know."

The boy's voice seemed to thicken. "Running through trees." Moaning, he tore himself from them and vomited on the floor. Hanging over the sofa, he gagged and groaned while Steve held his head. At last the boy stood up straight.

"I think he'll be okay now," said Steve. "We'd better get him upstairs."

"Matty?" She reached out a hand, but he moved away with wobbling steps. "Matty?"

Wordlessly, he began to mount the stairs, putting both feet on one step before going on to the next.

"Steve? What's wrong with him?"

They peered up through the banister spokes. "Look at his face," Steve whispered. "Like he's sleepwalking. Come on." They both followed, he making an effort to move quietly, she leaning heavily on the rail. "Where's he taking us?"

Strewn along the hall, piles of clothing spilled out of a room at the top of the stairs, many of them ripped and torn. Steve paused to examine them, then glanced at Athena. Her eyes never left the boy's back. Nearly reaching out to take her arm as she passed, he thought better of it and watched them move away from him, the limping woman and the slow, silent boy.

The boy disappeared into what looked like a closet, and his mother paused only a moment before following. Steve hurried to catch up. The alcove hid narrow stairs.

Moonlight streamed through the crusted window. Steve switched on the light and looked around in confusion, frowning at the clinging stench of dried urine.

"He sleeps here." She answered his unspoken question. "It used to be my husband's room when he was a boy, and when Matty was little, he used to make noises at night, so I thought . . ." She stopped. There was no justification for this. Revealed by the chilling glow, dirt lay thicker than she'd ever realized.

" 'Thena? Where is he?"

She wended her way between pieces of furniture, looking behind and under things as she passed. "I saw him go over this way."

Steve followed, shoving things aside and choking on the dust.

"Matty?" She reached the wall. "Where could . . . ?"

He pointed. "What's that?"

Against the wall, a massive chest of drawers partly blocked a dark area in the plaster.

"Matthew?"

It was a hole, a deep hole.

"Are you back there?" She squeezed through into the cobwebbed cave.

Too late, he put out a hand to stop her. "Athena?"

No sound came from within. Scraping his shoulder, he tried to pass through the opening but had to shove the high bureau aside. He stumbled over crumbling plaster. Almost no light found its way into the tunnel.

"Athena?" Beyond a tight corner, he found some sort of crawl space, possibly a ventilation passage between the inner wall and outer shell of the house. Slats poked through like broken ribs. He heard a sound, a muffled fluttering as of moths, and he lit a match. At the end of the narrow space, the boy sat hunched against the wall, mumbling to himself. Barely a foot away, Athena had been feeling her way along the bricks.

From outside and far below came a sound like the night

breathing through the trees, like waves pressing through the pines to break against the house.

Slowly, she raised her head and gazed at something just above the boy, and Steve raised the faltering match.

Crude iron manacles had been hammered into the ancient bricks of the chimney.

PART FOUR

DEVIL

. . . hatched for sport
Out of warm water and slime . . .

                                        Edgar Lee Masters

. . . his eyes have all the seeming of a demon's that is dreaming. . .

                                        Edgar Allen Poe

. . . departing dreams and shadowy forms
Of midnight vision . . .

                                        Henry David Thoreau

Wednesday, August 12

He was trapped. Ernie lay in the airless little room, languid heat pounding through the tiny window slit. Trapped. He lay on the cot, an arm flung over his face. One long brown hand throbbed with infection, and each breath brought pain.

The summer had peaked, and each day it seemed a relentless ball of flame blazed over the barrens. It was killing him, he knew.

"I brung ya some water."

One eye stuck shut, the other an opaque slit, he struggled to raise his head as the boy moved timidly into the room. Just since he'd been here, the youth had changed, grown. He seemed leaner, taller. The flesh was firm, the face clear. He carried a brown-caked mug, half-filled with tepid liquid. Gently, he held Ernie's head and put the cup to his lips, then took a wet rag from the basin and wiped Ernie's face with it, dabbing at his eyes.

Scratching the grit away with his fingertips, Ernie got his eyes entirely open and for a long moment just lay there, staring at the boy. Aching hunger darkened his face, and his breath became a slow bubbling. He gazed at pale hair so light it seemed a melted confection, spun and glistening, at flesh so thin it displayed a delicate tracing of blue.

"Your pop's gonna throw me outta here, Marl. Soon. If I don't get some more money from someplace."

The boy shook his head. "No, I won't let 'im." The face registered no emotion, but the childlike voice whined in a high pitch. "Won't let nobody! Yor 'bout the only friend I ever . . . anybody'd try to chase you 'way, I'd . . ."

Ernie reached out a hand for the cup, gulped down the rest of the water. "Who was that woman was here yesterday? I heard you talking. You thought I was asleep, but I heard you."

"J-Just some woman. Lives down that ways . . . inna big old house."

"What'd she want?"

Marl didn't answer at first. "She just . . . asking stuff."

"She ask about me?" He leaned forward, studying the boy's face. "She pretty?" Marl looked down in embarrassment, and Ernie laughed, the sound a liquid susurration, like cellophane melting. "Would you like to go to her house?" He leaned back with all his teeth showing, laughing in harsh, explosive little bursts. "Go over there and knock the cook pot over maybe? Start a little fire?" The laughter changed to raking coughs, and Ernie tasted blood as he hacked to clear his sleep-clogged breath. Marl tried to get him to lie back down, but he resisted, choking bloody phlegm into a bucket by the bed.

Marl forced him down on the cot. "You f-feel hot." Then Ernie lay still for a while, wheezing hard, and Marl glanced at the bucket. "I ain't had a nosebleed inna long time."

"Marl. Marl, please." He muttered feverishly, the damp slits of his eyes clouding over again. "Fucking dying. Get me outta here. We gotta get out. To the woods, Marl. Gotta get into the pines. Come out to the woods with me."

Marl held him down. "You need more water?" He glanced at the empty mug; then his gaze roamed to the window. "Hate the woods."

He struggled to sit up. "Please. Just once." Pushing at the boy's hands, he thrashed in the bed, but Marl held him firmly. "Just once. Come! Please!" Finally exhausted, he rested his head on the cot and just stared at the flies that stuck to the ceiling like tufts of black velvet.

Marl squinted at the window.

"There's nothing to be scared of, Marl." Desperation played across the vulpine face. "You don't hardly go out no more, getting pale as a worm. Look at you . . . hair so long, just like a girl. But look at your muscles." He ran his palm across smooth hardness. "You ever see a dragonfly?" His voice went soft with weariness, with surrender. "When it's little, I mean? Right after it hatches out in the water? The pond's all foul, stinks." He spoke in quick gasps. "Just a little thing, harmless. Nothing notices it in the mud on the bottom. Looks the same as all the other worms." Already little more than a whisper, his voice grew even softer, weaker, and as he spoke he stared intently at his swollen hand. "Then one day, all of a sudden, something happens. Gets hungry. Is hunger. Starts to eat everything it can catch, salamanders, leeches. Don't matter."

"You ain't seen my cat, has you?"

"Or fish, even if it's a great big sunny. Don't matter."

"Looked all over for 'er."

"One time, I scooped one out of a puddle. Scooped him right up in my hand, mud and all. After all the wet stuff leaked away, just lay there. All of a sudden, it felt like fire." He unclenched his fist, then gazed at the insects on the ceiling again. He fumbled with the empty cup, and his hand slipped to the boy's leg. "That's what it does. Kills and kills. Gorges till the wings burst outta the skin on his back, and he flies."

Marl wouldn't look at him. The hand on his leg moved.

". . . wings . . . in the sunlight . . . changing colors . . . so pretty . . ."

"Your hand bleeding?"

"Just draining a little. Be all right," Ernie told him, staring. The light faded. Marl's hair still glowed.

"Th–There's this bad dream I have." Marl stayed on the edge of the bed, his face turned away. "'Bout something hungry inna pines. They always making fun a me downstairs. But I know. It's out there. I use to try to drive it 'way, burn it out, make it go 'way." Beyond the window, a few tall pines prodded the sky. "You know?" He turned his head and looked down at the bed. The room had grown darker than the hot glitter of Ernie's eyes, and he watched as Ernie reached for him with a hungry languor.

★ ★ ★

In the mad jumble of the bedroom, clothes were piled on the floor and heaped on the bed. Beside her, nestled in laundry, he lay motionless.

His hair was damply plastered to his forehead, and beaded moisture ran down the side of his face. As she stroked him, she watched the pale lashes of his closed eyes and listened to his even breath. She kept her touch light, wanting to hold him tightly but fearing to wake him.

The room smelled of lovemaking. Sweating herself, she looked down his body at the muscular chest and stomach. She remembered the fierce rejoicing in his eyes when her jeans had finally peeled away, remembered how the sight of her one thinner leg had caused a violent tenderness to well up within him. Her breasts still ached slightly—he'd nearly crushed her to this chest her fingers trailed along. She toyed with the tightly curled and sweaty hairs, then caressed his head, smiling gently to herself.

It had been too fast and fumbling but incredibly intense, and she thought back to the shy formality of those first times with Wallace, when she'd been little more than a girl. Then her thoughts turned to Barry's pornographic posturings and she closed her eyes against the sudden sharpness of that memory. She smiled again. With Steve it had been rough and fast and loving and, yes, he'd hurt her a little, though she would never tell him.

Something, some dream of pain or sorrow washed across his face, distorting it. There came the low, ominous sound of his grinding teeth, and she held him until the tension passed.

With a murmuring groan, he turned heavily in the creaking bed to lay half upon her, momentarily squeezing away her breath. She stroked the trickling dampness of his hair.

Eyes still closed, he cradled her again, his lips finding her breasts.

They lay belly to back, drowsing in the heat, while twilight seeped through the windows of the still room. Was there a sound? Not sure whether he'd heard something, Steve listened. Her breath warm and soft on his face, she slept deeply, her body suffused with limp peacefulness at last.

Across the window, amber light spread like honey over the wall, growing orange as he watched. Long wavering ridges and cracks mapped the paint, and in the pleasant gloom, he lay thinking.

Until dawn, they'd sat up with the boy, calming him, questioning him, even making some attempts to repair the wreckage of the house. When Matthew had finally slipped into a natural sleep, Steve had carried him back to the attic, undressing the boy himself, while she waited below.

Damp sheet sculpted to his body, he stretched out a hand and laid it on her arm. *We've wasted so much time.* In sleep, her face was like a child's, all worries faded. He thought about her life, about the boy in the attic and, in spite of the warmth, slid a protective arm about her. She curled against him like a cat, and he smiled indulgently, glancing around at the ferocious disorder of the room. At first, he'd assumed that their visitor last night had savaged it. Only after quite a while had he realized this to be its normal state. Her belongings formed mounds everywhere, and he felt an intense pleasure at just being here among them in the heavy softness of this room.

Won't that window open farther? He felt the stagnant air lulling him, felt sleep stealing over him again as he inhaled the deep warm scent of her and listened to the flutter of her breath. Shadows stretched across the floor, crept up the walls.

He heard the sound again and thought of the dog, still hiding under the sofa when they'd gone to bed. Athena stirred slightly. "Sleep some more, babe," he told her, his voice hushed as he patted her gently. "Sleep." He rolled over, eased himself out of the bed. "You need it."

He wandered naked into the hallway. In the shadows, something breathed, and moved, and then came toward him.

Wearing only his ragged jeans, Matty stood halfway down the hall, and he glared at Steve with a look of absolute malevolence. *Oh Lord, letting the kid see me come out of his mother's room like this.* The boy's face was drawn and lined from hours of sickness. *Oh God, what's wrong with me?* Blinking, trying to clear his head, he heard again the sound that had awakened him.

"Uh . . . Matt . . . uh . . . are you all right?" He backed away with slow horror. "No, don't come any closer. Stay where you are!"

His arm shot out in a defensive reflex as Matty lunged. Teeth met with a click an inch from Steve's chest.

Lord God! His whole body trembled, wet with fear. *Oh dear Jesus.* He stared at the boy. *He went for my throat.* He backed into the bedroom, no longer protective, now seeking safety. *He tried to . . .*

The boy crouched in the shadowed hall, another growl boiling deep in his chest.

At last, even the final thread of purple fades, and vast shadows slide across the sky, enfolding the earth in a patchwork of darkness, velvety blackness overlapping thick gray.

Like a sentient creature, heat broods, hovering over Munro's Furnace. The stench of the garbage dump hums with vermin, and in a cold strike of moonlight, they swarm, a riot of life in the night.

Something sighs. Hot guttering breath grows more rapid as the night drips. Luminous eyes blink, recede to blackness again, then open, awake to the flicker of self-awareness.

Awake.

The sound of an owl hollows through. A seething lust, rabid in the dark, prowls the twisted scrub, its feral shadow like a hole in the night. It stalks the dump, then turns in an avalanche of refuse and creeps toward the center of town.

No lights show in any of the houses. No air stirs. Violent and frenzied images swim, screaming in the beast-mind: hooked fingers, nails splintering on bone; skin parts, bubbling throat; the fingers disappearing in flesh—spurting soft hot meat—teeth sink in, tearing, wet jets out. A memory flickers of being forced to abandon the one in the car when the big splashing thing— tractor?—approached on the flooded road. Blood and foam in his mouth then.

Running. Power shudders through. Force thuds, gigantic and irresistible, roars and leaps within. It grows. Always the wild joy surges stronger . . . changing . . . forcing. . . .

The beast stops moving. Outside the darkened gin mill, it lifts its head to regard the window slit: Marl's bedroom. An image of the sleeping blond head forms in its mind.

Then madly racing, leaping the barely moving sludge of the creek, it dashes through pines, branches slashed aside in the luminous night. Chaos now.

Pammy . . . trailer . . . that way. But it moves away, farther through the woods.

It finds the house, all sharpness dissolving in the rinse of stars: the crazily tilting chimneys and roof, the shed behind. Standing in the dark of the yard, it gazes at the boarded windows and yearns for the woman within.

Inside, Dooley begins to howl.

Thursday, August 13

She locked him in the house the night of the storm. Steve wiped his sweating neck with a crumpled handkerchief.

But there was a hole, practically a tunnel behind the stove. He paced the kitchen, then paused at the back door to watch mother and child play in the yard. *And he was alone with the sister-in-law.* The boy threw the stick for the stiffly moving dog—who mostly ignored it—while she clapped and called out encouragements. *Now she's missing.*

But he's just a boy. He thought about his observations that morning. When he'd returned from getting a new battery for Athena's car, she'd still been asleep, but Matty had been up and hungry, so he'd made him a sandwich. He'd watched the boy's face for any sign of the previous night's violence. *Nothing.* He'd made some lemonade from a can he'd found in the freezer, and as he'd stirred the clinking ice cubes, the boy had leaned his elbows on the table, staring at the frosted moisture on the pitcher, his overbright gaze fixed on the ripening drops, following them as they slid down. *A total blank.*

Just a boy. There'd been no indication that Matty even remembered seeing him come out of his mother's room.

He saw her fight with Lonny. Now Lonny's dead.

And last night he was in some kind of contact with Chabwok, whatever Chabwok is. He couldn't stop thinking about the books they'd been reading, especially the ones about psychotic killers.

What if Chabwok were just another part of the boy? Another personality? *What if . . . ?*

He shook his head. *I must be losing my mind.* There had to be another explanation. *All the talk of monsters and curses must be getting to me.* All that crazy stuff could confuse anyone.

But what if Lonny came here the night of the storm? Came looking for Athena to continue their argument about his moving in? What if he came here and found the boy alone?

He moved away from the back door. *Nobody's going to blame the boy.* He poured himself a glass of lemonade. It tasted warm and watery now, and feathery things like plastic shavings floated on the surface. *They blame me.* He grimaced as he downed the sweet liquid.

I go out on a routine assignment, and my partner winds up dead . . . and I've got some cock-and-bull story about going for a drive and coming back to find him torn apart. Not my fault. But I left him there. Knowing there was a killer in the woods, I took his gun and drove away.

I might as well have killed him. The phone was already in his hands. *It's just like with those pineys he was always going on about. I killed him and took his woman.*

"So, Steve, when you coming back to work?" Phone cradled on his shoulder, Frank Buzby shuffled papers while pretending to look for the bulletin Steve wanted. As he scratched the graying tangle of hair at his open shirt, his face bore an expression of annoyed curiosity. "So now tell me again why it is you want to know about this." Silently, he beckoned to the other cop in the office. "Uh-huh."

Billy Mills—a shy man with no neck and an upper body like a log—approached the desk. Listening in and trying to read his boss's signals, he passed paper and pencil when Frank motioned for them.

"Uh-huh." Buzby scribbled. "Yeah, sure. Where'd you say he was hiding again? Sure, I gotcha. You're gonna check it out yourself, and I'll wait to hear from you. Right." He grinned at Mills.

"So when you coming back? Huh? Oh, Cathy's fine, I guess. I ain't seen her. You know how busy we are, shorthanded like this. Well, listen, Steve, thanks a lot for checking in, and you'll call me soon as you know something, right?" He hung up and leaned back in his chair. "That moron." He crowed with laughter.

"What?"

"We done finally caught a break, that's what." Frank sat up straight, reached for the phone again. "And he wants to handle it hisself."

"You mean the cars? You hear something?"

"The police dick just told me how to get the heat off a us and the troopers outta the frigging woods." Buzby rummaged through his desk. "So we can get back to business."

" 'Bout time."

"Let me tell ya—ain't never been so frigging paralyzed. Got eighteen cars just sitting. What's the number for the state cops? Never mind." He dialed. "Listen, go outside and use the other phone. See if you can get hold a some a your buddies, then get your partner in here. Hello, operator? Connect me with the state police. Yeah, it's an emergency call from Chief of Police Frank Buzby."

Distant cries drifted down the road, then a cracking noise. As he twisted the steering wheel, he saw a puff of white smoke ahead.

He cursed himself. As a wave of uniformed troopers zig-zagged toward the central buildings, he spotted Frank's cowboy hat and a couple of people he recognized as Buzby's cronies.

The buildings were surrounded.

He should have guessed what Buzby would do, should have gotten here sooner. But Athena hadn't wanted to be left alone, and he'd promised to file a missing-persons report about Pamela, and then . . .

A trooper waved him back. He left the Volks on the road.

The clearing blazed white as Frank's vigilante buddies and the troopers converged on what had to be the gin mill. As Steve ran forward, someone yelled, "Hey you, get back! You up there, quit firing until I say so!"

He flashed his ID and was let through. An officer kept shouting at the paint-blistered building, ordering someone to come out, to throw down any weapons. "Nobody wants to hurt you now. Just do what I'm telling you."

The troopers began to mutter. Again, Steve spotted Frank's cowboy hat and moved toward it. Suddenly, the troopers grew silent.

The door to the gin mill slowly opened.

"That's it. Come on out now."

At first, nothing moved in the shadowed doorway, then a wild thing charged, a knife clutched about its head with both hands. With an animal cry, it streaked for the nearest cop.

Steve heard a nearby rookie whisper, "Oh Jesus." Then guns began to go off. He saw Buzby rock backward with the recoil of his rifle.

The redheaded man with the knife jerked from side to side, clouds of dust rising from his shabby clothing with each blast. It seemed he would never hit the ground.

"Stop firing!" Steve heard himself shouting. "For God's sake, stop firing!" Then others took up the cry. He was already running forward when a final burst rolled the body onto its back.

Steve reached it first. He knelt. He couldn't guess how many shots had struck their target, but only reddening shreds of clothing maintained the figure's shape. A bullet had cracked the skull open just above the left temple; yet the broken face smiled. Like seeds spilling from a sack, the contents of the split forehead seeped out and streaked the face, mingling with and becoming part of that horrid, secret smile.

He felt sand in his teeth. In all probability, this was the man who killed Barry. Yet he felt no hatred. Only pity and disgust. He could see the troopers cautiously entering the gin mill, and men gathered about him now as well, staring at the ruined corpse. And still he felt no sense that justice had been done, not even as he pried the knife from the man's clenched fist. It was an ordinary Buck knife, the handle mother-of-pearl, its milky opalescence spotted with blood.

"I don't know as you should be touching that."

"Leave him be. That's the guy whose partner got it."

He dropped the knife beside what remained of the stomach. He turned his back on the gathering men and caught a glimpse of Buzby—grinning, deep in a furtive-looking conversation with a state police captain. *We'll never know now, not for sure.* Sick and angry, Steve hurried away, not trusting himself to speak to anyone. *Never know the why or the how.*

"Hey! There's a kid up here!" A trooper stuck his head through the narrow second-story window. "He's all tied up!"

With a single movement, the crowd ran toward the building. From inside, somebody began screaming "Ernie!" over and over in a desperate panic. A cop bellowed at the trooper in the window.

"What? Yeah, he's all right," he shouted back. "Just looks a little spooky."

"Lucky to be alive," another trooper muttered. "Probably would've found him staked out in the woods next."

Steve pushed past him and kept walking.

Her car idled in the middle of the road. The motionless figure within just stared through the windshield, stared through the clot of people ahead, at the ruined thing at their feet, at red seepage in the sand.

"Athena?" She didn't seem aware of him. Gently, he reached through the window, putting a hand on her shoulder. " 'Thena?"

Madly battering at his vision, branches clawed at his jacket. His boots crashed through the brush. He looked back over his shoulder, and a tree knocked the cap from his head, but he never slowed, not even when his breath came in roaring stabs and his eyes felt ready to burst. He staggered and nearly collided with a pine but kept on with great stumbling strides, the sweat soaking through his jacket.

Spencer fled deeper into the woods. He'd seen the police approaching his home, seen their stealth and numbers, and had gotten out just in time.

Al knew revenuers when he saw them.

Though she'd been eating for some time, the bowl in front of her still seemed to be full. He watched her surreptitiously. Apparently engrossed with the soup, she never actually brought any of it to her mouth but solemnly spooned the dark liquid as though dredging for a corpse.

"Don't you like it?"

"Gritty. Sorry. Not your fault. I swear I can taste sand in everything anymore." At last, she put the spoon down. "It's beginning to get dark. We should start to lock up."

Water trickled loudly into the sink. He twisted the faucet shut and wiped soapy hands on his pants before touching her cheek with a damp palm. "Athena, it's over. They got him."

She said nothing, but studied his face with desperate hope.

He caressed her hair, dark with flickering lights trapped within its coils. He looked at her slim body beneath the man's shirt that hung so loosely on her. He watched her face. "Don't you understand? It's over."

In the dimming yard beyond the screen door, a cluster of starlings shrieked and flurried.

She closed her eyes. "Steve . . ." She laid her hand on his, trying to draw his sureness into herself. "There's nothing out there? Getting closer in the dark?"

He simply took hold of her hand.

"I chew my nails," she told him after a moment.

"So I see."

"You got sunburned today." She touched the side of his face.

He put his arms around her, and she laughed sadly against him. He pressed his lips to her forehead.

When the boy's cries came, she gently pushed him aside, nothing on her face betraying the least surprise. Not moving, he just listened to her mount the stairs. Then he turned the heat off under the coffee and rubbed a hand across his eyes.

Leaving the kitchen and climbing the stairs, he followed the shouts to the attic.

"Pammy's blood! My friend—Pammy's blood comin' outta his mouth!"

"It was a nightmare. Only a nightmare."

Steve found her rocking the boy in her arms.

"My poor baby. It's over. Oh Matty." Forcefully, she repeated, "All over."

Friday, August 14

Rattling the newspaper in irritation, she scanned an article about a local mayor's involvement in a toxic dumping scandal. "Now there's shocking news. A crooked politician. Imagine." A boxed follow-up story just below it described New Jersey's pollution problem in depressing detail. Continuing to mutter under her breath, Doris turned back to the front page and reread the account of the death of a serial killer at Munro's Furnace. The paper really played it up big—right across from the headline about the record heat wave, above the bit about the red tide near Brigantine.

At least Athena's safe now, she thought. Sighing, she lowered the paper and looked down at her bandaged foot. The trap had severed a muscle, which might easily take longer to heal than a broken bone. Her glance continued around the small hospital room, everything ice blue and smelling of disinfectant. The slanting windows looked down on a sun-pounded lot. Shifting on the bed, she tried to find a comfortable position and toyed with an unlit cigarette. She checked her watch: almost time for more medication.

She didn't like taking it. It made her brain fuzzy, and lately there'd been nightmares about that last drive with Steve, that night he'd driven her to the hospital. She'd been practically fainting at that point, barely able to make out his words, but in her dreams she heard him clearly. He seemed to be speaking about Barry, about fighting with Barry the day he died. ". . . squeezed and his eyes got very large, and that made me feel, not happy exactly, but like release was on the way, and the harder I squeezed the faster it came, and the feeling ran up my fingertips to my shoulders and then spread to . . ."

Just a dream. A drug dream. No, no more painkillers. She gritted her teeth and wished Athena would call.

Gazing at the pile of well-thumbed magazines on the night table, she sighed again, in boredom this time, and reopened the newspaper, amusing herself by reading about another casino scandal. Then her eyes wandered to a tiny account of a tractor-trailer driver arrested for drunk driving on the turnpike. The rig had turned out to contain radioactive materials. "Swell. Wipe out half the state that way." She began leafing through pages in exasperation, stopping at a headline that read GRAND-MOTHER KILLS BOY IN RITUAL. She skimmed the piece. After neighbors had complained of a bad smell, a woman in Newark had been arrested for murdering a four-year-old in some sort of exorcism. She read down a bit farther. The child's body was badly burned, and police had taken scrapings from the walls of the oven.

People are crazy, she thought and turned the page.

The lumps in the pancake batter wouldn't go away. Athena stabbed them with a fork. She stirred them furiously, tried squashing them under the surface as though to drown them, but they only stuck to the tines. "This doesn't look right." She glanced over at Matty to see if he was impatient for lunch, but he just sat at the table and stared out the screen door. She watched him without seeming to. He was so still, so quiet.

Dropping the fork, which immediately disappeared into the batter, she pulled a chair over and climbed up on it. She dug through the kitchen cabinet, trying to find where Pam had put the eggbeater. With one hand, she steadied herself against the wall—its texture like the flaking skin of an elderly lizard—as she crashed and rattled things around on the shelves. No eggbeater. She did, however, find a utensil that vaguely resembled a cross between a cheese grater and brass knuckles, the proper function of which she couldn't imagine. "Oh well, maybe this'll work." Hopping down, she got the oil out from under the sink and put the large skillet on the burner, turning the flame way up.

The dog lifted his head from the floor and sniffed the thin odor of scalded metal.

She tried mashing the lumps, and batter dribbled over the side of the bowl. She glanced over at the boy, who continued to sit in silence, still apparently traumatized by Pamela's . . . disappearance. She didn't know what to do to help. As she reached for the wooden spoon on a hook, heavy objects in her pockets banged against the stove. "Oh, I forgot. Look what I found while I was cleaning your room, Matthew. It's those stones you used to play with. Remember?" She hopped down, but he only stared impassively. "Don't you want them?" She felt his forehead again—no fever—but those hot, sunken eyes disturbed her. She touched the metallic sheen of his hair, lightly stroked the curling blades. "I'll just put them here for you." She laid the stones on the table.

"Oh well, here goes." Trying to watch the boy over her shoulder, she spooned batter into the skillet. But she'd filled the pan with cooking oil, the way she'd seen her grandmother do when making dumplings, and the pancake batter spattered and spread across the bottom, dry lumps bobbing to the surface. "Hell." She stirred the mess distractedly, then turned off the burner. "Pancake stew."

She looked around the kitchen at the litter of flour and spilled milk and eggshells. It seemed she'd dirtied every dish they owned. Even the old iron stove, which hadn't seen use since Wallace installed the reconditioned propane range ten years ago, looked filthy. It occurred to her that this might be the first time anyone had ever cooked in this kitchen without Dooley underfoot looking for handouts. She scowled at the dog who watched in plain dismay. "Might as well dump this mess." She took hold of the iron skillet, burning herself and cursing. Already singed brown at both ends, the dish towel she'd been using as a potholder lay soaking in the sink.

"Matthew?" She dragged the chair over to the cabinet again.

"How about a peanut-butter sandwich instead? Would you like that?" The five-pound peanut-butter jar sat on the top shelf—of course. Her leg twinging a bit, she reached it down, and the jar slipped from her fingers.

Dooley yelped as it crashed to the floor—a mass of tan putty and splintered glass. Before being blamed for anything, the dog hastily vacated the room as Athena glanced down at the boy.

He hadn't reacted, just kept staring out the door.

Steve gazed wistfully at the bourbon, then chucked it in with the rest. Several bottles clanked noisily as he set down the wastepaper basket. Bustling about, he stacked boxes of trash by the front door, then picked up another flattened cardboard box and began folding it into shape. His shirtsleeves were rolled up, and dirt smudged his red face. He smiled.

The barest of breezes passed the window. He'd taken down the massive, dusty venetian blinds, and the sunlight, laying thickly on the dust, looked strange in this faded room. He glanced around and nodded, figuring they'd sell this place and use the money to start fixing up her house. He finished folding boxes, set one on a chair and scraped the contents of the table into it.

Glass tinkled from a framed photograph. For just a moment, he paused to stare at the wedding picture. He scarcely needed to look, could have seen it through closed eyelids: Anna's pale, sharp-featured face, her black hair. The word "redemption" kept running through his mind. He shoved the picture in and closed the lid, then tossed the box toward the door.

He struck the chair with the flat of his hand, and dust lifted. He thought about putting all the old furniture outside to air, then thought about just putting it all out with the trash. Mopping his face and neck with a handkerchief, he glanced into the kitchen and groaned at the sight of the boxes stacked on everything.

Break time, he decided. Unbuttoning his shirt, he plopped into the chair he'd been about to move, and his eyes drifted toward one of the bottles in the trash. The fifth of scotch still held an inch of bright amber fluid.

His hand stopped, still outstretched, and he looked at it with annoyance . . . and then with wonder. He held up the other hand.

Steady.

Sitting back in the chair, he looked again at the bottle, then let his gaze wander about the room. Momentarily swamped by memories, he stared hopelessly at the mounds of junk. He rubbed a hand across his face, and the loud scratching startled him. He needed to shave. Needed to start taking better care of himself. For her.

He rose and resumed packing.

The sun became a ripe and bloody disk. Those adults who moved about outside did so only to perform tasks considered absolutely necessary. Children remained safely indoors. Locked within their shacks and trailers, men and women huddled and spoke little . . . and that little, in whispers.

Gradually, the hammering impact of the heat began to diminish.

Wes Shourd's panel truck bounced and clattered over the scorched earth. There was no mistaking the truck. He had no license plate, just a bumper sticker that read JESUS SAVES, and he'd lashed everything he owned to the back. Hot wind stirred whirlpools of dust in his wake. Those of his neighbors who still remained noted his passage through shuttered windows.

A flight of crows swept through the fading sky, leaving loud cawings to settle on the rooftops. Floating on the warmth, one of the crows hovered on rowing wings against the sun as another dented vehicle, crammed full of junk furniture and children, lumbered noisily along the road out of town.

Redness touched the horizon, then spread rapidly along it, and shadows scythed the woods. As dusk sifted down, Athena carried trash out to the heap, broken glass tinkling in the bag. Muffled heat rose from the earth around her. Chimney swifts, circling after insects overhead, twittered, a high-pitched chattering that sounded like bats above the blurring trees. Crossing the yard, she passed the shed.

Faintly, a sobbing cry swelled in the twilight landscape, rising, growing unmistakably bestial. Motionless, she listened, shaking her head in denial. It surrounded her—a long, demanding yowl. She took a step backward. At times it sounded hungry. At times it almost whimpered. Always it seemed to change direction, drifting with the breeze. Almost dying away, it would begin again—like the cry of cats—no less mournful for being entirely sexual.

She ran, the bag of trash scattered on the ground. A wail of painful joy and triumphant fear pursued her.

Evening poured across the landscape, flowing strong and dense until it filled the world. The shadows beneath the porch melted and spread, merging. She reached the house.

"Chabwok." Calmly, the child sat at the table and toyed with the white stones, while his mother stood gasping in the doorway.

"Chabwok's dead!" she cried. "It's over!"

"Ain't dead."

"I saw him die!"

The cry rolled again, louder now. The boy played with the pebbles, and his eyes, when he looked up, burned like living cinders.

Slammed the door, she bolted it. "It's all right." She backed away. "It's going to be all right, Matthew." She stumbled to the phone. "I'm going to call Steve." Hands trembling, she began to dial. "They'll just have to come and kill him again." Even her voice shook.

A stone struck the wall by her head.

"Matthew!" She spun around. Another stone hit the dial of the phone, produced a broken ringing. The boy seemed not to have moved.

From outside, the muffled cry penetrated the walls. And suddenly the air was full of objects.

The phone pulled from her hand, yanked to the end of its cord, then slammed back and struck her on the side of the neck. As she yelled, stones flew and the table overturned. "No!" Dishes shattered all around the room. "What's happening?" She cringed against the wall. "This can't be happening!" The sugar bowl smashed against the sink, and she watched in disbelief as the pipes of the old stove began to shudder. Black dust dribbled down.

As though battered by invisible fists, the stovepipe wrenched away from the wall, and a century's accumulation of soot cascaded, filling the kitchen, choking away the light.

"Matthew!" As the worst of the cloud settled, she saw the black dirt—still pouring from the ruptured pipe—slowly cover the boy's body where it writhed and convulsed on the floor.

Saturday, August 15

"You the one? The bitch that's been makin' all the trouble?" His face went a deep purple, the mouth very wet and red inside his beard. "Everbody look at 'er! She's the one 'at killed a whole town!" His hands clutched into gnarled fists.

"All right now, that'll do." Out of simple habit, Steve forced authority into his voice. "Leave the lady alone." Keeping one hand on the old man's shoulder, he didn't exactly push the shuddering frame but firmly held him down on the bench.

Though subdued, the grumbling continued. "You know what the price a meat is now the jackin's over with round here? Ain't no damn deers left. Place crawlin' with stateys and everything else. Man can't even make a living."

A ceiling fan turned with infinite slowness, and strips of fly-paper swayed in the corner of the Hobbston General Store. Candy and potato chips and a sparse selection of canned goods were ranged up and down the small aisles. A couple of barefoot kids lurked furtively in the back, while a group of elderly men hung close around the immensely fat woman at the cash register.

In a voice that strained after a reasonable tone, Athena tried to continue. "All we wanted to ask you about was . . ."

The old man's one eye held a steady glower like a watery flame, and Steve could see he would start shouting again in a minute. "Athena, why don't you go outside and check if the boy's all right?"

"But I just wanted to . . ."

"I think that would be best." He motioned her toward the door, keeping his voice low. " 'Thena, this is pointless—he's antagonistic toward you." To quell her objections, he went on rapidly. "I can calm this guy down and question him, but I can't do it if he's yelling at you. Okay?"

"All right. Yes." She glanced over at the pineys, knowing she'd made a mess of things again. The old man's friends all muttered, and the fat woman looked miserable about having a cop in the store at all. "Get, uh, get some cookies or something for Matthew." She began to fish in her pockets for money.

He patted her arm. "I'll get something. You go on outside and keep him company." She smiled and nodded, putting on her sunglasses.

He knew that the circles under her eyes meant she hadn't slept again, and as she went through the door into the bright daylight, he sighed. Her behavior wasn't hard to understand: simple hysteria, brought on by exhaustion, the aftereffect of all she'd been through, all they'd both been through. That's all it was. She'd get over it. In the meantime, he was stuck with questioning this geezer.

They'd spent all morning searching for him, banging on the doors of shacks and asking questions, Athena reasoning that if anyone could explain what was going on, the oldest living resident of Munro's Furnace should be able to. However, like so many of his neighbors, old Dan had already vanished. Finally, they'd traced him to a nearby town. Preparing to interview him, Steve shook his head and sighed. When would Athena realize it was over? He blamed the books he'd showed her when Barry died. He must have been near the breaking point himself to bring such madness into their lives.

She considered moving the car into the shade, then realized Steve had the keys. She didn't want to go back into the store for them, didn't want to interrupt his interrogation of the old man, even though she knew he was only doing it to humor her.

She looked around. By the door to the shop stood a rusting Coke machine that obviously hadn't worked in years. Trying to make out the words of a nearby sign, where yellow letters flaked and curled from a mildewed background, she finally deciphered KEROSENE. Pure heat seeped into the car, actually making it hard to breathe, and she leaned out the window. The little town looked deserted, drowned by the impossibly bright sunlight. But these days, even at noon, she could still feel the approaching night.

Across the seat from her, Matty hung out the window. She watched him. Since his . . . seizure . . . the previous evening, he'd been almost comatose, barely mumbling to himself. Up until that point, he'd been doing so well, so really well, even beginning to talk to her. She couldn't bear it.

The boy's T-shirt had hiked up, exposing the tanned small of his back. Halfway out the window, he stared down at the sand, waving his fingers vaguely. He glanced up, his face lighting with wonder as a red bird flashed above the square.

He continued to stare upward, squinting hard at the shapes of tumbling clouds. This one looked like a dog, just like Dooley—he could see the open mouth and the tail. And this one was . . . this one was . . .

His face darkened with recognition as he saw the lumpish mimicry of great leathery wings. He shut his eyes before he had to see its face.

"You need two things to go out in them woods these days—an automatic weapon and a damn good reason." Steve could feel his headache returning as old Dan rambled, repeating himself, contradicting himself, one minute insisting there was nothing in the woods, the next swearing he'd seen the monster. The few yellow butts of his teeth looked soft, like kernels of corn. "She's the one to see, all right, like I said."

"Could you repeat that last part? Who is this now?"

"What's the matter? Don't you hear good? Mother Jenks, I'm talking about. She got a shack about a quarter mile or two south a Munro's Hole." He grinned at his buddies. "That's what us old-timers calls it."

"And who is this woman again?"

"I told you wunst already. Midwife—been working these parts more'n eighty year, they say. Hell, she's older'n me even." At this, he chuckled and rubbed his rheumy eyes with a crooked knuckle. "She knows everything about everybody round here. Brought most of them into the world. Maybe she'll tell you what you wanna know. Maybe and maybe not too. You and that bitch—no offense—but if it hadn't been for her, Lonny'd still be alive. I knowed him since he was a little boy. And Wally too. You better watch yourself." He nudged the fat woman. "Yeah, Mother Jenks'll answer you. Course you liable to be sorry you asked. I can remember . . ."

His words were suddenly drowned out. From outside came violent bellowing, a dull pounding. Steve's mouth dropped open; then he ran for the door.

Doubled fists hammered at the car windows. The big man's face twisted with rage as he belched out an incoherent stream of filth.

"Hey, you!" Steve yelled, barreling out of the store. "What the devil . . . ?"

The man leaped up on the car, ran across the hood. Jumping down, he raced across the town square without looking back. In the mummifying heat, Steve began to give chase, then stopped, panting, and ran back to the car.

"Athena! Are you all right?" The doors were locked, the windows rolled tight. Inside, she hugged the boy. " 'Thena?" He called again and rapped on the window. Behind the dark glasses, her eyes might have been closed. He dug the car keys out of his pocket. "Who was he?" As he leaned in, the wave of escaping heat struck him like a blow.

Without releasing her hold on the child, she looked up. "His name is Al Spencer," she told him in a strangely calm voice.

"You mean he's the guy . . . ?"

"Yes. He owns the gin mill where they killed that man, where Lonny lived."

"But what happened here?"

"He was just walking up to the store. Then he saw us." She tightened her grip on the boy, whose expression registered nothing, neither alarm nor particular awareness. "It looked like he just went mad, screaming like that. He almost grabbed Matthew. If I hadn't pulled him back . . ."

Wincing at the brightness, Steve stared across the square. His shirt stuck to his chest and back, and the heated air seared his nostrils, throat, lungs. Yet he realized the man had been wearing a flannel jacket. That was pretty crazy, he decided, almost as crazy as looking for a monster. He thought about that while walking around to the other side of the car.

"Move over." He got behind the wheel. "I'm going to drop you home. You look exhausted. I've got some phone calls to make. I'll put out a report on this Spencer character. Then there's an errand I want to run. Okay?"

"You found out something in there? A lead?"

"I don't know." He rolled down the window. "Maybe." Starting the engine, he glanced around at the town square again, empty save for the faces at the store window.

"Steve? I wouldn't blame you if you just left us," she said softly, turning away as the boy squirmed against her. "You probably should."

"My head is splitting." He put the car in gear. "Let's not talk about it anymore right now."

"Last night. That howl."

" 'Thena, please."

"It was just . . . announcing itself."

"Stop this."

"Letting me know. Letting me know it would be coming for him. For Matthew. It wants him. Don't you feel that? For some reason, he's always been the center, the focus. And me. It wants me too."

This is the last, the last thing, and then it has to stop. He'd left the Volkswagen about a half mile back. *Insane to be out here in this heat.* His shirt was glued to his back. *A howling in the woods.* He hiked through the pines in what he hoped was the direction of Mother Jenks's. *Every dog for miles dead, and she says she heard . . .*

He trudged on, feeling foolish. *The man who did the killing is dead. If danger remains, it's back at that house.* But how to tell Athena? And what kind of future could they have together under these conditions? They must get help for the boy. Perhaps she'd consider sending him someplace, just for a time. *Just until they can figure out what's wrong with him.* He picked up the pace. *Lord, the mess in that kitchen.* She'd told him the dog had torn the place up, but that hadn't seemed likely. *And that bruise on her neck.* That really bothered him the most.

It had all been too much for her. *Finding her brother-in-law's body that way, then Barry's death, then seeing that poor son of a bitch blown away right in front of her the other day.* Too much for anyone. *She's not thinking clearly.* Yes, the boy must have professional help, and he'd make her see that.

And then perhaps they'd have some time for themselves.

He walked through the drugged quiet of the woods, trying to stay on the all-but-invisible trail. *This has to be the path the old guy meant.* He'd stick with it another five or ten minutes; then, if he still hadn't found the house, he'd turn back.

The ground grew rougher, and clumps of brownish moss scratched the soles of his shoes. Stumbling through a shallow depression, he kicked up a piece of brick burned black on one side. He chose a suitable walking stick from the dry litter of the forest floor. *Five more minutes, then I'll head back.*

But the woods drew him on.

He passed a small area of swampy ground, but even that looked dry, and many of the pines seemed lifeless, their branches ending in sharp brown clusters. Sand crunched softly underfoot, almost the only sound. Beginning to imagine that eyes followed him, he looked around. Matted vines, dried stiff, curved and knotted through the thicket, forming dense caves of vegetation all along the trail. The sensation of being watched intensified, and he spun around.

In the trees, darkness moved. A large crow stared from the pines, pointing with its beak. And another. Huge birds, silent and iridescent. Everywhere. Easily dozens of them watched him, some the size of small dogs. A few yards away, one clumsily glided down to the trail. It hopped toward him.

Lousy carrion birds. He turned away, and now they were in front of him as well. He stomped forward, waving the stick. In a glossy explosion, one cawed heavily away as he approached, beating its wings fiercely yet scarcely clearing the ground.

Ruined looking even from a distance, the shack stood well off the trail. Yet he knew this must be it. There didn't seem to be any easy approach. As he left the path, the footing grew onerous with slime and creepers and brambles, thorned vines perversely clutching at him. Spiked tentacles slashed at his face as he forced his way through. He stumbled into a ditch, rank with rotted leaves, and found himself ankle-deep in muck. Heaving against the shell of a tree, he boosted himself out of the gully, sand-scoured bark crumbling beneath his fingers.

Lord, no wonder the crows are here. One wall and the roof had gone entirely, and in a corner lay the twisted black mass. *Place could have burned weeks ago.* He gazed into the ruins, amazed that he felt no horror and no surprise. *The old lady might've already been dead when it happened.* Soft as charred honeycombs, sticks of wood crumbled underfoot. *She might've been. No telling.* And if he hadn't been looking for a corpse, he might never have seen it, burrowed there into the ash, nestled like an animal. *Place might have been struck by lightning during that last big storm.* A leg bone as small as a child's was exposed. Nearby an iron pot lay on its side by what had been a rough fireplace. *Or a cooking accident maybe.* But he knew Athena would never accept this. *Better look around.*

He walked behind the shack. His shoes squished as mud gripped his heels. The walking stick sank deeply and pulled out of his hand, as he sank to the calves in warm, vomitous muck, his legs disappearing into too-soft mud and sawgrass. He clawed at the trees, some of which had also partially burned, their blackened forms twisted as though with death agonies. He clawed at the stiff rushes, screaming through the surge of bile in his throat.

Catching at a thick root, he dragged himself out and hung against a trunk for a moment, waiting for his heart to slow.

The bog began to quake, and ripples spread in shivering circles across the surface as he stared. An earth tremor? Or did some huge creature stir in the depths of the quicksand? He peered around at the woods as if seeing them for the first time. A feeling of presence penetrated him, a sense of the pines: malignant, sentient, lethal.

The troopers only killed a man. This had not died. This could not die. He felt no breeze now, yet an animal moan stirred from the trees.

There on the ground before him, the moss looked squashed down. As he watched, it began to spring back. A few yards away, he saw more faint imprints. Freshly made. He recognized them for what they were immediately, having read their description a dozen times. *Humanlike.* Humanlike tracks surrounded him, bare footprints with slime just seeping in.

The woods grew dim and gray around him, color bleeding away with the rasping of his breath and the throbbing in his chest. And he grew aware of something more, a sense of . . . ripeness. It was ready now, no longer hiding, the pines now too dry to nurture it.

He took a step, then another. He began to run.

Sunday, August 16

"No!"

"'Thena, please, just one chance, that's all I ask."

"Can't you see? All you have to do is look at him." She wiped the boy's forehead with a damp cloth. He'd been uncontrollable all day, thrashing, convulsing, screaming wildly whenever they'd tried to move him. Finally they'd given up, afraid to touch him. At last, he seemed calmer.

Steve's gaze drifted to the boy, and he shuddered, recognizing the sickly gathering lump in his stomach as fear. All along, she'd been right, he knew. It was the boy. Somehow he'd always been the center of it.

Matty's face looked pallid and swollen, and the thick-lidded eyes seemed to stare inward. Perspiration oozed down him, and he shivered, periodically calling out in short, chattering sentences. ". . . coming . . . hurt-dark . . ."

"Help me throw some things in a suitcase. Or don't you believe me?" She confronted him. "Even now, don't you believe it's out there? Don't you believe it's coming here tonight?"

"I believe. That's why I'm asking you to let me do this."

"We have to go now. Leave the house." Determinedly, she marched across the room, then suddenly looked around instead, all her urgency bleeding away in small irresolute gestures. "Did I ever tell you how I met Wallace?"

He tried to smile for her. "No."

"My senior year at City College, my scholarship didn't cover everything, and I had to work after school on campus, and I was running late one night, so I cut through the park, running for my train. And there he was, looking lost, and so handsome in that uniform." She never turned toward him, but spoke as though to the room itself, to the house. "He was stationed at Fort Dix then. He and his friends had come into the city on leave." She laughed. "He'd gotten separated from them, had no idea where he was. I swear, we stared right in each other's eyes, and of course I dropped all my books. He helped me pick them up, and then I didn't care that I was late. He looked so shy, that smile. A natural gentleman, my grandmother would have said. My aunt practically screamed the place down because he was white. I left that night."

" 'Thena . . ."

"All those years, I wouldn't run because Wallace loved this place, and because I wouldn't be beaten, and because I really felt Matty would be, I don't know, safer here somehow." She clung to the twitching boy. "Look at him. He's been waiting for it all day." Her eyes probed every corner of the room. "This place . . . it's all we have." Finally, she faced him. "It'll start to get dark soon."

" 'Thena, one last time, I'm going to ask you to let me do this. Please, just hear me out. I promise there'll be no danger to you or the boy."

"Why do you go on with this?"

"You just said it yourself—it's almost dark. How far do you think we could get? Would you rather be caught out there?" He took a deep breath. "Yesterday in the woods, I ran in a blind panic from something I couldn't see." He watched disbelief grow on her face. "Do you understand? When Anna got sick, I should've helped her face it, but I ran away, dragged her out here with me, as though we could escape it. I don't want to run all my life."

"I can't believe this. Dear God! I can't believe you want to stay."

"This thing—whatever it is—it killed Barry. Don't you understand? It got my partner." He glanced at the boy. "And there's something else, something I can't even put into words. I have this feeling that, if we try to run now, we'll never be free of it. I want to nail it, 'Thena. Just give me one chance to kill it. If it doesn't work, then we'll go. I promise."

She looked at him a long time. "Tell me."

"I want you to keep a gun and lock yourself and the boy in the house."

"And where will you be?"

"Outside. Hiding. With a rifle. Because it is going to come for the boy. No matter where we go."

"You feel that?" In a corner, the sleeping dog jerked, and she started at the movement. "Where's the rifle?" She stroked the boy's hair.

"In the car."

"Get it."

Without speaking, he left the kitchen.

"One hour, Steve!" she called after him. "We'll wait one hour. Then we go."

He stomped across the porch and headed around the side of the house. The screen door didn't slam behind him, because the dog had followed, moving warily, tail stiff. "Good boy, Dooley," he muttered distractedly. In front of the house, the stone fragments of the driveway slid and crunched beneath his heavy tread. When he took the Remington automatic from the backseat of the Volkswagen, the dog whined eagerly. "What's the matter, boy? You want to go hunting?" He put the extra box of shells in his pocket, then scratched the broad head. "Shape you're in, doggy, I'd lay odds on the jackrabbits. But when all this is over, we'll go hunting. I promise." Dooley licked his hand and then, twitching toward the woods, began to growl softly.

He turned, weighing the rifle in his hands: the creek lay in that direction, and the town. He stood deliberating. That night in the storm, maybe Athena only saw that poor lunatic the troopers killed. Maybe the footprints he saw could have been . . . something else.

A hot breeze stirred, and he heard the strange keening. It was there. It was coming.

He glanced at the bristling animal beside him. Even the dog knew. He turned his gaze upward. The sky had begun to dim, and the wind blew stronger.

He hurried back to the house. When he pulled open the door, she spun around with a small cry. He put the rifle on the table, and for a moment, she leaned against him.

"I opened another can of soup. Are you hungry?"

"No." His gaze traveled to the boy. "No, thanks. Matty's feeling better?"

"A little, I think."

At the table, the boy just sat quietly. Steve placed a big hand on his shoulder. "Pal? You okay now?" Slowly, the boy looked up with something coiled in his eyes. Steve backed away. "I guess I'll get ready."

"It's not quite dark yet, is it? I'm only taking one suitcase. We can come back for the rest. If only Matty hadn't been so sick all day, we could've left earlier. We should have anyway." She brought a hand to her face. "I have to stop talking so fast. One hour after it gets dark, we're getting out of here. I mean it, Steve."

" 'Thena . . ."

"One hour. I don't know why I'm even . . ."

The child moaned, and his mother moved quickly to him. He pushed away and groaned again, doubling over. ". . . my friend . . . no, don't do that please don't . . . red coming out . . . help me . . . save . . ."

"Matty? What hurts?"

He groaned loudly, beginning to choke. Steve gently held his head while undigested vegetable soup spattered on the floor-boards. The boy spat a couple of times and continued to heave with nothing coming out. His nose ran, his eyes watered.

"That's a boy. Get it all out now." Steve rubbed his back. "Everything's going to be okay now. 'Thena, why don't you get him a glass of water? You're okay, Matty. Nothing to worry about. Want me to take you upstairs and get you cleaned up?" He used his handkerchief to wipe the boy's mouth. "Don't cry. You feel better now?" He reached for the glass of water and got the boy to drink, talking to him all the while and patting him.

She stood back, a thin smile playing across her lips, and listened to the soothing rumble of his voice. "You're good with him."

The boy stopped trembling and wiped his tears. He sat up straight in the chair, and his face grew calm.

Unnaturally calm, thought Steve. "That's a boy now. Take it easy. Don't worry about the mess. I'll take care of it. You just . . .'Thena? 'Thena, what's wrong with him?"

The boy stared with empty eyes. His breath evened out, grew fainter, became almost undetectable.

nnooooo

Gurglings built up within the boy with mounting pressure, ready to emerge in screaming protest and pleading. His face lit in a flushing surge of color, and saliva gathered on his slack lower lip and slowly dropped in one long bead while he struggled to speak.

where?

The adults hovered about him, and he heard the dwindling hum of their voices as the kitchen contracted and receded.

Darkness entered him: the sound of distant howling echoed in his mind, lonely and pathetic, waiting for him, wanting. The heat rose up inside him, spurting rancid from his nose and mouth, heat and blackness and the cries of wild animals within him. And something tingled behind his ears, a frenzied, unreachable itch. *Chabwok.*

("Look at his face. It's like he's in a trance.")

Now, the dim-lit room all but faded, remained in the sickening murk only as an afterimage. The world wavered. He seemed to be in two places. He could still hear his mother and the gruff, gentle man, but distantly, their voices barely penetrating. Round and pale, their faces swam in his thickening vision, dissolving in the depths. Blackness, thick with the stench of bile, even here, crushed all possibility of light.

Pain burned in his loins. The fever, the suffocation crushed his chest, climbed, rushing through him, and the sound of the night, the searching yowl of demons, bellowed and shook the fibers of the dark.

don wanna be here no

At last, he could hear his own voice and knew his droning words had gone on forever.

"Daddy . . . Daddy, d-don't, please, Daddy, no. N-Not again. I hear 'im? I can hear 'im! Yellin' and hollerin'! Gonna hurt me. Daddy?" A current of pain washed out of him, and his words flowed, only half heard, like the music of the insects that filtered to that lighted kitchen drifting in his mind. Then the kitchen vanished altogether. *Daddy?* He'd never been in this room before. He lay on the floor and glints of light flitted up through cracks in the boards, making his heart pound even more. He tried to understand why he felt so scared, then his mind gave up the struggle. *Might come up here. No, don't hurt me.* In the dark, the open window slit remained indistinguishable from the rest of the wall, yet he knew it was there, even before he felt the heavy air stir from that direction. He knew everything about this room. And from below the furious raging continued,

("Matthew? Why don't you answer me? Look at me! What's wrong?")

quaking the building with its very loudness. Slumped in the darkness of *my room, mine, only not*, he listened to shouts and cringed as from the gin mill below, something splintered noisily. He

("He can't hear you, 'Thena. My God I think I understand this. Matty, where are you? Can you tell me what you see? Try, boy. Can you hear me?")

whimpered. And now the fever, the suffocation began to come heavily over him, claiming him, pulling his limbs. It raged up his legs, climbing through the blood to his stomach. Saliva flowed unnoticed from his lips to run across his bare chest, and he trembled and bent forward, choking again and afraid to make a sound. He couldn't breathe anymore, and the burning pain in his groin made him weep.

Moaning softly, he pulled off the rest of his clothes. Marl leaned back against the bed and struggled for air. *Ernie's bed.* His chest stiffened, and he clutched the tightened knot of his belly. *Lonny's bed.* Hands clenched. His body hardened.

It was like drowning, the breath dammed deep within him, his lungs squeezed to bursting. Beyond his window, the night sighed softly.

His nostrils flared, vainly trying for oxygen, and the veins of his throat thickened and swelled, crushing his windpipe in anguished bulges. Burns exploded in his stomach, and he gritted back a scream. His teeth rattled as his head jerked spasmodically from side to side. He clutched at his swollen abdomen, fearing it would burst, and tears and spittle streaked his face.

Al Spencer rampaged and bellowed in the gin mill. He slammed a stool against the wall. He kicked a table over, and empty jars crashed to the dirt floor. The jars marked the last of his private stock; almost as an afterthought, the state troopers had smashed his still. But even before that, fewer and fewer of his customers had been venturing out. "Can't even make a buck. Where da fuck's Wes? Where's Lonny? Assholes. Man works hard all 'is life." At last he paused, panting heavily. Suddenly his face contorted with memory. He clawed away a loose board and extracted a jar half full of amber liquid. Leaning heavily on the wall, he gulped it down. "Gone." By the glow of candles stuck in beer bottles, he surveyed the wreckage of his establishment. "All gone." The slitted gleam returned to his eyes. "I know whose fault."

One thought guttered in his brain. "Took 'im in outta kindness. Jus' doin' 'im a favor. So?"

So he hurled the jar against the wall.

"Lost everthin'! Says 'is name is Ernie. Doesn't say the cops is after 'im! A favor! Up there—I knows what they was doin' up in 'at room. Unner my own roof. You get down here, Marl. You hear me? I know you listenin' up there! Thinks I don't know."

His eyes roamed to the calendar on the wall. December. Years ago. The woman's breasts impossibly huge and blubbery in the brown and yellow light. Hanging below it, the blade of the meat cleaver glowed softly.

"Shoulda made your mother take you with 'er." He paused, his breath labored. "When she went an lef' me 'lone, lef' me 'lone

with a kid. You hear me? I shoulda took you inna woods and lef'
you wi' half your head gone too. You think I done that?" Self-
pity rang through the rage now as he stood at the base of the stairs
and shrieked himself toward frenzy. "You think I done it? You
don't know what I done. Maybe I did and maybe I didn't. You
don't know. She left me. With a kid. My boy. Won't even come
near his old man no more but up there wi' that sumnabitch, that's
awright. I know!" He unscrewed the cap on a kerosene can and
slopped some into a lantern. "Punish 'im good. What? Who said
that? Somebody here?"

Something like a voice replied. Faintly. A tiny scraping noise.
A wordless whisper that could exist only in a nightmare.

Al's mouth opened, and no sound emerged. His eyes screwed
up in denial while his body went rigid with fear. "What? Can't
be? Wha's'at?" He took a step backward, then another. "Marl?"
Something like resignation seeped into his fury. "Marl? Where
you at, boy?"

The whisper scratched again, louder now, and nearer.

Al trembled . . . then took refuge in madness. Lantern in one
hand, he hooked the cleaver down from the nail. "I know wha'
you was doin' up there." He started back toward the stairs.
"Marl! You come here, boy! Fix you, you sumnabitch." Climbing, he clutched the cleaver tightly, and the dull blade caught
the light. "Won't even come down 'ere to 'is daddy no more, 'is
daddy who needs 'im, took care a him." His voice filled up with
tears. "Din' I always take care a you?" Halfway up the stairs, he
stopped. "Boy?"

Above him, something crouched . . . and cast a froglike
shadow on the wall.

Al blinked, silent now. All rage evaporated. Peering, he leaned
forward. With infinite slowness, he raised the lantern higher.

When he dropped it, flames engulfed the stairs.

Loud rustlings filled the dark pit of the shed.

Rats. Big ones, by the sound of them. Clutching the rifle,
Steve crouched behind the door. He touched the flashlight at
his side, still reluctant to switch it on. He needed a drink.

Across the grounds, the bright rectangle of the screen door glowed. He knew she sat waiting, revolver at her side, and he guessed she'd be holding Matthew's small firm hand in hers. Yet the yard isolated them as surely as if they'd been on separate islands.

There was no moon, there were no stars. He shifted his position slightly and heard the slitherings around him cease for a moment. He could almost feel the vermin listening. Seconds ticked by, and the electric, reverberating whine of crickets filled the minutes.

He thought about her alone with the boy, faraway in the snarl of the night. And again he remembered the childhood game of "Werewolf," the shame of being too afraid to come out of his hiding place when he'd been It, when they'd all been hunting him, remembered how he'd become the best one at the game when he grew older . . . because he'd been afraid still. He wiped sweat from his forehead with his sleeve, convinced now this waiting was insanity, that they should have run when Athena wanted to.

When her shouts came, the shock lasted only an instant. Then the flashlight beam swung weakly across the yard, the house, as he pelted toward the porch. Two voices rose, shattering the sound patterns of the crickets.

" 'Thena!" He thudded up the steps. "The door! Unlatch the—!" He ripped the screen door from its hinges, flinging it aside.

". . . running . . . coming now . . . blood running in the trees!" The boy twisted, shrieking on the floor. "Hide me! My friend, hu-hurting . . . !"

Down beside him, she struggled to restrain him. "He just fell," she gasped, looking up at Steve, who stood frozen in the doorway. ". . . and . . . and started to . . ."

The boy flailed and growled, froth at his mouth. In the far corner, Dooley crouched, shivering, with lips curled back. Together, the man and woman held the screaming, weeping child until his struggles grew weaker and his head dropped back, thudding on the floorboards.

". . . run . . ."

"Who's running?" Steve leaned over him, his face just a few inches from the boy's. "Is it Chabwok?"

". . . the trees . . ."

"Is Chabwok coming here?"

Matty's lips moved as he shuddered feebly. Steve released his hold on the boy's shoulders and looked to Athena.

Matty's eyes flew open.

"No, Steve! Don't let go of him!"

The boy struggled unsteadily to his feet, and when she moved to grab him, Steve waved her back.

As though drawn by invisible chains, Matty stumbled toward the open doorway. His arms swung limply at his sides, and his feet shuffled. Steve reached out gently and took hold of him by a belt loop. He stopped moving; slowly one arm rose. ". . . night-rushing . . ." The pointing finger described a small arc to the left.

"That's it then. It's over that way." Steve checked the flashlight. "Look at him. He knows. You were right. Somehow he's sensitive to it." He turned to her, confronting the fear in her eyes. "You take the rifle. We were wrong to wait. We're getting out now."

He allowed the trembling boy to lead him onto the porch, and she followed, pulling back just at the doorway. The dog also cowered, watching with eyes dull as slag.

"What is it, 'Thena? Do you hear something? Do you see . . . ?"

"Nothing." She stared past him. "Only the dark."

He stepped back and put a hand on her face, and then he was gone, beyond the spill of light, down the porch stairs and into the yard.

A moment passed before she could make herself follow. "Good-bye, house," she whispered, touching the kitchen wall. Taking the key ring from her pocket, she pulled the heavy inner door shut behind her, snuffing out the wedge of light. "Good-bye, Wallace." She fumbled with the flashlight. "Steve! Where did you go?"

"We're over here." Drowned in darkness, voices drifted on currents of warm air. She heard them walking away, the boy stumbling like a sleepwalker, and she hurried after them.

Around the side of the house, Steve waited for her. "We didn't bring the suitcases, Steven."

"Forget it. Get in the car. Where's the dog?"

"I thought you had him."

"Dooley! Dooley, come here, boy. Here, dog."

"Did he head over that way?"

"Dooley, come back here. Goddamn it!"

"I don't think I saw him come out of the house. Could he have gone back under the sofa again?"

" 'Thena, the dog will be all right. I'll pick him up in the morning when I get your suitcases. Let's just get to my house and try to rest."

They got in the Plymouth, Steve behind the wheel, the boy between them on the front seat. She handed Steve the keys and checked the locks on all the doors. When she turned the boy's face to her, his eyes twisted away to stare through the windshield.

"Chabwok would never hurt you, would he, baby?"

Awareness seemed to flicker on his face, then fade, leaving only ashes. The engine chattered, and the car rolled onto the winding sand. For a moment, headlights caught the silent house. Then it vanished, behind them in the night. They paused at the sand hill, the tires crackling over sticks.

She pointed. "That leads to the highway."

"What's down the other way?"

"I don't know, Steve. Nothing."

The boy's face stayed slack, but with a sudden bolt, he pointed his whole body toward the fork that led away from the highway.

"It's down that way, 'Thena. Whatever it is, it's down there."

The engine idled. The boy moaned with an agitated rumble in his throat.

"Steve?" She peered down the dark fork.

"Yeah, I see it."

"What is it?"

"A car, or a truck, I can't tell."

"Drive up a little farther," she told him.

He looked at her.

"We have to. If there's people in it, we have to warn them."

The car turned laboriously.

"Be careful of the sand here." Her voice was so soft, it was almost as though she were talking in her sleep. "The car gets stuck sometimes."

A small tree broken beneath it, the panel truck leaned against the woods off the road. Doorless and battered. No license plate. Broken windshield.

"Do you recognize it?"

"I'm not sure. I think I may have seen it around town." The boy knocked against her as he began rocking back and forth, faster and wilder, mumbling to himself.

Steve rolled down the window. "Anybody around?! Yo! Can anybody hear me?"

The boy's lips continued to move, his face lit by dashboard dials. He cocked his head to one side, listening to voices only he could hear, and his eyes never wavered from the night.

"You're going to make yourself sick again, baby. Try to calm down." In response, the boy murmured weakly, wildly. Trying not to hear, she took his face in her hands. "Matty, listen to me. It's going to be all right. Do you hear me? It's okay. Steve? What are you doing?"

"I have to get out and check."

"No!"

"Just stay put a minute. I could swear I see somebody in that truck." The door slammed behind him.

"Steven!"

A few quick steps brought him to the other vehicle. Then the smell hit him. "Oh my God."

Something headless slumped at the wheel.

Marl screamed away from it. He would not look up. Not for anything. Above him, impossibly huge, he knew its eyes glowed red with hellish fires, and its long tail whipped through the pines. Swaying, it spread wings that blacked out the night sky.

It hovered, taloned feet hanging just above the sand. A rope of saliva glistened as it opened its mouth and howled.

Dwarfed by the thing, he sobbed and rolled about the clearing, trying to escape the monstrous flapping, but all around, the hated pines pressed closer, trapping him. Each time the monster screamed, Marl hunched farther into himself, a tight ball, tearing soft hairs from his chest in fear and kicking at the dirt.

The woods wavered. He was safe elsewhere, gazing out through a windshield into the night as the woman's arms tightened around him.

They wavered again, and he hid his face in the sand. *Car bouncing in the . . . dark moving . . . coming here tonight or don't you believe? and if we run Dragonfly if we run we'll take it with us hatches out in the end all foul . . . don wanna . . . water all leaked away in the palm of my hand felt like fire No! Don't! Please! Wings burst outta the skin an it flies wet* Something moved in the wind and mounting heat. *You know what's out there, boy?* He remembered moonlight and the woman's voice as she held the book, murmuring in softness, remembered as though he'd been there. And the picture. *Chabwok.* The monster. *want I want I want my friend Ernie, where are you? Pammy-blood comin' outta my mouth*

It loomed before him, the picture from the page, eyes glistening, claws snapping, tearing away the tops of trees, and his stomach churned in terror. His head throbbed, lips stretched tight; his teeth felt too large.

come with me please to the woods Marl just once

The rising moon cast the dimmest of ground light. The reptilian tail lashed the sand near his face, and the wind it caused ruffled his hair. The yowling continued, sharp and inhuman.

Marl raised his head. No monster's tail slashed the air, only pine trees waving in the sudden wind. He stood up, his naked body soiled with ash. His left arm was burned, but he didn't feel it. The wind blew long whitish hair about his face, and it felt good. He looked around.

No Devil. And those were not spreading wings that billowed

and blotted out the sky. But still the howl poured forth as though from the Pit. He felt it vibrate in his chest, ripping through his throat. *Come with me, Marl.* Trembling tears streaked his face. *You don't have to be scared. Not scared.*

He spread wide his arms as though to embrace the woods, the long-hated woods, and reached for the smoke-stained sky.

The breeze carried a churning gurgle, as though floods rushed across the parched land. The wind flowed louder, roaring with a surge that hissed and lapped in suddenly shifting gusts. Even the sand stirred, rustling in the heated air, while in the low grasses insects shrilled louder, then stopped altogether.

Its topmost branches bent beneath a crushing wind; then Hanging Tree cracked with a drying sound. Above it, the night reddened with a false dawn.

Noises surrounded the Monroe house. It seemed all the birds were awake and shouting, stirred to panic by the acrid wind. Already, the smell of smoke hung thickly over the yard, and from inside the darkened house came barking and a frantic scrabbling at the door.

"I'm sorry, 'Thena. I shouldn't have gone this far." Slowly, the car pressed along the narrow road, scraping trees on both sides. "There's got to be a place to turn around."

"I'm frightened." She tightened her arms around the boy, who kept trying to jerk away from her. "I'm really frightened."

"Take it easy." He couldn't bring himself to look at them, and he cursed as he struggled with the wheel. "Do you know who it could have been? In the truck back there? No, forget it. I'm sorry. I'll get us out of here in a minute. Shit, I should've just backed up to the fork."

The boy's frenzy increased. Restraining him, she didn't answer at first. "We would've gotten stuck in the sand. Not your fault."

"Wait a minute. Was that a spot? Could I turn around there?" He stopped the car, backed up. "I can't tell. Is there enough room?"

She could see practically nothing through the window. "Yes, I think so." She unlocked the door and opened it to the moving ground. "Go back a little farther. Now cut your wheels."

The boy scrambled across her and out the door. She clutched at air.

"Jesus!" Instantly, Steve threw the brake and jumped out the other door. "Stop! Come back here! Matty!"

"Where are you?" She jumped out, staggered into the trees. "Matthew!"

"Athena!" He ran a few steps. "Stop right there. Don't chase him. He went up that way—running along the road. Get back in the car."

"But . . ."

"Hurry!"

His door slammed. Hesitating, she looked about wildly.

" 'Thena!" The car started moving. "Quick! Jump in!"

She threw herself across the seat. "Where is he?" They rolled after the boy. "Do you see him?"

"Athena, shut that door!"

"Where is he? Matthew, come back! Do you hear me? Go faster!"

"I'm afraid I'll hit him. Athena, close that door all the way!"

"Matthew? Oh God, oh my God, stop the car! Stop the car and let me go after him. Oh Matty!"

"Don't be stupid—you'll get lost. He went this way. Look up there! Is that him? I think I see . . ."

The road ended. Abruptly. A wall of trees.

"Oh please . . . Steve, catch him. . . . I can't run."

He stood in the road. "He went in that way. I saw him." He stood by the car and pounded his fist on the hood. "Matty! Matty! No, 'Thena, stay in the car. I'll go get him. Do you hear me? I said stay in the car."

"No."

"What if he comes back and there's nobody here?" He turned to look at her one last time. "One of us has to stay. Now don't argue with me. We can't waste the time. Roll up the windows and lock the doors. Keep the headlights on so I can find my way back." He slammed the door. "Keep the rifle in your hands. You remember what I told you about how to use it? Whatever you do, don't open the door to anybody but me and the boy."

"Steve?" She leaned out.

"And roll up those windows!" He hurried into the pines. "Matty! Where are you, boy? Answer me!" The headlights shone brightly behind him, striping the sand with pine shadows. He gripped the revolver. The breeze held a wisp of something; he shuddered with disgust, and the trees whispered like children all around him. It was here. He knew it. Flicking off the safety catch, he prayed that she wouldn't get out of the car.

He waited for the phantom children to surge toward him, waited for the clawing hands. He clutched the sweaty gun more tightly, and he stumbled, the ground breaking loose, soft. His stomach clenched. "Matty?" Already, the headlights behind him looked distant and foggy, and he cursed himself for not having brought the flashlight. He panted against the clamminess of his clothing. The hot silt of the dried swamp gave way beneath his feet with every step, and the air hummed around him. He heard a noise.

"Matty?" But he knew.

Something slogged toward him. He felt the strength drain from him with a steady, pulsing nausea, felt his guts roil and the sweat run down his sides.

The shot sounded so faint, so faraway.

She sat very still. *Please, be all right.* She could see only the reaching pines, frozen in the high beams. *Steven. Matthew.* She shut her eyes. *Help.* She heard nothing further. No shots. No cries. *I should go get help.* Even as she thought it, she knew there was no time, and as she sat motionless, an awareness filled her, a sense of her whole life, of everything that had brought her to this frozen moment, until her silent panic hardened into a feeling of rightness, of inevitability.

It's out there. Waiting. The way I always knew it was. It has the boy. And now I'm going to find him. To get him back. At last. All the nightmares rose in her mind. *It could be anything, anyone.* She remembered all those books they'd read and what Doris had said about people who change, who kill. *But I'm going to know it now.* The weight of the rifle surprised her. *I am.* She moved with an almost mechanical efficiency, as though she'd been preparing for this her whole life. *Now.*

She left the headlights on, and the merging shafts struck the blackness. *So we can all find our way back.* Getting out, she slammed the door tight and took a few steps, cutting through the swath of light. Beyond the bright island in front of the car lay only a void. Like the end of the world. Not limping, though her leg ached, she headed into the trees. "Steven?" Her shadow hurtled on ahead of her, startling her as it leaped from trunk to trunk. "Matthew?"

Hot wind gritted across the sand, and she listened to the night keening as it passed over her.

It knows. She switched off the flashlight and clipped it to her belt. *It's waiting.* Moonlight clawed through the trees, ran up the barrel of the rifle. In a few moments, her eyes grew accustomed to the dark, and she moved on.

She heard birds calling in agitation . . . and other noises now, tiny sounds, as though dozens of small slinking beasts scurried through the brush. Things crunched underfoot. *Please, be all right.* Her hand went numb, and she relaxed her grip on the rifle, felt the blood tingle back into her fingers.

A ticking of leaves and twigs became a heavy crunching.

"Steven?"

It grew louder.

She aimed the rifle at nothing she could see.

It growled.

She fired and ran, blinded, her shoulder aching from the recoil. *No dream.* Behind her, bulk shifted and rattled through the pines. *It's not a dream.* She spun around, fleetingly aware of an area of moving darkness.

Again, the gun rocked and roared, and she breathed the tang of gunpowder.

It grabbed her by the hair and yanked her head back.

She felt its talons, felt her scalp burn as hair ripped out. Crystals of pain tore through her skull, and her mouth pulled open, a gravid choke bursting in her throat. Whirling, she struck with the rifle butt, the blow containing all the terror-born fury of a thousand nightmares.

The dark shape staggered.

The gun wrenched from her grasp to go crashing into the dark.

She ran. Pain jolted in her leg as she broke through thick bracken. She could hear the thing crashing through the underbrush close behind her, and she stumbled, the flashlight on her belt banging against her thigh. She groped for the flashlight, pulled it loose. Switching it on, she cast it as far as she could into the pines. Instantly, she bolted in the opposite direction.

The pounding in her chest squeezed the breath from her until she could hear nothing but her own gasps. Sinking to the ground, she curled her body into a ball, found a bush to crawl beneath.

The night came in with wave after wave of terror; she felt it close above her head like a black foam. *Don't move.* Ragged tendrils of the dark wrapped themselves around her, and she hid herself in them. *Don't make a sound.* Wind hissed in her ears, and she felt safe, one with the night.

Where's the moon? When she opened her eyes, she could no longer see the stars. Her hands traveled over herself, feeling for blood, for gaping wounds. Her sides ached, and she trembled with a shock reaction from the pain in her scalp.

Something swirled in her vision, off in the trees, dim movement.

Mist shrouded the glow of the flashlight. *But I threw it farther than that, and I ran. How could . . . ?* The splaying beam swung through the trees. *Steve?* She stayed crouched, and her chest heaved.

In refracted brightness, she could almost see what held the flashlight, could almost make out the misshapen arm. *It's coming this way!*

The beam struck her eyes, and her night vision blanked out.

An unvoiced scream rattling in her brain, she turned her head until the beam passed on. She blinked. Dark and squat in the diffuse moonlight, something loomed behind her in the reeds.

A shack! Lurching to her feet, she almost pitched forward, and her leg exploded in pain. Gritting her teeth to keep herself silent, she hobbled toward the hut, looking back with every step.

The patch of brightness had stopped moving, still a good distance away, and she staggered on, gaining speed as the leg responded to her panicked demands. *It's back there. Way back there.* Peering over her shoulder, she noticed the light still had not moved . . . that it seemed curiously low to the ground.

The thing had thrown it away. *It could be anywhere now.* Pain loosened its grip on her side, and she limped rapidly toward the hut. *Could be right behind me!*

Off its hinges, the door leaned against a tree. *No shelter here. Nowhere to run.* Drying mud flats stretched all around in the faint moonlight.

A weapon—there could be something inside. She had to press against the wall and step across a bent sapling, and even as she entered, she realized this movement reminded her of something. *Matty at the shed that rainy morning, that pantomime he did.* She tried not to breathe through her nose, but a stench coated the roof of her mouth, gagging her. Mouth open, she peered back through the doorway. *Is it following?*

She stepped on something soft.

No. Moonlight leaked through the doorway, and the reeking shack swam about her. *Run!* Slowly, her eyes adjusted. *Get away from here!* She looked down at something like a black pudding stuffed into a dress and became aware that other things sprawled around her, vague shapes, some in advanced states of liquefaction. Something rustled.

Her eyes tracked across the moonlit floor.

From a dark corner inside the shack came a blubbering mockery of words. She backed away, slipped on a mound, fell, and a lump of something slimy as wet clay came away in her hand. She rolled. There was movement in the bulk she tumbled over, and she recoiled with a silent shriek.

" 'Th-Thena . . ." It spoke and reached for her.

"Steve!" She knelt by him, felt the wetness of his shirtfront. "You're hurt? Did you crawl in here? No, don't try to talk." She watched the doorway. "It's out there." She searched his pockets for matches, struck one, and the sulfurous stink found her throat. In the glow, his shirt glistened.

She looked around at hell, at madness.

The occupants of the shack lay in positions of abandon. Most had clothing peeled back to expose rotting carcasses. Pocked faces grinned pus yellow and mold green in the light of the tiny flame. Nearby, what appeared to be a male hunched on its face, coarsening gray buttocks exposed, and against the wall, a skeleton grin that fell away in maggots was no less obscene than the legs spread wide beneath a tattered skirt. Puddling flesh left the leg bones bare in spots.

The match went out, and she inhaled the horrible intimacy of the dark, the air so corrupt even it could probably kill. She pressed Steve's handkerchief to his throat, tried to stop the blood that gurgled there. "You'll be all right, Steve. I'll get you out of here." She lit another match but couldn't bring herself to look at his slashed belly. Tightening her jaw against the rising flow of nausea, she closed her eyes against the force of her mind's rejection. She couldn't move.

A distant flash of pain forced her eyes open. The match had gone out. With burned fingertips, she fumbled for another.

"Something under me . . . hurts . . ." Squirming, he shivered convulsively, and his arms jerked toward her.

"Don't try to move."

But he pulled her toward him. ". . . get out . . ."

"I'm not leaving you."

" 'Thena, run." His grip tightened. "Don't you know . . . where we . . . ?"

"We're in its . . . lair." Striking another match, she spoke softly. "My leg hurts. I can't run anymore."

A howl shook the walls.

She clutched him in terror. The sounds that emerged from his throat ceased to be words.

A weapon. Pulse throbbing in her head, she turned from him. *Find a weapon.* She forced herself to look beyond the ravaged bodies, the inflated faces.

Strange objects littered the shack. Damp sticks that might once have been furniture were heaped in the corners, and things twisted and partially devoured sprawled upon them, coated with a scum that seemed faintly to glow, a clinging putrescence. Oddly shaped devices hung from the rafters, bent stiff-wire cages and rotten leathern contraptions with tufts of fur adhering. *Must've been a trapper's hut. There have to be guns, guns and skinning knives and things.* But they'd be old, the guns, she knew—museum pieces. Useless.

Dust laden and cobwebbed, the largest object hung just above her head, and she struggled to pull it down with one hand, thick grime coating her fingers. It weighed more than she expected, and she almost dropped it. Rust ground into her palm. *What in the . . . ?*

As she hefted the object, examining it, match light gleamed off something on the floor, something bright.

Stooping, she brought the match low. A glistening caul of decay covered the face . . . but silver jewelry glittered on a bloated wrist. She recognized the design of interlocking leaves. *It's the bracelet Steve gave me, the one that belonged to his wife.*

Everything went black.

Oh, Pamela.

Choking, she held one hand across her nose and mouth and felt what remained of her sanity begin to splinter. A moment later, in the darkness, she realized what the heavy object in her hand must be.

"Steve?" Another match sparked. "I've found a bear trap."

In the flickering shadows, his mouth seemed to move.

"It's pretty rusted," she whispered. "Oh God, I think I hear it."

The thing howled again, louder, and dust rained down on her from the ceiling.

Oh God, let this be over. She pawed frantically across the corpses, finding canteens and camping gear, but no guns or knives. *I can't fight anymore. I can't.* Then she saw it. In the corner leaned an ax. She brushed away the silken tent that cocooned it, and black spiders dropped off. She hefted the ax. The handle was rotten, the head dull and loose, but it was something.

From outside, from just the other side of the wall, came the whispery scraping of heavy feet against the sand.

Almost. The match dropped, because she needed both hands now. Working in the dark, she struggled with the trap, trying to figure out how it opened. *I'm almost ready for you.*

Tugging and grunting, she managed to pull the ridged jaws a few inches apart, but they closed with a grind. She felt blood on her fingers. Taking hold of the ax handle, she pried the jaws open again, exerting all her strength, then worked the handle between the teeth. Holding the trap down with one foot, she levered it, slowly, all the way open. Then she put her lame foot on it and heard a click as the trap flattened.

" 'Thena, run."

"Ssh, Steve." Stepping back, she felt for the matches. *One left.* She set fire to the pack and examined the spring plate in the center of the trap. *This better work.* Holding the flame gingerly, she positioned the trap by the doorway.

She dropped the curling matchbook and watched the red fade. Then she stood out of the strike of moonlight and waited with the ax raised above her head.

The footsteps ceased.

It's just standing there, on the other side of the doorway. She could hear it breathing and realized with a sinking terror that it could hear her. Its breath became a slavering growl, a guttural snarl that ground thickly on and on.

"Thh thth thththenahthena"

Soft as spider's silk.

Then silence.

The damp wood of the ax handle began to crumble in her grip. *It . . . said . . . my . . . name.*

She heard a wet slithering.

Then Matthew's voice echoed clearly in her mind: *Behind . . . behind inna dark . . . turn around . . . right behind . . .*

From where Steve lay came a giggle that choked into a sob, and she spun, swinging with all her strength.

She heard a harsh animal shriek as the ax connected.

She swung again, shouting with a ferocity of her own. The handle snapped. She leaped for the doorway as fingers clawed at her. Her foot struck something hard and she went down, dragging the heavy object across the floor, feeling its metal teeth dig into her leg.

She scrambled outside and shoved at the leaning door, sent it toppling. For an instant, she glimpsed the blue-gray face above her in the moonlight, the wide, luminous eyes, the chin wet with drool. Then the door thudded, the thing disappearing beneath it.

Moonlight struck like a wave of energy. She plunged into it, stumbling, and fought her way against that current, still clutching the steel-jaw trap. *Too rusted.* It hadn't worked, hadn't snapped shut when she'd fallen on it. *Thank God.* She had to reach the pines—lose herself in them. *Steve, forgive me.*

At the edge of the woods stood the boy. His eyes shone white.

"Run! Matty, get away!" The wind blew strong against her as, limping heavily, she raced toward him.

The boy stood very still, and his gaze traveled past her.

"Run!" Yelling as she turned, she saw the thing burst from the hut and streak forward, blurring.

The gaping maw. The clutching hands.

"No!" She hurled the trap, falling to her knees, arms outstretched to shield the boy.

She heard a muffled clang, and the moonlight faded steadily, sinking the world in darkness.

Mired in the stench of the hut, Steve heard the awful screech and knew he had to help her. He tried to rise but felt the blood pool in his bowels and then leak out around the burning coil of pain. Again, his strength ebbed, receding into darkness. Something was sticking into him, sharp and hard at his back. He tried to squirm off it.

He couldn't die here, not now, couldn't abandon her when she needed him. He twisted over on his side, the pain searing him in half, his breath burning through his throat. Then his hand struck the thing he'd been lying on and fastened instantly on the familiar hardness.

The sky seemed to boil, the clouds strange and fleet.

She approached. It lay on the ground. A naked thing, it convulsed, shrieking and gibbering. She waited for it to die. In the dark, the feet looked horny and malformed. Cautiously, she bent closer. It breathed still but no longer growled, the worst of its death spasms over. Only as Matty drew forward did she recognize the long whitish hair that trailed about its shoulders.

The trap had stuck the abdomen, clamping shut on its stomach.

He's still alive. Heavy shadow lay across the face, but she could see the twitching of the lips, like the struggles of a dying bird. *I don't want to hear.*

Stench rose from the earth.

". . . kill anybody'd try ta chase you 'way . . . you 'bout the only friend I ever . . ."

The words grew even fainter, and she tried to hold Matty back from him.

". . . no don' tie me up! Wanna help ya. Ernie, they comin' . . . come to get Lonny's things she said you know what's out there, boy. My own son. You and yer ma out there inna woods . . ."

She watched his bowels looping out, listened to the pathetic ravings. *He's spilling his guts.* She wanted to scream or laugh. It seemed incredible he still could speak, incredible he could breathe, and in the weak light the entrails seemed to unclench and writhe on the ground like serpents.

His face. Moonlight raced, dappling over him. *I have to see.* Nothing of his features remained visible for more than a fleeting second, and the sibilant gasp of his voice ebbed, growing even more chaotic. *I have to know.*

". . . what'd you do to my father loony you ain't like them

others what are we sort of like cousins where's my old man I know you know where . . ."

Something buzzed in her skull. In confusion, she seemed to hear his voice duplicated by an echoing whisper.

". . . come with me please just once lef' me wi' a kid come with me to the woods Marl please . . ."

Speaking almost simultaneously, Matthew parroted every word, and when the other no longer had the strength, Matthew spoke alone.

". . . think you could take this alla this fer yer ole man shoulda blowed yer head off like I blowed hers off inna woods . . ."

She put her arms around her son's shoulders, tried to jerk him out of this communion. As though she'd touched a power line, awareness jolted through her; she drowned in unending misery as all the frightening filth of Marl's life poured through her. Sometimes it seemed more than words, more than just a sordid, horrible ramble. It entwined her, and she caught a sense of something that churned, deep and turbulent and hot, fuming over and obscured, a molten sadness that foamed upon the cold rawness of death. She smelled things, tasted things—jumbled memories—saw gigantic Spencer edge closer, leering, too close, the pores like craters in his bristling face, his clothes open. She saw the Devil loom transparent, and the pines breathed to her, moaning of the hunt and of wetness and of love. She broke away from the boy, and it ended.

". . . if I tie you you'll be safe here the stateys won't hurt you only I know Marl I found you only me but it's me they want put your whole head in 'is mouth and bite it off an' its wings glisten in the sunlight w-when it breaks free . . ."

His limbs trembled in a final convulsion, then Marl lay still.

She felt something twinge at the back of her consciousness; something like a whitish grub stirred blindly. Like a naked hatchling, fallen from the nest, it struggled to lift its head and gaze with still-shut eyes into a sky it would never know—struggled—then lay flattened on the ground.

"My friend! I can't hear 'im anymore. I won't! Chabwok! No! Not the chains!" He threw himself on Marl. "Please, not chains! Be good now! I'll be good!"

"Matty! No!" She couldn't pull him off.

He yelled and clawed at the body.

"My God, what are you doing? No, Matty!"

Sobbing, he bit it.

She tried to drag him away, but he backhanded her, knocking her down. He grunted and growled.

"Oh no, my baby. I won't let it happen." Soft things splashed on her, soaking the front of her shirt. "I promise you, I won't let it happen that way to you!"

Dried reeds rattled behind them. The boy shook her off and turned from the body, dark fluids pouring from his chin. He snarled.

Steve lay a few yards away, arched to one side as he crawled on his belly through the weeds. Mud covered him. Blood covered him. And the gun in his hand was leveled on the boy.

A wail tore from Athena as she hurled herself in front of her son.

Steve jerked the revolver away at the last instant, firing into the woods, then dropped it in front of his face. Instantly, he seemed to slip out of consciousness, his head falling to the soft ground.

An acrid stench washed over them with the hot, crushing wind. She smelled the smoke then, finally understood what was happening. The woods burned.

Her strength came from somewhere beyond her ability to comprehend, and she moved as in a dream, somehow half-rousing Steve, somehow getting him to his feet. She dragged and carried him through the pines. "Keep going, Steve. Just a little farther. Don't give up now. Stay with me, Matty. Don't cry. Stay with me."

Soon the pines had vanished, melting into a dense, featureless gray. Yet they stumbled onward, and many times she considered leaving the injured man and saving the boy. Somehow she led them. In silence, the boy clung to her clothing, sometimes helping her to bear the man along. They knew no direction, only movement and the effort to keep breathing.

The glow of baleful eyes filtered through the haze, though the headlights seemed to grow dimmer even as they watched.

With a final heaving effort, they reached the automobile. She got the back door open and tried to push the man onto the seat, and the boy tried to help by getting in the other side and dragging him in by the shoulders. Steve's eyes blinked open—he saw the boy.

He screamed once, then went limp.

They locked the doors, and rolled the windows tight. She clicked off the headlights and put her head down on the steering wheel. She wanted to sleep. Only the boy's coughing roused her.

The engine choked, then silence.

With no panic left, she tried again, turning the key, pumping the gas pedal.

Matty lay beside her on the seat. He was so very still. She drove through a world of blankness, eyes tearing, knowing she couldn't go on, knowing she could never stop. Vaguely, she wondered if they were already dead.

The car floated through an empty universe that separated into gray currents and eddies of reflected light.

"It bit me." Delirious, Steve gasped from the backseat. "I'm It." Each breath an ordeal, he kept repeating the same words. "I'm It now."

Coughing, she drove through a tunnel of smoke, the gleam of the headlights forming a bright, enveloping cocoon.

EPILOGUE/PROLOGUE

Those seriously injured had been taken elsewhere.

Filling the room, an irritating film coated their throats and burned their eyes, seeming to rise from the very clothing of the nearly two hundred refugees crowded into the high-school gymnasium. The volunteers, potbellied men in clerical collars, matronly women and earnest teenagers from rural churches, milled about, distributing sandwiches—mean circles of cold cuts wedged into dry bread—urging their charges to try some of the soft local apples.

Most of the people hunched on cots, dazed but eating—it was after all a free lunch. Others sprawled in exhaustion; some just wandered about.

The boy slept with his mouth pressed into the canvas, the rough woolen blanket bunched about his feet. "Dooley . . . save . . . ?" Some dark dream clotted in his face, and his voice held petulant wildness. ". . . find . . ." His hands clenched. ". . . come this way . . . come . . ."

The hall echoed, raucous with murmured complaints, with whining and crying and laughter, with the shuffling of feet and the blared chatter of a television and several radios, all amplified and distorted by the high ceiling and the polished floor.

"Old dogs are smart, baby. Dooley's all right. You hush now." Athena gazed down at the dreaming, rolling movement beneath his eyelids. "Just sleep." His face still looked red and puffy. A drop of blood at one nostril smeared toward his upper lip, and she wiped it away with her sleeve.

Finally, he seemed peaceful, and she stood up, easing a sharp twinge in her leg. After getting more coffee, she drifted toward the television set. The words and images jangled in her exhausted consciousness.

"Thirty-nine fire companies on the line . . . some from as faraway as Newark . . . smoke inhalation . . . list now stands at twelve known dead and thirty-one missing . . . governor has declared . . ."

She felt a moment's bitter rage at the mock-serious voice, the handsome face so composed in front of the projected image of an inferno. *They don't even know we exist.* Other faces flickered across the screen: sooty, dead-eyed firefighters; children impressed with the drama of their situations; broken-toothed men jubilant at being interviewed. Reeling slightly, she stared at the pulsating electron colors of the screen, trying to sort out the patterns.

". . . like the end of the world . . . thought I was dead . . . winds from the fire reached . . . barn just exploded like a bomb or something . . . couldn't reach her because the flames just . . . including two firemen overcome by . . . and the roof blew over to the next house and started that one burning . . . like the end of the world."

Larry and Jack. The thought brought her out of her stupor. *They're out there somewhere.* They'd be on the line, ditching with pick and shovel, racing before the blaze as it topped trees and leaped defense lines. *Was it really just a week ago I saw them last?* They seemed like people she'd known in another lifetime.

". . . already an estimated nine thousand acres have been . . ."

She wandered away. A placard at a table set up in a corner read INFORMATION. Behind it, a tight-faced man talked on a telephone. When he saw her again, he shook his head. Most Munro's Furnace residents remained unaccounted for. A stack of papers marked with scribbled lists, names of survivors, the missing, the dead covered the table in front of him. She turned away.

Scanning faces in the crowd, she realized with a shock that

most looked to some extent familiar, so strong were the similarities. Yet she recognized no individuals.

More people, some bent over with the weight of their possessions, shambled in through the double doors. She spotted one group and threaded through the crowd to reach them as they made their way toward a row of vacant cots along one wall. Wandering after their parents, the children hung together, silent, awed by their surroundings.

Manny set down the stuffed sack and began to rummage through it. She caught up with him just as he uncapped the jar.

"Where's the little girl?" She scanned the grimy faces of the other children. "The little blind girl?" The mother seemed furtive and scared as she fumbled with a snarl on one of the hastily tied bags. Athena couldn't tell if she was trying to open or tighten it.

"Where is she?" She stared at the bundles. Had they gathered up every scrap of trash they could find? Had they stopped to loot a neighbor's home?

"Hey, Miz Monroe. We made it, see? Thought we was burned for sure." Manny tilted his head back and let the jack run down his throat in a steady stream. "Damn shame 'bout the town."

"Answer me."

"Oh." He looked surprised. "Molly. Wasn't no time to get 'er. Happen so fast. Think it's true 'bout it startin' at the gin mill?"

"No time?" She heard her own voice rising. "No time?" The faces blurred. She pressed her fists roughly against her eyes. Burning. Melting. Release. She saw her hand strike at Manny's jaw. Stinking liquid sloshed across his chest as she knocked the jar away. She heard herself yell above the shouting all around her, saw herself punch the stupid, sullen face again and again. She caught him off guard, knocked him against the wall. She sobbed as she struck him.

And suddenly Doris was there, leaning unsteadily on one crutch, pulling her away.

Around them, people cursed, but Doris pushed through them. "Excuse us. Out of the way, please. Nothing to see." To

Athena, all the faces seemed uniformly hostile. "Honey, what the hell are you trying to do? What was that all about? I said, out of the way. Show's over."

They glimpsed white jackets with Red Cross insignias, and Doris waved a greeting to someone.

"Come on, honey, let's go outside for a while, get some air."

The wind hit them, rolling over them in invisible waves, buffeting them and blowing sand around their legs, sand pure as snow. The air felt cool in lungs that still ached with the memory of smoke. They walked in silence for a time, around the building, then across the shaggy road and into the trees.

"The heat's broken," Athena murmured, looking up at the sky. "Like a fever. I didn't think there'd ever be a morning like this again. And look at me. I'm crying. I'm really crying." The cooling tears still glistened like snail tracks on her cheeks.

"You feeling better now, honey?" Her leg in a partial cast, Doris hobbled beside her.

No sound hazed the crispness of the air; empty cicada husks clung hollowly to the nearby trees. "The summer's finally burned itself out," said Athena.

Doris stared. Her friend's face seemed almost colorless from strain, and she detected a weary sway to her movements. "Are you sure you're all right?"

"My leg hurts. My leg often hurts." She moved on. The pines held no menace for her now. "How are you?"

"Oh, I'm all right. I'll be out of this thing in a couple of weeks." They came to a slight rise in the ground. "I stopped off at the hospital to see Steve. He's stable now. They say he's doing real good."

She gazed off through the trees. "Thank God," she barely whispered. "When Matty wakes up, will you take us to see him?"

"They asked me a lot of questions. 'Thena? What did you tell them at the hospital?"

"The truth. That he was maimed by the Jersey Devil."

"And you . . . you killed it?"

She didn't answer, only watched the highway down below

them. "Sometimes, when I see that road, I just want to go down there and get in the first car that stops and never look back."

"'Thena?" They walked on.

"I'm not leaving, Doris. I thought you'd want to know. I'm staying in the barrens."

"Honey, Steve was pretty sedated still when I saw him. Really out of it. He said things. About the boy."

"It doesn't have to be a curse. Do you understand? You should've seen Steve's face. In the car, he came to for just a minute and saw Matty. He looked so terrified. But it could be a gift. I know it, feel it." She stopped walking. "The Spencer boy was one. It seems to happen when they reach puberty. One or two in every generation, down through the centuries. What happens to them in the end? Are they always killed or driven crazy? Do you see what I mean? What if they can be helped? Will the wildness pass in time? As they grow older? And then what?"

"I don't understand."

She made a noise like a laugh. "The funny thing is, it was all true, all those books we read, each with a little piece of the truth. Maybe that's all we ever get." She peered into the blue silence of the sky. "It doesn't have to be a curse, Doris. I . . . I sense it. They have, I don't know, abilities. They can move things with their minds. It happened in my kitchen, and I used to hear stories about Spencer's. They don't control it. It just seems to happen around them. That's one of the stages. And they can hear each other's thoughts. I felt that, heard it pass between them. And in the shack, I felt Matty try to warn me. He must have known all about Marl. Since he was a baby. Felt him as another part of himself. An imaginary playmate." She faltered, her voice low. "If the madness can be released somehow, controlled . . ."

The other woman just shook her head.

"You were right, Doris. Your theory. That night at my house. They brought it with them, the colonists. It was lurking deep within, waiting for the right combinations. They need someplace like this to survive, someplace isolated and wild. But it doesn't have to be. . . ." She took a deep breath. "I really feel that. We don't know anything about it yet. Only . . . only what I've pieced together. As children they have some kind of communications handicap. They seem backwards. But they're not. Not at all. Then the wildness comes. But what if one of them could pass beyond it? What's the final phase? Oh Doris, that poor damn boy." She took her by the arm. "Marl was his name. The hell he must've gone through. I think he tried to hold it back, to resist the change coming over him. Maybe that's the key. Maybe they all try to fight it. Maybe that's what twists them, warps them."

"I'm sorry, 'Thena. I just don't . . ."

"I made my son a promise. I'm not going to let it happen to him. I'm not. I don't care what it takes."

"I don't understand." Doris watched her face. "Are you and Steve . . . ?"

"There were probably other signs. I just didn't know what to look for. How could I? And what if Matty's not alone? What if he's not the only one out there?" She looked away. "Pamela's dead. Did you know?"

Doris nodded.

"And when he wakes up, I have to tell him . . . and tell him about the house . . . and the dog." Athena fell silent. The breeze caressed her face.

"What will you do now?" Doris went on. "Where will you go?"

"There was a reason I stayed all those years. I just didn't know what it was. He needs this place, needs to be protected, hidden . . . channeled."

"And Steve? What about Steve?"

"I don't know."

"Maybe the kid could use a father."

"I love Steve. I don't know. I can't think yet."

"Christ." Doris turned away. "You know, you and the kid, you're welcome to stay with me."

"Matty's awake. I have to go to him."

"What? How do you know that? Honey, wait up. I'm not too

good on these things yet." She hobbled through the trees. " 'Thena?"

". . . all right now, baby, I'm here . . ." Soft words drifted back, mingled with the whisper of the moving grains of sand.

" 'Thena, who you talking to?" She toiled to catch up. "I don't understand. Wait for me. 'Thena?"

But the other woman had already disappeared through the pines.

The beast moved stiffly, wobbling over the trail as though drugged. Fur had been scorched away to bright pink flesh in places, and the bandages had blackened. One scarlet ear still oozed.

Head raised, the animal tested the breeze. It was there: the troubled and troubling scent of humanity.

And, yes, the boy.

Head lowered, paws scuffing at the sand, the dog shuffled along the trail toward the school building.

And the pines hissed faintly in the wind.

Master of terror

RICHARD LAYMON

has one word of advice for you:

BEWARE

Elsie knew something weird was happening in her small supermarket when she saw the meat cleaver fly through the air all by itself. Everyone else realized it when they found Elsie on the butcher's slab the next morning—neatly jointed and wrapped. An unseen horror has come to town, and its victims are about to learn a terrifying lesson: what you can't see can very definitely hurt you.

ISBN 13: 978-0-8439-6137-9

WATER WITCH

Dunny knew from an early age what it meant to be an outsider. Her special abilities earned her many names, like freak and water witch. So she vowed to keep her powers a secret. But now her talents may be the only hope of two missing children. A young boy and girl have vanished, feared lost in the mysterious bayous of Louisiana. But they didn't just disappear; they were taken. And amid the ghosts and spirits of the swamp, there is a danger worse than any other, one with very special plans for the children—and for anyone who dares to interfere.

DEBORAH LEBLANC

ISBN 13: 978-0-8439-6039-6

EDWARD LEE

What bloodthirsty evil lies buried in the basement of a New York City brownstone, waiting for its chance to be reborn?

When Cristina and her husband moved in, they thought they had found their dream house. But Cristina can feel something calling her, luring her, filling her dreams with unbridled lust and promises of ecstasies she'd never thought possible. The time has come for the unholy ritual performed by the...

BRIDES OF THE IMPALER

ISBN 13: 978-0-8439-5807-2

COVENANT

WINNER OF THE BRAM STOKER AWARD!

The cliffs of Terrel's Peak are a deadly place, an evil place where terrible things happen. Like a series of mysterious teen suicides over the years, all on the same date. Or other deaths, usually reported as accidents. Could it be a coincidence? Or is there more to it?

Reporter Joe Kieran is determined to find the truth.

Kieran will uncover rumors and whispered legends—including the legend of the evil entity that lives and waits in the caves below Terrel's Peak....

JOHN EVERSON

ISBN 13: 978-0-8439-6018-1

What would you be willing to do for
TWO MILLION DOLLARS?

Michael Fox answered that question for himself. He was
just about to commit suicide when a stranger approached
him and offered him two million in cold, hard cash. All he
wanted in return was Fox's right arm....

But the mysterious surgeon's plans go far, far beyond one
simple limb. And Fox is not his only "donor." Once Fox
is trapped behind the operating room doors, he discovers
there is no escape from the madness, as bit by bloody bit
his body is taken from him...and gradually replaced....

THE JIGSAW MAN

GORD
ROLLO

ISBN 13: 978-0-8439-6012-9

✂ ☐ **YES!**

Sign me up for the Leisure Horror Book Club and send my
FREE BOOKS! If I choose to stay in the club, I will pay only
$8.50* each month, a savings of $7.48!

NAME: _____

ADDRESS: _____

TELEPHONE: _____

EMAIL: _____

☐ I want to pay by credit card.

☐ **VISA**　　☐ **MasterCard.**　　☐ **DISCOVER**

ACCOUNT #: _____

EXPIRATION DATE: _____

SIGNATURE: _____

Mail this page along with $2.00 shipping and handling to:
**Leisure Horror Book Club
PO Box 6640
Wayne, PA 19087**
Or fax (must include credit card information) to:
610-995-9274

You can also sign up online at **www.dorchesterpub.com.**

*Plus $2.00 for shipping. Offer open to residents of the U.S. and Canada only. Canadian
residents please call 1-800-481-9191 for pricing information.

If under 18, a parent or guardian must sign. Terms, prices and conditions subject to
change. Subscription subject to acceptance. Dorchester Publishing reserves the right to
reject any order or cancel any subscription.